S. Baring Gould

Eve - A Novel

S. Baring Gould

Eve - A Novel

ISBN/EAN: 9783337031732

Printed in Europe, USA, Canada, Australia, Japan

Cover: Foto ©Andreas Hilbeck / pixelio.de

More available books at **www.hansebooks.com**

EVE

A Novel

BY THE

REV. S. BARING GOULD

AUTHOR OF

'JOHN HERRING' 'MEHALAH' 'RED SPIDER'
ETC.

London

CHATTO & WINDUS, PICCADILLY

1891

PRINTED BY

SPOTTISWOODE AND CO., NEW-STREET SQUARE

LONDON

CONTENTS.

EVE.

CHAPTER I.

MORWELL.

THE river Tamar can be ascended by steamers as far as Morwell, one of the most picturesque points on that most beautiful river. There also, at a place called ' New Quay,' barges discharge their burdens of coal, bricks, &c., which thence are conveyed by carts throughout the neighbourhood. A new road, admirable as one of those of Napoleon's construction in France, gives access to this quay— a road constructed at the outlay of a Duke of Bedford, to whom belongs all the land that was once owned by the Abbey of Tavistock. This skilfully engineered road descends by zigzags from the elevated moorland on the Devon side of the Tamar, through dense woods of oak and fir, under crags of weathered rock wreathed with heather. From the summit of the moor this road runs due north, past mine shafts and ' ramps,' or rubble heaps thrown out of the mines, and meets other roads uniting from various points under the volcanic peak of Brent Tor, that rises in solitary dignity out of the vast moor to the height of twelve hundred feet, and is crowned by perhaps the tiniest church in England.

Seventy or eighty years ago no such roads existed. The vast upland was all heather and gorse, with tracks across it. An old quay had existed on the river, and the

B

ruins remained of the buildings about it erected by the abbots of Tavistock; but quay and warehouses had fallen into decay, and no barges came so far up the river.

The crags on the Devon side of the Tamar rise many hundred feet in sheer precipices, broken by gulfs filled with oak coppice, heather, and dogwood.

In a hollow of the down, half a mile from the oak woods and crags, with an ancient yew and Spanish chestnut before it, stood, and stands still, Morwell House, the hunting-lodge of the abbots of Tavistock, built where a moor-well—a spring of clear water—gushed from amidst the golden gorse brakes, and after a short course ran down the steep side of the hill, and danced into the Tamar.

Seventy or eighty years ago this house was in a better and worse condition than at present: worse, in that it was sorely dilapidated; better, in that it had not suffered tasteless modern handling to convert it into a farm with labourers' cottages. Even forty years ago the old banquetting hall and the abbot's parlour were intact. Now all has been restored out of recognition, except the gatehouse that opens into the quadrangle. In the interior of this old hall, on the twenty-fourth of June, just eighty years ago, sat the tenant: a tall, gaunt man with dark hair. He was engaged cleaning his gun, and the atmosphere was foul with the odour exhaled by the piece that had been recently discharged, and was now being purified. The man was intent on his work, but neither the exertion he used, nor the warmth of a June afternoon, accounted for the drops that beaded his brow and dripped from his face.

Once—suddenly—he placed the muzzle of his gun against his right side under the rib, and with his foot touched the lock. A quiver ran over his face, and his dim eyes were raised to the ceiling. Then there came from near his feet a feeble sound of a babe giving token with its lips that it was dreaming of food. The man sighed, and looked down at a cradle that was before him. He placed the gun between his knees, and remained for a moment gazing at the child's crib, lost in a dream, with the evening sun shining through the large window and illumining his face. It was a long face with light blue eyes, in which lurked anguish mixed with cat-like treachery. The mouth was tremulous, and betrayed weakness.

Presently, recovering himself from his abstraction, he laid the gun across the cradle, from right to left, and it rested there as a bar sinister on a shield, black and ominous. His head sank in his thin shaking hands, and he bowed over the cradle. His tears or sweat, or tears and sweat combined, dropped as a salt rain upon the sleeping child, that gave so slight token of its presence.

All at once the door opened, and a man stood in the yellow light, like a mediæval saint against a golden ground. He stood there a minute looking in, his eyes too dazzled to distinguish what was within, but he called in a hard, sharp tone, 'Eve! where is Eve?'

The man at the cradle started up, showing at the time how tall he was. He stood up as one bewildered, with his hands outspread, and looked blankly at the new comer.

The latter, whose eyes were becoming accustomed to the obscurity, after a moment's pause repeated his question, 'Eve! where is Eve?'

The tall man opened his mouth to speak, but no words came.

'Are you Ignatius Jordan?'

'I am,' he answered with an effort.

'And I am Ezekiel Babb. I am come for my daughter.'

Ignatius Jordan staggered back against the wall, and leaned against it with arms extended and with open palms. The window through which the sun streamed was ancient; it consisted of two lights with a transom, and the sun sent the shadow of mullion and transom as a black cross against the further wall. Ignatius stood unconsciously spreading his arms against this shadow like a ghastly Christ on his cross. The stranger noticed the likeness, and said in his harsh tones, 'Ignatius Jordan, thou hast crucified thyself.' Then again, as he took a seat unasked, 'Eve! where is Eve?'

The gentleman addressed answered with an effort, 'She is no longer here. She is gone.'

'What!' exclaimed Babb; 'no longer here? She was here last week. Where is she now?'

'She is gone,' said Jordan in a low tone.

'Gone!—her child is here. When will she return?'

'Return!'—with a sigh—'never.'

'Cursed be the blood that flows in her veins!' shouted the new comer. 'Restless, effervescing, fevered, fantastic! It is none of it mine, it is all her mother's.' He sprang to his feet and paced the room furiously, with knitted brows and clenched fists. Jordan followed him with his eye. The man was some way past the middle of life. He was strongly and compactly built. He wore a long dark coat and waistcoat, breeches, and blue worsted stockings. His hair was grey; his protruding eyebrows met over the nose. They were black, and gave a sinister expression to his face. His profile was strongly accentuated, hawklike, greedy, cruel.

'I see it all,' he said, partly to himself; 'that cursed foreign blood would not suffer her to find rest even here, where there is prosperity. What is prosperity to her? What is comfort? Bah! all her lust is after tinsel and tawdry.' He raised his arm and clenched fist. 'A life accursed of God! Of old our forefathers, under the righteous Cromwell, rose up and swept all profanity out of the land, the jesters, and the carol singers, and theatrical performers, and pipers and tumblers. But they returned again to torment the elect. What saith the Scripture? Make no marriage with the heathen, else shall ye be unclean, ye and your children.'

He reseated himself. 'Ignatius Jordan,' he said, 'I was mad and wicked when I took her mother to wife;

and a mad and wicked thing you did when you took the
daughter. As I saw you just now—as I see you at present—standing with spread arms against the black shadow
cross from the window, I thought it was a figure of
what you chose for your lot when you took my Eve. I
crucified myself when I married her mother, and now
the iron enters your side.' He paused; he was pointing at Ignatius with out-thrust finger, and the shadow
seemed to enter Ignatius against the wall. 'The blood
that begins to flow will not cease to run till it has all run
out.'

Again he paused. The arms of Jordan fell.

'So she has left you,' muttered the stranger, 'she has
gone back to the world, to its pomps and vanities, its lusts,
its lies, its laughter. Gone back to the players and dan-
cers.'

Jordan nodded; he could not speak.

'Dead to every call of duty,' Babb continued with a
scowl on his brow, 'dead to everything but the cravings of
a cankered heart; dead to the love of lawful gain; alive to
wantonness, and music, and glitter. Sit down, and I will
tell you the story of my folly, and you shall tell me the
tale of yours.' He looked imperiously at Jordan, who sank
into his chair beside the cradle.

'I will light my pipe.' Ezekiel Babb struck a light
with flint and steel. 'We have made a like experience, I
with the mother, you with the daughter. Why are you
downcast? Rejoice if she has set you free. The mother
never did that for me. Did you marry her?'

The pale man opened his mouth, and spread out, then
clasped, his hands nervously, but said nothing.

'I am not deaf that I should be addressed in signs,'
said Babb. 'Did you marry my daughter?'

'No.'

'The face of heaven was turned on you,' said Babb
discontentedly, 'and not on me. I committed myself, and
could not break off the yoke. I married,'

The child in the cradle began to stir. Jordan rocked it with his foot.

'I will tell you all,' the visitor continued. 'I was a young man when I first saw Eve—not your Eve, but her mother. I had gone into Totnes, and I stood by the cloth market at the gate to the church. It was the great fair-day. There were performers in the open space before the market. I had seen nothing like it before. What was performed I do not recall. I saw only her. I thought her richly, beautifully dressed. Her beauty shone forth above all. She had hair like chestnut, and brown eyes, a clear, thin skin, and was formed delicately as no girl of this country and stock. I knew she was of foreign blood. A carpet was laid in the market-place, and she danced on it to music. It was like a flame flickering, not a girl dancing. She looked at me out of her large eyes, and I loved her. It was witchcraft, the work of the devil. The fire went out of her eyes and burnt to my marrow; it ran in my veins. That was witchcraft, but I did not think it then. There should have been a heap of wood raised and fired, and she cast into the flames. But our lot is fallen in evil days. The word of the Lord is no longer precious, and the Lord has said, "Thou shalt not suffer a witch to live." That was witchcraft. How else was it that I gave no thought to Tamsine Bovey, of Buncombe, till it was too late, though Buncombe joins my land, and so Buncombe was lost to me for ever? Quiet that child if you want to hear more. Hah! Your Eve has deserted you and her babe, but mine had not the good heart to leave me.'

The child in the cradle whimpered. The pale man lifted it out, got milk and fed it, with trembling hand, but tenderly, and it dozed off in his arms.

'A girl?' asked Babb. Jordan nodded.

'Another Eve—a third Eve?' Jordan nodded again. 'Another generation of furious, fiery blood to work confusion, to breed desolation. When will the earth open her mouth and swallow it up, that it defile no more the habitations of Israel?'

Jordan drew the child to his heart, and pressed it so passionately that it woke and cried.

'Still the child or I will leave the house,' said Ezekiel Babb. 'You would do well to throw a wet cloth over its mouth, and let it smother itself before it work woe on you and others. When it is quiet, I will proceed.' He paused. When the cries ceased he went on: 'I watched Eve as she danced. I could not leave the spot. Then a rope was fastened and stretched on high, and she was to walk that. A false step would have dashed her to the ground. I could not bear it. When her foot was on the ladder, I uttered a great cry and ran forward; I caught her, I would not let her go. I was young then.' He remained silent, smoking, and looking frowningly before him. 'I was not a converted man then. Afterwards, when the word of God was precious to me, and I saw that I might have had Tamsine Bovey, and Buncombe, then I was sorry and ashamed. But it was too late. The eyes of the unrighteous are sealed. I was a fool. I married that dancing girl.'

He was silent again, and looked moodily at his pipe.

'I have let the fire die out,' he said, and rekindled as before. 'I cannot deny that she was a good wife. But what availed it me to have a woman in the house who could dance like a feather, and could not make scald cream? What use to me a woman who brought the voice of a nightingale with her into the house, but no money? She knew nothing of the work of a household. She had bones like those of a pigeon, there was no strength in them. I had to hire women to do her work, and she was thriftless and thoughtless, so the money went out when it should have come in. Then she bore me a daughter, and the witchery was not off me, so I called her Eve—that is your Eve, and after that she gave me sons, and then '—angrily —'then, when too late, she died. Why did she not die half a year before Tamsine Bovey married Joseph Warmington ? If she had, I might still have got Buncombe—now it is gone, gone for ever.'

He knocked the ashes out of his pipe, and put it into his pocket.

'Eve was her mother's darling ; she was brought up like a heathen to love play and pleasure, not work and duty. The child sucked in her mother's nature with her mother's milk. When the mother died, Eve—your Eve—was a grown girl, and I suppose home became unendurable to her. One day some play actors passed through the place on their way from Exeter, and gave a performance in our village. I found that my daughter, against my command, went to see it. When she came home, I took her into the room where is my great Bible, and I beat her. Then she ran away, and I saw no more of her ; whether she went after the play actors or not I never inquired. '

'Did you not go in pursuit ? '

'Why should I ? She would have run away again. Time passed, and the other day I chanced to come across a large party of strollers, when I was in Plymouth on business. Then I learned from the manager about my child, and so, for the first time, heard where she was. Now tell me how she came here.'

Ignatius Jordan raised himself in his chair, and swept back the hair that had fallen over his bowed face and hands.

'It is passed and over,' he said.

'Let me hear all. I must know all,' said Babb. 'She is my daughter. Thanks be, that we are not called to task for the guilt of our children. The soul that sinneth it shall surely die. She had light and truth set before her on one side as surely as she had darkness and lies on the other, Ebal and Gerizim, and she went after Ebal. It was in her blood. She drew it of her mother. One vessel is for honour—such am I ; another for dishonour—such are all the Eves from the first to the last, that in your arms. Vessels of wrath, ordained to be broken. Ah ! you may cherish that little creature in your arms. You may strain it to your heart, you may wrap it round with love, but it is in vain that you seek to save it, to shelter it. It is wayward, wanton, wicked clay; ordained from eternity to be broken. I stood between the first Eve and the shattering that should have come to her. That is the cause of all my woes. Where is the second Eve? Broken in soul, broken may-be in body. There lies the third, ordained to be broken.' He folded his arms, was silent a while, and then said: ' Tell me your tale. How came my daughter to your house ? '

CHAPTER II.

THE LITTLE MOTHER.

' Last Christmas twelvemonth,' said Ignatius Jordan slowly, ' I was on the moor—Morwell Down it is called. Night was falling. The place—where the road comes along over the down, from Beer Alston and Beer Ferris. I dare say you came along it, you took boat from Plymouth to Beer Ferris, and thence the way runs--the packmen travel it—to the north to Launceston. It was stormy weather, and the snow drove hard ; the wind was so high that a man might hardly face it. I heard cries for help. I found a party of players who were on their way to Launceston, and were caught by the storm and darkness on the moor. They had a sick girl with them——' His voice broke down.

' Eve ? ' asked Ezekiel Babb.

Jordan nodded. After a pause he recovered himself and went on. ' She could walk no further, and the party was distressed, not knowing whither to go or what to do. I invited them to come here. The house is large enough to hold a score of people. Next day I set them on their way forward, as they were pressed to be at Launceston for the Christmas holidays. But the girl was too ill to proceed, and I offered to let her remain here till she re-covered. After a week had passed the actors sent here from Launceston to learn how she was, and whether she could rejoin them, as they were going forward to Bodmin, but she was not sufficiently recovered. Then a month later, they sent again, but though she was better I would not let her go. After that we heard no more of the players. So she remained at Morwell, and I loved her, and she became my wife.'

'You said that you did not marry her.'

'No, not exactly. This is a place quite out of the world, a lost, unseen spot. I am a Catholic, and no priest comes this way. There is the ancient chapel here where the Abbot of Tavistock had mass in the old time. It is bare, but the altar remains, and though no priest ever comes here, the altar is a Catholic altar. Eve and I went into the old chapel and took hands before the altar, and I gave her a ring, and we swore to be true to each other'—his voice shook, and then a sob broke from his breast. 'We had no priest's blessing on us, that is true. But Eve would never tell me what her name was, or whence she came. If we had gone to Tavistock or Brent Tor to be married by a Protestant minister, she would have been forced to tell her name and parentage, and that, she said, nothing would induce her to do. It mattered not, we thought. We lived here out of the world, and to me the vow was as sacred when made here as if confirmed before a minister of the established religion. We swore to be all in all to each other.'

He clasped his hands on his knees, and went on with bent head: 'But the play-actors returned and were in Tavistock last week, and one of them came up here to see her, not openly, but in secret. She told me nothing, and he did not allow me to see him. She met him alone several times. This place is solitary and sad, and Eve of a lively nature. She tired of being here. She wearied of me.'

Babb laughed bitterly. 'And now she is flown away with a play-actor. As she deserted her father, she deserts her husband and child, and the house that housed her. See you,' he put out his hand and grasped the cradle: 'Here lies vanity of vanities, the pomps of the flesh, the lust of the eye, and the pride of life, nestled in that crib, that self-same strain of leaping, headlong, wayward blood, that never will rest till poured out of the veins and rolled down into the ocean, and lost—lost—lost!'

Jordan sprang from his seat with a gasp and a stifled cry, and fell back against the wall.

Babb stooped over the cradle and plucked out the child. He held it in the sunlight streaming through the window, and looked hard at it. Then he danced it up and down with a scoffing laugh.

'See, see!' he cried; 'see how the creature rejoices and throws forth its arms. Look at the shadow on the wall, as of a Salamander swaying in a flood of fire. Ha! Eve—blood! wanton blood! I will crucify thee too!' He raised the babe aloft against the black cross made by the shadow of the mullion and transom, as the child had thrown up its tiny arms.

'See,' he exclaimed, 'the child hangs also!'

Ignatius Jordan seized the babe, snatched it away from the rude grasp of Babb, clasped it passionately to his breast, and covered it with kisses. Then he gently replaced it, crowing and smiling, in its cradle, and rocked it with his foot.

'You fool!' said Babb; 'you love the strange blood in spite of its fickleness and falseness. I will tell you something further. When I heard from the players that Eve was here, at Morwell, I did not come on at once, because I had business that called me home. But a fortnight after I came over Dartmoor to Tavistock. I did not come, as you supposed, up the river to Beer Ferris and along the road over your down; no, I live at Buckfast·

leigh by Ashburton, right away to the east across Dartmoor. I came thence as far as Tavistock, and there I
found the players once more, who had come up from
Plymouth to make sport for the foolish and ungodly in
Tavistock. They told me that they had heard you lived
with my Eve, and had not married her, so I did not visit
you, but waited about till I could speak with her alone, and
I sent a message to her by one of the players that I was
wanting a word with her. She came to me at the place I
had appointed once - ay! and twice—and she feigned to
grieve that she had left me, and acted her part well as if
she loved me—her father. I urged her to leave you and
come back to her duty and her God and to me, but she
would promise nothing. Then I gave her a last chance.
I told her I would meet her finally on that rocky platform
that rises as a precipice above the river, last night, and
there she should give me her answer.'

Ignatius Jordan's agitation became greater, his lips
turned livid, his eyes were wide and staring as though
with horror, and he put up his hands as if warding off a
threatened blow.

'You—you met her on the Raven Rock?'

'I met her there twice, and I was to have met her
there again last night, when she was to have given me
her final answer, what she would do—stay here, and be
lost eternally, or come back with me to Salvation. But I
was detained, and I could not keep the engagement, so I
sent one of the player-men to inform her that I would
come to-day instead. So I came on to-day, as appointed,
and she was not there, not on the Raven Rock, as you call
it, and I have arrived here,—but I am too late.'

Jordan clasped his hands over his eyes and moaned.
The babe began to wail.

'Still the yowl of that child!' exclaimed Babb. 'I tell
you this as a last instance of her perfidy.' He raised his
voice above the cry of the child. 'What think you was
the reason she alleged why she would not return with me

at once—why did she ask time to make up her mind? She told me that you were a Catholic, she told me of the empty, worthless vow before an old popish altar in a deserted chapel, and I knew her soul would be lost if she remained with you; you would drag her into idolatry. And I urged her, as she hoped to escape hell fire, to flee Morwell and not cast a look behind, desert you and the babe and all for the Zoar of Buckfastleigh. But she was a dissembler. She loved neither me nor you nor her child. She loved only idleness and levity, and the butterfly career of a player, and some old sweetheart among the play company. She has gone off with him. Now I wipe my hands of her altogether.'

Jordan swayed himself, sitting as one stunned, with an elbow on each knee and his head in the hollow of his hands.

'Can you not still the brat?' cried Ezekiel Babb. 'now that the mother is gone, who will be the mother to it?'

'I—I—I!' the cry of an eager voice. Babb looked round, and saw a little girl of six, with grey eyes and dark hair, a quaint, premature woman, in an old, long, stiff frock. Her little arms were extended; 'Baby-sister!' she called, 'don't cry!' She ran forward, and, kneeling by the cradle, began to caress and play with the infant.

'Who is this?' asked Ezekiel.

'My Barbara,' answered Ignatius in a low tone; 'I was married before, and my wife died, leaving me this little one.'

The child, stooping over the cradle, lifted the babe carefully out. The infant crowed and made no resistance, for the arms that held it, though young, were strong. Then Barbara seated herself on a stool, and laid the infant on her lap, and chirped and snapped her fingers and laughed to it, and snuggled her face into the neck of the babe. The latter quivered with excitement, the tiny arms were held up, the little hands clutched in the child's long hair and tore at it, and the feet kicked with delight. 'Father! father!' cried Barbara, 'see little Eve; she is dancing and singing.'

'Dancing and singing!' echoed Ezekiel Babb, 'that is all she ever will do. She comes dancing and singing into the world, and she will go dancing and singing out of it—and then then,' he brushed his hand through the air, as though drawing back a veil. The girl-nurse looked at the threatening old man with alarm.

'Keep the creature quiet,' he said impatiently; 'I cannot sit here and see the ugly, evil sight. Dancing and singing! she begins like her mother, and her mother's mother. Take her away, the sight of her stirs my bile.'

At a sign from the father Barbara rose, and carried the child out of the room, talking to it fondly, and a joyous chirp from the little one was the last sound that reached Babb's ears as the door shut behind them.

'Naught but evil has the foreign blood, the tossing fever-blood, brought me. First it came without a dower, and that was like original sin. Then it prevented me from marrying Tamsine Bovey and getting Buncombe. That was like sin of malice. Now Tamsine is dead and her husband, Joseph Warmington, wants to sell. I did not want Tamsine, but I wanted Buncombe; at one time I could not see how Buncombe was to be had without Tamsine. Now the property is to be sold, and it joins on to mine as if it belonged to it. What Heaven has joined together let not man put asunder. It was wicked witchcraft stood in the way of my getting my rightful own.'

'How could it be your rightful own?' asked Ignatius; 'was Tamsine Bovey your kinswoman?'

'No, she was not, but she ought to have been my wife, and so Buncombe have come to me. I seem as if I could see into the book of the Lord's ordinance that so it was written. There's some wonderful good soil in Buncombe.

But the Devil allured me with his Eve, and I was be-witched by her beautiful eyes and little hands and feet. Cursed be the day that shut me out of Buncombe. Cursed be the strange blood that ran as a dividing river between Owlacombe and Buncombe, and cut asunder what Provi-dence ordained to be one. I tell you,' he went on fiercely, ' that so long as all that land remains another's and not mine, so long shall I feel only gall, and no pity nor love, for Eve, and all who have issued from her— for all who inherit her name and blood. I curse——' his voice rose to a roar, and his grey hair bristled like the fell of a wolf, ' I curse them all with——'

The pale man, Jordan, rushed at him and thrust his hand over his mouth.

' Curse not,' he said vehemently ; then in a subdued tone, ' Listen to reason, and you will feel pity and love for my little one who inherits the name and blood of your Eve. I have laid by money : I am in no want. It shall be the portion of my little Eve, and I will lend it you for seventeen years. This day, the 24th of June, seventeen years hence, you shall repay me the whole sum without interest. I am not a Jew to lend on usury. I shall want the money then for my Eve, as her dower. *She* '—he held up his head for a moment—' *she* shall not be portionless. In the meantime take and use the money, and when you walk over the fields you have purchased with it,—bless the name.'

A flush came in the sallow face of Ezekiel Babb. He rose to his feet and held out his hand.

' You will lend me the money, two thousand pounds ? '

' I will lend you fifteen hundred.'

' I will swear to repay the sum in seventeen years. You shall have a mortgage.'

' On this day.'

' This 24th day of June, so help me God.'

A ray of orange light, smiting through the window, was falling high up the wall. The hands of the men met in the beam, and the reflection was cast on their faces,—on the dark hard face of Ezekiel, on the white quivering face of Ignatius.

'And you bless,' said the latter, 'you bless the name of Eve, and the blood that follows it.'

'I bless. Peace be to the restless blood.'

CHAPTER III.

THE WHISH-HUNT.

On a wild and blustering evening, seventeen years after the events related in the two preceding chapters, two girls were out, in spite of the fierce wind and gathering darkness, in a little gig that accommodated only two, the body perched on very large and elastic springs. At every jolt of the wheels the body bounced and swayed in a manner likely to trouble a bad sailor. But the girls were used to the motion of the vehicle, and to the badness of the road. They drove a very sober cob, who went at his leisure, picking his way, seeing ruts in spite of the darkness.

The moor stretched in unbroken desolation far away on all sides but one, where it dropped to the gorge of the Tamar, but the presence of this dividing valley could only be guessed, not perceived by the crescent moon. The distant Cornish moorland range of Hingston and the dome of Kit Hill seemed to belong to the tract over which the girls were driving. These girls were Barbara and Eve Jordan. They had been out on a visit to some neighbours, if those can be called neighbours who lived at a distance of five miles, and were divided from Morwell by a range of desolate moor. They had spent the day with their friends, and were returning home later than they had intended.

'I do not know what father would say to our being abroad so late, and in the dark, unattended,' said Eve, 'were he at home. It is well he is away.'

'He would rebuke me, not you,' said Barbara.

'Of course he would; you are the elder, and responsible.'

'But I yielded to your persuasion.'

'Yes, I like to enjoy myself when I may. It is vastly
dull at Morwell, Tell me, Bab, did I look well in my
figured dress?'

'Charming, darling; you always are that.'

'You are a sweet sister,' said Eve, and she put her arm
round Barbara, who was driving.

Mr. Jordan, their father, was tenant of the Duke of
Bedford. The Jordans were the oldest tenants on the
estate which had come to the Russells on the sequestration
of the abbey. The Jordans had been tenants under the
abbot, and they remained on after the change of religion
and owners, without abandoning their religion or losing
their position. The Jordans were not accounted squires,
but were reckoned as gentry. They held Morwell on long
leases of ninety-nine years, regularly renewed when the
leases lapsed. They regarded Morwell House almost as
their freehold; it was bound up with all their family traditions and associations.

As a vast tract of country round belonged to the duke,
it was void of landed gentry residing on their estates, and
the only families of education and birth in the district were
those of the parsons, but the difference in religion formed
a barrier against intimacy with these. Mr. Jordan, moreover, was living under a cloud. It was well-known throughout the country that he had not been married to Eve's
mother, and this had caused a cessation of visits to Morwell. Moreover, since the disappearance of Eve's mother,
Mr. Jordan had become morose, reserved, and so peculiar
in his manner, that it was doubted whether he were in his
right mind.

Like many a small country squire, he farmed the
estate himself. At one time he had been accounted an
active farmer, and was credited with having made a great
deal of money, but for the last seventeen years he had

c

neglected agriculture a good deal, to devote himself to mineralogical researches. He was convinced that the rocks were full of veins of metal—silver, lead, and copper, and he occupied himself in searching for the metals in the wood, and on the moor, sinking pits, breaking stones, washing and melting what he found. He believed that he would come on some vein of almost pure silver or copper, which would make his fortune. Bitten with this craze, he neglected his farm, which would have gone to ruin had not his eldest daughter, Barbara, taken the management into her own hands.

Mr. Jordan was quite right in believing that he lived on rocks rich with metal: the whole land is now honey-combed with shafts and adits: but he made the mistake in thinking that he could gather a fortune out of the rocks unassisted, armed only with his own hammer, drawing only out of his own purse. His knowledge of chemistry and mineralogy was not merely elementary, but incorrect; he read old books of science mixed up with the fantastic alchemical notions of the middle ages, believed in the sympathies of the planets with metals, and in the virtues of the divining rod.

'Does a blue or a rose ribbon suit my hair best, Bab?' asked Eve. 'You see my hair is chestnut, and I doubt me if pink suits the colour so well as forget-me-not.'

'Every ribbon of every hue agrees with Eve,' said Barbara.

'You are a darling.' The younger girl made an attempt to kiss her sister, in return for the compliment.

'Be careful,' said Barbara, 'you will upset the gig.'

'But I love you so much when you are kind.'

'Am not I always kind to you, dear?'

'O yes, but sometimes much kinder than at others.'

'That is, when I flatter you.'

'O if you call it flattery——' said Eve, pouting.

'No—it is plain truth, my dearest.'

'Bab,' broke forth the younger suddenly, 'do you not think Bradstone a charming house? It is not so dull as ours.'

'And the Cloberrys—you like them?'

'Yes, dear, very much.'

'Do you believe that story about Oliver Cloberry, the page?'

'What story?'

'That which Grace Cloberry told me.'

'I was not with you in the lanes when you were talking together. I do not know it.'

'Then I will tell you. Listen, Bab, and shiver.'

'I am shivering in the cold wind already.'

'Shiver more shiveringly still. I am going to curdle your blood.'

'Go on with the story, but do not squeeze up against me so close, or I shall be pushed out of the gig.'

'But, Bab, I am frightened to tell the tale.'

'Then do not tell it.'

'I want to frighten you.'

'You are very considerate.'

'We share all things, Bab, even our terrors. I am a loving sister. Once I gave you the measles. I was too selfish to keep it all to myself. Are you ready? Grace told me that Oliver Cloberry, the eldest son, was page boy to John Copplestone, of Warleigh, in Queen Elizabeth's reign, you know—wicked Queen Bess, who put so many Catholics to death. Squire Copplestone was his godfather, but he did not like the boy, though he was his godchild and page. The reason was this: he was much attached to Joan Hill, who refused him and married Squire Cloberry, of Bradstone, instead. The lady tried to keep friendly with her old admirer, and asked him to stand godfather to her first boy, and then take him as his page; but Copplestone was a man who long bore a grudge, and the boy grew up the image of his father, and so—Copplestone hated him. One day, when Copplestone was going out hunting, he called for his stirrup cup, and young Cloberry ran and brought it to him. But as the squire raised the wine to his lips he saw a spider in it; and in a rage he dashed the cup and the contents in the face of the boy. He hit Oliver Cloberry on the brow, and when the boy staggered to his feet, he muttered something. Copplestone heard him, and called to him to speak out, if he were not a coward. Then the lad exclaimed, " Mother did well to throw you over for my father." Some who stood by laughed, and Copplestone flared up; the boy, afraid at what he had said, turned to go, then Copplestone threw his hunting dagger at him, and it struck him in the back, entered his heart, and he fell dead. Do you believe this story, Bab?'

'There is some truth in it, I know. Prince, in his "Worthies," says that Copplestone only escaped losing his head for the murder by the surrender of thirteen manors.'

'That is not all,' Eve continued; 'now comes the creepy part of the story. Grace Cloberry told me that every stormy night the Whish Hounds run over the downs, breathing fire, pursuing Copplestone, from Warleigh to Bradstone, and that the murdered boy is mounted behind Copplestone, and stabs him in the back all along the way. Do you believe this?'

'Most assuredly not.'

'Why should you not, Bab? Don't you think that a man like Copplestone would be unable to rest in his grave? Would not that be a terrible purgatory for him to be hunted night after night? Grace told me that old Squire Cloberry rides and blows his horn to egg-on the Whish Hounds, and Copplestone has a black horse, and he strikes spurs into its sides when the boy stabs him in the back, and screams with pain. When the Judgment Day comes, then only will his rides be over. I am sure I believe it all, Bab. It is so horrible.'

'It is altogether false, a foolish superstition.'

'Look there, do you see, Bab, we are at the white stone with the cross cut in it that my father put up where he first saw my mother. Is it not strange that no one knows whence my mother came? You remember her just a little. Whither did my mother go?'

'I do not know, Eve.'

'There, again, Bab. You who sneer and toss your chin when I speak of anything out of the ordinary, must admit this to be passing wonderful. My mother came, no one knows whence; she went, no one knows whither. After that, is it hard to believe in the Whish Hounds, and Black Copplestone?'

'The things are not to be compared.'

'Your mother was buried at Buckland, and I have seen her grave. You know that her body is there, and that her soul is in heaven. But as for mine, I do not even know whether she had a human soul.'

'Eve! What do you mean?'

'I have read and heard tell of such things. She may have been a wood-spirit, an elf-maid. Whoever she was, whatever she was, my father loved her. He loves her still. I can see that. He seems to me to have her ever in his thoughts.'

'Yes,' said Barbara sadly, 'he never visits my mother's grave; I alone care for the flowers there.'

'I can look into his heart,' said Eve. 'He loves me so dearly because he loved my mother dearer still.'

Barbara made no remark to this.

Then Eve, in her changeful mood, went back to the former topic of conversation.

'Think, think, Bab! of Black Copplestone riding nightly over these wastes on his black mare, with her tail streaming behind, and the little page standing on the crupper, stabbing, stabbing, stabbing; and the Whish Hounds behind, giving tongue, and Squire Cloberry in the rear urging them on with his horn. O Bab! I am sure father believes in this. I should die of fear were

Copplestone hunted by dogs to pass this way. Hold! Hark ! ' she almost screamed.

The wind was behind them; they heard a call, then the tramp of horses' feet.

Barbara even was for the moment startled, and drew the gig aside, off the road upon the common. A black cloud had rolled over the sickle of the moon, and obscured its feeble light. Eve could neither move nor speak. She quaked at Barbara's side like an aspen.

In another moment dark figures of men and horses were visible, advancing at full gallop along the road. The dull cob the sisters were driving plunged, backed, and was filled with panic. Then the moon shone out, and a faint, ghastly light fell on the road, and they could see the black figures sweeping along. There were two horses, one some way ahead of the other, and two riders, the first with slouched hat. But what was that crouched on the crupper, clinging to the first rider ?

As he swept past, Eve distinguished the imp-like form of a boy. That wholly unnerved her. She uttered a piercing shriek, and clasped her hands over her eyes.

The first horse had passed, the second was abreast of the girls when that cry rang out. The horse plunged, and in a moment horse and rider crashed down, and appeared to dissolve into the ground.

CHAPTER IV.

EVE'S RING.

SOME moments elapsed before Barbara recovered her surprise, then she spoke a word of encouragement to Eve, who was in an ecstasy of terror, and tried to disengage herself from her arms, and master the frightened horse sufficiently to allow her to descend. A thorn tree tortured by the winds stood solitary at a little distance, at a mound which indicated the presence of a former embankment. Barbara brought the cob and gig to it, there descended, and fastened the horse to the tree. Then she helped her sister out of the vehicle.

'Do not be alarmed, Eve. There is nothing here supernatural to dismay you, only a pair of farmers who have been drinking, and one has tumbled off his horse. We must see that he has not broken his neck.' But Eve clung to her in frantic terror, and would not allow her to disengage herself. In the meantime, by the sickle moon, now sailing clear of the clouds, they could see that the first rider had reined in his horse and turned.

'Jasper!' he called, 'what is the matter?'

No answer came. He rode back to the spot where the second horse had fallen, and dismounted.

'What has happened?' screamed the boy. 'I must get down also.'

The man who had dismounted pointed to the white stone and said, 'Hold the horse and stay there till you are wanted. I must see what cursed mischance has befallen Jasper.'

Eve was somewhat reassured at the sound of human voices, and she allowed Barbara to release herself, and advance into the road.

'Who are you?' asked the horseman.

'Only a girl. Can I help? Is the man hurt?'

'Hurt, of course. He hasn't fallen into a feather bed, or—by good luck—into a furze brake.'

The horse that had fallen struggled to rise.

'Out of the way,' said the man, 'I must see that the brute does not trample on him.' He helped the horse to his feet; the animal was much shaken and trembled. 'Hold the bridle, girl.' Barbara obeyed. Then the man went to his fallen comrade and spoke to him, but received no answer. He raised his arms, and tried if any bones were broken, then he put his hand to the heart. 'Give the boy the bridle, and come here, you girl. Help me to loosen his neck-cloth. Is there water near?'

'None; we are at the highest point of the moor.'

'Damn it! There is water everywhere in over-abundance in this country, except where it is wanted.'

'He is alive,' said Barbara, kneeling and raising the head of the prostrate, insensible man. 'He is stunned, but he breathes.'

'Jasper!' shouted the man who was unhurt, 'for God's sake, wake up. You know I can't remain here all night.'

No response.

'This is desperate. I must press forward. Fatalities always occur when most inconvenient. I was born to ill-luck. No help, no refuge near.'

'I am by as help; my home not far distant,' said Barbara, 'for a refuge.'

'O yes—*you!* What sort of help is that? Your house! I can't diverge five miles out of my road for that.'

'We live not half an hour from this point.'

'O yes—half an hour multiplied by ten. You women don't know how to calculate distances, or give a decent direction.'

'The blood is flowing from his head,' said Barbara: 'it is cut. He has fallen on a stone.'

'What the devil is to be done? I cannot stay.'

'Sir,' said Barbara, 'of course you stay by your comrade. Do you think to leave him half dead at night to the custody of two girls, strangers, on a moor?'

'You don't understand,' answered the man; 'I cannot and I will not stay.' He put his hand to his head. 'How far to your home?'

'I have told you, half-an-hour.'

'Honour bright—no more?'

'I said, half-an-hour.'

'Good God, Watt! always a fool?' He turned sharply towards the lad who was seated on the stone. The boy

had unslung a violin from his back, taken it from its case,
had placed it under his chin, and drawn the bow across the
strings.

'Have done, Watt! Let go the horses, have you?
What a fate it is for a man to be cumbered with helpless,
useless companions.'

'Jasper's horse is lame,' answered the boy, 'so I have
tied the two together, the sound and the cripple, and
neither can get away.'

'Like me with Jasper. Damnation—but I must go!
I dare not stay.'

The boy swung his bow in the moonlight, and above
the raging of the wind rang out the squeal of the instrument. Eve looked at him, scared. He seemed some
goblin perched on the stone, trying with his magic fiddle
to work a spell on all who heard its tones. The boy
satisfied himself that his violin was in order, and then put
it once more in its case, and cast it over his back.

'How is Jasper?' he shouted; but the man gave him
no answer.

'Half-an-hour! Half an eternity to me,' growled the
man. 'However, one is doomed to sacrifice self for others.
I will take him to your house and leave him there. Who
live at your house? Are there many men there?'

'There is only old Christopher Davy at the lodge, but
he is ill with rheumatics. My father is away.' Barbara
regretted having said this the moment the words escaped
her.

The stranger looked about him uneasily, then up at the
moon. 'I can't spare more than half-an-hour.'

Then Barbara said undauntedly, 'No man, under any
circumstances, can desert a fellow in distress, leaving him,
perhaps, to die. You must lift him into our gig, and we
will convey him to Morwell. Then go your way if you
will. My sister and I will take charge of him, and do our
best for him till you can return.'

'Return!' muttered the man scornfully. 'Christian

cast his burden before the cross. He didn't return to pick it up again.'

Barbara waxed wroth.

'If the accident had happened to you, would your friend have excused himself and deserted you?'

'Oh!' exclaimed the man carelessly, 'of course *he* would not.'

'Yet you are eager to leave him.'

'You do not understand. The cases are widely different.' He went to the horses. 'Halloo!' he exclaimed as he now noticed Eve. 'Another girl springing out of the turf! Am I among pixies? Turn your face more to the light. On my oath, and I am a judge, you are a beauty!' Then he tried the horse that had fallen; it halted. 'The brute is fit for dogs' meat only,' he said. 'Let the fox-hounds eat him. Is that your gig? We can never lift my brother——'

'Is he your brother?'

'We can never pull him up into that conveyance. No, we must get him astride my horse; you hold him on one side, I on the other, and so we shall get on. Come here, Watt, and lend a hand; you help also, Beauty, and see what you can do.'

With difficulty the insensible man was raised into the saddle. He seemed to gather some slight consciousness when mounted, for he muttered something about pushing on.

'You go round on the further side of the horse,' said the man imperiously to Barbara. 'You seem strong in the arm, possibly stronger than I am. Beauty! lead the horse.'

'The boy can do that,' said Barbara.

'He don't know the way,' answered the man. 'Let him come on with your old rattletrap. Upon my word, if Beauty were to throw a bridle over my head, I would be content to follow her through the world.'

Thus they went on; the violence of the gale had somewhat abated, but it produced a roar among the heather and gorse of the moor like that of the sea. Eve, as commanded, went before, holding the bridle. Her movements were easy, her form was graceful. She tripped lightly along with elastic step, unlike the firm tread of her sister. But then Eve was only leading, and Barbara was sustaining.

For some distance no one spoke. It was not easy to speak so as to be heard, without raising the voice ; and now the way led towards the oaks and beeches and pines about Morwell, and the roar among the branches was fiercer, louder than that among the bushes of furze.

Presently the man cried imperiously 'Halt!' and stepping forward caught the bit and roughly arrested the horse. 'I am certain we are followed.'

'What if we are?' asked Barbara.

'What if we are!' echoed the man. 'Why, everything to me.' He put his hands against the injured man ; Barbara was sure he meant to thrust him out of the saddle, leap into it himself, and make off. She said, 'We are followed by the boy with our gig.'

Then he laughed. 'Ah! I forgot that. When a man has money about him and no firearms, he is nervous in such a blast-blown desert as this, where girls who may be decoys pop out of every furze bush.'

'Lead on, Eve,' said Barbara, affronted at his insolence. She was unable to resist the impulse to say, across the horse, 'You are not ashamed to let two girls see that you are a coward.'

The man struck his arm across the crupper of the horse, caught her bonnet-string and tore it away.

'I will beat your brains out against the saddle if you insult me.'

'A coward is always cruel,' answered Barbara ; as she said this she stood off, lest he should strike again, but he took no notice of her last words, perhaps had not caught them. She said no more, deeming it unwise to provoke such a man.

Presently, turning his head, he asked, 'Did you call that girl—Eve?'

'Yes; she is my sister.'

'That is odd,' remarked the man. 'Eve! Eve!'

'Did you call me?' asked the young girl who was leading.

'I was repeating your name, sweet as your face.'

'Go on, Eve,' said Barbara.

The path descended, and became rough with stones.

'He is moving,' said Barbara. 'He said something.'

'Martin!' spoke the injured man.

'I am at your side, Jasper.'

'I am hurt—where am I?'

'I cannot tell you; heaven knows. In some God-forgotten waste.'

'Do not leave me!'

'Never, Jasper.'

'You promise me?'

'With all my heart.'

'I must trust you, Martin,—trust you.'

Then he said no more, and sank back into half-consciousness.

'How much farther?' asked the man who walked. 'I call this a cursed long half-hour. To women time is nought; but every moment to me is of consequence. I must push on.'

'You have just promised not to desert your friend, your brother.'

'It pacified him, and sent him to sleep again.'

'It was a promise.'

'You promise a child the moon when it cries, but it never gets it. How much farther?'

'We are at Morwell.'

They issued from the lane, and were before the old gatehouse of Morwell; a light shone through the window over the entrance door.

'Old Davy is up there, ill. He cannot come down. The gate is open ; we will go in,' said Barbara.

'I am glad we are here,' said the man called Martin ; 'now we must bestir ourselves.'

Thoughtlessly he struck the horse with his whip, and the beast started, nearly precipitating the rider to the ground. The man on it groaned. The injured man was lifted down.

'Eve!' said Barbara, 'run in and tell Jane to come out, and see that a bed be got ready at once, in the lower room.'

Presently out came a buxom womanservant, and with her assistance the man was taken off the horse and carried indoors.

A bedroom was on the ground-floor opening out of the hall. Into this Eve led the way with a light, and the patient was laid on a bed hastily made ready for his reception. His coat was removed, and Barbara examined the head.

'Here is a gash to the bone,' she said, 'and much blood is flowing from it. Jane, come with me, and we will get what is necessary.'

Martin was left alone in the room with Eve and the man called Jasper. Martin moved, so that the light fell over her ; and he stood contemplating her with wonder and admiration. She was marvellously beautiful, slender, not tall, and perfectly proportioned. Her hair was of the richest auburn, full of gloss and warmth. She had the exquisite complexion that so often accompanies hair of this colour. Her eyes were large and blue. The pure oval face was set on a delicate neck, round which hung a kerchief, which she now untied and cast aside.

'How lovely you are!' said Martin. A rich blush overspread her cheek and throat, and tinged her little ears. Her eyes fell. His look was bold.

Then, almost unconscious of what he was doing, as an act of homage, Martin removed his slouched hat, and for the first time Eve saw what he was like, when she timidly raised her eyes. With surprise she saw a young face. The man with the imperious manner was not much above twenty, and was remarkably handsome. He had dark hair, a pale skin, very large, soft dark eyes, velvety, enclosed within dark lashes. His nose was regular, the nostrils delicately arched and chiselled. His lip was fringed with a young moustache. There was a remarkable refinement and tenderness in the face. Eve could hardly withdraw her wondering eyes from him. Such a face she had never seen, never even dreamed of as possible. Here was a type of masculine beauty that transcended all her imaginings. She had met very few young men, and those she did meet were somewhat uncouth, addicted to the stable and the kennel, and redolent of both, more at home following the hounds or shooting than associating with ladies. There was so much of innocent admiration in the gaze of simple Eve that Martin was flattered, and smiled.

'Beauty!' he said, ' who would have dreamed to have stumbled on the likes of you on the moor ? Nay, rather let me bless my stars that I have been vouchsafed the privilege of meeting and speaking with a real fairy. It is said that you must never encounter a fairy without taking of her a reminiscence, to be a charm through life.'

Suddenly he put his hand to her throat. She had a delicate blue riband about it, disclosed when she cast aside her kerchief. He put his finger between the riband and her throat, and pulled.

'You are strangling me!' exclaimed Eve, shrinking away, alarmed at his boldness.

'I care not,' he replied, ' this I will have.'

He wrenched at and broke the riband, and then drew it from her neck. As he did so a gold ring fell on the floor. He stooped, picked it up, and put it on his little finger.

'Look,' said he with a laugh, 'my hand is so small, my fingers so slim—I can wear this ring.'

'Give it me back! Let me have it! You must not take it!' Eve was greatly agitated and alarmed. 'I may not part with it. It was my mother's.'

Then, with the same daring insolence with which he ha s taken the ring, he caught the girl to him, and kissed her.

CHAPTER V.

THE LIMPING HORSE.

EVE drew herself away with a cry of anger and alarm, and with sparkling eyes and flushed cheeks. At that moment her sister returned with Jane, and immediately Martin re-assumed his hat with broad brim. Barbara did not notice the excitement of Eve ; she had not observed the incident, because she entered a moment too late to do so, and no suspicion that the stranger would presume to take such a liberty crossed her mind.

Eve stood back behind the door, with hands on her bosom to control its furious beating, and with head depressed to conceal the heightened colour.

Barbara and the maid stooped over the unconscious man, and whilst Martin held a light, they dressed and bandaged his head.

Presently his eyes opened, a flicker of intelligence passed through them, they rested on Martin ; a smile for a moment kindled the face, and the lips moved.

'He wants to speak to you,' said Barbara, noticing the direction of the eyes, and the expression that came into them.

'What do you want, Jasper?' asked Martin, putting his hand on that of the other.

The candle-light fell on the two hands, and Barbara noticed the contrast. That of Martin was delicate as the hand of a woman, narrow, with taper fingers, and white ; that of Jasper was strong, darkened by exposure.

'Will you be so good as to undress him,' said Barbara, 'and put him to bed? My sister will assist me in the kitchen. Jane, if you desire help, is at your service.'

'Yes, go,' said Martin, 'but return speedily, as I cannot stay many minutes.'

Then the girls left the room.

'I do not want you,' he said roughly to the serving woman. 'Take yourself off; when I need you I will call. No prying at the door.' He went after her, thrust Jane forth and shut the door behind her. Then he returned to Jasper, removed his clothes, somewhat ungently, with hasty hands. When his waistcoat was off, Martin felt in the inner breast-pocket, and drew from it a pocket-book. He opened it, and transferred the contents to his own purse, then replaced the book and proceeded with the undressing.

When Jasper was divested of his clothes, and laid at his ease in the bed, his head propped on pillows, Martin went to the door and called the girls. He was greatly agitated, Barbara observed it. His lower lip trembled. Eve hung back in the kitchen, she could not return.

Martin said in eager tones, 'I have done for him all I can, now I am in haste to be off.'

'But,' remonstrated Barbara, 'he is your brother.'

'My brother!' laughed Martin. 'He is no relation of mine. He is naught to me and I am naught to him.'

'You called him your brother.'

'That was tantamount to comrade. All sons of Adam are brothers, at least in misfortune. I do not even know the fellow's name.'

'Why,' said Barbara, 'this is very strange. You call him Jasper, and he named you Martin.'

'Ah!' said the man hesitatingly, 'we are chance travellers, riding along the same road. He asked my name and I gave it him—my surname. I am a Mr. Martin—he mistook me; and in exchange he gave me his Christian name. That is how I knew it. If anyone asks about this event, you can say that Mr. Martin passed this way and halted awhile at your house, on his road to Tavistock.

'You are going to Tavistock?'

'Yes, that is my destination.'

'In that case I will not seek to detain you. Call up Doctor Crooke and send him here.'

'I will do so. You furnish me with an additional motive for haste to depart.'

'Go,' said Barbara. 'God grant the poor man may not die.'

'Die! pshaw! die!' exclaimed Martin. 'Men aren't such brittle ware as that pretty sister of yours. A fall from a horse don't kill a man. If it did, fox-hunting would not be such a popular sport. To-morrow, or the day after, Mr. Jasper What's-his-name will be on his feet again. Hush! What do I hear?'

His cheek turned pale, but Barbara did not see it; he kept his face studiously away from the light.

'Your horse which you hitched up outside neighed, that is all.'

'That is a great deal. It would not neigh at nothing.'

He went out. Barbara told the maid to stay by the sick man, and went after Martin, She thought that in all probability the boy had arrived driving the gig.

Martin stood irresolute in the doorway. The horse that had borne the injured man had been brought into the courtyard, and hitched up at the hall door. Martin looked across the quadrangle. The moon was shining into it. A yellow glimmer came from the sick porter's window over the great gate. The large gate was arched, a laden waggon might pass under it. It was unprovided with doors. Through it the moonlight could be seen on the paved ground in front of the old lodge.

A sound of horse-hoofs was audible approaching slowly, uncertainly, on the stony ground; but no wheels.

D

'What can the boy have done with our gig?' asked Barbara.

'Will you be quiet?' exclaimed Martin angrily.

'I protest—you are trembling,' she said.

'May not a man shiver when he is cold?' answered the man.

She saw him shrink back into the shadow of the entrance as something appeared in the moonlight outside the gatehouse, indistinctly seen, moving strangely.

Again the horse neighed.

They saw the figure come on haltingly out of the light into the blackness of the shadow of the gate, pass through, and emerge into the moonlight of the court.

Then both saw that the lame horse that had been deserted on the moor had followed, limping and slowly, as it was in pain, after the other horse. Barbara went at once to the poor beast, saying, 'I will put you in a stall,' but in another moment she returned with a bundle in her hand.

'What have you there?' asked Martin, who was mounting his horse, pointing with his whip to what she carried.

'I found this strapped to the saddle.'

'Give it to me.'

'It does not belong to you. It belongs to the other— to Jasper.'

'Let me look through the bundle; perhaps by that means we may discover his name.'

'I will examine it when you are gone. I will not detain you; ride on for the doctor.'

'I insist on having that bundle,' said Martin. 'Give it me, or I will strike you.' He raised his whip.

'Only a coward would strike a woman. I will not give you the bundle. It is not yours. As you said, this man Jasper is naught to you, nor you to him.'

'I will have it,' he said with a curse, and stooped from the saddle to wrench it from her hands. Barbara was too quick for him; she stepped back into the doorway and slammed the door upon him, and bolted it.

He uttered an ugly oath, then turned and rode through the courtyard. 'After all,' he said, 'what does it matter? We were fools not to be rid of it before.'

As he passed out of the gatehouse, he saw Eve in the moonlight, approaching timidly.

'You must give me back my ring!' she pleaded; 'you have no right to keep it.'

'Must I, Beauty? Where is the compulsion?'

'Indeed, indeed you must.'

'Then I will—but not now; at some day in the future, when we meet again.'

'O give it me now! It belonged to my mother, and she is dead.'

'Come! What will you give me for it? Another kiss?'

Then from close by burst a peal of impish laughter, and the boy bounded out of the shadow of a yew tree into the moonlight.

'Halloo, Martin! always hanging over a pretty face, detained by it when you should be galloping. I've upset the gig and broken it; give me my place again on the crupper.'

He ran, leaped, and in an instant was behind Martin. The horse bounded away, and Eve heard the clatter of the hoofs as it galloped up the lane to the moor.

CHAPTER VI.

A BUNDLE OF CLOTHES.

BARBARA JORDAN sat by the sick man with her knitting on her lap, and her eyes fixed on his face. He was asleep, and the sun would have shone full on him had she not drawn a red curtain across the window, which subdued

the light, and diffused a warm glow over the bed. He
was breathing calmly; danger was over.

On the morning after the eventful night, Mr. Jordan
had returned to Morwell, and had been told what had
happened—at least, the major part—and had seen the sick
man. He, Jasper, was then still unconscious. The doctor
from Tavistock had not arrived. The family awaited him
all day, and Barbara at last suspected that Martin had not
taken the trouble to deliver her message. She did not like
to send again, expecting him hourly. Then a doubt rose
in her mind whether Doctor Crooke might not have refused
to come. Her father had made some slighting remarks
about him in company lately. It was possible that these
had been repeated and the doctor had taken umbrage.

The day passed, and as he did not arrive, and as the
sick man remained unconscious, on the second morning
Barbara sent a foot messenger to Beer Alston, where
was a certain Mr. James Coyshe, surgeon, a young man,
reputed to be able, not long settled there. The gig was
broken, and the cob in trying to escape from the upset
vehicle had cut himself about the legs, and was unfit for a
journey. The Jordans had but one carriage horse. The
gig lay wrecked in the lane; the boy had driven it against
a gate-post of granite, and smashed the axle and the
splashboard and a wheel.

Coyshe arrived; he was a tall young man, with hair
cut very short, very large light whiskers, prominent eyes,
and big protruding ears.

'He is suffering from congestion of the brain,' said the
surgeon; 'if he does not awake to-morrow, order his grave
to be dug.'

'Can you do nothing for him?' asked Miss Jordan.

'Nothing better than leave him in your hands,' said
Coyshe with a bow.

This was all that had passed between Barbara and the
doctor. Now the third day was gone, and the man's brain
had recovered from the pressure on it.

As Barbara knitted, she stole many a glance at Jasper's face; presently, finding that she had dropped stitches and made false counts, she laid her knitting in her lap, and watched the sleeper with undivided attention and with a face full of perplexity, as though trying to read the answer to a question which puzzled her, and not finding the answer where she sought it, or finding it different from what she anticipated.

In appearance Barbara was very different from her sister. Her face was round, her complexion olive, her eyes very dark. She was strongly built, without grace of form, a sound, hearty girl, hale to her heart's core. She was not beautiful, her features were without chiselling, but her abundant hair, her dark eyes, and the sensible, honest expression of her face redeemed it from plainness. She had practical common sense; Eve had beauty. Barbara was content with the distribution; perfectly satisfied to believe herself destitute of personal charms, and ready to excuse every act of thoughtlessness committed by her sister. Barbara rose from her seat, laid aside the knitting, and went to a carved oak box that stood against the wall, ornamented with the figure of a man in trunk hose, with a pair of eagles' heads in the place of a human face. She raised the lid and looked in. There lay, neatly folded, the contents of Jasper's bundle, a coarse grey and yellow suit—a suit so peculiar in cut and colour that there was no mistaking whence it had come, and what he was who had worn it. Barbara shut the chest and returned to her place, and her look was troubled. Her eyes were again fixed on the sleeper. His face was noble. It was pale from loss of blood. The hair was black, the eyes were closed, but the lashes were long and dark. His nose was aquiline without being over-strongly characterised, his lips were thin and well moulded. The face, even in sleep, bore an expression of gravity, dignity, and integrity. Barbara found it hard to associate such a face with crime, and yet how else could

she account for that convict garb she had found rolled up
and strapped to his saddle, and which she had laid in the
trunk?

Prisoners escaped now and again from the great jail on
Dartmoor. This was one of them. As she sat watching
him, puzzling her mind over this, his eyes opened, and he
smiled. The smile was remarkably sweet. His eyes were
large, dark and soft, and from being sunken through sickness, appeared to fill his face. Barbara rose hastily, and,
going to the fireplace, brought from it some beef-tea that
had been warming at the small fire. She put it to his
lips; he thanked her, sighed, and lay back. She said not
a word, but resumed her knitting.

From this moment their positions were reversed. It
was now she who was watched by him. When she looked
up, she encountered his dark eyes. She coloured a little,
and impatiently turned her chair on one side, so as to conceal her face. A couple of minutes after, sensible in every
nerve that she was being observed, unable to keep her
eyes away, spell-drawn, she glanced at him again. He
was still watching her. Then she moved to her former
position, bit her lip, frowned, and said, 'Are you in want
of anything?'

He shook his head.

'You are sufficiently yourself to remain alone for a few
minutes,' she said, stood up, and left the room. She had
the management of the house, and, indeed, of the farm on
her hands; her usual assistant in setting the labourers
their work, old Christopher Davy, was ill with rheumatism. This affair had happened at an untoward moment,
but is it not always so? A full hour had elapsed before
Miss Jordan returned. Then she saw that the convalescent's eyes were closed. He was probably again asleep,
and sleep was the best thing for him. She reseated herself by his bedside, and resumed her knitting. A moment
after she was again aware that his eyes were on her. She
had herself watched him so intently whilst he was asleep

that a smile came involuntarily to her lips. She was being repaid in her own coin. The smile encouraged him to speak.

' How long have I been here ? '

' Four days.'

' Have I been very ill ? '

' Yes, insensible, sometimes rambling.'

' What made me ill ? What ails my head ? ' He put his hand to the bandages.

' You have had a fall from your horse.'

He did not speak for a moment or two. His thoughts moved slowly. After a while he asked, ' Where did I fall ? '

' On the moor—Morwell Down.'

' I can remember nothing. When was it ? '

' Four days ago.'

' Yes—you have told me so. I forgot. My head is not clear, there is singing and spinning in it. To-day is——? '

' To-day is Monday.'

' What day was that—four days ago ? '

' Thursday.'

' Yes, Thursday. I cannot think to reckon backwards. Monday, Tuesday, Wednesday. I can go on, but not backward. It pains me. I can recall Thursday.' He sighed and turned his head to the wall. ' Thursday night—yes, I remember no more.'

After a while he turned his head round to Barbara and asked, ' Where am I now ? '

' At Morwell House.'

He asked no more questions for a quarter of an hour. He was taking in and turning over the information he had received. He lay on his back and closed his eyes. His face was very pale, like marble, but not like marble in this, that across it travelled changes of expression that stirred the muscles. Do what she would Barbara could not keep her eyes off him. The horrible mystery about the man, the lie given to her thoughts of him by his face, forced her to observe him.

Presently he opened his eyes, and met hers; she recoiled as if smitten with a guilty feeling at her heart.

'You have always been with me whilst I was unconcious and rambling,' he said earnestly.

'I have been a great deal with you, but not always. The maid, Jane, and an old woman who comes in occasionally to char, have shared with me the task. You have not been neglected.'

'I know well when you have been by me and when you have been away. Sometimes I have felt as if I lay on a bank with wild thyme under me——'

'That is because we put thyme with our linen,' said the practical Barbara.

He did not notice the explanation, but went on, ' And the sun shone on my face, but a pleasant air fanned me. At other times all was dark and hot and miserable.

'That was according to the stages of your illness.'

'No, I think I was content when you were in the room, and distressed when you were away. Some persons exert a mesmeric power of soothing.'

'Sick men get strange fancies,' said Barbara.

He rose on his elbow, and held out his hand.

'I know that I owe my life to you, young lady. Allow me to thank you. My life is of no value to any but myself. I have not hitherto regarded it much. Now I shall esteem it, as saved by you. I thank you. May I touch your hand?'

He took her fingers and put them to his lips.

'This hand is firm and strong,' he said, ' but gentle as the wing of a dove.'

She coldly withdrew her fingers.

'Enough of thanks,' she said bluntly. 'I did but my duty.'

'Was there——' he hesitated—'anyone with me when I was found, or was I alone?'

'There were two—a man and a boy.'

His face became troubled. He began a question, then let it die in his mouth, began another, but could not bring it to an end.

'And they—where are they?' he asked at length.

'That one called Martin brought you here.'

'He did!' exclaimed Jasper, eagerly.

'That is—he assisted in bringing you here.' Barbara was so precise and scrupulous about truth, that she felt herself obliged to modify her first assertion. 'Then, when he saw you safe in our hands, he left you.'

'Did he—did he say anything about me?'

'Once—but that I suppose was by a slip, he called you brother. Afterwards he asserted that you were nothing to him, nor he to you.'

Jasper's face was moved with painful emotions, but it soon cleared, and he said, 'Yes, I am nothing to him—nothing. He is gone. He did well. I was, as he said—and he spoke the truth—nothing to him.'

Then, hastily, to turn the subject, 'Excuse me. Where am I now? And, young lady, if you will not think it rude of me to inquire, who are you to whom I owe my poor life?'

'This, as I have already said, is Morwell, and I am the daughter of the gentleman who resides in it, Mr. Ignatius Jordan.'

He fell back on the bed, a deadly greyness came over his face, he raised his hands: 'My God! my God! this is most wonderful. Thy ways are past finding out.'

'What is wonderful?' asked Barbara.

He did not answer, but partially raised himself again in bed.

'Where are my clothes?' he asked.

'Which clothes?' inquired Barbara, and her voice was hard, and her expression became stern. She hesitated for a moment, then went to the chest and drew forth the suit that had been rolled up on the pommel of the saddle; also that which he had worn when he met with the accident. She held one in each hand, and returned to the bed.

'Which?' she asked gravely, fixing her eyes on him.

He looked from one to the other, and his pale face turned a chalky white. Then he said in a low tremulous tone, 'I want my waistcoat.'

She gave it him. He felt eagerly about it, drew the pocket-book from the breast-pocket, opened it and fell back.

'Gone!' he moaned, 'gone!'

The garment dropped from his fingers upon the floor, his eyes became glassy and fixed, and scarlet spots of colour formed in his cheeks.

After this he became feverish, and tossed in his bed, put his hand to his brow, plucked at the bandages, asked for water, and his pulse quickened.

Towards evening he seemed conscious that his senses were slipping beyond control. He called repeatedly for the young lady, and Jane, who attended him then, was obliged to fetch Barbara.

The sun was setting when she came into the room. She despatched Jane about some task that had to be done, and, coming to the side of the bed, said in a constrained voice, 'Yes, what do you require? I am here.'

He lifted himself. His eyes were glowing with fever; he put out his hand and clasped her wrist; his hand was burning. His lips quivered; his face was full of a fiery eagerness.

'I entreat you! you are so good, so kind! You have surprised a secret. I beseech you let no one else into it—no one have a suspicion of it. I am hot. I am in a fever. I am afraid what I may say when others are by me. I would go on my knees to you could I rise. I pray you, I pray you——' he put his hands together, 'do not leave me if I become delirious. It is a hard thing to ask. I have no claim on you; but I fear. I would have none but you know what I say, and I may say strange things if my mind becomes deranged with fever. You feel my hand, is it not like a red-hot-coal? You know that I am likely to wander. Stay by me—in pity—in mercy—for the love of God—for the love of God!'

His hand, a fiery hand, grasped her wrist convulsively. She stood by his bed, greatly moved, much stung with self-reproach. It was cruel of her to act as she had done, to show him that convict suit, and let him see that she knew his vileness. It was heartless, wicked of her, when the poor fellow was just returned to consciousness, to cast him back into his misery and shame by the sight of that degrading garment.

Spots of colour came into her cheeks almost as deep as those which burnt in the sick man's face.

'I should have considered he was ill, that he was under my charge,' she said, and laid her left hand on his to intimate that she sought to disengage her wrist from his grasp.

At the touch his eyes, less wild, looked pleadingly at her.

'Yes, Mr. Jasper,' she said, 'I——'

'Why do you call me Mr. Jasper?'

'That other man gave you the name.'

'Yes, my name is Jasper. And yours?'

'Barbara. I am Miss Barbara Jordan.'

'Will you promise what I asked?'

'Yes,' she said, 'I will stay by you all night, and whatever passes your lips shall never pass mine.'

He smiled, and gave a sigh of relief.

'How good you are! How good! Barbara Jordan.'

He did not call her Miss, and she felt slightly piqued. He, a convict, to speak of her thus! But she pacified her wounded pride with the consideration that his mind was disturbed by fever.

CHAPTER VII.

A NIGHT-WATCH.

BARBARA had passed her word to remain all night with the sick man, should he prove delirious; she was scrupulously conscientious, and in spite of her father's remonstrance and assurance that old Betty Westlake could look after the fellow well enough, she remained in the sick room after the rest had gone to bed.

That Jasper was fevered was indubitable; he was hot and restless, tossing his head from side to side on the pillow, and it was not safe to leave him, lest he should disarrange his bandage, lest, in an access of fever, he should leap from his bed and do himself an injury.

After everyone had retired the house became very still. Barbara poked and made up the fire. It must not become too large, as the nights were not cold, and it must not be allowed to go out.

Jasper did not speak, but he opened his eyes occasionally, and looked at his nurse with a strange light in his eyes that alarmed her. What if he were to become frantic? What—worse—were he to die? He was only half conscious, he did not seem to know who she was. His lips twitched and moved, but no voice came. Then he clasped both hands over his brow, and moaned, and plucked at the bandages. 'You must not do that,' said Barbara Jordan, rising from her chair and going beside him. He glared at her from his burning eyes without intelligence. Then she laid her cool hand on his strapped brow, and he let his arms fall, and lay still, and the twitching of his mouth ceased. The pressure of her hand eased, soothed him. Directly she withdrew her hand he began to murmur and move, and cry out, 'O Martin! Martin!'

Then he put forth his hand and opened it wide, and closed it again, in a wild, restless, unmeaning manner.

Next he waved it excitedly, as if in vehement conversation or earnest protest. Barbara spoke to him, but he did not hear her. She urged him to lie quiet and not excite himself, but her words, if they entered his ear, conveyed no message to the brain. He snatched at his bandage.

'You shall not do that,' she said, and caught his hand, and held it down firmly on the coverlet. Then, at once, he was quiet. He continued turning his head on the pillow, but he did not stir his arm. When she attempted to withdraw her hand he would not suffer her. Once, when almost by main force, she plucked her hand away, he became excited and tried to rise in his bed. In terror, to pacify him, she gave him her hand again. She moved her chair close to the bed, where she could sit facing him, and let him hold her left hand with his left. He was quiet at once. It seemed to her that her cool, calmly flowing blood poured its healing influence through her hand up his arm to his tossing, troubled head. Thus she was obliged to sit all night, hand in hand with the man she was constrained to pity, but whom, for his guilt, she loathed.

He became cooler, his pulse beat less fiercely, his hand was less burning and dry. She saw him pass from vexing dreams into placid sleep. She was unable to knit, to do any work all night. She could do nothing other than sit, hour after hour, with her eyes on his face, trying to unravel the riddle, to reconcile that noble countenance with an evil life. And when she could not solve it, she closed her eyes and prayed, and her prayer was concerned, like her thoughts, with the man who lay in fever and pain, and who clasped her so resolutely. Towards dawn his eyes opened, and there was no more vacancy and fire in them. Then she went to the little casement and opened it. The fresh, sweet air of early morning rushed in, and with the air came the song of awakening thrushes, the spiral twitter of the lark. One fading star was still shining in a sky that was laying aside its sables.

She went back to the bedside and said gently, 'You are better.'

'Thank you,' he answered. 'I have given you much trouble.'

She shook her head, she did not speak. Something rose in her throat. She had extinguished the lamp. In the grey dawn the face on the bed looked death-like, and a gush of tenderness, of pity for the patient, filled Barbara's heart. She brought a basin and a sponge, and, leaning over him, washed his face. He thanked her with his sweet smile, a smile that told of pain. It affected Barbara strangely. She drew a long breath. She could not speak. If she had attempted to do so she would have sobbed; for she was tired with her continued watching. To be a nurse to the weak, whether to a babe or a wounded man, brings out all the sweet springs in a woman's soul; and poor Barbara, against her judgment, felt that every gentle vein in her heart was oozing with pity, love, solicitude, mercy, faith and hope. What eyes that Jasper had! so gentle, soft, and truthful. Could treachery, cruelty, dishonesty lurk beneath them?

A question trembled on Barbara's lips. She longed to ask him something about himself, to know the truth, to have that horrible enigma solved. She leaned her hand on the back of the chair, and put the other to her lips.

'What is it?' he asked suddenly.

She started. He had read her thoughts. Her eyes met his, and, as they met, her eyes answered and said, 'Yes, there is a certain matter. I cannot rest till I know.'

'I am sure,' he said, 'there is something you wish to say, but are afraid lest you should excite me.'

She was silent.

'I am better now; the wind blows cool over me, and the morning light refreshes me. Do not be afraid. Speak.'

She hesitated.

'Speak,' he said. 'I am fully conscious and self-possessed now.'

'Yes,' she said slowly. 'It is right that I should know for certain what you are.' She halted. She shrank from the question. He remained waiting. Then she asked with a trembling voice, 'Is that convict garment yours?'

He turned away his face sharply.

She waited for the answer. He did not reply. His breast heaved and his whole body shook, the very bed quivered with suppressed emotion.

'Do not be afraid,' she said, in measured tones. 'I will not betray you. I have nursed you and fed you, and bathed your head. No, never! never! whatever your crime may have been, will I betray you. No one in the house suspects. No eyes but mine have seen that garment. Do not mistrust me; not by word or look will I divulge the secret, but I must know all.'

Still he did not reply. His face was turned away, but she saw the working of the muscles of his cheek-bone, and the throb of the great vein in his temple. Barbara felt a flutter of compunction in her heart. She had again over-agitated this unhappy man when he was not in a condition to bear it. She knew she had acted precipitately, unfairly, but the suspense had become to her unendurable.

'I have done wrong to ask the question,' she said.

'No,' he answered, and looked at her. His large eyes, sunken and lustrous with sickness, met hers, and he saw that tears were trembling on her lids.

'No,' he said, 'you did right to ask;' then paused. The garment—the prison garment is mine.'

A catch in Barbara's breath; she turned her head hastily and walked towards the door. Near the door stood the oak chest carved with the eagle-headed man. She stooped, threw it open, caught up the convict clothes, rolled them together, and ran up into the attic, where she secreted them in a place none but herself would be likely to look into.

A moment after she reappeared, composed.

'A packman came this way with his wares yesterday,' said Miss Jordan gravely. 'Amongst other news he brought was this, that a convict had recently broken out from the prison at Prince's Town on Dartmoor, and was thought to have escaped off the moor.' He listened and made no answer, but sighed heavily. 'You are safe here,' she said; 'your secret remains here'-- she touched her breast. 'My father, my sister, none of the maids suspect anything. Never let us allude to this matter again, and I hope that as soon as you are sufficiently recovered you will go your way.'

The door opened gently and Eve appeared, fresh and lovely as a May blossom.

'Bab, dear sister,' said the young girl, 'let me sit by him now. You must have a nap. You take everything upon you—you are tired. Why, Barbara, surely you have been crying?'

'I——crying!' exclaimed the elder angrily. 'What have I had to make me cry? No; I am tired, and my eyes burn.'

'Then close them and sleep for a couple of hours.'

Barbara left the room and shut the door behind her. In the early morning none of the servants could be spared to sit with the sick man.

Eve went to the table and arranged a bunch of oxlips, dripping with dew, in a glass of water.

'How sweet they are!' she said, smiling. 'Smell them, they will do you good. These are of the old monks' planting; they grow in abundance in the orchard, but nowhere else. The oxlips and the orchis suit together perfectly. If the oxlip had been a little more yellow and the orchis a little more purple, they would have made an ill-assorted posy.'

Jasper looked at the flowers, then at her.

'Are you her sister?'

'What, Barbara's sister?'

'Yes, her name is Barbara.'

'Of course I am.'

He looked at Eve. He could trace in her no likeness to her sister. Involuntarily he said, 'You are very beautiful.'

She coloured—with pleasure. Twice within a few days the same compliment had been paid her.

'What is your name, young lady?'

'My name is Eve.'

'Eve!' repeated Jasper. 'How strange!'

Twice also, within a few days, had this remark been passed on her name.

'Why should it be strange?'

'Because that was also the name of my mother and of my sister.'

'Is your mother alive?'

He shook his head.

'And your sister?'

'I do not know. I remember her only faintly, and my father never speaks of her.' Then he changed the subject. 'You are very unlike Miss Barbara. I should not have supposed you were sisters.'

'We are half-sisters. We had not the same mother.'

He was exhausted with speaking, and turned towards the wall. Eve seated herself in the chair vacated by Barbara. She occupied her fingers with making a cowslip ball, and when it was made she tossed it. Then, as he moved, she feared that she disturbed him, so she put the ball on the table, from which, however, it rolled off.

Jasper turned as she was groping for it.

'Do I trouble you?' she said. 'Honour bright, I will sit quiet.'

How beautiful she looked with her chestnut hair; how delicate and pearly was her lovely neck; what sweet eyes were hers, blue as a heaven full of sunshine!

'Have you sat much with me, Miss Eve, whilst I have seen ill?'

E

'Not much; my sister would not suffer me. I am such a fidget that she thought I might irritate you; such a giddypate that I might forget your draughts and compresses. Barbara is one of those people who do all things themselves, and rely on no one else.'

'I must have given Miss Barbara much trouble. How good she has been!'

'Oh, Barbara is good to everyone! She can't help it. Some people are born good-tempered and practical, and others are born pretty and poetical; some to be good needlewomen, others to wear smart clothes.'

'Tell me, Miss Eve, did anyone come near me when I met with my accident?'

'Your friend Martin and Barbara brought you here.'

'And when I was here who had to do with my clothes?'

Martin undressed you whilst my sister and I got ready what was necessary for you.'

'And my clothes—who touched them?'

'After your friend Martin, only Barbara; she folded them and put them away. Why do you ask?'

Jasper sighed and put his hand to his head. Silence ensued for some time; had not he held his hand to the wound Eve would have supposed he was asleep. Now, all at once, Eve saw the cowslip ball; it was under the table, and with the point of her little foot she could touch it and roll it to her. So she played with the ball, rolling it with her feet, but so lightly that she made no noise.

All at once he looked round at her. Startled, she kicked the cowslip ball away. He turned his head away again.

About five minutes later she was on tiptoe, stealing across the room to where the ball had rolled. She picked it up and laid it on the pillow near Jasper's face. He opened his eyes. They had been closed.

'I thought,' explained Eve, 'that the scent of the

flowers might do you good. They are somewhat bruised and so smell the stronger.'

He half nodded and closed his eyes again.

Presently she plucked timidly at the sheet. As he paid no attention she plucked again. He looked at her. The bright face, like an opening wild rose, was bending over him.

' Will it disturb you greatly if I ask you a question ? '

He shook his head.

' Who was that young man whom you called Martin ? '

He looked earnestly into her eyes, and the colour mounted under the transparent skin of her throat, cheeks, and brow.

' Eve,' he said gravely, ' have you ever been ill—cut, wounded '—he put out his hand and lightly indicated her heart—' there ? '

She shook her pretty head with a smile.

' Then think and ask no more about Martin. He came to you out of darkness, he went from you into darkness. Put him utterly and for ever out of your thoughts as you value your happiness.'

CHAPTER VIII.

BAB.

As Jasper recovered, he saw less of the sisters. June had come, and with it lovely weather, and with the lovely weather the haysel. The air was sweet about the house with the fragrance of hay, and the soft summer breath wafted the pollen and fine strands on its wings into the court and in at the windows of the old house. Hay harvest was a busy time, especially for Barbara Jordan. She engaged extra hands, and saw that cake was baked and beer brewed for the harvesters. Mr. Jordan had become, as years passed, more abstracted from the cares of the farm, and more steeped in his fantastic semi-scientific pursuits. As his eldest daughter put her strong shoulder to the wheel of business, Mr. Jordan edged his from under it and left the whole pressure upon her. Consequently Barbara was very much engaged. All that was necessary to be done for the convalescent was done, quietly and considerately; but Jasper was left considerably to himself. Neither Barbara nor Eve had the leisure, even if they had the inclination, to sit in his room and entertain him with conversation. Eve brought Jasper fresh flowers every morning, and by snatches sang to him. The little parlour opened out of the room he occupied, and in it was her harpsichord, an old instrument, without much tone, but it served to accompany her clear fresh voice. In the evening she and Barbara sang duets. The elder sister had a good alto voice that contrasted well with the warble of her sister's soprano.

Mr. Jordan came periodically into the sick room, and saluted his guest in a shy, reserved manner, asked how he progressed, made some common remark about the weather, fidgeted with the backs of the chairs or the brim of his hat, and went away. He was a timid man with strangers, a man who lived in his own thoughts, a man with a frightened, far-off look in his eyes. He was ungainly in his movements, through nervousness. He made no friends, he had acquaintances only.

His peculiar circumstances, the connection with Eve's mother, his natural reserve, had kept him apart from the gentlefolks around. His reserve had deepened of late, and his shyness had become painful to himself and to those with whom he spoke.

As Eve grew up, and her beauty was observed, the neighbours pitied the two girls, condemned through no fault of their own to a life of social exclusion. Of Barbara everyone spoke well, as an excellent manager and thrifty housekeeper, kind of heart, in all things reliable. Of Eve everyone spoke as a beauty. Some little informal conclaves had been held in the neighbourhood, and one good lady had said to the Cloberrys, 'If you will call, so will I.' So the Cloberrys of Bradstone, as a leading county family, had taken the initiative and called. As the Cloberry family coach drove up to the gate of Morwell, Mr. Jordan was all but caught, but he had the presence of mind to slip behind a laurel bush, that concealed his body, whilst exposing his legs. There he remained motionless, believing himself unseen, till the carriage drove away. After the Cloberrys had called, other visitors arrived, and the girls received invitations to tea, which they gladly accepted. Mr. Jordan sent his card by his daughters ; he would make no calls in person, and the neighbours were relieved not to see him. That affair of seventeen years ago was not forgiven.

Mr. Jordan was well pleased that his daughters should go into society, or rather that his daughter Eve should be received and admired. With Barbara he had not much in common, only the daily cares of the estate, and these worried him. To Eve, and to her alone, he opened out, and spoke of things that lived within, in his mind, to her alone did he exhibit tenderness. Barbara was shut out from his heart ; she felt the exclusion, but did not resent the preference shown to Eve. That was natural, it was Eve's due, for Eve was so beautiful, so bright, so perfect a little fairy. But, though Barbara did not grudge her young sister the love that was given to her, she felt an ache in her heart, and a regret that the father's love was not so full that it could embrace and envelop both.

One day, when the afternoon sun was streaming into the hall, Barbara crossed it, and came to the convalescent's room.

'Come,' she said, 'my father and I think you had better sit outside the house ; we are carrying the hay, and it may amuse you to watch the waggons. The sweet air will do you good. You must be weary of confinement in this little room.'

'How can I be weary where I am so kindly treated !—

where all speaks to me of rest and peace and culture!
Jasper was dressed, and was sitting in an arm-chair reading, or pretending to read, a book.

'Can you rise, Mr. Jasper?' she asked.

He tried to leave the chair, but he was still very weak,
so she assisted him.

'And now,' she said kindly, 'walk, sir!'

She watched his steps. His face was pale, and the
pallor was the more observable from the darkness of his
hair. 'I think,' said he, forcing a smile, 'I must beg a
little support.'

She went without hesitation to his side, and he put his
arm in hers. He had not only lost much blood, but had
been bruised and severely shaken, and was not certain of
his steps. Barbara was afraid, in crossing the hall, lest he
should fall on the stone floor. She disengaged his hand,
put her arm about his waist, bade him lean on her shoulder. How strong she seemed!

'Can you get on now?' she asked, looking up. His
deep eyes met her.

'I could get on for ever thus,' he answered.

She flushed scarlet.

'I dislike such speeches,' she said; and disengaged herself from him. Whilst her arm was about him her hand
had felt the beating of his heart.

She conducted him to a bench in the garden near a bed
of stocks, where the bees were busy.

'How beautiful the world looks when one has not seen
it for many days!' he said.

'Yes, there is a good shear of hay, saved in splendid
order.'

'When a child is born into the world there is always
a gathering, and a festival to greet it. I am born anew
into the beautiful world to-day. I am on the threshold of
a new life, and you have nursed me into it. Am I too
presumptuous if I ask you to sit here a very little while,
and welcome me into it? That will be a festival indeed.'

She smiled good-humouredly, and took her place on the bench. Jasper puzzled her daily more and more. What was he? What was the temptation that had led him away? Was his repentance thorough? Barbara prayed for him daily, with the excuse to her conscience that it was always well to pray for the conversion of a sinner, and that she was bound to pray for the man whom Providence had cast broken and helpless at her feet. The Good Samaritan prayed, doubtless, for the man who fell among thieves. She was interested in her patient. Her patient he was, as she was the only person in the house to provide and order whatever was done in it. Her patient, Eve and her father called him. Her patient he was, somehow her own heart told her he was; bound to her doubly by the solicitude with which she had nursed him, by the secret of his life which she had surprised.

He puzzled her. He puzzled her more and more daily There was a gentleness and refinement in his manner and speech that showed her he was not a man of low class, that if he were not a gentleman by birth he was one in mind and culture. There was a grave religiousness about him, moreover, that could not be assumed, and did not comport with a criminal.

Who was he, and what had he done? How far had he sinned, or been sinned against? Barbara's mind was fretted with these ever-recurring questions. Teased with the enigma, she could not divert her thoughts for long from it—it formed the background to all that occupied her during the day. She considered the dairy, but when the butter was weighed, went back in mind to the riddle. She was withdrawn again by the demands of the cook for groceries from her store closet; when the closet door was shut she was again thinking of the puzzle. She had to calculate the amount of cake required for the harvesters, and went on from the calculations of currants and sugar to the balancing of probabilities in the case of Jasper.

She had avoided seeing him of late more than was necessary, she had resolved not to go near him, and let the maid Jane attend to his requirements, aided by Christopher Davy's boy, who cleaned the boots and knives, and ran errands, and weeded the paths, and was made generally useful. Yet for all her resolve she did not keep it: she discovered that some little matter had been neglected, which forced her to enter the room.

When she was there she was impatient to be out of it again, and she hardly spoke to Jasper, was short, busy, and away in a moment.

'It does not do to leave the servants to themselves,' soliloquised Barbara. 'They half do whatever they are set at. The sick man would not like to complain. I must see to everything myself.'

Now she complied with his request to sit beside him, but was at once filled with restlessness. She could not speak to him on the one subject that tormented her. She had herself forbidden mention of it.

She looked askance at Jasper, who was not speaking. He had his hat off, on his lap; his eyes were moist, his lips were moving. She was confident he was praying. He turned in a moment, re-covered his head, and said with his sweet smile, 'God is good. I have already thanked you. I have thanked him now.'

Was this hypocrisy? Barbara could not believe it.

She said, 'If you have no objection, may we know your name? I have been asked by my father and others. I mean,' she hesitated, 'a name by which you would care to be called.'

'You shall have my real name,' he said, slightly colouring.

'For myself to know, or to tell others?'

'As you will, Miss Jordan. My name is Babb.'

'Babb!' echoed Barbara. She thought to herself that it was a name as ugly as it was unusual. At that moment Eve appeared, glowing with life, a wreath of wild roses wound about her hat.

'Bab! Bab dear!' she cried, referring to her sister.

Barbara turned crimson, and sprang from her seat.

'The last cartload is going to start,' said Eve eagerly, 'and the men say that I am the Queen and must sit on the top; but I want half-a-crown, Bab dear, to pay my footing up the ladder to the top of the load.'

Barbara drew her sister away. 'Eve! never call me by that ridiculous pet-name again. When we were children it did not matter. Now I do not wish it.'

'Why not?' asked the wondering girl. 'How hot you are looking, and yet you have been sitting still!'

'I do not wish it, Eve. You will make me very angry, and I shall feel hurt if you do it again. Bab—think, darling, the name is positively revolting, I assure you. I hate it. If you have any love for me in your heart, any regard for my feelings, you will not call me by it again. Bab——!'

CHAPTER IX.

THE POCKET-BOOK.

JASPER drew in full draughts of the delicious air, leaning back on the bench, himself in shade, watching the trees, hearing the hum of the bees, and the voices of the harvesters, pleasant and soft in the distance, as if the golden sun had subdued all the harshness in the tones of the rough voices. Then the waggon drew nigh; the garden was above the level of the farmyard, terraced so that Jasper could not see the cart and horses, or the men, but he saw the great load of grey-green hay move by, with Eve and Barbara seated on it, the former not only crowned with roses, but holding a pole with a bunch of roses and a flutter of ribands at the top. Eve's golden hair had fallen loose and was about her shoulders. She was in an ecstasy of gaiety. As the load travelled along before the garden,

both Eve and her sister saw the sick man on his bench.
He seemed so thin, white, and feeble in the midst of a fresh
and vigorous nature that Barbara's heart grew soft, and
she had to bite her lip to control its quiver. Eve waved
her staff topped with flowers and streamers, stood up in
the hay and curtsied to him, with a merry laugh, and then
dropped back into the hay, having lost her balance through
the jolting of the wheels. Jasper brightened, and, removing his hat, returned the salute with comic majesty. Then,
as Eve and Barbara disappeared, he fell back against the
wall, and his eyes rested on the fluttering leaves of a white
poplar, and some white butterflies that might have been
leaves reft from the trees, flickering and pursuing each
other in the soft air. The swallows that lived in a colony
of inverted clay domes under the eaves were darting about,
uttering shrill cries, the expression of exuberant joy of life.
Jasper sank into a summer dream.

He was roused from his reverie by a man coming between him and the pretty garden picture that filled his
eyes. He recognised the surgeon, Mr.—or as the country
people called him, Doctor—Coyshe. The young medical
man had no objection to being thus entitled, but he very
emphatically protested against his name being converted
into Quash, or even Squash. Coyshe is a very respectable
and ancient Devonshire family name, but it is a name that
lends itself readily to phonetic degradation, and the young
surgeon had to do daily battle to preserve it from being
vulgarised. 'Good afternoon, patient!' said he cheerily;
'doing well, thanks to my treatment.'

Jasper made a suitable reply.

'Ah! I dare say you pull a face at seeing me now,
thinking I am paying visits for the sake of my fee, when
need for my attendance is past. That, let me tell you, is
the way of some doctors; it is, however, not mine. Lord
love you, I know a case of a man who sent for a doctor
because his wife was ill, and was forced to smother her
under pillows to cut short the attendance and bring the

bill within the compass of his means. Bless your stars, my man, that you fell into my hands, not into those of old Crooke.'

'I am assured,' said Jasper, ' that I am fallen into the best possible hands.'

'Who assured you of that?' asked Coyshe sharply; ' Miss Eve or the other?'

'I am assured by my own experience of your skill.'

'Ah! an ordinary practitioner would have trepanned you; the whole run of them, myself and myself only excepted, have an itch in their fingers for the saw and the scalpel. There is far too much bleeding, cupping, and calomel used in the profession now—but what are we to say? The people love to have it so, to see blood and have a squeal for their money. I've had before now to administer a bread pill and give it a Greek name.'

Mr. Jordan from his study, the girls from the stackyard (or moway, as it is locally called), saw or heard the surgeon. He was loud in his talk and made himself heard. They came to him into the garden. Eve, with her natural coquetry, retained the crown of roses and her sceptre.

'You see,' said Mr. Coyshe, rubbing his hands, 'I have done wonders. This would have been a dead man but for me. Now, sir, look at me,' he said to Jasper; 'you owe me a life.'

'I know very well to whom I owe my life,' answered Jasper, and glanced at Barbara. ' To my last hour I shall not forget the obligation.'

'And do you know *why* he owes me his life?' asked the surgeon of Mr. Jordan. ' Because I let nature alone, and kept old Crooke away. I can tell you the usual practice. The doctor comes and shrugs his shoulders and takes snuff. When he sees a proper impression made, he says, " However; we will do our best, only we don't work miracles." He sprinkles his victim with snuff, as if about to embalm the body. If the man dies, the reason is clear. Crooke was not sent for in time. If he recovers, Crooke has wrought a miracle. That is not my way, as you all know.' He looked about him complacently.

'What will you take, Mr. Coyshe?' asked Barbara; 'some of our haysel ale, or claret? And will you come indoors for refreshment?'

'Indoors! O dear me, no!' said the young doctor; 'I keep out of the atmosphere impregnated with four or five centuries of dirt as much as I can. If I had my way I would burn down every house with all its contents every ten years, and so we might get rid of half the diseases which ravage the world. I wouldn't live in your old ramshackle Morwell if I were paid ten guineas a day. The atmosphere must be poisoned, charged with particles of dust many centuries old. Under every cupboard, ay, and on top of it, is fluff, and every stir of a gown, every tread of a foot, sets it floating, and the currents bring it to your lungs or pores. What is that dust made up of? Who can tell? The scrapings of old monks, the scum of Protestant reformers, the detritus of any number of Jordans for ages, some of whom have had measles, some scarlet-fever, some small-pox. No, thank you. I'll have my claret in the garden. I can tell you without looking what goes to make up the air in that pestilent old box; the dog has carried old bones behind the cupboard, the cat has been set a saucer of milk under the chest, which has been forgotten and gone sour. An old stocking which one of the ladies was mending was thrust under a sofa cushion, when the front door bell rang, and she had to receive callers—and that also was forgotten.'

Miss Jordan waxed red and indignant. 'Mr. Coyshe,' she said, 'I cannot hear you say this, it is not true. Our house is perfectly sweet and clean; there is neither a store of old bones, nor a half-darned stocking, nor any of the other abominations you mentioned about it.'

'Your eyes have not seen the world through a microscope. Mine have,' answered the unabashed surgeon.

'When a ray of sunlight enters your rooms, you can see the whole course of the ray.'

'Yes.

'Very well, that is because the air is dirty. If it were clean you would be unable to see it. No, thank you. I will have my claret in the garden; perhaps you would not mind having it sent out to me. The air out of doors is pure compared to that of a house.'

A little table, wine, glasses and cake were sent out. Barbara and Eve did not reappear.

Mr. Jordan had a great respect for the young doctor. His self-assurance, his pedantry, his boasting, imposed on the timid and half-cultured mind of the old man. He hoped to get information from the surgeon about tests for metals, to interest him in his pursuits without letting him into his secrets; he therefore overcame his shyness sufficiently to appear and converse when Mr. Coyshe arrived.

'What a very beautiful daughter you have got!' said Coyshe; 'one that is only to be seen in pictures. A man despairs of beholding such loveliness in actual life, and see, here, at the limit of the world, the vision flashes on one! Not much like you, Squire, not much like her sister; looks as if she belonged to another breed.'

Jasper Babb looked round startled at the audacity and rudeness of the surgeon. Mr. Jordan was not offended; he seemed indeed flattered. He was very proud of Eve.

'You are right. My eldest daughter has almost nothing in common with her younger sister—only a half-sister.'

'Really,' said Coyshe, 'it makes me shiver for the future of that fairy being. I take it for granted she will be yoked to some county booby of a squire, a Bob Acres. Good Lord! what a prospect! A jewel of gold in a swine's snout, as Solomon says.'

'Eve shall never marry one unworthy of her,' said Ignatius Jordan vehemently. 'She will be under no constraint. She will be able to afford to shape her future according to her fancy. She will be comfortably off.'

'Comfortably off fifty years ago means pinched now, and pinched now means screwed flat fifty years hence. Everything is becoming costly. Living is a luxury only for the well-to-do. The rest merely exist under sufferance.'

'Miss Eve will not be pinched,' answered Mr. Jordan, unconscious that he was being drawn out by the surgeon. 'Seventeen years ago I lent fifteen hundred pounds, which is to be returned to me on Midsummer Day. To that I can add about five hundred; I have saved something since—not much, for somehow the estate has not answered as it did of old.'

'You have two daughters.'

'Oh, yes, there is Barbara,' said Jordan in a tone of indifference. 'Of course she will have something, but then—she can always manage for herself - with the other it is different.'

'Are you ill?' asked Coyshe, suddenly, observing that Jasper had turned very pale, and dark under the eyes. 'Is the air too strong for you?'

'No, let me remain here. The sun does me good.'

Mr. Jordan was rather glad of this opportunity of publishing the fortune he was going to give his younger daughter. He wished it to be known in the neighbourhood, that Eve might be esteemed and sought by suitable young men. He often said to himself that he could die content were Eve in a position where she would be happy and admired.

'When did Miss Eve's mother die?' asked Coyshe abruptly. Mr. Jordan started.

'Did I say she was dead? Did I mention her?'

Coyshe mused, put his hand through his hair and ruffled it up; then folded his arms and threw out his legs.

'Now tell me, squire, are you sure of your money?'

'What do you mean?'

'That money you say you lent seventeen years ago. What are your securities?'

'The best. The word of an honourable man.'

'The word!' Mr. Coyshe whistled. 'Words! What are words?'

'He offered me a mortgage, but it never came,' said Mr. Jordan. 'Indeed, I never applied for it. I had his word.'

'If you see the shine of that money again, you are lucky.' Then looking at Jasper: 'My patient is upset again—I thought the air was too strong for him. He must be carried in. He is going into a fit.'

Jasper was leaning back against the wall, with distended eyes, and hands and teeth clenched as with a spasm.

'No,' said Jasper faintly, 'I am not in a fit.'

'You looked much as if going into an attack of lock-jaw.'

At that moment Barbara came out, and at once noticed the condition of the convalescent.

'Here,' said she, 'lean on me as you did coming out. This has been too much for you. Will you help me, Doctor Coyshe?'

'Thank you,' said Jasper. 'If Miss Jordan will suffer me to rest on her arm, I will return to my room.'

When he was back in his arm-chair and the little room he had occupied, Barbara looked earnestly in his face and said, 'What has troubled you? I am sure something has.'

'I am very unhappy,' he answered, 'but you must ask me no questions.'

Miss Jordan went in quest of her sister. 'Eve,' she said, 'our poor patient is exhausted. Sit in the parlour and play and sing, and give a look into his room now and then. I am busy.'

The slight disturbance had not altered the bent of Mr. Jordan's thoughts. When Mr. Coyshe rejoined him, which he did the moment he saw Jasper safe in his room, Mr. Jordan said, ' I cannot believe that I ran any risk with the money. The man to whom I lent it is honourable. Besides, I have his note of hand acknowledging the debt; not that I would use it against him.'

' A man's word,' said Coyshe, ' is like india-rubber that can be made into any shape he likes. A word is made up of letters, and he will hold to the letters and permute their order to suit his own convenience, not yours. A man will stick to his word only so long as his word will stick to him. It depends entirely on which side it is licked. Hark! Is that Miss Eve singing? What a voice! Why, if she were trained and on the stage——'

Mr. Jordan stood up, agitated and angry.

' I beg your pardon,' said Coyshe. ' Does the suggestion offend you? I merely threw it out in the event of the money lent not turning up.'

Just then his eyes fell on something that lay under the seat. ' What is that? Have you dropped a pocket-book?'

A rough large leather pocket-book that was to which he pointed. Mr. Jordan stooped and took it up. He examined it attentively and uttered an exclamation of surprise.

' Well,' said the surgeon mockingly, ' is the money come, dropped from the clouds at your feet?'

' No,' answered Mr. Jordan, under his breath, ' but this is most extraordinary, most mysterious! How comes this case here? It is the very same which I handed over, filled with notes, to that man seventeen years ago! See! there are my initials on it; there on the shield is my crest. How comes it here?'

' The question, my dear sir, is not how comes it here? but what does it contain?'

' Nothing.'

The surgeon put his hands in his pockets, screwed up his lips for a whistle, and said, ' I foretold this, I am always right.'

'The money is not due till Midsummer-day.'

'Nor will come till the Greek kalends. Poor Miss Eve!'

CHAPTER X.

BARBARA'S PETITION.

MIDSUMMER-DAY was come. Mr. Jordan was in suspense and agitation. His pale face was more livid and drawn than usual. The fears inspired by the surgeon had taken hold of him.

Before the birth of Eve he had been an energetic man, eager to get all he could out of the estate, but for seventeen years an unaccountable sadness had hung over him, damping his ardour; his thoughts had been carried away from his land, whither no one knew, though the results were obvious enough.

With Barbara he had little in common. She was eminently practical. He was always in a dream. She was never on an easy footing with her father, she tried to understand him and failed, she feared that his brain was partially disturbed. Perhaps her efforts to make him out annoyed him; at any rate he was cold towards her, without being intentionally unkind. An ever-present restraint was upon both in each other's presence.

At first, after the disappearance of Eve's mother, things had gone on upon the old lines. Christopher Davy had superintended the farm labours, but as he aged and failed, and Barbara grew to see the necessity for supervision, she took the management of the farm as well as of the house upon herself. She saw that the men dawdled over their work, and that the condition of the estate was going back. The coppices had not been shredded in winter and the oak was grown into a tangle. The rending for bark in spring was done unsystematically. The hedges became ragged,

the ploughs out of order, the thistles were not cut periodically and prevented from seeding. There were not men
sufficient to do the work that had to be done. She had
not the time to attend to the men as well as the maids, to
the farmyard as well as the house. She had made up her
mind that a proper bailiff must be secured, with authority
to employ as many labourers as the estate required. Barbara was convinced that her father, with his lost, dreamy
head, was incapable of managing their property, even if he
had the desire. Now that the trusty old Davy was ill,
and breaking up, she had none to advise her.

She was roused to anger on Midsummer-day by discovering that the hayrick had never been thatched, and
that it had been exposed to the rain which had fallen
heavily, so that half of it had to be taken down because
soaked, lest it should catch fire or blacken. This was the
result of the carelessness of the men. She determined to
speak to her father at once. She had good reason for
doing so.

She found him in his study arranging his specimens of
lunudic and peacock copper.

'Has anyone come, asking for me?' he said, looking
up with fluttering face from his work.

'No one, father.'

'You startled me, Barbara, coming on me stealthily
from behind. What do you want with me? You see I
am engaged, and you know I hate to be disturbed.'

'I have something I wish to speak about.'

'Well, well, say it and go.' His shaking hands resumed their work.

'It is the old story, dear papa. I want you to engage
a steward. It is impossible for us to go on longer in the
way we have. You know how I am kept on the run from
morning to night. I have to look after all your helpless
men, as well as my own helpless maids. When I am in
the field, there is mischief done in the kitchen; when I
am in the house, the men are smoking and idling on the

farm. Eve cannot help me in seeing to domestic matters,
she has not the experience. Everything devolves on me.
I do not grudge doing my utmost, but I have not the time
for everything, and I am not ubiquitous.'

'No,' said Mr. Jordan, 'Eve cannot undertake any sort
of work. That is an understood thing.'

'I know it is. If I ask her to be sure and recollect
something, she is certain with the best intentions to forget; she is a dear beautiful butterfly, not fit to be har-
nessed. Her brains are thistledown, her bones cherry
stalks.'

'Yes, do not crush her spirits with uncongenial work.'

'I do not want to. I know as well as yourself that I
must rely on her for nothing. But the result is that I am
overtasked. Now—will you credit it? The beautiful hay
that was like green tea is spoiled. Those stupid men did
not thatch it. They said they had no reed, and waited to
comb some till the rain set in. When it did pour, they
were all in the barn talking and making reed, but at the
same time the water was drenching and spoiling the hay.
Oh, papa, I feel disposed to cry!'

'I will speak to them about it,' said Mr. Jordan, with
a sigh, not occasioned by the injury to his hay, but because
he was disturbed over his specimens.

'My dear papa,' said the energetic Barbara, 'I do not
wish you to be troubled about these tiresome matters.
You are growing old, daily older, and your strength is not
gaining. You have other pursuits. You are not heartily
interested in the farm. I see your hand tremble when
you hold your fork at dinner; you are becoming thinner
every day. I would spare you trouble. It is really necessary, I must have it—you must engage a bailiff. I shall
break down, and that will be the end, or we shall all go to
ruin. The woods are running to waste. There are trees
lying about literally rotting. They ought to be sent away
to the Devonport dockyard where they could be sold. Last
spring, when you let the rending, the barbers shaved a

whole copse wood, as if shaving a man's chin, instead of leaving the better sticks standing.'

'We have enough to live on.'

'We must do our duty to the land on which we live. I cannot endure to see waste anywhere. I have only one head, one pair of eyes, and one pair of hands. I cannot think of, see to, and do everything. I lie awake night after night considering what has to be done, and the day is too short for me to do all I have determined on in the night. Whilst that poor gentleman has been ill, I have had to think of him in addition to everything else; so some duties have been neglected. That is how, I suppose, the doctor came to guess there was a stocking half-darned under the sofa cushion. Eve was mending it, she tired and put it away, and of course forgot it. I generally look about for Eve's leavings, and tidy her scraps when she has gone to bed, but I have been too busy. I am vexed about that stocking. How those protruding eyes of the doctor managed to see it I cannot think. He was, however, wrong about the saucer of sour milk.'

Mr. Jordan continued nervously sorting his minerals into little white card boxes.

'Well, papa, are you going to do anything?'

'Do—do—what?'

'Engage a bailiff. I am sure we shall gain money by working the estate better. The bailiff will pay his cost, and something over.'

'You are very eager for money,' said Mr. Jordan sulkily; 'are you thinking of getting married, and anxious to have a dower?'

Barbara coloured deeply, hurt and offended.

'This is unkind of you, papa; I am thinking of Eve I think only of her. You ought to know that'—the tears came into her eyes. 'Of course Eve will marry some day;' then she laughed, 'no one will ever come for me.'

'To be sure,' said Mr. Jordan.

'I have been thinking, papa, that Eve ought to be sent to some very nice lady, or to some very select school, where she might have proper finishing. All she has learnt has been from me, and I have had so much to do, and I have been so unable to be severe with Eve—that—that— I don't think she has learned much except music, to which she takes instinctively as a South Sea islander to water.'

'I cannot be parted from Eve. It would rob my sky of its sun. What would this house be with only you—I mean without Eve to brighten it?'

'If you will think the matter over, father, you will see that it ought to be. We must consider Eve, and not ourselves. I would not have her, dear heart, anywhere but in the very best school,—hardly a school, a place where only three or four young ladies are taken, and they of the best families. That will cost money, so we must put our shoulders to the wheel, and push the old coach on.' She laid her hands on the back of her father's chair and leaned over his shoulder. She had been standing behind him. Did she hope he would kiss her? If so, her hope was vain.

'Do, dear papa, engage an honest, superior sort of man to look after the farm. I will promise to make a great deal of money with my dairy, if he will see to the cows in the fields. Try the experiment, and, trust me, it will answer.'

'All in good time.'

'No, papa, do not put this off. There is another reason why I speak. Christopher Davy is bedridden. You are sometimes absent, then we girls are left alone in this great house, all day, and occasionally nights as well. You know there was no one here on that night when the accident happened. There were two men in this house, one, indeed, insensible. We know nothing of them, who they were, and what they were about. How can you tell that bad characters may not come here? It is thought that you have saved money, and it is known that Morwell is unprotected. You, papa, are so frail, and with your shaking hand a gun would not be dangerous.'

He started from his chair and upset his specimens.

' Do not speak like that,' he said, trembling.

' There, I have disturbed you even by alluding to it. If you were to level a gun, and had your finger——'

He put his hand, a cold, quivering hand, on her lips: 'For God's sake—silence ! ' he said.

She obeyed. She knew how odd her father was, yet his agitation now was so great that it surprised her. It made her more resolute to carry her point.

' Papa, you are expecting to have about two thousand pounds in the house. Will it be safe? You have told the doctor, and that man, our patient, heard you. Excuse my saying it, but I think it was not well to mention it before a perfect stranger. You may have told others. Mr. Coyshe is a chatterbox, he may have talked about it throughout the neighbourhood—the fact may be known to everyone, that to-day you are expecting to have a large sum of money brought you. Well—who is to guard it ? Are there no needy and unscrupulous men in the county who would rob the house, and maybe silence an old man and two girls who stood in their way to a couple of thousand pounds ? '

' The sum is large. It must be hidden away,' said Mr. Jordan, uneasily. ' I had not considered the danger '—he paused—' if it be paid——'

' *If*, papa ? I thought you were sure of it.'

' Yes, quite sure; only Mr. Coyshe disturbed me by suggesting doubts.'

' Oh, the doctor ! ' exclaimed Barbara, shrugging her shoulders.

' Well, the doctor,' repeated Mr. Jordan, captiously. ' He is a very able man. Why do you turn up your nose at him ? He can see through a stone wall, and under a cushion to where a stocking is hidden, and under a cupboard to where a saucer of sour milk is thrust away; and he can see into the human body through the flesh and behind the bones, and can tell you where every nerve and vein is, and what is wrong with each. When things are wrong, then it is like stockings and saucers where they ought not to be in a house.'

'He was wrong about the saucer of sour milk, utterly wrong,' persisted Barbara.

'I hope and trust the surgeon was wrong in his forecast about the money—but my heart fails me——'

'He was wrong about the saucer,' said the girl encouragingly.

'But he was right about the stocking,' said her father dispiritedly.

CHAPTER XI.

GRANTED!

As the sun declined, Mr. Jordan became uneasy. He could not remain in his study. He could not rest anywhere. The money had not been returned. He had taken out of his strong box Ezekiel Babb's acknowledgment and promise of payment, but he knew that it was so much waste-paper to him. He could not or would not proceed against the borrower. Had he not wronged him cruelly by living with his daughter as if she were his wife, without having been legally married to her? Could he take legal proceedings for the recovery of his money, and so bring all the ugly story to light and publish it to the world? He had let Mr. Babb have the money to pacify him, and make some amends for the wrong he had done. No! If Mr. Babb did not voluntarily return the money, Ignatius Jordan foresaw that it was lost to him, lost to Eve, and poor Eve's future was unprovided for. The estate must go to Barbara, that is, the reversion in the tenure of it; the ready money he had intended for Eve.

Mr. Jordan felt a bitterness rise in his heart against Barbara, whose future was assured, whilst that of Eve was not. He would have liked to leave Morwell to his younger daughter, but he was not sure that the Duke would approve of this, and he was quite sure that Eve was incompetent to manage a farm and dairy.

At the time of which we treat, it was usual for every squire to farm a portion of his own estate, his manor house was backed with extensive outbuildings for cattle, and his wife and daughters were not above superintending the dairy. Indeed, an ancestress of the author took farm after farm into her own hands as the leases fell in, and at last farmed the entire parish. She died in 1795. The Jordans were not squires, but perpetual tenants under the Dukes of Bedford, and had been received by the country gentry on an equal footing, till Mr. Jordan compromised his character by his union with Eve's mother. The estate of Morwell was a large one for one man to farm; if the Duke had exacted a large rent, of late years Mr. Jordan would have fallen into arrears, but the Duke had not raised his rent at the last renewal. The Dukes were the most indulgent of landlords.

Mr. Jordan came into the hall. It was the same as it had been seventeen years before; the same old clock was there, ticking in the same tone, the same scanty furniture of a few chairs, the same slate floor. Only the cradle was no longer to be seen. The red light smote into the room just as it had seventeen years before. There against the wall it painted a black cross as it had done seventeen years ago.

Ignatius Jordan looked up over the great fireplace. Above it hung the musket he had been cleaning when Ezekiel Babb entered. It had not been taken down and used since that day. Seventeen years! It was an age. The little babe that had lain in the cradle was now a beautiful marriageable maiden. Time had made its mark upon himself. His back was more bent, his hand **more**

shaky, his walk less steady ; a careful, thrifty man had
been converted into an abstracted, half-crazed dreamer.
Seventeen years of gnawing care and ceaseless sorrow ! How
had he been able to bear it ? Only by the staying wings of
love, of love for his little Eve—for *her* child. Without
his Eve, *her* child, long ago he would have sunk and been
swallowed up, the clouds of derangement of intellect would
have descended on his brain, or his bodily health would
have given way.

Seventeen years ago, on Midsummer-day, there had
stood on the little folding oak table under the window a
tumbler full of china roses, which were drooping, and had
shed their leaves over the polished, almost black, table
top. They had been picked some days before by his wife.
Now, in the same place stood a glass, and in it were roses
from the same tree, not drooping, but fresh and glistening,
placed that morning there by *her* daughter. His eye
sought the clock. At five o'clock, seventeen years ago,
Ezekiel Babb had come into that hall through that doorway, and had borrowed his money. The clock told that
the time was ten minutes to five. If Mr. Babb did not
appear to the hour, he would abandon the expectation of
seeing him. He must make a journey to Buckfastleigh
over the moor, a long day's journey, and seek the
defaulter, and know the reason why the loan was not
repaid.

He thought of the pocket-book on the gravel. How
came it there ? Who could have brought it ? Mr. Jordan
was too fully impressed with belief in the supernatural not
to suppose it was dropped at his feet as a warning that his
money was gone.

Mr. Jordan's eyes were fixed on the clock. The works
began to whir-r. Then followed the strokes. One—two
—three—four—FIVE.

At the last stroke the door of Jasper's sickroom opened,
and the convalescent slowly entered the hall and con-
fronted his host.

The last week had wrought wonders in the man. He had rapidly recovered flesh and vigour after his wounds were healed.

As he entered, and his eyes met those of Mr. Jordan, the latter felt that a messenger from Ezekiel Babb stood before him, and that his money was not forthcoming.

'Well, sir?' he said.

'I am Jasper, the eldest son of Ezekiel Babb, of Owla-combe in Buckfastleigh,' he said. 'My father borrowed money of you this day seventeen years ago, and solemnly swore on this day to repay it.'

'Well?'

'It is not well. I have not got the money.'

A moan of disappointment broke from the heart of Ignatius Jordan, then a spasm of rage, such as might seize on a madman, transformed his face; his eye blazed, and he sprang to his feet and ran towards Jasper. The latter, keeping his eye on him, said firmly, 'Listen to me, Mr. Jordan. Pray sit down again, and I will explain to you why my father has not sent the money.'

Mr. Jordan hesitated. His face quivered. With his raised hand he would have struck Jasper, but the composure of the latter awed him. The paroxysm passed, and he sank into his chair, and gave way to depression.

'My father is a man of honour. He gave you his word, and he intended to keep it. He borrowed of you a large sum, and he laid it out in the purchase of some land. He has been fairly prosperous. He saved money enough to repay the debt, and perhaps more. As the time drew nigh for repayment he took the sum required from the bank in notes, and locked them in his bureau. Others knew of this. My father was not discreet: he talked about the repayment, he resented having to make it, complained that he would be reduced to great straits without it.'

'The money was not his, but mine.'

'I know that,' said Jasper, sorrowfully. 'But my

father has always been what is termed a close man, has
thought much of money, and cannot bear to part with it.
I do not say that this justifies, but it explains, his dissatis-
faction. He is an old man, and becoming feeble, and
clings through force of habit to his money.'

'Go on ; nothing can justify him.'

'Others knew of his money. One day he was at
Totnes, at a great cloth fair. He did not return till the
following day. During his absence his bureau was broken
open, and the money stolen.'

'Was the thief not caught? Was the money not recovered?' asked Mr. Jordan, trembling with excitement.

'The money was in part recovered.'

'Where is it?'

'Listen to what follows. You asked if the—the person
who took the money was caught. He was.'

'Is he in prison?'

'The person who took the money was caught, tried,
and sent to jail. When taken, some of the money was
found about him ; he had not spent it all. What remained
I was bringing you.'

'Give it me.'

'I have not got it.'

'You have not got it?'

'No, I have lost it.'

Again did Mr. Jordan start up in a fit of rage. He
ground his teeth, and the sweat broke out in drops on his
brow.

'I had the money with me when the accident happened, and I was thrown from my horse, and became unconscious. It was lost or taken then.'

'Who was your companion? He must have robbed
you.'

'I charge no one. I alone am to blame. The money
was entrusted to my keeping.'

'Why did your father give you the money before the
appointed day?'

'When my father recovered part of the money, he would no longer keep it in his possession, lest he should again lose it; so he bade me take it to you at once.'

'You have spent the money, you have spent it yourself!' cried Mr. Jordan wildly.

'If I had done this, should I have come to you to-day with this confession? I had the money in the pocket-book in notes. The notes were abstracted from the book. As I was so long insensible, it was too late to stop them at the bank. Whoever took them had time to change them all.'

'Cursed be the day I lent the money,' moaned Ignatius Jordan. 'The empty, worthless case returns, the precious contents are gone. What is the shell without the kernel? My Eve, my Eve!' He clasped his hands over his brow.

'And now once more hearken to me,' pursued Jasper. 'My father cannot immediately find the money that he owes you. He does not know of this second loss. I have not communicated with him since I met with my accident. The blame attaches to me. I must do what I can to make amends for my carelessness. I put myself into your hands. To repay you now, my father would have to sell the land he bought. I do not think he could be persuaded to do this, though, perhaps, you might be able to force him to it. However, as you say the money is for your daughter, will you allow it to lie where it is for a while? I will undertake, should it come to me after my father's death, to sell it or transfer it, so as to make up to Miss Eve at the rate of five per cent. on the loan. I will do more. If you will consent to this, I will stay here and work for you. I have been trained in the country, and know about a farm. I will act as your foreman, overlooker, or bailiff. I will put my hand to anything. Reckon what my wage would be. Reckon at the end of a year whether I have not earned my wage and much more. If you like, I will work for you as long as my father lives; I will serve you now faithfully as no hired bailiff would serve you. My presence here will be a guarantee to you that I will be true to my undertaking to repay the whole sum with interest. I can see that this estate needs an active man on it; and you, sir, are too advanced in age, and too much given up to scientific pursuits, to cope with what is required.'

Those words, 'scientific pursuits,' softened Mr. Jordan. Jasper spoke in good faith; he had no idea how worthless those pursuits were, how little true science entered into them. He knew that Mr. Jordan made mineralogical studies, and he supposed they were well directed.

'Order me to do what you will,' said Jasper, 'and I will do it, and will double your gains in the year.'

'I accept,' said Ignatius Jordan. 'There is no help for it. I must accept or be plundered of all.'

'You accept! let us join hands on the bargain.'

It was strange; as once before, seventeen years ago, hands had met in the golden gleam of sun that shot through the window, ratifying a contract, so was it now. The hands clasped in the sunbeam, and the reflected light from their illuminated hands smote up into the faces of the two men, both pale, one with years and care, the other with sickness.

Mr. Jordan withdrew his hand, clasped both palms over his face and wept. 'Thus it comes,' he said. 'The shadow is on me and on my child. One sorrow follows another.'

At that moment Barbara and Eve entered from the court.

'Eve! Eve!' cried the father excitedly, 'come to me, my angel! my ill-treated child! my martyr!' He caught her to his heart, put his face on her shoulder, and sobbed. 'My darling, you have had your money stolen, the money put away for you when you were in the cradle.'

'Who has stolen it, papa?' asked Barbara.

'Look there!' he cried; 'Jasper Babb was bringing

me the money, and when he fell from his horse, it was stolen.'

Neither Barbara nor Eve spoke.

'Now,' continued Mr. Jordan, 'he has offered himself as my hind to look after the farm for me, and promises, if I give him time——'

'Father, you have refused!' interrupted Barbara.

'On the contrary, I have accepted.'

'It cannot, it must not be!' exclaimed Barbara vehemently. 'Father, you do not know what you have done.'

'This is strange language to be addressed by a child to a father,' said Mr. Jordan in a tone of irritation. 'Was there ever so unreasonable a girl before? This morning you pressed me to engage a bailiff, and now that Mr. Jasper Babb has volunteered, and I have accepted him, you turn round and won't have him.'

'No,' she said, with quick-drawn breath, 'I will not. Take anyone but him. I entreat you, papa. If you have any regard for my opinion, let him go. For pity's sake do not allow him to remain here!'

'I have accepted him,' said her father coldly. 'Pray what weighty reasons have you got to induce me to alter my resolve?'

Miss Jordan stood thinking; the colour mounted to her forehead, then her brows contracted. 'I have none to give,' she said in a low tone, greatly confused, with her eyes on the ground. Then, in a moment, she recovered her self-possession and looked Jasper full in the face, but without speaking, steadily, sternly. In fact, her heart was beating so fast, and her breath coming so quick, that she could not speak. 'Mr. Jasper,' she said at length, controlling her emotions by a strong effort of will, 'I entreat you—go.'

He was silent.

'I have nursed you; I have given my nights and days to you. You confessed that I had saved your life. If you have any gratitude in your heart, if you have any respect for the house that has sheltered you – go !'

'Barbara,' said her father, 'you are a perverse girl. He shall not go. I insist on his fulfilling his engagement. If he leaves I shall take legal proceedings against his father to recover the money.'

'Do that rather than retain him.'

'Miss Jordan,' said Jasper, slowly, and with sadness in his voice, ' it is true that you have saved my life. Your kind hand drew me from the brink of the grave whither I was descending. I thank you with all my heart, but I cannot go from my engagement to your father. Through my fault the money was lost, and I must make what amends I may for my negligence.'

' Go back to your father.'

' That I cannot do.'

She considered with her hand over her lips to hide her agitation. ' No,' she said, ' I understand that. Of course you cannot go back to your native place and to your home; but you need not stay here.' Then suddenly, in a burst of passion, she extended her hands to her father, ' Papa !'— then to the young man, ' Mr. Jasper !—Papa, send him away! Mr. Jasper, do not remain !'

The young man was hardly less agitated than herself. He took a couple of steps towards the door.

' Stuff and fiddlesticks !' shouted Mr. Jordan. ' He shall not go. I forbid him.'

Jasper turned. ' Miss Barbara,' he said, humbly, 'you are labouring under a mistake which I must not explain. Forgive me. I stay.'

She looked at him with moody anger, and muttered, ' Knowing what you do--that I am not blind—that you should dare to settle here under this *honourable* roof. It is unjust! it is ungrateful ! it is wicked! God help us ! I have done what I could.'

CHAPTER XII.

CALLED AWAY.

JASPER was installed in Morwell as bailiff in spite of the remonstrances of Barbara. He was given a room near the gatehouse, and was attended by Mrs. Davy, but he came for his dinner to the table of the Jordans. Barbara had done what she could to prevent his becoming an inmate of the house. She might not tell her father her real reasons for objecting to the arrangement.

She was rendered more uneasy a day or two after by receiving news that an aunt, a sister of her mother, who lived beyond Dartmoor, was dying, and she was summoned to receive her last sigh. She must leave Morwell, leave her father and sister in the house with a man whom she thoroughly mistrusted. Her only comfort was that Jasper was not sufficiently strong and well to be dangerous. What was he? Was there any truth in that story he had told her father? She could not believe it, because it would not fit in with what she already knew. What place had the convict's garb in that tale? She turned the narrative about in her mind, and rejected it. She was inclined to disbelieve in Jasper being the son of old Mr. Babb. He had assumed the name and invented the story to deceive her father, and form an excuse for remaining in the house.

She hardly spoke to Jasper when they met. She was cold and haughty, she did not look at him ; and he made no advances to gain her goodwill.

When she received the summons to her aunt's death-bed, knowing that she must go, she asked where Mr. Babb was, and, hearing that he was in the barn, went thither with the letter in her hand.

He had been examining the horse turned winnowing

machine, which was out of order. As she came to the
door he looked up and removed his hat, making a formal
salute. The day was hot; he had been taking the machine
to pieces, and was warm, so he had removed his coat. He
at once drew it on his back again.

Barbara had a curt, almost rough, manner at times.
She was vexed now, and angry with him, so she spoke
shortly, 'I am summoned to Ashburton. That is close to
Buckfastleigh, where, you say, you lived, to make my
father believe it is your home.'

'Yes, Miss Jordan, that is true.'

'You have not written to your home since you have
been with us. At least—' she hesitated, and slightly
coloured—'you have sent no letter by our boy. Perhaps
you were afraid to have it known where you are. No
doubt you were right. It is essential to you that your
presence here should not be known to anyone but your
father. A letter might be opened, or let lie about, and so
your whereabouts be discovered. Supposing your story to
be true, that is how I account for your silence. If it be
false——'

'It is not false, Miss Jordan.'

'I am going to Ashburton, I will assure myself of
it there. If it be false I shall break my promise to you,
and tell my father everything. I give you fair warning.
If it be true——'

'It is true, dear young lady.'

'Do not be afraid of my disclosing your secret, and
putting you in peril.'

'I am sure you cannot do that,' he said, with a smile
that was sad. 'If you go to Buckfastleigh, Miss Jordan,
I shall venture to send word by you to my father where I
am, that the money is lost, and what I have undertaken.'

Barbara tossed her head, and flashed an indignant
glance at him out of her brown eyes.

'I cannot, I will not be a porter of lies.'

'What lies?'

G

'You did not lose the money. Why deceive me? I know your object in lurking here, in the most out-of-the-way nook of England you could find. You think that here you are safe from pursuit. You made up the story to impose on my father, and ·induce him to engage you. O, you are very honourable ! discharging a debt!—I hate crime, but I hate falsehood even more.'

'You are mistaken, Miss Jordan. The story is true.'

'You have told the whole honest truth ? '

'I do not profess to have told the whole truth. What I have told has been true, though I have not told all.'

'A pinch of truth is often more false than a bushel of lies. It deceives, the other does not.'

'It is true that I lost the money confided to me. If you are going to Ashburton, I ask you, as a matter of kindness—I know how kind you can be, alas, and I know also how cruel—to see my father.'

She laughed haughtily. 'This is a fine proposition. The servant sends the mistress to do his dirty work. I thank you for the honour.' She turned angrily away.

'Miss Barbara,' said Jasper, 'you are indeed cruel.'

'Am I cruel ? ' She turned and faced him again, with a threatening brow. 'I have reason to be just. Cruel I am not.'

'You were all gentleness at one time, when I was ill. Now——'

'I will not dispute with you. Do you expect to be fed with a spoon still ? When you were ill I treated you as a patient, not more kindly than I would have treated my deadliest enemy. I acted as duty prompted. There was no one else to take care of you, that was my motive—my only motive.'

'When I think of your kindness then, I wish I were sick again.'

'A mean and wicked wish. Tired already, I suppose, of doing *honest* work.'

'Miss Barbara,' he said, 'pray let me speak.'

'Cruel,'—she recurred to what he had said before, without listening to his entreaty, 'It is you who are cruel coming here—you, with the ugly stain on your life, coming here to hide it in this innocent household. Would it not be cruel in a man with the plague poison in him to steal into a home of harmless women and children, and give them all the pestilence? Had I suspected that you intended making Morwell your retreat and skulking den, I would never have passed my promise to keep silence. I would have taken the hateful evidence of what you are in my hand, and gone to the first constable and bid him arrest you in your bed.'

'No,' said Jasper, 'you would not have done it. I know you better than you know yourself. Are you lost to all humanity? Surely you feel pity in your gentle bosom, notwithstanding your bitter words.'

'No,' she answered, with flushed cheeks and sparkling eyes, 'no, I have pity only for myself, because I was weak enough to take pains to save your worthless life.'

'Miss Jordan,' he said, looking sorrowfully at her— and her eyes fell—'surely I have a right to ask some pity of you. Have you considered what the temptations must be that beset a young man who has been roughly handled at home, maltreated by his father, reared without love—a young man with a soul bounding with hopes, ambition, love of life, with a heart for pleasure, all which are beaten back and trampled down by the man who ought to direct them? Can you not understand how a lad who has been thwarted in every way, without a mother to soothe him in trouble, and encourage him in good, driven desperate by a father's harshness, may break away and transgress? Con-sider the case of one who has been taught that everything beautiful—laughter, delight in music, in art, in nature, a merry gambol, a joyous warble—is sinful; is it not likely that the outlines of right and wrong would be so blurred in his conscience, that he might lapse into crime without criminal intent?'

'Are you speaking of yourself, or are you excusing another?'

'I am putting a case.'

Barbara sighed involuntarily. Her own father had been unsympathetic. He had never been actually severe, he had been indifferent.

'I can see that there were temptations to one so situated to leave his home,' she answered, 'but this is not a case of truancy, but of crime.'

'You judge without knowing the circumstances.'

'Then tell me all, that I may form a more equitable judgment.'

'I cannot do that now. You shall be told—later.'

'Then I must judge by what I know——'

'By what you guess,' he said, correcting her.

'As you will.' Her eyes were on the ground. A white spar was there. She turned it over with her foot, and turned it again.

She hesitated what to say.

'Should you favour me so far as to visit my father,' said Jasper, 'I beg of you one thing most earnestly. Do not mention the name of my companion—Martin.'

'Why not?'

'He may suspect him of having robbed me. My father is an energetic, resolute man. He might pursue him, and I alone am to blame. I lost the money.'

'Who was that Martin?'

'He told you—that I was nothing to him.'

'Then why do you seek to screen him?'

'Can I say that he took the money? If my father gets him arrested—I shall be found.'

Barbara laughed bitterly.

'Of course, the innocent must not be brought into suspicion because he has ridden an hour alongside of the guilty. No! I will say nothing of Martin.'

She was still turning over the piece of spar with her foot. It sparkled in the sun.

'How are you going to Ashburton, Miss Jordan?'

'I ride, and little John Ostler rides with me, conveying my portmanteau.'

Then she trifled with the spar again. There was some peacock copper on it that glistened with all the colours of the rainbow. Abruptly, at length, she turned away and went indoors.

Next morning early she came in her habit to the gate where the boy who was to accompany her held the horses. She had not seen Jasper that morning, but she knew where he was. He had gone along the lane toward the common to set the men to repair fences and hedges, as the cattle that strayed on the waste-land had broken into the wheat field.

She rode along the lane in meditative mood. She saw Jasper awaiting her on the down, near an old quarry, the rubble heap from which was now blazing with gorse in full bloom. She drew rein, and said, 'I am going to Ashburton. I will take your message, not because you asked me, but because I doubt the truth of your story.'

'Very well, Miss Jordan,' he said respectfully; 'I thank you, whatever your motive may be.'

'I expect and desire no thanks,' she answered, and whipped her horse, that started forward.

'I wish you a favourable journey,' he said. 'Good-bye.'

She did not turn her head or respond. She was very angry with him. She stooped over her pommel and buckled the strap of the little pocket in the leather for her kerchief. But, before she had ridden far, an intervening gorse bush forced her to bend her horse aside, and then she looked back, without appearing to look, looked back out of her eye-corners. Jasper stood where she had left him, with his hat in his hand.

CHAPTER XIII.

MR. BABB AT HOME.

A LOVELY July day in the fresh air of Dartmoor, that seems to sparkle as it enters the lungs : fresh, but given a sharpness of salt : pure, but tinged with the sweetness of heather bloom and the honey of gorse. Human spirits bound in this air. The scenery of Dartmoor, if bare of trees, is wildly picturesque with granite masses and bold mountain peaks. Barbara could not shake off the anxiety that enveloped her spirits like the haze of a valley till she rose up a long ascent of three miles from the wooded valley of the Tavy to the bald, rock-strewn expanse of Dartmoor. She rode on, attended by her little groom, till she reached Prince's Town, the highest point attained by the road, where, in a desolate plain of bog, but little below the crests of some of the granite tors, stands a prison surrounded by a few mean houses. From Prince's Town Barbara would have a rough moor-path, not a good road, before her ; and, as the horses were exhausted with their long climb, she halted at the little inn, and ordered some dinner for herself, and required that the boy and the horses should be attended to.

Whilst ham and eggs—nothing else was procurable— were being fried, Barbara walked along the road to the prison, and looked at the gloomy, rugged gate built of un-trimmed granite blocks. The unbroken desolation swept to the very walls of the prison.[1] At that height the wind moans among the rocks and rushes mournfully ; the air is never still. The landlady of the inn came to her.

'That is the jail,' she said. 'There was a prisoner broke out not long ago, and he has not yet been caught.

---

[1] The author has allowed himself a slight anachronism. The prison was not a convict establishment at the period of this tale.

How he managed it none can tell. Where he now is no one knows. He may be still wandering on the moor. Every road from it is watched. Perhaps he may give himself up, finding escape impossible. If not, he will die of hunger among the rocks.'

'What was the crime for which he was here?' asked Barbara; but she spoke with an effort.

'He was a bad man; it was no ordinary wickedness he committed. He robbed his own father.'

'His own father!' echoed Barbara, starting.

'Yes, he robbed him of nigh on two thousand pounds. The father acted sharp, and had him caught before he had spent all the money. The assizes were next week, so it was quick work; and here he was for a few days, and then —he got away.'

'Robbed his own father!' murmured Barbara, and now she thought she saw more clearly than before into a matter that looked blacker the more she saw.

'There's a man in yonder who set fire to his house to get the insurance. Folks say his house was but a rummagy old place. 'Tis a pity. Now, if he had got away it would not have mattered; but, a rascal who did not respect his own father!—not that I hold with a man prosecuting his own son. That was hard. Still, if one was to escape, I don't see why the Lord blessed the undertaking of the man who robbed his father, and turned His face away from him who only fired his house to get the insurance.'

The air ceased to sparkle as Miss Jordan rode the second stage of her journey: the sun was less bright, the fragrance of the gorse less sweet. She did not speak to her young groom the whole way, but rode silently, with compressed lips and moody brow. The case was worse than she had anticipated. Jasper had robbed his father, and all that story of his coming as a messenger from Mr. Babb with the money was false.

One evening, unattended, Barbara Jordan rode to

Buckfastleigh, asked for the house of Mr. Babb, and dismounted at the door. The house was a plain, ugly, square modern erection, almost an insult to the beauty of the surroundings. The drive from the entrance gate was grass-grown. There was a stucco porch. The door was painted drab, and the paint was blistered, and had flaked off. The house also was mottled. It had been painted over plaster and cement, and the paint had curled and come off in patches. The whole place had an uncared-for look. There were no flower beds, no creepers against the walls; the rain-shoots to the roof were choked, and the overflowing water had covered the walls where it reached with slime, black and green. At the back of the house was a factory, worked by a water-wheel, for cloth, and a gravel well-trodden path led from the back door of the house to the factory.

Barbara had descended from her cob to open the gate into the drive; and she walked up to the front door, leading her horse. There she rang the bell, but had doubts whether the wire were sound. She waited a long time, and no one responded. She tried the bell again, and then rapped with the handle of her whip against the door.

Then she saw a face appear at a side window, observe her and withdraw. A moment after, a shuffling tread sounded in the hall, chains and bolts were undone, the door was cautiously opened, and in it stood an old man with white hair, and black beady eyes.

'What do you want? Who are you?' he asked.

'Am I speaking to Mr. Babb?'

'Yes, you are.'

'May I have a few words with you in private?'

'Oh, there is no one in the house, except my housekeeper, and she is deaf. You can say what you want here.'

'Who is there to take my horse?'

'You can hold him by the bridle, and talk to me where you stand. There's no occasion for you to come in.'

Barbara saw into the hall; it was floored with stone, the Buckfastleigh marble, but unpolished. The walls had been papered with glazed imitation panelling, but the paper had peeled off, and hung in strips. A chair with wooden seat, that had not been wiped for weeks, a set of coat and hat pegs, some broken, on one a very discoloured great coat and a battered hat. In a corner a bulging green umbrella, the silk detached from the whalebone.

'You see,' said the old man grimly, half turning, as he noticed that Barbara's eyes were observing the interior; 'you see, this is no place for ladies. It is a weaving spider's web, not a gallant's bower.'

'But——' the girl hesitated, 'what I have to say is very particular, and I would not be overheard on any account.'

'Ah! ah!' he giggled, 'I'll have no games played with me. I'm no longer susceptible to fascination, and I ain't worth it; on my sacred word I'm not. I'm very poor, very poor now. You can see it for yourself. Is this house kept up, and the garden? Does the hall look like a lap of luxury? I'm too poor to be a catch, so you may go away.'

Barbara would have laughed had not the nature of her visit been so serious.

'I am Miss Jordan,' she said, 'daughter of Mr. Jordan of Morwell, from whom you borrowed money seventeen years ago.'

'Oh!' he gave a start of surprise. 'Ah, well, I have sent back as much as I could spare. Some was stolen. It is not convenient to me after this reverse to find all now.'

'My father has received nothing. What you sent was lost or stolen on the way.'

The old man's jaw fell, and he stared blankly at her.

'It is as I say. My father has received nothing.'

'I sent it by my son.'

'He has lost it.'

'It is false. He has stolen it.

'What is to be done?'

'Oh, that is for your father to decide. When my son robbed me, I locked him up. Now let your father see to it. I have done my duty, my conscience is clear.'

Barbara looked steadily, with some curiosity, into his face. The face was repulsive. The strongly marked features which might have been handsome in youth, were exaggerated by age. His white hair was matted and uncombed. He had run his fingers through it whilst engaged on his accounts, and had divided it into rat's-tails. His chin and jaws were frouzy with coarse white bristles. In his black eyes was a keen twinkle of avarice and cunning. Old age and the snows of the winter of life soften a harsh face, if there be any love in it; but in this there was none. If a fire had burnt on the hearth of the old man's heart, not a spark remained alive, the hearth was choked with grey ashes. Barbara traced a resemblance between the old man and his son. From his father, Jasper had derived his aquiline nose, and the shape of mouth and chin. But the expression of the faces was different. That of Jasper was noble, that of his father mean. The eyes of the son were gentle, those of Mr. Babb hard as pebbles that had been polished.

As Barbara talked with and observed the old man she recalled what Jasper had said of ill-treatment and lack of love. There was no tenderness to be got out of such a man as that before her.

'Now look you here,' said Mr. Babb. 'Do you see that stretch of field yonder where the cloth is strained in the sun? Very well. That cloth is mine. It is woven in my mill yonder. That field was purchased seventeen years ago for my accommodation. I can't repay the money now without selling the factory or the field, and neither is worth a shilling without the other. No—we must all put up with losses. I have mine; the Lord sends your father his. A wise Providence orders all that. Tell him so. His heart has been hankering after mammon, and now Heaven has deprived him of it. I've had losses too. I've learned to

bear them. So must he. What is your name?—I mean
your Christian name?'

'Barbara.'

'Oh! not Eve—dear, no. You don't look as if that
were your name.'

'Eve is my sister—my half-sister.'

'Ah, ha! the elder daughter. And what has become of
the little one?'

'She is well, at home, and beautiful as she is good.
She is not at all like me.'

'That is a good job—for you. I mean, that you are not
like her. Is she lively?'

'Oh, like a lark, singing, dancing, merry.'

'Of course, thoughtless, light, a feather that flies and
tosses in the breath.'

'To return to the money. It was to have been my
sister's.'

'Well,' said the old man with a giggle, 'let it so remain. It *was* to have been. Now it cannot be. Whoso
fault is that? Not mine. I kept the money for your
father. I am a man of my word. When I make a cove-
nant I do not break it. But my son—my son!'

'Your son is now with us.'

'You say he has stolen the money. Let your father
not spare him. There is no good in being lenient. Be
just. When my son robbed me, I did not spare him. I will
not lift a little finger to save Jasper, who now, as you say,
has robbed your father. Wait where you are; I will run
in, and write something, which will perhaps satisfy Mr.
Jordan; wait here, you cannot enter, or your horse would
run away. What did you give for that cob? not much.
Do you want to sell him? I don't mind ten pounds. He's
not worth more. See how he hangs his off hind leg. That's
a blemish that would stand in your way of selling. Would
you like to go over the factory? No charge, you can tip
the foreman a shilling. No cloth weaving your way, only
wool growing; and—judging from what I saw of your

father-wool-gathering.' With a cackle the old man slipped in and shut the door in Barbara's face.

Miss Jordan stood patting the neck of her disparaged horse. ' You are not to be parted with, are you, Jock, to an old skinflint who would starve you?'

The cob put his nose on her shoulder, and rubbed it. She looked round. Everything spoke of sordidness, only the factory seemed cared for, where money was made. None was wasted on the adornment, even on the decencies, of life.

The door opened. Mr. Babb had locked it after him as he went in. He came out with a folded letter in his hand.

'Here,' he said, 'give that to your father.'

'I must tell you, Mr. Babb, that your son Jasper is with us. He professes to have lost the money. He met with an accident and was nearly killed. He remains with us, as a sort of steward to my father, for a while, only for a while.'

'Let him stay. I don't want him back, I won't have him back. I dare say, now, it would do him good to have his Bible. I'll give you that to take to him. He may read and come to repentance.'

'It is possible that there may be other things of his he will want. If you can make them up into a bundle, I will send for them. No,' she said after a pause, 'I will not send for them. I will take them myself.'

'You will not mind staying there whilst I fetch them?' said Mr. Babb. 'Of course you won't. You have the horse to hold. If you like to take a look round the garden you may, but there is nothing to see. Visit the mill if you like. You can give twopence to a boy to hold the horse.' Then he slipped in again and relocked the door.

Barbara was only detained ten minutes. Mr. Babb came back with a jumble of clothes, a Bible, and a violin, not tied together, but in his arms anyhow. He threw everything on the doorstep.

'There,' he said, 'I will hold the bridle, whilst you make this into a bundle. I'm not natty with my fingers.' He took the horse from her. Barbara knelt under the portico and folded Jasper's clothes, and tied all together in an old table cover the father gave for the purpose. 'Take the fiddle,' he said, 'or I'll smash it.'

She looked up at him gravely, whilst knotting the ends.

'Have you a message for your son—of love and forgiveness?'

'Forgiveness! it is your father he has robbed. Love —— There is no love lost between us.'

'He is lonely and sad,' said Barbara, not now looking up, but busy with her hands, tightening the knots and intent on the bundle. 'I can see that his heart is aching; night and day there is a gnawing pain in his breast. No one loves him, and he seems to me to be a man who craves for love, who might be reclaimed by love.'

'Don't forget the letter for your father,' said Mr. Babb.

'What about your son? Have you no message for him?'

'None. Mind that envelope. What it contains is precious.'

'Is it a cheque for fifteen hundred pounds?'

'Oh, dear me, no! It is a text of scripture.'

Then, hastily, Mr. Babb stepped back, shut the door, and bolted and chained it.

CHAPTER XIV.

A SINE QUÂ NON.

Barbara was on her way home from Ashburton. She had attended her aunt's funeral, and knew that a little sum of about fifty pounds per annum was hers, left her by her aunt. She was occupied with her thoughts. Was there any justification for Jasper? The father was hateful. She could excuse his leaving home; that was nothing; such a home must be intolerable to a young man of spirit —but to rob his father was another matter. Barbara could not quite riddle the puzzle out in her mind. It was clear that Mr. Babb had confided the fifteen hundred pounds to Jasper, and that Jasper had made away with them. He had been taken and sent to prison at Prince's Town. Thence he had escaped, and whilst escaping had met with the accident which had brought him to become an inmate of Morwell House. Jasper's story that he had lost the money was false. He had himself taken it. Barbara could not quite make it out; she tried to put it from her. What mattered it how the robbery had been committed?—sufficient that the man who took the money was with her father. What had he done with the money? That no one but himself could tell, and that she would not ask him.

It was vain crying over spilt milk. Fifteen hundred pounds were gone, and the loss of that money might affect Eve's prospects. Eve was already attracting admiration, but who would take her for her beauty alone? Eve, Barbara said to herself, was a jewel that must be kept in a velvet and morocco case, and must not be put to rough usage. She must have money. She must marry where nothing would be required of her but to look and be—charming.

It was clear to Barbara that Mr. Coyshe was struck with her sister, and Mr. Coyshe was a promising, pushing man, sure to make his way. If a man has a high opinion of himself he impresses others with belief in him. Mr. Jordan was loud in his praises; Barbara had sufficient sense to dislike his boasting, but she was influenced by it. Though his manner was not to her taste, she was convinced that Mr. Coyshe was a genius, and a man whose name would be known through England.

What was to be done? The only thing she could think of was to insist on her father making over Morwell to Eve on his death; as for herself—she had her fifty pounds, and she could go as housekeeper to some lady; the Duchess of Bedford would recommend her. *She* was was not likely to be thought of by any man with only fifty pounds, and with a plain face.

When Barbara reached this point she laughed, and then she sighed. She laughed because the idea of her being married was so absurd. She sighed because she was tired. Just then, quite uncalled for and unexpected, the form of Jasper Babb rose up before her mind's eye, as she had last seen him, pale, looking after her, waving his hat.

She was returning to him without a word from his father, of forgiveness, of encouragement, of love. She was scheming a future for herself and for Eve; Jasper had no future, only a horrible past, which cast its shadow forward, and took all hope out of the present, and blighted the future. If she could but have brought him a kind message it would have inspired him to redeem his great fault, to persevere in well-doing. She knew that she would find him watching for her return with a wistful look in his dark full eyes, asking her if she brought him consolation.

Then she reproached herself because she had left his parting farewell unacknowledged. She had been ungracious; no doubt she had hurt his feelings.

She had passed through Tavistock, with her groom riding some way behind her, when she heard the sound of a trotting horse, and almost immediately a well-known voice called, 'Glad to see your face turned homewards, Miss Jordan.'

'Good evening, Mr. Coyshe.'

'Our roads run together, to my advantage. What is that you are carrying? Can I relieve you?'

'A violin. The boy is careless, he might let it fall. Besides he is burdened with my valise and a bundle.'

'What? has your aunt bequeathed a violin to you?'

A little colour came into Barbara's cheeks, and she

answered, 'I am bringing it home from over the moor.' She blushed to have to equivocate.

'I hope you have had something more substantial left you than an old fiddle,' said the surgeon.

'Thank you, my poor aunt has been good enough to leave me something comfortable, which will enable my dear father to make up to Eve for the sum that has been lost.'

'I am glad to hear it,' said Mr. Coyshe. 'Charmed!'

'By the way,' Barbara began, 'I wanted to say something to you, but I have not had the opportunity. You were quite in the wrong about the saucer of sour milk, though I admit there was a stocking—but how you saw that, passes my comprehension.'

'I did not see it, I divined it,' said the young man, with his protruding light eyes staring at her with an odd mischievous expression in them. 'It is part of the mysteries of medicine—a faculty akin to inspiration in some doctors, that they see with their inner eyes what is invisible to the outer eye. For instance, I can see right into your heart, and I see there something that looks to me very much like the wound I patched up in Mr. Jasper's pate. Whilst his has been healing, yours has been growing worse.'

Barbara turned cold and shivered. 'For heaven's sake, Mr. Coyshe, do not say such things; you frighten me.'

He laughed.

She remained silent, uneasy and vexed. Presently she said, 'It is not true; there is nothing the matter with me.'

'But the stocking was under the sofa cushion, and you said, Not true, at first. Wait and look.'

'Doctor, it is not true at all. That is, I have a sort of trouble or pain, but it is all about Eve. I have been very unhappy about the loss of her money, and that has fretted me greatly.'

'I foresaw it would be lost.'

'Yes, it is lost, but Eve shall be no loser.'

'Look here, Miss Jordan, a beautiful face is like a

beautiful song, charming in itself, but infinitely better with an accompaniment.'

'What do you mean, Mr. Coyshe?'

'A sweet girl may have beauty and amiability, but though these may be excellent legs for the matrimonial stool, a third must be added to prevent an upset, and that —metallic.'

Barbara made no reply. The audacity and impudence of the young surgeon took the power to reply from her.

'You have not given me that fiddle,' said Coyshe.

'I am not sure you will carry it carefully,' answered Barbara; nevertheless she resigned it to him. 'When you part from me let the boy have it. I will not ride into Morwell cumbered with it.'

'A doctor,' said Coyshe, 'if he is to succeed in his profession, must be endowed with instinct as well as science. A cat does not know what ails it, but it knows when it is out of sorts; instinct teaches it to swallow a blade of grass. Instinct with us discovers the disorder, science points out the remedy. I may say without boasting that I am brimming with instinct—you have had a specimen or two—and I have passed splendid examinations, so that testifies to my science. Beer Alston cannot retain me long, my proper sphere is London. I understand the Duke has heard of me, and said to someone whom I will not name, that if I come to town he will introduce me. If once started on the rails I must run to success. Now I want a word with you in confidence, Miss Jordan. That boy is sufficiently in the rear not to hear. You will be mum, I trust?'

Barbara slightly nodded her assent.

'I confess to you that I have been struck with your sister, Miss Eve. Who could fail to see her and not become a worshipper? She is a radiant star; I have never seen anyone so beautiful, and she is as good as she is beautiful.'

'Indeed, indeed she is,' said Barbara, earnestly.

'Montecuculli said,' continued the surgeon, 'that in

H

war three things are necessary: money; secondly, money; thirdly, money. In love it is the same. We may regret it, but it is undeniable.'

Barbara did not know what to say. The assurance of the young man imposed on her; she did not like him particularly, but he was superior in culture to most of the young men she knew, who had no ideas beyond hunting and shooting.

After a little while of consideration, she said, 'Do you think you would make Eve happy?'

'I am sure of it. I have all the instincts of the family-man in me. A man may marry a score of times and be father of fifty children, without instinct developing the special features of domesticity. They are born in a man, not acquired. *Pater-familias nascitur, non fit.*'

'Have you spoken to my father?'

'No, not yet; I am only feeling my way. I don't mind telling you what brought me into notice with the Duke. He was ill last autumn when down at Endsleigh for the shooting, and his physician was sent for. I met the doctor at the Bedford Inn at Tavistock; some of us of the faculty had an evening together, and his Grace's condition was discussed, casually of course. I said nothing. We were smoking and drinking rum and water. There was something in his Grace's condition which puzzled his physician, and he clearly did not understand how to treat the case. *I* knew. I have instinct. Some rum had been spilled on the table; I dipped the end of my pipe in it, and scribbled a prescription on the mahogany. I saw the eye of the doctor on it. I have reason to believe he used my remedy. It answered. He is not ungrateful. I say no more. A city set on a hill cannot be hid. Beer Alston is a bushel covering a light. Wait.'

Barbara said nothing. She rode on, deep in thought. The surgeon jogged at her side, his protruding water-blue eyes peering in all directions.

'You think your sister will not be penniless?' he said.

'I am certain she will not. Now that my aunt has provided for me, Eve will have Morwell after my father's death, and I am sure she is welcome to what comes to me from my aunt till then.'

'Halt!' exclaimed the surgeon.

Barbara drew rein simultaneously with Mr. Coyshe.

'Who are you there, watching, following us, skulking behind bushes and hedges?' shouted Coyshe.

'What is it?' asked Miss Jordan, surprised and alarmed.

The surgeon did not answer, but raised to his shoulder a stick he carried.

'Answer! Who are you? Show yourself, or I fire!'

'Doctor Coyshe,' exclaimed Barbara, 'forbear in pity!'

'My dear Miss Jordan,' he said in a low tone, 'set your mind at rest. I have only an umbrella stick, of which all the apparatus is blown away except the catch. Who is there?' he cried, again presenting his stick.

'Once, twice!'—click went the catch. 'If I call three and fire, your blood be on your own head!'

There issued in response a scream, piercing in its shrillness, inhuman in its tone.

Barbara shuddered, and her horse plunged.

A mocking burst of laughter ensued, and then forth from the bushes into the road leaped an impish boy, who drew a bow over the catgut of a fiddle under his chin, and ran along before them, laughing, leaping, and evoking uncouth and shrill screams from his instrument.

'A pixy,' said the surgeon. 'I knew by instinct one was dodging us. Fortunately I could not lay my hand on a riding whip this morning, and so took my old umbrella stick. Now, farewell. So you think Miss Eve will have Morwell, and the matrimonial stool its golden leg? That is right.'

CHAPTER XV.

AT THE QUAY.

ON the day of Barbara's departure Eve attended diligently to the duties of the house, and found that everything was in such order that she was content to believe that all would go on of its own accord in the old way, without her supervision, which declined next day, and was pretermitted on the third.

Jasper did not appear for mid-day dinner ; he was busy on the old quay. He saw that it must be put to rights. The woods could be thinned, the coppice shredded for bark, and bark put on a barge at the bottom of the almost precipitous slope, and so sent to the tanyards at Devonport. There was waste of labour in carrying the bark up the hills and then carting it to Beer Ferris, some ten miles.

No wonder that, as Mr. Jordan complained, the bark was unremunerative. The profit was eaten up by the wasteful transport. It was the same with the timber. There was demand for oak and pine at the dockyards, and any amount was grown in the woods of Morwell.

So Jasper asked leave to have the quay put to rights, and Mr. Jordan consented. He must supervise proceedings himself, so he remained the greater part of the day by the river edge. The ascent to Morwell House was arduous if attempted directly up the steep fall, long if he went by the zigzag through the wood. It would take him a stiff three-quarters of an hour to reach the house and half-an-hour to return. Accordingly he asked that his dinner might be sent him.

On the third day, to Eve's dismay, she found that she had forgotten to let him have his food, both that day and the preceding. He had made no remark when he came

back the day before. Eve's conscience smote her—a convalescent left for nine or ten hours without food.

When she recalled her promise to send it him she
found that there was no one to send. In shame and self-
reproach, she packed a little basket, and resolved to carry
it to him. The day was lovely. She put her broad-
brimmed straw hat, trimmed with forget-me-not bows, on
her head, and started on her walk.

The bank of the Tamar falls from high moorland many
hundreds of feet to the water's edge. In some places the
rocks rise in sheer precipices with gullies of coppice and
heather between them. Elsewhere the fall is less abrupt,
and allows trees to grow, and the richness of the soil and
the friable nature of the rock allows them to grow to con-
siderable dimensions. From Morwell House a long *détour*
through beautiful forest, affording peeps of mountains and
water, gave the easiest descent to the quay, but Eve
reserved this road for the ascent, and slid merrily down
the narrow corkscrew path in the brushwood between the
crags, which afforded the quickest way down to the water's
edge.

'Oh, Mr. Jasper!' she exclaimed, 'I have sinned,
through my forgetfulness; but see, to make amends, I
have brought you a little bottle of papa's Burgundy and a
wee pot of red currant jelly for the cold mutton.'

'And you have come yourself to overwhelm me with a
sense of gratitude.'

'Oh, Mr. Jasper, I am so ashamed of my naughtiness.
I assure you I nearly cried. Bab I mean Barbara—
would never have forgotten. She remembers everything.
Her head is a perfect store-closet, where all things are in
place and measured and weighed and on their proper
shelves. You had no dinner yesterday.'

'To-day's is a banquet that makes up for all defi-
ciencies.'

Eve liked Jasper; she had few to converse with, very
few acquaintances, no friends, and she was delighted to be

able to have a chat with anyone, especially if that person flattered her—and who did not? Everyone naturally offered incense before her; she almost demanded it as a right. The Tamar formed a little bay under a wall of rock. A few ruins marked the site of the storehouses and boatsheds of the abbots. The sun glittered on the water, forming of it a blazing mirror, and the dancing light was reflected back by the flower-wreathed rocks.

'Where are the men?' asked Eve.

'Gone into the wood to fell some pines. We must drive piles into the bed of the river, and lay beams on them for a basement.'

'Oh,' said Eve listlessly, 'I don't understand about basements and all that.' She seated herself on a log. 'How pleasant it is here with the flicker of the water in one's face and eyes, and a sense of being without shadow! Mr. Jasper, do you believe in pixies?'

'What do you mean, Miss?'

'The little imps who live in the mines and on the moors, and play mischievous tricks on mortals. They have the nature of spirits, and yet they have human shapes, and are like old men or boys. They watch treasures and veins of ore, and when mortals approach the metal, they decoy the trespassers away.'

'Like the lapwing that pretends to be wounded, and so lures you from its precious eggs. Do *you* believe in pixies?'

Eve laughed and shook her pretty head. 'I think so, Mr. Jasper, for I have seen one.'

'What was he like?'

'I do not know, I only caught glimpses of him. Do not laugh satirically. I am serious. I did see something, but I don't know exactly what I saw.'

'That is not a very convincing reason for the existence of pixies.'

Eve drew her little feet together, and folded her arms in her lap, and smiled, and tossed her head. She had taken off her hat, and the sun glorified her shining head.

Jasper looked admiringly at her.

'Are you not afraid of a sunstroke, Miss Eve?'

'O dear no! The sun cannot harm me. I love him so passionately. O Mr. Jasper! I wish sometimes I lived far away in another country where there are no wet days and grey skies and muggy atmospheres, and where the hedges do not drip, and the lanes do not stand ankle deep in mud, and the old walls exude moisture indoors, and one's pretty shoes do not go mouldy if not wiped over daily. I should like to be in a land like Italy, where all the people sing and dance and keep holiday, and the bells in the towers are ever ringing, and the lads have bunches of gold and silver flowers in their hats, and the girls have scarlet skirts, and the village musicians sit in a cart adorned with birch branches and ribands and roses, and the trumpets go tu-tu! and the drums bung-bung!—I have read about it, and cried for vexation that I was not there.'

'But the pixy?'

'I would banish all pixies and black Copplestones and Whish hounds; they belong to rocks and moors and darkness and storm. I hate gloom and isolation.'

'You are happy at Morwell, Miss Eve. One has but to look in your face and see it. Not a crabbed line of care, not the track of a tear, all smoothness and smiles.'

The girl twinkled with pleasure, and said, 'That is because we are in midsummer; wait till winter and see what becomes of me. Then I am sad enough. We are shut in for five months—six months—seven almost, by mud and water. O, how the winds howl! How the trees toss and roar! How the rain patters! That is not plea-sant. I wish, I do wish, I were a squirrel; then I would coil myself in a corner lined with moss, and crack nuts in a doze till the sun came again and woke me up with the flowers. Then I would throw out all my cracked nutshells with both paws, and leap to the foot of a tree, run up it, and skip from branch to branch, and swing in the summer sunshine on the topmost twig. O, Mr. Jasper, how much wiser than we the swallows are! I would rather be a swallow than a squirrel, and sail away when I felt the first frost to the land of eternal summer, into the blazing eye of the sun.'

'But as you have no wings——'

'I sit and mope and talk to Barbara about cows and cabbages, and to father about any nonsense that comes into my head.'

'As yet you have given me no description of the pixy.'

'How can I, when I scarce saw him? I will tell you exactly what happened, if you will not curl up the corner of your lips, as though mocking me. That papa never does. I tell him all the rhodomontade I can, and he listens gravely, and frightens and abashes me sometimes by swallowing it whole.'

'Where did you see, or not see, the pixy?'

'On my way to you. I heard something stirring in the wood, and I half saw what I took to be a boy, or a little man the size of a boy. When I stood still, he stood; when I moved, I fancied he moved. I heard the crackle of sticks and the stir of the bushes. I am sure of nothing.'

'Were you frightened?'

'No; puzzled, not frightened. If this had occurred at night, it would have been different. I thought it might have been a red-deer; they are here sometimes, strayed from Exmoor, and have such pretty heads and soft eyes; but this was not. I fancied once I saw a queer little face peering at me from behind a pine tree. I uttered a feeble cry and ran on.'

'I know exactly what it was,' said Jasper, with a grave smile. 'There is a pixy lives in the Raven Rock; he has r smithy far down in the heart of the cliff, and there he works all winter at a vein of pure gold, hammering and turning the golden cups and marsh marigolds with which to strew the pastures and watercourses in spring. But it is dull for the pixy sitting alone without light; he has no one to love and care for him, and, though the gold glows in his forge, his little heart is cold. He has been dreaming all winter of a sweet fairy he saw last summer wearing a crown of marigold, wading in cuckoo flowers, and now he has come forth to capture that fairy and draw her down into his stony palace.'

'To waste her days,' laughed Eve, 'in sighing for the sun, whilst her roses wither and her eyes grow dim, away from the twitter of the birds and the scent of the gorse. He shan't have me.' Then, after a pause, during which she gathered some marigolds and put them into her hat, she said, half seriously, half jestingly, 'Do you believe in pixies?'

'You must not ask me. I have seen but one fairy in all my life, and she now sits before me.'

'Mr. Jasper,' said Eve, with a dimple in her cheek, in recognition of the compliment,—'Mr. Jasper, do you know my mother is a mystery to me as much as pixies and fairies and white ladies?'

'No, I was not aware of that.'

'She was called, like me, Eve.'

'I had a sister of that name who is dead, and my mother's name was Eve. She is dead.'

'I did not think the name was so common,' said the girl. 'I fancied we were the only two Eves that ever were. I do not know what my mother's other name was. Is not that extraordinary?'

Jasper Babb made no reply.

'I have been reading "Undine." Have you read that story? O, it has made me so excited. The writer says that it was founded on what he read in an old author, and that author, Paracelsus, is one papa believes in. So, I suppose, there is some truth in the tale. The story of my mother is quite like that of Undine. One night my father heard a cry on the moor, and he went to the place, and found my mother all alone. She was with him for a year and a day, and would have stayed longer if my father could have refrained from asking her name. When he did that she was forced to leave him. She was never seen again.'

'Miss Eve, this cannot be true.'

'I do not know. That is what old Betsy Davy told me. Papa never speaks of her. He has been an altered man since she left him. He put up the stone cross on the moor at the spot where he found her. I like to fancy there was something mysterious in her. I can't ask papa, and Bab was—I mean Barbara—was too young at the time to remember anything about it.'

'This is very strange.'

'Betsy Davy says that my father was not properly married to her, because he could not get a priest to perform the ceremony without knowing what she was.'

'My dear Miss Eve, instead of listening to the cock-and-bull stories——'

'Mr. Jasper! How can you—how can you use such an expression? The story is very pretty and romantic, and not at all like things of this century. I dare say there is some truth in it.'

'I am far from any intention of offending you, dear young lady; but I venture to offer you a piece of advice. Do not listen to idle tales; do not encourage people of a lower class to speak to you about your mother; ask your father what you want to know, he will tell you; and take my word for it, romance there always must be in love, but there will be nothing of what you imagine, with a fancy set on fire by " Undine."'

Her volatile mind had flown elsewhere.

'Mr. Jasper,' she said, 'have you ever been to a theatre?'

'Yes.'

'O, I should like it above everything else. I dream of it. We have Inchbald's " British Theatre " in the library, and it is my dearest reading. Barbara likes a cookery

book or a book on farming; I cannot abide them. Do
you know what Mr. Coyshe said the other day when I was
rattling on before him and papa? He said I had missed
my vocation, and ought to have been on the stage. What
do you think?'

'I think a loving and merciful Providence has done
best to put such a precious treasure here where it can
best be preserved.'

'I don't agree with you at all,' said Eve, standing up.
'I think Mr. Coyshe showed great sense. Anyhow, I
should like to see a theatre—O, above everything in the
world! Papa thinks of Rome or the Holy Land; but I
say—a theatre. I can't help it; I think it, and must say
it. Good-bye! I have things my sister left that I must
attend to. I wish she were back. Oh, Mr. Jasper, do
not you?'

'Everyone will be pleased to welcome her home.'

'Because I have let everything go to sixes and sevens,
eh?'

'For her own sake.'

'Well, I do miss her dreadfully, do not you?'

He did not answer. She cast him another good-bye,
and danced off into the wood, swinging her hat by the blue
ribands.

CHAPTER XVI.

WATT.

THE air under the pines was balmy. The hot July sun
brought out their resinous fragrance. Gleams of fire fell
through the boughs and dappled the soil at intervals, and
on these sun-flakes numerous fritillary butterflies with
silver under-wings were fluttering, and countless flies were
humming. The pines grew only at the bottom of the
crags, and here and there in patches on the slopes. The

woods were composed for the most part of oak, now in its richest, fullest foliage, the golden hue of early spring changing to the duller green of summer. Beech also abounded with their clean stems, and the soil beneath them bare of weed, and here and there a feathery birch with erect silver stem struggled up in the overgrowth to the light. The wood was full of foxgloves, spires of pink dappled bells, and of purple columbine. Wild roses grew wherever a rock allowed them to wreath in sunshine and burst into abundant bloom over its face. Eve carried her straw hat on her arm, hung by its blue ribands. She needed its shelter in the wood no more than in her father's hall.

She came to a brook, dribbling and tinkling on its way through moss and over stone. The path was fringed with blazing marigolds. Eve had already picked some, she now halted, and brimmed the extemporised basket with more of the golden flowers.

The gloom, the fragrant air, the flicker of colour made her think of the convent chapel at Lanherne, whither she had been sent for her education, but whence, having pined under the restraint, she had been speedily removed. As she walked she swung her hat like a censer. From it rose the fresh odour of flowers, and from it dropped now and then a marigold like a burning cinder. Scarce thinking what she did, Eve assumed the slow and measured pace of a religious procession, as she had seen one at Lanherne, still swinging her hat, and letting the flowers fall from it whilst she chanted meaningless words to a sacred strain. Then she caught her straw hat to her, and holding it before her in her left arm, advanced at a quicker pace, still singing. Now she dipped her right hand in the crown and strewed the blossoms to left and right, as did the little girls in the Corpus Christi procession round the convent grounds at Lanherne. Her song quickened and brightened, and changed its character as her flighty thoughts shifted to other topics, and her changeful mood assumed another complexion. Her tune became that of the duet *Là ci darem la mano*, in 'Don Giovanni,' which she had often sung with her sister. She sang louder and more joyously, and her feet moved in rhythm to this song, as they had to the ecclesiastical chant ; her eyes sparkled, her cheeks flushed.

It seemed to her that a delicate echo accompanied her —very soft and spiritual, now in snatches, then low, rolling, long-drawn-out. She stopped and listened, then went on again. What she heard was the echo from the rocks and tree boles.

But presently the road became steeper, and she could no longer spare breath for her song ; now the sacred chant was quite forgotten, but the sweet air of Mozart clung to her memory, as the scent of pot-pourri to a parlour, and there it would linger the rest of the day.

As she walked on she was in a dream. What must it be to hear these songs accompanied by instruments, and with light and scenery, and acting on the stage? Oh, that she could for once in her life have the supreme felicity of seeing a real play!

Suddenly a flash of vivid golden light broke before her, the trees parted, and she stood on the Raven Rock, a precipice that shoots high above the Tamar and commands a wide prospect over Cornwall—Hingston Hill, where Athelstan fought and beat the Cornish in the last stand the Britons made, and Kitt Hill, a dome of moorclad mountain. As she stepped forth on the rock to enjoy the light and view and air, there rushed out of the oak and dog-wood bushes a weird boy, who capered and danced, brandished a fiddle, clapped it under his chin, and still dancing, played *Là ci darem* fast, faster, till his little arms went faster than Eve could see.

The girl stood still, petrified with terror. Here was the Pixy of the Raven Rock Jasper had spoken of. The malicious boy saw and revelled in her fear, and gambolled round her, grimacing and still fiddling till his tune led up to and finished in a shriek.

'There, there,' said he, at length, lowering the violin and bow ; 'how I have scared you, Eve!'

Eve trembled in every limb, and was too alarmed to speak. The scenery, the rock, the boy, swam in a blue haze before her eyes.

'There, Eve, don't be frightened. You led me on with your singing. I followed in your flowery traces. Don't you know me ?'

Eve shook her head. She could not speak.

'You have seen me. You saw me that night when I came riding over your downs at the back of Martin, when poor Jasper fell—you remember me. I smashed your rattle-trap gig. What a piece of good luck it was that Jasper's horse went down and not ours. I might have broken my fiddle. I'd rather break a leg, especially that of another person.'

Eve had not thought of the boy since that eventful night. Indeed, she had seen little of him then.

'I remember,' she said, 'there was a boy.'

'Myself. Watt is my name, or in full, Walter. If you doubt my humanity touch my hand ; feel, it is warm.' He grasped Eve and drew her out on the rocky platform.

'Sit down, Eve. I know you better than you know me. I have heard Martin speak of you. That is how I know about you. Look me in the face.'

Eve raised her eyes to his. The boy had a strange countenance. The hair was short-cropped and black, the skin olive. He had protruding and large ears, and very black keen eyes.

'What do you think is my age ?' asked the boy. 'I am nineteen. I am an ape. I shall never grow into a man.' He began again to skip and make grimaces. Eve shrank away in alarm.

'There ! Put your fears aside, and be reasonable,' said Watt, coming to a rest. 'Jasper is below, munching his dinner. I have seen him. He would not eat whilst you were by. He did not suspect I was lying on the rock overhead in the heath, peering down on you both whilst you were talking. I can skip about, I can scramble anywhere, I can almost fly. I do not wish Jasper to know I am here. No one must know but yourself, for I have come here on an errand to you.'

'To me!' echoed Eve, hardly recovered from her terror.

'I am come from Martin. You remember Martin? Oh! there are not many men like Martin. He is a king of men. Imagine an old town, with ancient houses and a church tower behind, and the moon shining on it, and in the moonlight Martin in velvet, with a hat in which is a white feather, and his violin, under a window, thinking you are there, and singing *Deh, vieni alla finestra*. Do you know the tune? Listen.' The boy took his fiddle, and touching the strings with his fingers, as though playing a mandolin, he sang that sweet minstrel song.

Eve's blue eyes opened wonderingly, this was all so strange and incomprehensible to her.

'See here, Miss Zerlina, you were singing *Là ci darem* just now, try it with me. I can take Giovanni's part and you that of Zerlina.'

'I cannot. I cannot, indeed.'

'You shall. I shall stand between you and the wood. You cannot escape over the rock, you would be dashed to pieces. I will begin.'

Suddenly a loud voice interrupted him as he began to play—'Watt!'

Standing under the shadow of the oaks, with one foot on the rocky platform, was Jasper.

'Watt, how came you here?'

The boy lowered his violin and stood for a moment speechless.

'Miss Eve,' said Jasper, 'please go home. After all, you have encountered the pixy, and that a malicious and dangerous imp. Stand aside, Watt.'

The boy did not venture to resist. He stood back near the edge of the rock and allowed Eve to pass him.

When she was quite gone, Jasper said gravely to the boy, 'What has brought you here?'

'That is a pretty question to ask me, Jasper. We left you here, broken and senseless, and naturally Martin and I want to know what condition you are in. How could we tell whether you were alive or dead? You know very well that Martin could not come, so I have run here to obtain information.'

'I am well,' answered Jasper, 'you may tell Martin, everywhere but here,' he laid his hand on his heart.

'With such a pretty girl near I do not wonder,' laughed the boy. 'I shall tell poor Martin of the visits paid you at the water's edge.'

'That will do,' said Jasper; 'this joking offends me. Tell Martin I am here, but with my heart aching for him.'

'No occasion for that, Jasper. Not a cricket in the grass is lighter of spirit than he.'

'I dare say,' said the elder, 'he does not feel matters acutely. Tell him the money must be restored. Here I stay as a pledge that the debt shall be paid. Tell him that I insist on his restoring the money.'

'Christmas is coming, and after that Easter, and then, all in good time, Christmas again; but money once passed, returns no more.'

'I expect Martin to restore what he took. He is good at heart, but inconsiderate. I know Martin better than you. You are his bad angel. He loves me and is generous. He knows what I have done for him, and when I tell him that I must have the money back he will return it if he can.'

'If he can!' repeated the boy derisively. 'It is well you have thrown in that proviso. I once tossed my cap into the Dart and ran two miles along the bank after it. I saw it for two miles bobbing on the ripples, but at last it went over the weir above Totnes and disappeared. I believe that cap was fished up at Dartmouth and is now worn by the mayor's son. It is so with money. Once let it out of your hands and it avails nothing to run after it. It disappears and comes up elsewhere to profit others.'

' Where is Martin now ? '

' Anywhere and everywhere.'

' He is not in this county, I trust.'

' Did you never hear of the old lady who lost the store closet key and hunted everywhere except in her own pocket ? What is under your nose is overlooked.'

' Go back to Martin. Tell him, as he values his safety and my peace of mind, to keep out of the country, certainly out of the county. Tell him to take to some honest work and stick to it, and to begin his repentance by ——'

' There ! if I carry a preachment away with me I shall never reach Martin. I had a surfeit of this in the olden days, Jasper. I know a sailor lad who has been fed on salt junk at sea till if you put but as much as will sit on the end of your knife under his nose when he is on land he will upset the table. It is the same with Martin and me. No sermons for us, Jasper. So—see, I am off at the first smell of a text.'

He darted into the wood and disappeared, singing at the top of his voice ' Life let us cherish.'

CHAPTER XVII.

FORGET-ME-NOT !

THAT night Eve could not sleep. She thought of her wonderful adventure. Who was that strange boy ? And who was Martin ? And, what was the link between these two and Jasper ?

Towards morning, when she ought to have been stirring, she fell asleep, and laughed in her dreams. She

I

woke with the sun shining in on her, and her father standing by her bed, watching her.

After the visions in which she had been steeped full of
fair forms and brilliant colours, it was a shock to her to
unclose her eyes on the haggard face of her father, with
sunken eyes.

'What is it, papa?'

'My dear, it is ten o'clock. I have waited for my
breakfast. The tea is cold, the toast has lost its crispness,
and the eggs are like the tea—cold.'

'O papa!' she said sorrowfully, sitting up in bed; 'I
have overslept myself. But, you will not begrudge me the
lovely dreams I have had. Papa! I saw a pixy yesterday.'

'Where, child?'

'On the Raven Rock.'

He shut his eyes, and put his hand over his mouth.
Then he heaved a deep sigh, said nothing, turned, and
went out of the room.

Eve was the idol of her father's heart. He spoiled her,
by allowing her her own way in everything, by relieving
her of every duty, and heaping all the responsibilities on
the shoulders of his eldest daughter.

Eve was so full of love and gaiety, that it was impossible to be angry with her when she made provoking
mistakes; she was so penitent, so pretty in her apologies,
and so sincere in her purpose of amendment.

Eve was warmly attached to her father. She had an
affectionate nature, but none of her feelings were deep.
Her rippling conversation, her buoyant spirits, enlivened
the prevailing gloom of Mr. Jordan. His sadness did not
depress her. Indeed, she hardly noticed it. Hers was not
a sympathetic nature. She exacted the sympathy of others,
but gave nothing more in return than prattle and laughter.

She danced down the stairs when dressed, without any
regret for having kept her father waiting. He would eat a
better breakfast for a little delay, she said to herself, and
satisfied her conscience.

She came into the breakfast-room in a white muslin dress, covered with little blue sprigs, and with a blue riband in her golden hair. The lovely roses of her complexion, the sparkling eyes, the dimple in her cheeks, the air of perfect content with herself, and with all the world, disarmed what little vexation hung in her father's mood.

'Do you think Bab will be home to-day?' she asked, seating herself at the tea-tray without a word of apology for the lateness of her appearance.

'I do not know what her movements are.'

'I hope she will. I want her home.'

'Yes, she must return, to relieve you of your duties.'

'I am sure the animals want her home. The pigeons find I am not regular in throwing them barley, and I sometimes forget the bread-crumbs after a meal. The little black heifer always runs along the paddock when Bab goes by, and she is indifferent to me. She lows when I appear, as much as to say, Where is Miss Barbara? Then the cat has not been himself for some days, and the little horse is in the dumps. Do you think brute beasts have souls?'

'I do not know.' Then after a pause, 'What was that you said about a pixy?'

'O papa! it was a dream.' She coloured. Something rose in her heart to check her from confiding to him what in her thoughtless freedom she was prepared to tell on first awaking.

He pressed her no further. He doubtless believed she had spoken the truth. She had ever been candid. Now, however, she lacked courage to speak. She remembered that the boy had said 'I come to you with a message.' He had disappeared without giving it. What was that message? Was he gone without delivering it?

Mr. Jordan slowly ate his breakfast. Every now and then he looked at his daughter, never steadily, for he could look fixedly long at nothing.

'I will tell you all, papa,' said Eve suddenly, shaking

her head, to shake off the temptation to be untrue. Her better nature had prevailed. 'It was not a dream, it was a reality. I did see a pixy on the Raven Rock, the maddest, merriest, ugliest imp in the world.'

'We are surrounded by an unseen creation,' said Mr. Jordan. 'The microscope reveals to us teeming life in a drop of water. Another generation will use an instrument that will show them the air full of living things. Then the laugh will be no more heard on earth. Life will be grave, if not horrible. This generation is sadder than the last because less ignorant.'

'O papa! He was not a pixy at all. I have seen him before, when Mr. Jasper was thrown. Then he was perched like an ape, as he is, on the cross you set up, where my mother first appeared to you. He was making screams with his fiddle.'

Mr. Jordan looked at her with flickering, frightened eyes. 'It was a spirit—the horse saw it and started—that was how Jasper was thrown,' he said gravely.

'Here Jasper comes,' said Eve, laughing; 'ask him.' But instead of waiting for her father to do this, she sprang up, and danced to meet him with the simplicity of a child, and clapping her palms, she asked, 'Mr. Jasper! My father will have it that my funny little pixy was a spirit of the woods or wold, and will not believe that he is flesh and blood.'

'My daughter,' said Mr. Jordan, 'has told me a strange story. She says that she saw a boy on the the Raven Rock, and that you know him.'

'Yes, I do.'

'Whence comes he?'

'That I cannot say.'

'Where does he live?'

'Nowhere.'

'Is he here still?'

'I do not know.'

'Have you seen him before?'

'Yes—often.'

'That will do.' Mr. Jordan jerked his head and waved his hand, in sign that he did not wish Jasper to remain.

He treated Jasper with rudeness; he resented the loss of Eve's money, and being a man of narrow mind and vindictive temper, he revenged the loss on the man who was partly to blame for the loss. He brooded over his misfortune, and was bitter. The sight of Jasper irritated him, and he did not scruple at meals to make allusions to the lost money which must hurt the young man's feelings. When Barbara was present, she interposed to turn the conversation or blunt the significance of her father's words. Eve, on the other hand, when Mr. Jordan spoke in a way she did not like to Jasper or Barbara, started up and left the room, because she could not endure discords. She sprang out of the way of harsh words as she turned from a brier. It did not occur to her to save others, she saved herself.

Barbara thought of Jasper and her father, Eve only of herself.

When Jasper was gone, Mr. Jordan put his hand to his head. 'I do not understand, I cannot think,' he said, with a vacant look in his eyes. 'You say one thing, and he another.'

'Pardon me, dearest papa, we both say the same, that the pixy was nothing but a real boy of flesh and blood, but—there, let us think and talk of something else.'

'Take care!' said Mr. Jordan gloomily; 'take care! There are spirits where the wise see shadows; the eye of the fool sees farther than the eye of the sage. My dear Eve, beware of the Raven Rock.'

Eve began to warble the air of the serenade in 'Don Giovanni' which she had heard the boy Watt sing.

Then she threw her arms round her father's neck. 'Do not look so miserable, papa. I am the happiest little

being in the world, and I will kiss your cheeks till they
dimple with laughter.' But instead of doing so, she
dashed away to pick flowers, for she thought, seeing herself in the glass opposite, that a bunch of forget-me-not in
her bosom was what lacked to perfect her appearance in
the blue-sprigged muslin.

She knew where wild forget-me-nots grew. The Abbot's Well sent its little silver rill through rich grass
towards the wood, where it spilled down the steep descent
to the Tamar. She knew that forget-me-not grew at the
border of the wood, just where the stream left the meadow
and the glare of the sun for its pleasant shadow. As she
approached the spot she saw the imp-like boy leap from
behind a tree.

He held up his finger, put it to his lips, then beckoned
her to follow him. This she would not do. She halted
in the meadow, stooped, and, pretending not to see him,
picked some of the blue flowers she desired.

He came stealthily towards her, and pointed to a stone
a few steps further, which was hidden from the house by
the slope of the hill. 'I will tell you nothing unless you
come,' he said.

She hesitated a moment, looked round, and advanced
to the place indicated.

'I will go no farther with you,' said she, putting her
hand on the rock. 'I am afraid of you.'

'It matters not,' answered the boy ; 'I can say what I
want here.'

'What is it ? Be quick, I must go home.'

'Oh, you little puss ! Oh, you came out full of business ! I can tell you, you came for nothing but the chance
of hearing what I forgot to tell you yesterday. I must
give the message I was commissioned to bear before I can
leave.'

'Who from ? '

'Can you ask ? From Martin.'

'But who is Martin ? '

'Sometimes he is one thing, then another; he is Don Giovanni. Then he is a king. There—he is an actor. Will that content you?'

'What is his surname?'

'O Eve! daughter of Eve!' jeered the boy, 'all inquisitiveness! What does that matter? An actor takes what name suits him.'

'What is his message? I must run home.'

'He stole something from you—wicked Martin.'

'Yes; a ring.'

'And you—you stole his heart away. Poor Martin has had no peace of mind since he saw you. His conscience has stung him like a viper. So he has sent me back to you with the ring.'

'Where is it?'

'Shut your blue eyes, they dazzle me, and put out your finger.'

'Give me the ring, please, and let me go.'

'Only on conditions—not my conditions—those of Martin. He was very particular in his instructions to me. Shut your eyes and extend your dear little finger. Next swear never, never to part with the ring I put on your finger.'

'That I never will. Mr. Martin had no right to take the ring. It was impertinent of him; it made me very angry. Once I get it back I will never let the ring go again.' She opened her eyes.

'Shut! shut!' cried the boy: 'and now swear.'

'I promise,' said the girl. 'That suffices.'

'There, then, take the ring.' He thrust the circlet on her finger. She opened her eyes again and looked at her hand.

'Why, boy!' she exclaimed, 'this is not my ring. It is another.'

'To be sure it is, you little fool. Do you think that Martin would return the ring you gave him? No, no. He sends you this in exchange for yours. It is prettier,

Look at the blue flower on it, formed of turquoise. Forget-me-not.'

'I cannot keep this. I want my own,' said Eve, pouting, and her eyes filling.

'You must abide Martin's time. Meanwhile retain this pledge.'

'I cannot! I will not!' she stamped her foot petulantly on the oxalis and forget-me-not that grew beneath the rock, tears of vexation brimming in her eyes. 'You have not dealt fairly by me. You have cheated me.'

'Listen to me, Miss Eve,' said the boy in a coaxing tone. 'You are a child, and have to be treated as such. Look at the beautiful stones, observe the sweet blue flower. You know what that means—Forget-me-not. Our poor Martin has to ramble through the world with a heart-ache, yearning for a pair of sparkling blue eyes, and for two wild roses blooming in the sweetest cheeks the sun ever kissed, and for a head of hair like a beech tree touched by frost in a blazing autumn's sun. Do you think he can forget these? He carries that face of yours ever about with him, and now he sends you this ring, and that means—"Miss, you have made me very unhappy. I can never forget the little maid with eyes of blue, and so I send her this token to bid her forget me not, as I can never forget her."'

And as Eve stood musing with pouting lips, and troubled brow, looking at the ring, the boy took his violin, and with the fingers plucked the strings to make an accompaniment as he sang :—

A maiden stood beside a river,
  And with her pitcher seemed to play ;
Then sudden stooped and drew up water,
  But drew my heart as well away.

And now I sigh beside the river,
  I dream about that maid I saw,
I wait, I watch, am restless, weeping,
  Until she come again to draw.

A flower is blooming by the river,
  A floweret with a petal blue,
Forget me not, my love, my treasure !
  My flower and heart are both for you.

He played and sang a sweet, simple and plaintive air. It touched Eve's heart; always susceptible to music. Her lips repeated after the boy, 'My flower and heart are both for you.'

She could not make up her mind what to do. While she hesitated, the opportunity of returning the ring was gone. Watt had disappeared into the bushes.

CHAPTER XVIII.

DISCOVERIES.

A BEAUTIFUL summer evening. Eve from her window saw Jasper in the garden; he was trimming the flower-beds which had been neglected since Christopher Davy had been ill. The men were busy on the farm, too busy to be taken off for flower gardening. Barbara had said one day that it was a pity the beds were not put to rights; and now Jasper was attending to her wishes during her absence. Mr. Jordan was out. He had gone forth with his hammer, and there was no telling when he would return. Eve disliked being alone. She must talk to someone. She brushed her beautiful hair, looked in the glass, adjusted a scarf round her shoulders, and in a coquettish way tripped into the garden and began to pick the flowers, peeping at Jasper out of the corners of her eyes, to see if he were observing her. He, however, paid no attention to what she was doing. In a fit of impatience, she flung the auriculas and polyanthus she had picked on the path, and threw herself pouting into the nearest garden seat.

'Mr. Jasper!' she called; 'are you so mightily busy that you cannot afford me a word?'

'I am always and altogether at your service, dear Miss Eve.'

'Why have you taken to gardening? Are you fond of flowers?'

'I am devoted to flowers.'

'So am I. I pick them.'

'And throw them away,' said Jasper, stooping and collecting those she had strewn on the path.

'Well—I have not the patience to garden. I leave all that to Barbara and old Christopher. I wish things generally, gardens included, would go along without giving trouble. I wish my sister were home.'

'To relieve you of all responsibility and trouble.'

'I hate trouble,' said Eve frankly, 'and responsibility is like a burr in one's clothes—detestable. There! you are laughing at me, Mr. Jasper.'

'I am not laughing, I am sighing.'

'Oh, you are always sad.'

'I do not like to hear you talk in this manner. You cannot expect to have your sister at your elbow throughout life, to fan off all the flies that tease you.'

'If I have not Bab, 1 shall have someone else.'

'Miss Barbara might marry—and then——'

'Barbara marry!' exclaimed Eve, and clapped her hands. 'The idea is too absurd. Who would marry her? She is a dear, darling girl, but——'

'But what, missie?'

'I dare say I shall marry.'

'Miss Eve! listen to me. It is most likely that you will be married some day, but what then? You will have a thousand more cares on your shoulders than you have now, duties you will be forced to bear, troubles which will encompass you on all sides.'

'Do you know,' said Eve, with a twinkling face, and a sly look in her eyes, 'do you know, Mr. Jasper, I don't think I shall marry for ever so long. But I have a glorious scheme in my head. As my money is gone, if anything should happen to us, I should dearly like to go on the stage. That would be simply splendid!'

'The young crows,' said Jasper gravely, 'live on the dew of heaven, and then they are covered with a soft shining down. After a while the old birds bring them carrion, and when they have tasted flesh, they no longer have any liking for dew. Then the black feathers sprout, then only.' He raised his dark eyes to those of Eve, and said in a deep, vibrating voice, ' I would have this sweet fledgling sit still in her beautiful Morwell nest, and drink only the sparkling drops that fall into her mouth from the finger of God. I cannot bear to think of her growing black feathers, and hopping about —a carrion crow.'

Eve fidgeted on her seat. She had thrust her pretty feet before her, clad in white stockings and blue leather slippers, one on the other ; she crossed and recrossed them impatiently.

' I do not like you to talk to me like this. I am tired of living in the wilds where one sees nobody, and where I can never go to theatre or concert or ball. I should—oh, I should like to live in a town.'

' You are a child, Miss Eve, and think and talk like a child. But the time is coming when you must put away childish things, and face life seriously.'

' It is not wicked to want to go to a town. There is no harm in dreaming that I am an actress. Oh !' she exclaimed, held up her hands, and laughed, 'that would be too delightful ! '

' What has put this mad fancy into your head ? '

' Two or three things. I will confide in you, dear Mr. Jasper, if you can spare the time to listen. This morning as I had nothing to do, and no one to talk to, I thought I would search the garrets here. I have never been over them, and they are extensive. Barbara has always dissuaded me from going up there because they are so dusty and hung with cobwebs. There is such a lot of rubbish heaped up and packed away in the attics. I don't believe that Barbara knows what is there. I don't fancy papa does. Well ! I went up to-day and found treasures.'

' Pray, what treasures ? '

' Barbara is away, and there is no one to scold.

There are boxes there, and old chairs, all kinds of things, some are so heavy I could hardly move them. I could not get them back into their places again, if I were to try.'

'So you threw the entire garret into disorder?'

'Pretty well, but I will send up one of the men or maids to tidy it before Barbara comes home. Behind an old broken winnowing machine—fancy a winnowing machine up there!—and under a pile of old pans and bottomless crocks is a chest, to which I got with infinite trouble, and not till I was very hot and dirty. I found it was locked, but the rust had eaten through the hinges, or the nails fastening them; and after working the lid about awhile I was able to lift it. What do you suppose I found inside?'

'I cannot guess.'

'No, I am sure you cannot. Wait—go on with your gardening. I will bring you one of my treasures.'

She darted into the house, and after a few minutes, Jasper heard a tinkling as of brass. Then Eve danced out to him, laughing and shaking a tambourine.

'I suppose it belonged to you or Miss Jordan when you were children, and was stowed away under the mistaken impression that you had outgrown toys.'

'No, Mr. Jasper, it never belonged to either Barbara or me. I never had one. Barbara gave me everything of her own I wanted. I could not have forgotten this. I would have played with it till I had broken the parchment, and shaken out all the little bells.'

'Give it to me. I will tighten the parchment, and then you can drum on it with your fingers.' He took the instrument from her, and strained the cover. 'Do you know, Miss Eve, how to use a tambourine?'

'No. I shake it, and then all the little bells tingle.'

'Yes, but you also tap the drum. You want music as an accompaniment, and to that you dance with this toy.'

'How do you mean?'

'I will show you how I have seen it played by Italian

and gipsy girls.' He took the tambourine, and singing a lively dance air, struck. the drum and clinked the brasses. He danced before Eve gravely, with graceful movements.

'That is it!' cried Eve, with eyes that flashed with delight, and with feet that itched to dance. 'Oh, give it me back. I understand thoroughly now, thank you, thank you so heartily, dear Mr. Jasper. And now—I have not done. Come up into the garret when I call.'

'What for? To help you to make more rummage, and find more toys?'

'No! I want you to push the winnowing machine back, and to make order in the litter I have created.'

Jasper nodded good-humouredly.

Then Eve, rattling her tambourine over her head, ran in; and Jasper resumed his work at the flower-beds. Barbara's heliotrope, from which she so often wore a fragrant flower, had not been planted many weeks. It was straggling, and needed pinning down. Her seedling asters had not been pricked out in a bed, and they were crowding each other in their box. He took them out and divided their interlaced roots.

'Mr. Jasper!' A little face was peeping out of the small window in the gable that lighted the attic. He looked up, waved his hand, and laid down the young asters with a sigh, but covered their roots with earth before leaving them.

Then he washed his hands at the Abbot's Well, and slowly ascended the stair to the attic. It was a newel stone flight, very narrow, in the thickness of the wall.

When he reached the top he threw up a trap in the floor, and pushed his head through.

Then, indeed, he was surprised. The inconsiderate Eve had taken some candle ends and stuck them on the binding beam of the roof, and lighted them. They cast a yellow radiance through the vast space, without illumining its recesses. All was indistinct save within the radius of a few feet around the candles. In the far off blackness was one silvery grey square of light—the little gable window. On the floor the rafter cast its shadow as a bar of ink.

Jasper was not surprised at the illumination, though vexed at the careless manner in which Eve had created it. What surprised him was the appearance of the young girl. She was transfigured. She was dressed in a saffron-yellow skirt with a crimson lattice of ribbon over it, fastened with bows, and covered with spangles. She wore a crimson velvet bodice, glittering with gold lace and bullion thread embroidery. But her eyes sparkled brighter than the tarnished spangles.

The moment Jasper's head appeared through the trap in the floor, she struck the timbrel, and clattered the jingles, and danced and laughed. Then seeing how amazed he was she skipped coquettishly towards him, rattled her drum in his ear, and danced back again under her row of candles. She had caught the very air he had sung recently, when showing her how to manage the instrument. She had heard it that once, but she had seized the melody, and she sang it, and varied it after her own caprice, but without losing the leading thread, and always coming back to the burden with a similar set gesture of arms and feet, and stroke of drum and clash of bells. Then, all at once, one of the candles fell over on the rafter and dropped to the floor. Eve brought her tambourine down with a crash and jangle; Jasper sprang forward, and extinguished the candle with his foot.

'There! Is not this witchcraft?' exclaimed Eve. 'Go down through the trap again, Mr. Jasper, and I will rejoin you. Not a word to papa, or to Barbie when she returns.'

'I will not go till the candles are put out and the risk of a fire is past. You can see by the window to take off this trumpery.'

'Trumpery! Oh, Mr. Jasper! Trumpery!' she exclaimed in an injured, disappointed tone.

'Call it what you will. Where did you find it?'

'In yonder box. There is more in it. Do go now, Mr. Jasper; I will put out the candles, I will, honour bright.'

The bailiff descended, and resumed his work with the asters. He smiled and yet was vexed at Eve's giddiness. It was impossible to be angry with her, she was but a child. It was hard not to look with apprehension to her future.

Suddenly he stood up, and listened. He heard the clatter of horse's hoofs in the lane. Who could be coming? The evening had closed in. The sun was set. It was not dark so near midsummer, but dusk. He went hastily from the garden into the lane, and saw the young groom urging on his fagged horse, and leading another by the bridle, with a lady's saddle on it.

'Where is your mistress? Is anything the matter?'

'Nothing,' answered the lad. 'She is behind. In taking off her glove she lost her ring, and now I must get a lantern to look for it.'

'Nelly,' that was the horse, 'is tired. I will get a light and run back. Whereabouts is she?'

'Oh, not a thousand yards from the edge of the moor. The doctor rode with us part of the way from Tavistock. After he left, Miss Barbara took off her glove and lost her ring. She won't leave the spot till it be found.'

'Go in. I will take the light to her. Tell the cook to prepare supper. Miss Jordan must be tired and hungry.'

CHAPTER XIX.

BARBARA'S RING.

JASPER quickly got the lantern out of the stable, and lighted the candle in the kitchen. Then he ran with it along the rough, stone-strewn lane, between walls of moor-stone, till he came to the moor. He followed the track rather than road which traversed it. With evening, clouds had gathered and much obscured the light. Nevertheless the north was full of fine silvery haze, against which stood up the curious conical hill of Brent Tor, crowned with its little church.

When suddenly Jasper came up to Miss Jordan, he took her unawares. She was stooping, searching the ground, and, in her dark-green riding habit, he had mistaken her for a gorse bush. When he arrived with the lantern she arose abruptly, and on recognising the young man the riding-whip dropped from her hand.

'Mr. Jasper!' she exclaimed.

'Miss Barbara!'

They stood still looking at each other in the twilight. One of her white hands was gloveless.

'What has brought you here?' asked Barbara, stooping and picking up her whip with one hand, and gathering her habit with the other.

'I heard that you had lost something.'

'Yes; I was thoughtless. I was warm, and I hastily whisked off my glove that I might pass my hand over my brow, and I felt as I plucked the glove away that my aunt's ring came off. It was not a good fit. I was so foolish, so unnerved, that I let drop the glove—and now can find neither. The ring, I suspect, is in the glove, but I cannot find that. So I sent on Johnny Ostler for the lantern. I supposed he would return with it.'

'I took the liberty of coming myself. He is a boy and tired with his long journey; besides, the horses have to be attended to. I hope you are not displeased.'

'On the contrary,' she replied, in her frank, kindly tone, 'I am glad to see you. When one has been from home a long distance, it is pleasant to meet a messenger from home to say how all are.'

'And it is pleasant for the messenger to bring good

tidings. Mr. Jordan is well; Miss Eve happy as a butterfly in summer over a clover field.'

If it had not been dusk, and Barbara had not turned her
head aside, Jasper would have seen a change in her face.
She suddenly bowed herself and recommenced her search.

'I am very, very sorry,' she said, in a low tone, 'I am
not able to be a pleasant messenger to you. I am——'
she half raised herself, her voice was full of sympathy. 'I
am more sorry than I can say.'

He made no reply; he had not, perhaps, expected
much. He threw the light of the lantern along the ground,
and began to search for the glove.

'You are carrying something,' he said; 'let me relieve
you, Miss Jordan.'

'It is—your violin.'

'Miss Barbara! how kind, how good! You have
carried it all the way?'

'Not at all. Johnny Ostler had it most part. Then
Mr. Coyshe carried it. The boy *could* not take it at the
same time that he led my horse; you understand that?'
Her voice became cold, her pride was touched; she did not
choose that he should know the truth.

'But you thought of bringing it.'

'Not at all. Your father insisted on its being taken
from his house. The boy has the rest of your things, as
many as could be carried.'

Nothing further was said. They searched together for
the glove. They were forced to search closely together because the lantern cast but a poor light round. Where the
glare did fall, there the tiny white clover leaves, fine moor
grass, small delicately-shaped flowers of the milkwort,
white and blue, seemed a newly-discovered little world of
loveliness. But Barbara had other matters to consider,
and scarcely noticed the beauty. She was not susceptible
as Eve to the beautiful and picturesque. She was looking
for her glove, but her thoughts were not wholly concerned
with the glove and ring.

K

'Mr. Jasper, I saw your father.' She spoke in a low voice, their heads were not far asunder. 'I told him where you were.'

'Miss Barbara, did he say anything to you about me? Did he say anything about the—the loss of the money?'

'He refused to hear about you. He would hardly listen to a word I said.'

'Did he tell you who took the money?'

'No.' She paused. 'Why should he? I know—it was you——'

Jasper sighed.

'I can see,' pursued Barbara, 'that you were hard tried. I know that you had no happy home, that you had no mother, and that your father may have been harsh and exacting, but—but—' her voice shook. 'Excuse me, I am tired, and anxious about my ring. It is a sapphire surrounded with diamonds. I cannot speak much. I ought not to have put the ring on my finger till the hoop had been reduced. It was a very pretty ring.'

Then the search was continued in silence, without result.

'Excuse me,' she said, after a while, 'I may seem engrossed in my loss and regardless of your disappointment. I expected that your father would have been eager to forgive you. The father of the prodigal in the Gospel ran to meet his repentant son. I am sure—I am sure you are repentant.'

'I will do all in my power to redress the wrong that has been done,' said Jasper calmly.

'I entreated Mr. Babb to be generous, to relax his severity, and to send you his blessing. But I could not win a word of kindness for you, Mr. Jasper, not a word of hope and love!'

'Oh, Miss Jordan, how good and kind you are!'

'Mr. Jasper,' she said in a soft tremulous voice, 'I would take the journey readily over again. I would ride back at once, and alone over the moor, if I thought that

would win the word for you. I believe, I trust, you are repentant, and I would do all in my power to strengthen
your good resolution, and save your soul.'

Then she touched a gorse bush and made her hand
smart with the prickles. She put the ungloved hand within
the radius of the light, and tried to see and remove the
spines.

'Never mind,' she said, forcing a laugh. 'The ring,
not the prickles, is of importance now. If I do not find
it to-night, I shall send out all the men to-morrow, and
promise a reward to quicken their interest and sharpen
their eyes.'

She put her fingers where most wounded to her lips.
Then, thinking that she had said too much, shown too great
a willingness to help Jasper, she exclaimed, 'Our holy religion requires us to do our utmost for the penitent. There
is joy in heaven over one sinner that is contrite.'

'I have found your glove,' exclaimed Jasper joyously.
He rose and held up a dog-skin riding-glove with
gauntlet.

'Feel inside if the ring be there,' said Barbara. 'I
cannot do so myself, one hand is engaged with my whip
and skirt.'

'I can feel it—the hoop—through the leather.'

'I am so glad, so much obliged to you, Mr. Jasper.'
She held out her white hand with the ring-finger extended.
'Please put it in place, and I will close my fist till I reach
home.'

She made the request without thought, considering
only that she had her whip and gathered habit in her
right, gloved hand.

Jasper opened the lantern and raised it. The diamonds
sparkled. 'Yes, that is my ring,' said Barbara.

He set the lantern on a stone, a slab of white felspar
that lay on the grass. Then he lightly held her hand with
his left, and with the right placed the ring on her finger.

But the moment it was in place and his fingers held it

K 2

there, a shock of terror and shame went to Barbara's heart. What inconsiderateness had she been guilty of! The reflection of the light from the white felspar was in their faces. In a moment, unable to control herself, Barbara burst into tears. Jasper stooped and kissed the fingers he held.

She started back, snatched her hand from him, clenched her fist, and struck her breast with it. 'How dare you! You—you—the escaped convict! Go on ; I will follow. You have insulted me.'

He obeyed. But as he walked back to Morwell ahead of her, he was not cast down. Eve, in the garret, had that day opened a coffer and made a discovery. He, too, on the down, had wrenched open for one moment a fast-closed heart, had looked in, and made a discovery.

When Barbara reached her home she rushed to her room, where she threw herself on her bed, and beat and beat again, with her fists, her head and breast, and said, 'I hate—I hate and despise myself! I hate—oh, how I hate myself!'

CHAPTER XX.

PERPLEXITY.

BARBARA was roused early next morning by Eve; Eve had overslept herself when she ought to be up ; she woke and rose early when another hour of rest would have been a boon to poor Barbara. The sisters occupied adjoining rooms that communicated, and the door was always open between them. When Eve was awake she would not suffer her sister to sleep on. She stooped over her and kissed her closed eyes till she woke. Eve had thrown open the window, and the sweet fresh air blew in. The young girl was not more than half dressed. She stood by Barbara's bed with her lovely hair dishevelled about her head, forming a halo of red-gold glory to her face. That face was lovely with its delicate roses of health and happiness, and the blue eyes twinkling in it full of life and fun. Her neck was exposed. She folded her slender arms round Barbara's head and shook it, and kissed again, till the tired, sleep-stupefied girl awoke.

'I cannot sleep this lovely morning,' said Eve; then, with true feminine *non-sequitur*; 'So you must get up, Barbie.'

'Oh, Eve, is it time?' Barbara sat up in bed instantly wide awake. Her sister seated herself on the side of the bed and laid her hand in her lap.

'Eve!' exclaimed Barbara suddenly, 'what have you there—on your finger? Who gave you that?'

'It is a ring, Bab. Is it not beautiful, a forget-me-not of turquoise set in a circlet of gold?'

'Who gave it you, Eve?'

'A pixy gift!' laughed the girl carelessly.

'This will not do. You must answer me. Where did you get it?'

'I found it, Barbie.'

'Found it—where?'

'Where are forget-me-nots usually found?' Then hastily, before her sister could speak, 'But what a lovely ring you have got on your pincushion, Bab! Mine cannot compare with it. Is that the ring I heard the maids say you lost?'

'Yes, dear.'

'How did you recover it? Who found it for you?'

'Jasper.'

Eve turned her ring on her finger.

'My darling,' said Barbara, 'you have not been candid with me about that ring. Did Dr. Coyshe give it to you?'

'Dr. Coyshe! Oh, Barbara, that ever you should think of me as aspiring to be Mrs. Squash!'

'When did you get the ring?'

'Yesterday.

'Who gave it to you? You must tell me.'

'I have already told you—I found it by the wood, as truly as you found yours on the down.'

Suddenly Barbara started, and her heart beat fast.

'Eve!—where is the ribbon and your mother's ring? You used to have that ring always in your bosom. Where is it? Have you parted with that?'

Eve's colour rose, flushing face and throat and bosom.

'Oh, darling!' exclaimed Barbara, 'answer me truly. To whom have you given that ring?'

'I have not given it; I have lost it. You must not be angry with me, Bab. You lost yours.' Eve's eyes sank as she spoke, and her voice faltered.

The elder sister did not speak for a moment; she looked hard at Eve, who stood up and remained before her in a pretty penitential attitude, but unable to meet her eye.

Barbara considered. Whom could her sister have met? There was no one, absolutely no one she could think of, if Mr. Coyshe were set aside, but Jasper. Now Barbara had disapproved of the way in which Eve ran after Jasper before she departed for Ashburton. She had remonstrated, but she knew that her remonstrances carried small weight. Eve was a natural coquette. She loved to be praised, admired, made much of. The life at Morwell was dull, and Eve sought society of any sort where she could chatter and attract admiration and provoke a compliment. Eve had not made any secret of her liking for Jasper, but Barbara had not thought there was anything serious in the liking. It was a child's fancy. But then, she considered, would any man's heart be able to withstand the pretty wiles of Eve? Was it possible for Jasper to be daily associated with this fairy creature and not love her?'

'Eve,' said Barbara gravely, 'it is of no use trying concealment with me. I know who gave you the ring. I know more than you suppose.'

'Jasper has been telling tales,' exclaimed Eve.

Barbara winced but did not speak.

Eve supposed that Jasper had informed her sister about the meeting with Watt on the Raven Rock.

' Are you going to sleep again ? ' asked Eve, as Barbara had cast herself back on her pillow with the face in it. The elder sister shook her head and made a sign with her hand to be left alone.

When Barbara was nearly dressed, Eve stole on tiptoe out of her own room into that of her sister. She was uneasy at Barbara's silence ; she thought her sister was hurt and offended with her. So she stepped behind her, put her arms round her waist, as Barbara stood before the mirror, and her head over her sister's shoulder, partly that she might kiss her cheek, partly also that she might see her own face in the glass and contrast it with that of Barbara. ' You are not cross with me ? ' she said coaxingly.

' No, Eve, no one can be cross with you.' She turned and kissed her passionately. ' Darling ! you must give back the little ring and recover that of your mother.'

' It is impossible,' answered Eve.

' Then I must do what I can for you,' said Barbara. Barbara was resolved what to do. She would speak to her father, if necessary ; but before that she must have a word on the matter with Jasper. It was impossible to tolerate an attachment and secret engagement between him and her sister.

She sought an opportunity of speaking privately to the young man, and easily found one. But when they were together alone, she discovered that it was not easy to approach the topic that was uppermost in her mind.

' I was very tired last night, Mr. Jasper,' she said, ' over-tired, and I am hardly myself this morning. The loss of my aunt, the funeral, the dividing of her poor little treasures, and then the lengthy ride, upset me. It was very ridiculous of me last night to cry, but a girl takes refuge in tears when overspent, it relieves and even refreshes her.'

Then she hesitated and looked down. But Barbara had

a strong will, and when she had made up her mind to do what she believed to be right, allowed no weakness to interfere with the execution.

'And now I want to speak about something else. I must beg you will not encourage Eve. She is a child, thoughtless and foolish.'

'Yes; she should be kept more strictly guarded. I do not encourage her. I regret her giddiness, and give her good advice, which she casts to the winds. Excuse my saying it, but you and Mr. Jordan are spoiling the child.'

'My father and I spoil Eve! That is not possible.'

'You think so; I do not. The event will prove which is right, Miss Jordan.'

Barbara was annoyed. What right had Jasper to dictate how Eve was to be treated?

'That ring,' began Barbara, and halted.

'It is not lost again, surely!' said Jasper.

Barbara frowned. 'I am not alluding to my ring which you found along with my glove, but to that which you gave to Eve.'

'I gave her no ring; I do not understand you.'

'It is a pretty little thing, and a toy. Of course you only gave it her as such, but it was unwise.'

'I repeat, I gave her no ring, Miss Jordan.'

'She says that she found it, but it is most improbable.'

Jasper laughed, not cheerfully; there was always a sadness in his laughter. 'You have made a great mistake, Miss Jordan. It is true that your sister found the ring. That is, I conclude she did, as yesterday she found a chest in the garret full of old masquerading rubbish, and a tambourine, and I know not what besides.'

A load was taken off Barbara's mind. So Eve had not deceived her.

'She showed me a number of her treasures,' said Jasper. 'No doubt whatever that she found the ring along with the other trumpery.'

Barbara's face cleared. She drew a long breath.
'Why did not Eve tell me all?' she said.

'Because,' answered the young man, 'she was afraid you would be angry with her for getting the old tawdry stuff out of the box, and she asked me not to tell you of it. Now I have betrayed her confidence, I must leave to you, Miss Jordan, to make my peace with Miss Eve.'

'She has also lost something that hung round her throat.'

'Very likely. She was, for once, hard at work in the garret, moving boxes and hampers. It is lying somewhere on the floor. If you wish it I will search for her ornament, and hope my success will be equal to that of last night.' He looked down at her hand. The ring was not on it. She observed his glance and said coldly, 'My ring does not fit me, and I shall reserve it till I am old, or till I find some young lady friend to whom I must make a wedding present.' Then she turned away. She walked across the Abbot's Meadow, through which the path led to the rocks, because she knew that Eve had gone in that direction. Before long she encountered her sister returning with a large bunch of foxgloves in her hand.

'Do look, Bab!' exclaimed Eve, 'is not this a splendid sceptre? A wild white foxglove with thirty-seven bells on it.'

'Eve!' said Barbara, her honest face alight with pleasure; 'my dearest, I was wrong to doubt you. I know now where you found the ring, and I am not in the least cross about it. There, kiss and make peace.'

'I wish the country folk had a prettier name for the foxglove than *flop-a-dock*,' said Eve.

'My dear,' said Barbara, 'you shall show me the pretty things you have found in the attic.'

'What—Bab?'

'I know all about it. Jasper has proved a traitor.'

'What has he told you?'

'He has told me where you found the turquoise ring, together with a number of fancy ball dresses.'

Eve was silent. A struggle went on in her innocent heart. She hated falsehood. It pained her to deceive her sister, who had such perfect faith in her. She felt inclined to tell her all, yet she dared not do so. In her heart she longed to hear more of Martin. She remembered his handsome face, his flattering and tender words, the romance of that night. No! she could not tell Barbara.

'We will go together into the garret,' said Barbara, ' and search for your mother's ring. It will easily be found by the blue ribbon to which it is attached.'

Then Eve laughed, held her sister at arms' length, thrusting the great bunch of purple and white foxgloves against her shoulder, so that their tall heads nodded by her cheek and ear. 'No, Bab, sweet, I did not find the ring in the chest with the gay dresses. I did not lose the ring of my mother's in the loft. I tell you the truth, but I tell you no more.'

'Oh, Eve!' Barbara's colour faded. 'Who was it? I implore you, if you love me, tell me.'

'I love you dearly, but no.' She curtsied. 'Find out if you can.' Then she tripped away, waving her foxgloves.

CHAPTER XXI.

THE SCYTHE OF TIME.

'My papa! my darling papa!' Eve burst into her father's room. 'I want you much to do something for me. Mr. Jasper is so kind. He has promised to have a game of bowls with me this evening on the lawn, and the grass is not mown.'

'Well, dear, get it mown,' said Mr. Jordan dreamily.

'But there is no man about, and old Davy is in bed. What am I to do?'

'Wait till to-morrow.'

'I cannot; I shall die of impatience. I have set my heart on a game of bowls. Do you not see, papa, that the weather may change in the night and spoil play for to-morrow?'

'Then what do you wish?'

'Oh! my dear papa,' Eve nestled into his arms, 'I don't want much, only that you would cut the grass for me. It really will not take you ten minutes. I will promise to sweep up what is cut.'

'I am engaged, Eve, on a very delicate test.'

'So am I, papa.'

Mr. Ignatius Jordan looked up at her with dull surprise in his eyes.

'I mean, papa, that if you really love me you will jump up and mow the grass. If you don't love me you will go on muddling with those minerals and chemicals.'

The gaunt old man stood up. Eve knew her power over him. She could make him obey her slightest caprice. She ran before him to the gardener's tool-house and brought him the scythe.

In the quadrangle was a grass plat, and on this Eve had decided to play her game.

'All the balls are here except the Jack,' said she. 'I shall have to rummage everywhere for the black-a-moor; I can't think where he can be.' Then she ran into the house in quest of the missing ball.

The grass had been left to grow all spring and had not been cut at all, so that it was rank. Mr. Jordan did not well know how to wield a scythe. He tried and met with so little success that he suspected the blade was blunt. Accordingly he went to the tool-house for the hone, and, standing the scythe up with the handle on the swath, tried to sharpen the blade.

The grass was of the worst possible quality. The

quadrangle was much in shadow. The plots were so exhausted that little grew except daisy and buttercup. Jasper had already told Barbara to have the wood-ashes thrown on the plots, and had promised to see that they were limed in winter. Whilst Mr. Jordan was honing the scythe slowly and clumsily Barbara came to him. She was surprised to see him thus engaged. Lean, haggard, with deep-sunken eyes, and hollow cheeks, he lacked but the hour-glass to make him stand as the personification of Time. He was in an ill-humour at having been disturbed and set to an uncongenial task, though his ill-humour was not directed towards Eve. Barbara was always puzzled by her father. That he suffered, she saw, but she could not make out of what and where he suffered, and he resented inquiry. There were times when his usually dazed look was exchanged for one of keenness, when his eyes glittered with a feverish anxiety, and he seemed to be watching and expecting with eye and ear something or some person that never came. At table he was without conversation ; he sat morose, lost in his own thoughts till roused by an observation addressed to him. His temper was uncertain. Often, as he observed nothing, he took offence at nothing ; but occasionally small matters roused and unreasonably irritated him. An uneasy apprehension in Barbara's mind would not be set at rest. She feared that her father's brain was disturbed, and that at any time, without warning, he might break out into some wild, unreasonable, possibly dreadful, act, proclaiming to everyone that what she dreaded in secret had come to pass—total derangement. Of late his humour had been especially changeful, but his eldest daughter sought to convince herself that this could be accounted for by distress at the loss of Eve's dowry.

Barbara asked her father why he was mowing the grass plot, and when he told her that Eve had asked him to do so that she might play bowls that evening on it, she remonstrated, ' Whom is she to play with ? '

'Jasper Babb has promised her a game. I suppose you and I will be dragged out to make up a party.'

'O papa, there is no necessity for your mowing! You do not understand a scythe. Now you are honing the wrong way, blunting, not sharpening, the blade.'

'Of course I am wrong. I never do right in your eyes.'

'My dear father,' said Barbara, hurt at the injustice of the remark, 'that is not true.'

'Then why are you always watching me? I cannot walk in the garden, I cannot go out of the door, I cannot eat a meal, but your eyes are on me. Is there anything very frightful about me? Anything very extraordinary? No—it is not that. I can read the thoughts in your head. You are finding fault with me. I am not doing useful work. I am wasting valuable hours over empty pursuits. I am eating what disagrees with me, too much, or too little. Understand this, once for all. I hate to be watched. Here is a case in point, a proof if one were needed. I came out here to cut this grass, and at once you are after me. You have spied my proceedings. I must not do this. If I sharpen the scythe I am all in the wrong, blunting the blade.'

The tears filled Barbara's eyes.

'I am told nothing,' continued Mr. Jordan. 'Everything I ought to know is kept concealed from me, and you whisper about me behind my back to Jasper and Mr. Coyshe.'

'Indeed, indeed, dear papa——'

'It is true. I have seen you talking to Jasper, and I know it was about me. What were you trying to worm out of him about me? And so with the doctor. You rode with him all the way from Tavistock to the Down the other day; my left ear was burning that afternoon. What did it burn for? Because I was being discussed. I object to being made the topic of discussion. Then, when you parted with the doctor, Jasper Babb ran out to meet you, that you might learn from him how I had behaved, what I had done, whilst you were away. I have no rest in my own house because of your prying eyes. Will you go now, and leave me.'

'I will go now, certainly,' said Barbara, with a gulp in her throat, and swimming eyes.

'Stay!' he said, as she turned. He stood leaning his elbow on the head of the scythe, balancing it awkwardly. 'I was told nothing of your visit to Buckfastleigh. You told Eve, and you told Jasper but I who am most concerned only heard about it by a side-wind. You brought Jasper his fiddle, and when I asked how he had got it, Eve told me. You visited his father. Well! am I nobody that I am to be kept in the dark?'

'I have nothing of importance to tell,' said Barbara. 'It is true I saw Mr. Babb, but he would not let me inside his house.'

'Tell me, what did that man say about the money?'

'I do not think there is any chance of his paying unless he be compelled. He has satisfied his conscience. He put the money away for you, and as it did not reach you the loss is yours, and you must bear it.'

'But good heavens! that is no excuse at all. The base hypocrite! He is a worse thief than the man who stole the money. He should sell the fields he bought with my loan.'

'They were fields useful to him for the stretching of the cloth he wove in his factory.'

'Are you trying to justify him for withholding payment?' asked Mr. Jordan. 'He is a hypocrite. What was he to cry out against the strange blood, and to curse it?—he, Ezekiel Babb, in whose veins ran fraud and guile?'

Barbara looked wonderingly at him through the veil of tears that obscured her sight. What did he mean?

'He is an old man, papa, but hard as iron. He has white hair, but none of the reverence which clings to age attaches to him.'

'White hair!' Mr. Jordan turned the scythe, and with the point aimed at, missed, aimed at again, and cut down a white-seeded dandelion in the grass. 'That is white, but the neck is soft, even if the head be hard,' said Mr. Jordan, pointing to the dandelion. 'I wish that were his head, and I had cut through his neck. But then——' he seemed to fall into a bewildered state—'the blood should run red—run, run, dribble over the edge, red. This is milky, but acrid.' He recovered himself. 'I have only cut down a head of dandelion.' He reversed the scythe again, and stood leaning his arm on the back of the blade, and staying the handle against his knee.

'My dear father, had you not better put the scythe away?'

'Why should I do that? I have done no harm with it. No one can set on me for what I have cut with it—only a white old head of dandelion with a soft neck. Think—if it had been Ezekiel Babb's head sticking out of the grass, with the white hair about it, and the sloe-black wicked eyes, and with one cut of the scythe—swish, it had tumbled over, with the stalk upwards, bleeding, bleeding, and the eyes were in the grass, and winking because the daisies teased them and made them water.'

Barbara was distressed. She must change the current of his thoughts. To do this she caught at the first thing that came into her head.

'Papa! I will tell you what Mr. Coyshe was talking to me about. It is quite right, as you say, that you should know all; it is proper that nothing should be kept from you.'

'It is hardly big enough,' said Mr. Jordan.

'What, papa?'

'The dandelion. I can't feel towards it as if it were Mr. Babb's head.'

'Papa,' said Barbara, speaking rapidly, and eager to divert his mind into another channel, 'papa dear, do you know that the doctor is much attached to our pet?'

'It could not be otherwise. Everyone loves Eve; if they do not, they deserve to die.'

'Papa! He told me as much as that. He admires her greatly, and would dearly like to propose for her, but, though I do not suppose he is bashful, he is not quite sure that she cares for him.'

'Eve shall have whom she will. If she does not like Coyshe, she shall have anyone else.'

Then he hinted that, though he had no doubt he would make himself a great name in his profession, and in time be very wealthy, that yet he could not afford as he is now circumstanced to marry a wife without means.

'There! there!' exclaimed Mr. Jordan, becoming again excited. 'See how the wrong done by Ezekiel Babb is beginning to work. There is a future, a fine future offering for my child, but she cannot accept it. The gate is open, but she may not pass through, because she has not the toll-money in her hand.'

'Are you sure, papa, that Mr. Coyshe would make Eve happy?'

'I am sure of it. What is this place for her? She should be in the world, be seen and received, and shine. Here she is like one hidden in a nook. She must be brought out, she must be admired by all.'

'I do not think Eve cares for him.'

But her father did not hear her; he went on, and as he spoke his eyes flashed, and spots of dark red colour flared on his cheek-bones. 'There is no chance for poor Eve! The money is gone past recovery. Her future is for ever blighted. I call on heaven to redress the wrong. I went the other day to Plymouth to hear Mass, and I had but one prayer on my lips, Avenge me on my enemy! When the choir sang "*Gloria in Excelsis, Deo,*" I heard my heart sing a bass, "On earth a curse on the man of ill-will." When they sang the Hosanna! I muttered, Cursed is he that cometh to defraud the motherless! I could not hear the Benedictus. My heart roared out "*Imprecatus!*

Imprecatus sit!" I can pray nothing else. All my prayers turn sour in my throat, and I taste them like gall on my tongue.'

' O papa! this is horrible ! '

Now he rested both his elbows on the back of the blade and raised his hands, trembling with passion, as if in prayer. His long thin hair, instead of hanging lank about his head, seemed to bristle with electric excitement, his cheeks and lips quivered. Barbara had never seen him so greatly moved as now, and she did not know what to do to pacify him. She feared lest any intervention might exasperate him further.

' I pray,' he began, in a low, vibrating monotone, ' I pray to the God of justice, who protecteth the orphan and the oppressed, that He may cause the man that sinned to suffer; that He will whet his gleaming sword, and smite and not spare—smite and not spare the guilty.' His voice rose in tone and increased in volume. Barbara looked round, in hopes of seeing Eve, trusting that the sight of her might soothe her father, and yet afraid of her sister seeing him in this condition.

' There was a time, seventeen years ago,' continued Mr. Jordan, not noticing Barbara, looking before him as if he saw something far beyond the boundary walls of the house, ' there was a time when he lifted up his hand and voice to curse my child. I saw the black cross, and the shadow of Eve against it, and he with his cruel black hands held her there, nailed her with his black fingers to the black cross. And now I lift my soul and my hands to God against him. I cry to Heaven to avenge the innocent. Raise Thy arm and Thy glittering blade, O Lord, and smite ! '

Suddenly the scythe slipped from under his elbows. He uttered a sharp cry, staggered back and fell.

As he lay on the turf, Barbara saw a dark red stain ooze from his right side, and spread as ink on blotting-paper. The point of the scythe had entered his side. He put his hand to the wound, and then looked at his palm. His face turned livid. At that moment, just as Barbara sprang to her father, having recovered from the momentary paralysis of terror, Eve bounded from the hall-door, holding a ball over her head in both her hands, and shouting joyously, 'I have the Jack! I have the Jack!'

CHAPTER XXII.

THE RED STREAK.

BARBARA was not a girl to allow precious moments to be lost; instead of giving way to emotion and exclamations, she knelt and tore off her father's waistcoat, ripped his shirt, and found a gash under the rib; tearing off her kerchief she ran, sopped it in cold water, and held it tightly to the wound.

'Run, Eve, run, summon help!' she cried. But Eve was powerless to be of assistance; she had turned white to the lips, had staggered back to the door, and sent the Jack rolling over the turf to her father's feet.

'I am faint,' gasped poor Eve. 'I cannot see blood.'

'You must,' exclaimed Barbara, 'command yourself. Ring the alarm bell: Jasper—someone—will hear.'

'The power is gone from my arms,' sobbed Eve, shivering.

'Call one of the maids. Bid her ring,' ordered the elder.

Eve, holding the sides of the door to prevent herself from falling, deadly white, with knees that yielded under her, staggered into the house.

Presently the old bell hung in a pent-house over the roof of the chapel began to give tongue.

Barbara, kneeling behind her father, raised his head on her bosom, and held her kerchief to his side. The first token of returning consciousness was given by his hands, which clutched at some grass he had cut. Then he opened his eyes.

'Why is the bell tolling?'

'Dear papa! it is calling for help. You must be moved. You are badly hurt.'

'I feel it. In my side. How was it? I do not remember. Ah! the scythe. Has the blade cut deep?'

'I cannot tell, papa, till the doctor comes. Are you easier now?'

'You did it. Interfering with me when I was mowing. Teasing me. You will not leave me alone. You are always watching me. You wanted to take the scythe from me. If you had left me alone this would not have happened.'

'Never mind, darling papa, how it happened. Now we must do our best to cure you.'

'Am I badly hurt? What are these women coming crowding round me for? I do not want the maids here. Drive them back, Barbara.'

Barbara made a sign to the cook and house and kitchen maids to stand back.

'You must be moved to your room, papa.'

'Am I dying, Barbara?'

'I hope and trust not, dear.'

'I cannot die without speaking; but I will not speak till I am on the point of death.'

'Do not speak, father, at all now.'

He obeyed and remained quiet, with his eyes looking up at the sky. Thus he lay till Jasper arrived breathless. He had heard the bell, and had run, suspecting some disaster.

'Let me carry him, with one of the maids,' said Jasper,

'No,' answered Barbara. 'You shall take his shoulders, I his feet. We will carry him on a mattress. Cook and Jane have brought one. Help me to raise him on to it.'

Jasper was the man she wanted. He did not lose his

L 2

head. He did not ask questions, how the accident had happened; he did not waste words in useless lamentation. He sent a maid at once to the stable to saddle the horse. A girl, in the country, can saddle and bridle as well as a boy.

'I am off for the doctor,' he said shortly, as soon as he had seen Mr. Jordan removed to the same downstairs room in which he had so recently lain himself.

'Send for the lawyer,' said Mr. Jordan, who had lain with his eyes shut.

'The lawyer, papa!'

'I must make my will. I might die, and then what would become of Eve?'

'Ride on to Tavistock after you have summoned Mr. Coyshe,' said Barbara.

When Jasper was gone, Eve, who had been fluttering about the door, came in, and threw herself sobbing on her knees by her father's bed. He put out his hand, stroked her brow, and called her tender names.

She was in great distress, reproaching herself for having asked him to mow the grass for her; she charged herself with having wounded him.

'No—no, Eve!' said her father. 'It was not your fault. Barbara would not let me alone. She interfered, and I lost my balance.'

'I am so glad it was not I,' sobbed Eve.

'Let me look at you. Stand up,' he said.

She rose, but averted her face somewhat, so as not to see the blood on the sheet. He had been caressing her. Now, as he looked at her, he saw a red streak across her forehead.

'My child! what is that? You are hurt! Barbara, help! She is bleeding.'

Barbara looked.

'It is nothing,' she said; 'your hand, papa, has left some of its stains on her brow. Come with me, Eve, and I will wash it clean.'

The colour died completely out of Eve's face, and she

seemed again about to faint. Barbara hastily bathed a napkin in fresh water, and removed all traces of blood from her forehead, and then kissed it.

'Is it gone?' whispered Eve.

'Entirely.'

'I feel it still. I cannot remain here.' Then the young girl crept out of the room, hardly able to sustain herself on her feet.

When Barbara was alone with her father, she said to him, in her quiet, composed tones, 'Papa, though I do not in the least think this wound will prove fatal, I am glad you have sent for Lawyer Knighton, because you ought to make your will, and provide for Eve. I made up my mind to speak to you when I was on my way home from Ashburton.'

'Well, what have you to say?'

'Papa! I've been thinking that as the money laid by for Eve is gone for ever, and as my aunt has left me a little more than sixteen hundred pounds, you ought to give Morwell to Eve – that is, for the rest of your term of it, some sixty-three years, I think. If you like to make a little charge on it for me, do so, but do not let it be much. I shall not require much to make me happy. I shall never marry. If I had a good deal of money it is possible some man would be base enough to want to marry me for it; but if I have only a little, no one will think of asking me. There is no one whom I care for whom I would dream of taking—under no circumstances—nothing would move me to it—nothing. And as an old maid, what could I do with this property? Eve must marry. Indeed, she can have almost anyone she likes. I do not think she cares for the doctor, but there must be some young squire about here who would suit her.'

'Yes, Barbara, you are right.'

'I am glad you think so,' she said, smiled, and coloured, pleased with his commendation, so rarely won. 'No one can see Eve without loving her. I have my little scheme. Captain Cloberry is coming home from the army this ensuing autumn, and if he is as nice as his sisters say—then something may come of it. But I do not know whether Eve cares or does not care for Mr. Coyshe. He has not spoken to her yet. I think, papa, it would be well to let him and everyone know that Morwell is not to come to me, but is to go to Eve. Then everyone will know what to expect.

'It shall be so. If Mr. Knighton comes, I will get the doctor to be in the room when I make my will, and Jasper Babb also.' He considered for a while, and then said, ' In spite of all—there is good in you, Barbara. I forgive you my wound. There—you may kiss me.'

As Barbara wished, and Mr. Jordan intended, so was the will executed. Mr. Knighton, the solicitor, arrived at the same time as the surgeon; he waited till Mr. Coyshe had bandaged up the wound, and then he entered the sick man's room, summoned by Barbara.

' My second daughter,' said Mr. Jordan, ' is, in the eye of the law, illegitimate. My elder daughter has urged me to do what I likewise feel to be right—to leave my title to Morwell estate to Eve.'

' What is her surname—I mean her mother's name ? '

' That you need not know. I leave Morwell to my daughter Eve, commonly called Eve Jordan. That is Barbara's wish.'

' I urged it on my father,' said Barbara.

Jasper, who had been called in, looked into her face with an expression of admiration. She resented it, frowned, and averted her head.

When the will had been properly executed, the doctor left the room with Jasper. He had already given his instructions to Barbara how Mr. Jordan was to be treated. Outside the door he found Eve fluttering, nervous, alarmed, entreating to be reassured as to her father's condition.

' Dear Barbie disturbed him whilst he was mowing,' she said, ' and he let the scythe slip, and so got hurt.' She was readily consoled when assured that the old gentleman lay in no immediate danger. He must, however, be kept quiet, and not allowed to leave his bed for some time. Then Eve bounded away, light as a roe. The reaction set in at once. She was like a cork in water, that can only be kept depressed by force; remove the pressure and the cork leaps to the surface again.

Such was her nature. She could not help it.

'Mr. Jasper,' said the surgeon, 'I have never gone over this property. If you have a spare hour and would do me a favour, I should like to look about me. The quality of the land is good?'

'Excellent.'

'Is there anywhere a map of the property that I could run my eye over?'

'In the study.'

'What about the shooting, now?'

'It is not preserved. If it were it would be good, the cover is so fine.'

'And there seems to be a good deal of timber.'

After about an hour Mr. Coyshe rode away. 'Some men are Cyclopses, as far as their own interests are concerned,' said he to himself; 'they carry but a single eye. I invariably use two.'

In the evening, when Barbara came to her sister's room to tell her that she intended to sit up during the night with her father, she said: 'Mr. Jasper is very kind. He insists on taking half the watch, he will relieve me at two o'clock. What is the matter with you, Eve?'

'I can see nothing, Barbie, but it is there still.'

'What is?'

'That red mark. I have been rubbing, and washing, and it burns like fire.'

'I can see, my dear Eve, that where you have rubbed your pretty white delicate skin, you have made it red.'

'I have rubbed it in. I feel it. I cannot get the feel away. It stains me. It hurts me. It burns me.'

CHAPTER XXIII.

A BUNCH OF ROSES.

Mr. Jordan's wound was not dangerous, but the strictest rest was enjoined. He must keep his bed for some days. As when Jasper was ill, so now that her father was an invalid, the principal care devolved on Barbara. No reliance could be placed on Eve, who was willing enough, but too thoughtless and forgetful to be trusted. When Barbara returned from Ashburton she found her store closet in utter confusion: bags of groceries opened and not tied up again, bottles of sauces upset and broken, coffee berries and rice spilled over the floor, lemons with the sugar, become mouldy, and dissolving the sugar. The linen cupboard was in a similar disorder: sheets pulled out and thrust back unfolded in a crumpled heap, pillow-cases torn up for dusters, blankets turned out and left in a damp place, where the moth had got to them. Now, rather than give the keys to Eve, Barbara retained them, and was kept all day engaged without a moment's cessation. She was not able to sit much with her father, but Eve could do that, and her presence soothed the sick man. Eve, however, would not remain long in the room with her father. She was restless, her spirits flagged, and Mr. Jordan himself insisted on her going out. Then she would run to Jasper Babb, if he were near. She had taken a great fancy to him. He was kind to her; he treated her as a child, and accommodated himself to her humours. Barbara could not now be with her. Besides, Barbara had not that craving for colour and light, and melody and poetry, that formed the very core of Eve's soul. The elder sister was severely practical. She liked what was beautiful, as a well-educated young lady is required by society to have such a liking, but it was not instinctive in her, it was in no way a passion. Jasper, on the other hand, responded to the æsthetic longings of Eve. He could sympathise with her raptures ; Barbara laughed at them. It is said that everyone sees his own rainbow, but there are many who are colour-blind and see no rainbows, only raindrops. Wherever Eve looked she saw rainbows. Jasper had a strong fibre of poetry in him, and he was able to read the girl's character and understand the uncertain aspirations of her heart. He thought that Barbara was mistaken in laughing down and showing no interest in her enthusiasms, and he sought to give her vague aspirations some direction, and her cravings some satisfaction.

Eve appreciated his efforts. She saw that he understood her, which Barbara did not ; she and Jasper had a world of ideas in common from which her sister was shut out. Eve took great delight in talking to Jasper, but her chief delight was in listening to him when he played the violin, or in accompanying him on the piano. Old violin music was routed out of the cupboards, fresh was ordered. Jasper introduced her to a great deal of very beautiful classical music of which she was ignorant. Hitherto she had been restrained to a few meagre collections : the ' Musical Treasury,' the ' Sacred Harmonist,' and the like. Now, with her father's consent, she ordered the operas of Mozart, Beethoven's sonatas, Rossini, Boieldieu, and was guided, a ready pupil, by Jasper into this new and enchanted world. By this means Jasper gave Eve an interest, which hitherto she had lacked—a pursuit which she followed with eagerness.

Barbara was dissatisfied. She thought Jasper was encouraging Eve in her frivolity, was diverting her from the practical aims of life. She was angry with Jasper, and misinterpreted his motives. The friendship subsisting between her sister and the young steward was too warm. How far would it go ? How was it to be arrested ? Eve was inexperienced and wilful. Before she knew

where she was, Jasper would have gained her young heart.
She was so headstrong that Barbara doubted whether a
word of caution would avail anything. Nevertheless, convinced that it was her duty to interfere, she did speak,
and, of course, gained nothing by so doing. Barbara
lacked tact. She spoke to Eve plainly, but guardedly.

'Why, Bab! what are you thinking of? Why should
I not be with Mr. Jasper?' answered Eve to her sister's
expostulation. 'I like him vastly; he talks delightfully,
he knows so much about music, he plays and sings the
tears into my eyes, and sets my feet tingling to dance.
Papa does not object. When we are practising I leave the
parlour door open for papa to hear. He says he enjoys
listening. Oh, Barbie! I wish you loved music as I do.
But as you don't, let me go my way with the music, and
you go your way with the groceries.'

'My dearest sister,' said Barbara, 'I do not think it
looks well to see you running after Mr. Jasper.'

'Looks well!' repeated Eve. 'Who is to see me?
Morwell is quite out of the world. Besides,' she screwed
up her pretty mouth to a pout, 'I don't run after him, he
runs after me, of course.'

'My dear, dear Eve,' said Barbara earnestly, 'you
must not suffer him to do so.'

'Why not?' asked Eve frankly. 'You like Ponto and
puss to run after you, and the little black calf, and the
pony in the paddock. What is the difference? You care
for one sort of animals, and I for another. I detest dogs
and cats and bullocks.'

'Eve, sweetheart'—poor Barbara felt her powerlessness
to carry her point, even to make an impression, but in her
conscientiousness believed herself bound to go on—'your
conduct is indiscreet. We must never part with our self-
respect. That is the guardian angel given to girls by God.'

'Oh, Bab!' Eve burst out laughing. 'What a dear,
grave old Mother Hubbard you are! I am always doing,
and always will do, exactly opposite to what you intend

and expect. I know why you are lecturing me now. I
will tell Mr. Jasper how jealous you have become.'

'For heaven's sake!' exclaimed Barbara, springing to
her feet—she had been sitting beside Eve—'do nothing
of the sort. Do not mention my name to him. I
am not jealous. It is an insult to me to make such a
suggestion. Do I ever seek his company? Do I not shun
it? No, Eve, I am moved only by uneasiness for you.
You are thoughtless, and are playing a dangerous game
with that man. When he sees how you seek his society,
it flatters him, and his vanity will lead him to think of
you with more warmth than is well. Understand this,
Eve—there is a bar between him and you which should
make the man keep his distance, and he shows a wicked
want of consideration when he draws near you, relying on
your ignorance.'

'What are you hinting at?'

'I cannot speak out as I wish, but I assure you of this,
Eve, unless you are more careful of your conduct, I shall
be forced to take steps to get Jasper Babb dismissed.'

Eve laughed, clapped her hands on her sister's cheeks,
kissed her lips and said, 'You dear old Mother Hubbard,
you can't do it. Papa would not listen to you if I told
him that I wanted Jasper to stay.'

Barbara was hurt. This was true, but it was unkind
of Eve to say it. The young girl was herself aware that
she had spoken unfeelingly, was sorry, and tried to make
amends by coaxing her sister.

'I want you to tell me,' said Barbara, very gravely,
'for you have not told me yet, who gave you the ring?'

'I did not tell you because you said you knew. No one
carries water to the sea or coals to Newcastle.'

'Be candid with me, Eve.'

'Am not I open as the day? Why should you complain?'

'Eve, be serious. Was it Mr. Jasper who gave you
the turquoise ring?'

'Jasper!' Eve held out her skirts daintily, and danced and made curtsies round her sister, in the prettiest, most coquettish, laughing way. 'You dearest, you best, you most jealous of sisters; we will not quarrel over poor good Jasper. I don't mind how much you pet the black calf. How absurd you are! You make me laugh sometimes at your density. There, do not cry. I would tell you all if I dared.' Then warbling a strain, and still holding her skirts out, she danced as in a minuet, slowly out of the room, looking back over her shoulder at her distressed sister.

That was all Barbara had got by speaking—nothing, absolutely nothing. She knew that Eve would not be one wit more guarded in her conduct for what had been said to her. Barbara revolved in her mind the threat she had rashly made of driving Jasper away. That would necessitate the betrayal of his secret. Could she bring herself to this? Hardly. No, the utmost she could do was to threaten him that, unless he voluntarily departed, she would reveal the secret to her father.

A day or two after this scene, Barbara was again put to great distress by Eve's conduct.

She knew well enough that she and her sister were invited to the Cloberrys to an afternoon party and dance. Eve had written and accepted before the accident to Mr. Jordan. Barbara had let her write, because she was herself that day much engaged and could not spare time. The groom had ridden over from Bradstone manor, and was waiting for an answer, just whilst Barbara was weighing out sago and tapioca. When Mr. Jordan was hurt, Barbara had wished to send a boy to Bradstone with a letter declining the party, but Mr. Coyshe had said that her father was not in danger, had insisted on Eve promising him a couple of dances, and had so strictly combated her desire to withdraw that she had given way.

In the afternoon, when the girls were ready to go, they came downstairs to kiss their father, and let him see them in their pretty dresses. The little carriage was at the door.

In the hall they met Jasper Babb, also dressed for the party. He held in his hands two lovely bouquets, one of yellow tea-scented roses, which he handed to Barbara, the other of Malmaison, delicate white, with a soft inner blush, which he offered to Eve. Whence had he procured them? No doubt he had been for them to a nursery at Tavistock.

Eve was in raptures over her Malmaison; it was a new rose, quite recently introduced, and she had never seen it before. She looked at it, uttered exclamations of delight, smelt at the flowers, then ran off to her father that she might show him her treasures.

Barbara thanked Jasper somewhat stiffly; she was puzzled. Why was he dressed?

'Are you going to ride, or to drive us?' asked Eve, skipping into the hall again. She had put her bunch in her girdle. She was charmingly dressed, with rose satin ribands in her hair, about her throat, round her waist. Her face was, in colour, itself like a souvenir de la Malmaison rose.

'Whom are you addressing?' asked Barbara seriously.

'I am speaking to Jasper,' answered Eve.

'*Mr.* Jasper,' said Barbara, 'was not invited to Bradstone.'

'Oh, that does not matter!' said the ready Eve. 'I accepted for him. You know, dear Bab—I mean Barbie—that I had to write, as you were up to your neck in tapioca. Well, at these parties there are so many girls and so few gentlemen, that I thought I would give the Cloberry girls and Mr. Jasper a pleasure at once, so I wrote to say that you and I accepted and would bring with us a young gentleman, a friend of papa, who was staying in the house. Mr. Jasper ought to know the neighbours, and get some pleasure.'

Barbara was aghast.

'I think, Miss Eve, you have been playing tricks with

me,' said Jasper. 'Surely I understood you that I had been specially invited, and that you had accordingly accepted for me.'

'Did I?' asked Eve carelessly; 'it is all the same. The Cloberry girls will be delighted to see you. Last time I was there they said they hoped to have an afternoon dance, but were troubled how to find gentlemen as partners for all the pretty Misses.'

'That being so,' said Barbara sternly, turning as she spoke to Jasper, 'of course you do not go?'

'Not go!' exclaimed Eve; 'to be sure he goes. We are engaged to each other for a score of dances.' Then, seeing the gloom gathering on her sister's brow, she explained, 'It is a plan between us so as to get free from Doctor Squash. When Squash asks my hand, I can say I am engaged. I have been booked by him for two dances, and he shall have no more.'

'You have been inconsiderate,' said Barbara. 'Unfortunately Mr. Babb cannot leave Morwell, as my father is in his bed—it is not possible.'

'I have no desire to go,' said Jasper.

'I do not suppose you have,' said Barbara haughtily, turning to him. 'You are judge of what is right and fitting— in every way.'

Then Eve's temper broke out. Her cheeks flushed, her lips quivered, and the tears started into her eyes. 'I will not allow Mr. Jasper to be thus treated,' she exclaimed. 'I cannot understand you, Barbie; how can you, who are usually so considerate, grudge Mr. Jasper a little pleasure? He has been working hard for papa, and he has been kind to me, and he has made your garden pretty, and now you are mean and ungrateful, and send him back to his room when he is dressed for the party. I'll go and ask papa to interfere.'

Then she ran off to her father's room.

The moment Eve was out of hearing, Barbara's anger blazed forth. 'You are not acting right. You forget your position ; you forget who you are. How dare you allow my sister—— ? If you had a spark of honour, a grain of good feeling in your heart, you would keep her at arm's length. She is a child, inconsiderate and confiding ; you are a man with such a foul stain on your name, that you must not come near those who are clean, lest you smirch them. Keep to yourself, sir ! Away ! '

' Miss Jordan,' he answered, with a troubled expression on his face and a quiver in his voice, ' you are hard on me. I had no desire whatever to go to this dance, but Miss Eve told me it was arranged that I was to go, and I am obedient in this house. Of course, now I withdraw.'

'Of course you do. Good heavens ! In a few days some chance might bring all to light, and then it would be the scandal of the neighbourhood that we had introduced—that Eve had danced with—an escaped jail-bird—a vulgar thief.'

She walked out through the door, and threw the bunch of yellow roses upon the plot of grass in the quadrangle.

CHAPTER XXIV.

WHERE THEY WITHERED.

BARBARA did not enjoy the party at the Cloberrys. She was dull and abstracted. It was otherwise with Eve. During the drive she had sulked ; she was in a pet with Barbara, who was a stupid, tiresome marplot. But when she arrived at Bradstone and was surrounded by admirers, when she had difficulty, not in getting partners, but in selecting among those who pressed themselves on her, Eve's spirits were elated. She forgot about Jasper, Barbara, her father, about everything but present delight. With sparkling eyes, heightened colour, and dimples that came and went in her smiling face, she sailed past Barbara without observing her, engrossed in the pleasure of the dance, and in playing with her partner.

Barbara was content to be unnoticed. She sat by herself in a corner, scarce noticing what went on, so wrapped up was she in her thoughts. Her mood was observed by her hostess, and atrributed to anxiety for her father. Mrs. Cloberry went to her, seated herself at her side, and talked to her kindly about Mr. Jordan and his accident.

'You have a friend staying with you. We rather expected him,' said Mrs. Cloberry.

'Oh!' Barbara answered, 'that was dear Eve's nonsense. She is a child, and does not think. My father has engaged a steward; of course he could not come.'

'How lovely Eve is!' said Mrs. Cloberry. 'I think I never saw so exquisite a creature.'

'And she is as good and sweet as she is lovely,' answered Barbara, always eager to sing her sister's praises.

Eve's roses were greatly admired. She had her posy out of her waistband showing the roses, and many a compliment was occasioned by them. 'Barbara had a beautifull bouquet also,' she said, and looked round. 'Oh, Bab! where are your yellow roses?'

'I have dropped them,' answered Barbara.

Besides dancing there was singing. Eve required little pressing.

'My dear Miss Jordan,' said Mrs. Cloberry, 'how your sister has improved in style. Who has been giving her lessons?'

The party was a pleasant one; it broke up early. It began at four o'clock and was over when the sun set. As the sisters drove home, Eve prattled as a brook over stones. She had perfectly enjoyed herself. She had outshone every girl present, had been much courted and greatly flattered. Eve was not a vain girl; she knew she was pretty, and accepted homage as her right. Her father and sister had ever been her slaves; and she expected to find everyone wear chains before her. But there was no vulgar conceit about her. A queen born to wear the crown grows up to expect reverence and devotion. It is her due. So with Eve; she had been a queen in Morwell since infancy.

Barbara listened to her talk and answered her in monosyllables, but her mind was not with the subject of Eve's conversation. She was thinking then, and she had been thinking at Bradstone, whilst the floor throbbed with dancing feet, whilst singers were performing, of that bouquet of yellow roses which she had flung away. Was it still lying on the grass in the quadrangle? Had Jane, the housemaid, seen it, picked it up, and taken it to adorn the kitchen table?

She knew that Jasper must have taken a long walk to procure those two bunches of roses. She knew that he could ill afford the expense. When he was ill, she had put aside his little purse containing his private money, and had counted it, to make sure that none was lost or taken. She knew that he was poor. Out of the small sum he owned he must have paid a good deal for these roses.

She had thrown her bunch away in angry scorn, under his eyes. She had been greatly provoked; but—had she behaved in a ladylike and Christian spirit? She might have left her roses in a tumbler in the parlour or the hall. That would have been a courteous rebuff—but to fling them away!

There are as many conflicting currents in the human soul as in the ocean; some run from east to west, and some from north to south, some are sweet and some bitter, some hot and others cold. Only in the Sargasso Sea are there no currents—and that is a sea of weeds. What we believe to-day we reject to-morrow; we are resentful at one moment over a wrong inflicted, and are repentant the next for having been ourselves the wrong-doer. Barbara had been in fiery indignation at three o'clock against Jasper; by five she was cooler, and by six reproached herself.

As the sisters drove into the little quadrangle, Barbara

turned her head aside, and whilst she made as though she were unwinding the knitted shawl that was wrapt about her head, she looked across the turf, and saw lying, where she had cast it, the bunch of roses.

The stable-boy came with his lantern to take the horse and carriage, and the sisters dismounted. Jane appeared at the hall door to divest them of their wraps.

'How is papa?' asked Eve; then, without waiting for an answer, she ran into her father's room to kiss him and tell him of the party, and show herself again in her pretty dress, and again receive his words of praise and love.

But Barbara remained at the door, leisurely folding her cloak. Then she put both her own and her sister's parasols together in the stand. Then she stood brushing her soles on the mat—quite unnecessarily, as they were not dirty.

'You may go away, Jane,' said Barbara to the maid, who lingered at the door.

'Please, Miss, I'm waiting for you to come in, that I may lock up.'

Then Barbara was obliged to enter.

'Has Mr. Babb been with my father?' she asked.

'No, Miss. I haven't seen him since you left.'

'You may go to bed, Jane. It is washing-day to-morrow, and you will have to be up at four. Has not Mr. Babb had his supper?'

'No, Miss. He has not been here at all.'

'That will do.' She signed the maid to leave.

She stood in the hall, hesitating. Should she unbar the door and go out and recover the roses? Eve would leave her father's room in a moment, and ask questions which it would be inconvenient to answer. Let them lie. She went upstairs with her sister, after having wished her father good-night.

'Barbie, dear!' said Eve, 'did you observe Mr. Squash?'

'Do not, Eve. That is not his name.'

'I think he looked a little disconcerted. I repudiated.'

'What do you mean?'

'I refused to be bound by the engagements we had made for a quadrille and a waltz. I did not want to dance with him, and I did not.'

'Run back into your room, darling, and go to bed.'

When Barbara was alone she went to her window and opened it. The window looked into the court. If she leaned her head out far, she could see where the bunch of roses ought to be. But she could not see them, though she looked, for the grass lay dusk in the shadows. The moon was rising, and shone on the long roof like steel, and the light was creeping down the wall. That long roof was over the washhouse, and next morning at early dawn the maids would cross the quadrangle with the linen and carry fuel, and would either trample on or pick up and appropriate the bunch of yellow roses.

Barbara remembered every word that she had said to Jasper. She could not forget—and now could not forgive herself. Her words had been cruel; how they must have wounded him! He had not been seen since. Perhaps he was gone and would not return again. They and she would see him no more. That would be well in one way, it would relieve her of anxiety about Eve; but, on the other hand, Jasper had proved himself most useful, and, above all—he was repentant. Her treatment of him might make him desperate, and cause him to abandon his resolutions to amend. Barbara knelt at the window, and prayed.

The white owls were flying about the old house. They had their nests in the great barn. The bats were squeaking as they whisked across the quadrangle, hunting gnats.

When Barbara rose from her knees her eyes were moist. She stood on tiptoe and looked forth from the casement again. The moonlight had reached the sward, drawing a sharp line of light across it, broken by one brighter speck—the bunch of roses.

Then Barbara, without her shoes, stole downstairs. There was sufficient light in the hall for her to find her way across it to the main door. She very softly unbarred it, and still in her stockings, unshod, went out on the doorstep, over the gravel, the dewy grass, and picked up the cold wet bunch.

Then she slipped in again, refastened the door, and with beating heart regained her room.

Now that she had the roses, what should she do with them? She stood in the middle of her room near the candle, looking at them. They were not much faded. The sun had not reached them, and the cool grass had kept them fresh. They were very delicately formed, lovely roses, and freshly sweet. What should she do with them? If they were put in a tumbler they would flourish for a few days, and then the leaves would fall off, and leave a dead cluster of seedless rose-hearts.

Barbara had a desk that had belonged to her mother, and this desk had in it a secret drawer. In this drawer Barbara preserved a few special treasures; a miniature of her mother, a silver cold-cream capsule with the head of Queen Anne on it, that had belonged to her grandmother, the ring of brilliants and sapphire that had come to her from her aunt, and a lock of Eve's hair when she was a baby. Barbara folded the roses in a sheet of white paper, wrote in pencil on it the date, and placed them in the secret drawer, there to wither along with the greatest treasures she possessed.

Barbara's heart was no Sargasso Sea. In it ran currents strong and contrary. What she cast away with scorn in the afternoon, she sought and hid as a treasure in the night.

CHAPTER XXV.

LEAH AND RACHEL.

SUNDAY was a quiet day at Morwell. As the Jordans were Catholics they did not attend their parish church, which was Tavistock, some four miles distant. The servants went, or pretended to go. Morwell was quiet on all days, it was most quiet of all on a bright Sunday, for then there were fewest people about the old house.

Jasper Babb had not run away, offended at Barbara's rudeness. He went about his work as usual, was as little seen of the sisters as might be, and silent when in their company.

On Sunday evening Barbara and Eve strolled out together; it was their wont to do so on that day, when the weather permitted. Jane, the housemaid, was at home with their father.

They directed their steps as usual to the Raven Rock, which commanded so splendid a view to the west, was so airy, and so sunny a spot that they liked to sit there and talk. It was not often that Barbara had the leisure for such a ramble; on Sundays she made a point of it. As the two girls emerged from the wood, and came out on the platform of rock, they were surprised to see Jasper seated there with a book on his knee. He rose at once on hearing their voices and seeing them. If he had wished to escape, escape was impossible, for the rock descends on all sides sheer to great depths, except where the path leads to it.

'Do not let us disturb you,' said Barbara; 'we will withdraw if we interrupt your studies.'

'What is the book?' asked Eve. 'If it be poetry, read us something from it.'

He hesitated a moment, then with a smile said, 'It contains the noblest poetry—it is my Bible.'

'The Bible!' exclaimed Barbara. She was pleased. He certainly was sincere in his repentance. He would not have gone away to a private spot to read the sacred volume unless he were in earnest.

'Let us sit down, Barbie!' said Eve. 'Don't run away, Mr. Jasper.'

'As Mr. Jasper was reading, and you asked him to give you something from the book, I will join in the request.'

'I thought it was perhaps—Byron,' said Eve.

'As it is not Byron, but something better, we shall be all the better satisfied to have it read to us,' said Barbara.

'Well, then, some of the story part, please,' asked Eve, screwing up her mouth, 'and not much of it.'

'I should prefer a Psalm,' said Barbara; 'or a chapter from one of the Epistles.'

'I do not know what to read,' Jasper said smiling, 'as each of you asks for something different.'

'I have an idea,' exclaimed Eve. 'He shall hold the book shut. I will close my eyes and open the volume at hap-hazard, and point with my finger. He shall read that, and we can conjure from it, or guess our characters, or read our fate. Then you shall do the same. Will that please you?'

'I do not know about guessing characters and reading our fate; our characters we know by introspection, and the future is hidden from our eyes by the same Hand that sent the book. But if you wish Mr. Jasper to be guided by this method what to read, I do not object.'

'Very well,' said Eve, in glee; 'that will be fun! You will promise, Barbie, to shut your eyes when you open and put your finger on a page? And, Mr. Jasper, you promise to read exactly what my sister and I select?'

'Yes,' answered both to whom she appealed.

'But mind this,' pursued the lively girl; 'you must stop as soon as I am tired.'

Then first, eager in all she did that promised entertainment or diversion, she took the Bible from Mr. Babb's hands, and closed her eyes; a pretty smile played about her flexible lips as she sat groping with her finger among the pages. Then she opened the book and her blue orbs together.

'There!' she exclaimed, 'I have made my choice; yet—wait! I will mark my place, and then pass the book to Bab—I mean, Barbie.' She had a wild summer rose in her bosom. She pulled off a petal, touched it with her tongue, and put the leaf at the spot she had selected.

Then she shut the Bible with a snap, laughed, and handed it to her sister.

'I need not shut my eyes,' said Barbara; 'I will look you full in the face, Eve.' Then she took the book and felt for the end pages that she might light on an Epistle; just as she saw that Eve had groped for an early part of the book that she might have a story from the times of the patriarchs. She did not know that Eve in handing her the book had not turned it; consequently she held the Bible reversed. Barbara held a buttercup in her hand. She was so accustomed to use her fingers, that it was strange to her to have nothing to employ them. As they came through the meadows she had picked a few flowers, broken the stalks and thrown them away. There remained in her hand but one buttercup.

Barbara placed the Bible on her lap; she, like Eve, had seated herself on the rocky ledge. Then she opened near what she believed to be the end of the book, and laid the golden cup on a page.

Eve leaned towards her and looked, and uttered an exclamation.

'What is it?' asked Barbara, and looked also.

Behold! the golden flower of Barbara was shining on the pink petal of Eve's rose.

'We have chosen the same place. Now, Barbie, what do you say to this? Is it a chance, or are we going to learn our fate, which is bound up together, from the passage Mr. Jasper is about to read?'

'There is no mystery in the matter,' said Barbara quietly; 'you did not turn the book when you gave it to me, and it naturally opened where your flower lay.'

'Go on, Mr. Jasper,' exhorted Eve. But the young man seemed ill-disposed to obey.

'Yes,' said Barbara; 'begin. We are ready.'

Then Jasper began to read:—

'Jacob went on his journey, and came into the land of the people of the east. And he looked, and behold a well in a field, and, lo, there were flocks of sheep lying by it.'

'I am glad we are going to have this story,' said Eve; 'I like it. It is a pretty one. Jacob came to that house of Laban just as you, Mr. Babb, have come to Morwell.'

Jasper read on:—

'And Laban had two daughters: now the name of the elder was Leah, and the name of the younger was Rachel. Leah was tender eyed; but Rachel was beautiful and well-favoured.'

Barbara was listening, but as she listened she looked away into the blue distance over the vast gulf of the Tamar valley towards the Cornish moors, the colour of cobalt, with a salmon sky above them. Something must at that moment have struck the mind of Jasper, for he paused in his reading, and his eyes sought hers.

She said in a hard tone, 'Go on.'

Then he continued in a low voice, 'And Jacob loved Rachel; and said, I will serve thee seven years for Rachel, thy younger daughter. And Laban said, It is better that I give her to thee, than that I should give her to another man: abide with me. And Jacob served seven years for Rachel; and they seemed unto him but a few days, for the love he had to her.'

The reader again paused; and again with a hard voice Barbara bade him proceed.

'And Jacob said unto Laban, Give me my wife, for my

days are fulfilled. And Laban gathered together all the men of the place, and made a feast. And it came to pass in the evening, that he took Leah his daughter, and brought her to Jacob.'

'That will do,' said Eve, 'I am tired.'

'It seems to me,' said Barbara, in a subdued tone, 'that Leah was a despicable woman, a woman without self-respect. She took the man, though she knew his heart was set on Rachel, and that he did not care a rush for her. No!—I do not like the story. It is odious.' She stood up and, beckoning to Eve, left the platform of rock.

Jasper remained where he had been, without closing the book, without reading further, lost in thought. Then a small head appeared above the side of the rock where it jutted out of the bank of underwood, also a pair of hands that clutched at the projecting points of stone; and in another moment a boy had pulled himself on to the platform, and lay on it with his feet dangling over the edge, his head and breast raised on his hands. He was laughing.

'What! dreaming, Master Jasper Jacob? Of which? Of the weak-eyed Leah or the blue-orbed Rachel?'

The young man started as if he had been stung.

'What has brought you here, Watt? No good, I fear.'

'O my dear Jasper, there you are out. Goodness personified has brought me here—even your own pious self, sitting Bible-reading to two pretty girls. How happy could I be with either! Eh, Jasper?'

'What do you want with me?' asked Jasper, reddening; 'I detest your fun.'

'Which is it?' taunted the mischievous boy. 'Which —the elder, plain and dark; or the younger, beautiful as dawn? or—like the patriarch Jacob—both?

'Enough of this, Watt. What has brought you here?'

'To see you, of course. I know you think me void of all Christianity, but I have that in me yet, I like to know the whereabouts of my brother, and how he is getting on. I am still with Martin—ever on the move, like the sun, like the winds, like the streams, like everything that does not stagnate.'

'It is a hard thing for me to say,' said Jasper, 'but it is true. Poor Martin would be better without you. He would be another man, and his life not blighted, had it not been for your profane and mocking tongue. He was a generous-hearted fellow, thoughtless, but not wicked; you, however, have gained complete power over him, and have used it for evil. Your advice is for the bad, your sneers for what is good.'

'I do not know good from bad,' said the boy, with a contemptuous grin.

'Watt, you have scoffed at every good impulse in Martin's heart, you have drowned the voice of his conscience by your gibes. It is you who have driven him with your waspish tongue along the road of ruin.'

'Not at all, Jasper; there you wrong me. It was you who had the undoing of Martin. You have loved him and screened him since he was a child. You have taken the punishment and blame on you which he deserved by his misconduct. Of course he is a giddy-pate. It is you who have let him grow up without dread of the consequences of wrong-doing, because the punishment always fell on you. You, Jasper, have spoiled Martin, not I.'

'Well, Watt, this may be so. Father was unduly harsh. I had no one else to love at home but my brother Martin. You were such a babe as to be no companion. And Martin I did—I do love. Such a noble, handsome, frank-hearted brother! All sunshine and laughter! My childhood had been charged with grief and shadow, and I did my best to screen him. One must love something in this world, or the heart dies. I loved my brother.'

'Love, love!' laughed Watt. 'Now you have that

heart so full that it is overflowing towards two nice girls. I suppose that, enthralled between blue eyes and brown, you have no thought left for Martin, none for father—who, by the way, is dying.'

'Dying!' exclaimed Jasper, springing to his feet.

'There, now!' said the boy; 'don't in your astonishment topple over the edge of the precipice into kingdom come.'

'How do you know this, Watt?' asked Jasper in great agitation.

'Because I have been to Buckfastleigh and seen the beastly old hole, and the factory, and the grey rat in his hole, curled up, gnawing his nails and squealing with pain.'

'For shame of you, Watt! you have no reverence even for your father.'

'Reverence, Jasper! none in the world for anybody or anything. Everything like reverence was killed out of me by my training.'

'What is the matter with father?'

'How should I tell? I saw him making contortions and yowling. I did not approach too near lest he should bite.'

'I shall go at once,' said Jasper earnestly.

'Of course you will. You are the heir. Eh! Jasper! When you come in for the house and cloth mill, you will extend to us the helping hand. O you saint! Why don't you dance as I do? Am I taken in by your long face? Ain't I sure that your heart is beating because now at last you will come in for the daddy's collected money? Poor Martin! He can't come and share. You won't be mean, but divide, Jasper? I'll be the go-between.'

'Be silent, you wicked boy!' said Jasper angrily; 'I cannot endure your talk. It is repugnant to me.'

'Because I talk of sharing. You, the saint! He sniffs filthy mammon and away he flies like a crow to carrion. Good-bye, Jasper! Away you go like an arrow from the bow. Don't let that old housekeeper rummage the stockings stuffed with guineas out of the chimney before you get to Buckfastleigh!'

Jasper left the rock and strode hastily towards Morwell, troubled at heart at the news given him. Had he looked behind him as he entered the wood, he would have seen the boy making grimaces, capering, clapping his hands and knees, whistling, screaming snatches of operatic tunes, laughing, and shouting 'Which is it to be, Rachel or Leah?'

CHAPTER XXVI.

AN IMP OF DARKNESS.

JASPER went immediately to Mr. Jordan. He found Eve with her father. Jane, the housemaid, had exhibited signs of restlessness and impatience to be off. Joseph Woodman, the policeman from Tavistock, a young and sleepy man who was paying her his addresses, had appeared at the kitchen window and coughed. He was off duty, and Jane thought it hard that she should be on when he was off. So Eve had let her depart with her lover.

'Well,' said Mr. Jordan, who was still in bed, 'what is it? Do you want me?'

'I have come to ask your permission to leave for a few days. I must go to my father, who is dying. I will return as soon as I can.'

Eve's great blue eyes opened with amazement. 'You said nothing about this ten minutes ago.'

'I did not know it then.'

'What!' exclaimed Mr. Jordan, trying to rise on his elbow, and his eyes brightening, 'Ezekiel Babb dying! Is justice overtaking him at last?'

'I hear that he is dying,' said Jasper; 'it is my duty to go to him.'

'If he dies,' said Mr. Jordan, 'to whom will his property go?'

'Probably to me; but it is premature to inquire.'

'Not at all. My Eve has been robbed——'

'Sir!' said Jasper gravely, 'I undertook to repay that sum as soon as it should be in my power to do so, principal and interest. I have your permission, sir?' He bowed and withdrew.

At supper Barbara looked round, and noticed the absence of Jasper Babb, but she said nothing.

'You need not look at that empty chair,' said Eve; 'Mr. Jasper will not be here. He is gone.'

'Gone where?'

'Called away suddenly. His father is dying.'

Barbara raised her eyebrows. She was greatly puzzled. She sat playing with her fork, and presently said, 'This is very odd—who brought the news?'

'I saw no one. He came in almost directly after we left him on the Raven Rock.'

'But no one came up to the house.'

'Oh, yes—Joseph Woodman, Jane's sweetheart, the policeman.'

'He cannot have brought the news.'

'I do not think Mr. Jasper saw him, but I cannot say.'

'I cannot understand it, Eve,' mused Barbara. 'What is more, I do not believe it.'

Barbara was more puzzled and disturbed than she chose to show. How could Jasper have received news of his father? If the old man had sent a messenger, that messenger would have come to the house and rested there, and been refreshed with a glass of cider and cake and cold beef. No one had been to the house but the policeman, and a policeman was not likely to be made the vehicle of communication between old Babb and his son, living in concealment. More probably Jasper had noticed that a policeman was hovering about Morwell, had taken alarm, and absented himself.

Then that story of Jacob serving for Rachel and being given Leah came back on her. Was it not being in part enacted before her eyes? Was not Jasper there acting as steward to her father, likely to remain there for some years, and all the time with the love of Eve consuming his heart? 'And the seven years seemed unto him but a few days for the love that he had to her.' What of Eve? Would she come to care for him, and in her wilfulness insist on having him? It could not be. It must not be. Please God, now that Jasper was gone, he would not return. Then, again, her mind swung back to the perplexing question of the reason of Jasper's departure. He *could* not go home. It was out of the question his showing his face again at Buckfastleigh. He would be recognised and taken immediately. Why did he invent and pass off on her father such a falsehood as an excuse for his disappearance? If he were made uneasy by the arrival of the Tavistock policeman at the house, he might have found some other excuse, but to deliberately say that his father was dying and that he must attend his death-bed, this was monstrous.

Eve remained till late, sitting in the parlour without a light. The servant maids were all out. Their eagerness to attend places of worship on Sunday—especially Sunday evenings—showed a strong spirit of devotion; and the lateness of the hour to which those acts of worship detained them proved also that their piety was of stubborn and enduring quality. Generally, one of the maids remained at home, but on this occasion Barbara and Eve had allowed Jane to go out when she had laid the table for supper, because her policeman had come, and there was to be a love-feast at the little dissenting chapel which Jane attended. The lover having turned up, the love-feast must follow.

As the servants had not returned, Barbara remained below, waiting till she heard their voices. Her father was dozing. She looked in at him and then returned to her place by the latticed window. The room was dark, but there was silvery light in the summer sky, becoming very white towards the north. Outside the window was a jessamine; the scent it exhaled at night was too strong. Barbara shut the window to exclude the fragrance. It made her head ache. A light air played with the jessamine, and brushed some of the white flowers against the glass. Barbara was usually sharp with the servants when they returned from their revivals, and love-feasts, and missionary meetings, late; but this evening she felt no impatience. She had plenty to occupy her mind, and the time passed quickly with her. All at once she heard a loud prolonged hoot of an owl, so near and so loud that she felt sure the bird must be in the house. Next moment she heard her father's voice calling repeatedly and excitedly. She ran to him and found him alarmed and agitated. His window had been left open, as the evening was warm.

'I heard an owl!' he said. 'It was at my ear; it called, and roused me from my sleep. It was not an owl—I do not know what it was. I saw something, I am not sure what.'

'Papa dear, I heard the bird. You know there are several about. They have their nests in the barn and old empty pigeon-house. One came by the window hooting. I heard it also.'

'I saw something,' he said.

She took his hand. It was cold and trembling.

'You were dreaming, papa. The owl roused you, and dreams mixed with your waking impressions, so that you cannot distinguish one from another.'

'I do not know,' he said, vacantly, and put his hand to his head. 'I do see and hear strange things. Do not leave me alone, Barbara. Kindle a light, and read me one of Challoner's Meditations. It may compose me.'

Eve was upstairs, amusing herself with unfolding and trying on the yellow and crimson dress she had found in the garret. She knew that Barbara would not come up-

stairs yet. She would have been afraid to masquerade
before her. She put her looking-glass on a chair, so that
she might see herself better in it. Then she took the timbrel, and poised herself on one foot, and held the instrument over her head, and lightly tingled the little bells.
She had put on the blue turquoise ring. She looked at it,
kissed it, waved that hand, and rattled the tambourine,
but not so loud that Barbara might hear. Eve was quite
happy thus amusing herself. Her only disappointment
was that she had not more such dresses to try on.

All at once she started, stood still, turned and uttered
a cry of terror. She had been posturing hitherto with her
back to the window. A noise at it made her look round.
She saw, seated in it, with his short legs inside, and his
hands grasping the stone mullions—a small dark figure.

'Well done, Eve! Well done, Zerlina!

> Là ci darem la mano,
> Là mi dirai di sì !'

Then the boy laughed maliciously; he enjoyed her confusion and alarm.

'The weak-eyed Leah is away, quieting Laban,' he
said; 'Leah shall have her Jacob, but Rachel shall get
Esau, the gay, the handsome, whose hand is against every
man, or rather one against whom every man's hand is
raised. I am going to jump into your room.'

'Keep away!' cried Eve in the greatest alarm.

'If you cry out, if you rouse Leah and bring her here,
I will make such a hooting and howling as will kill the
old man downstairs with fear.'

'In pity go. What do you want?' asked Eve, backing
from the window to the farthest wall.

'Take care! Do not run out of the room. If you attempt it, I will jump in, and make my fiddle squeal, and
caper about, till even the sober Barbara—Leah I mean—
will believe that devils have taken possession, and as for
the old man, he will give up his ghost to them without a
protest.'

'I entreat you—I implore you—go!' pleaded Eve, with tears of alarm in her eyes, cowering back against the wall, too frightened even to think of the costume she wore.

'Ah!' jeered the impish boy. 'Run along down into the room where your sister is reading and praying with the old man, and what will they suppose but that a crazy opera-dancer has broken loose from her caravan and is rambling over the country.'

He chuckled, he enjoyed her terror.

'Do you know how I have managed to get this little talk with you uninterrupted? I hooted in at the window of your father, and when he woke made faces at him. Then he screamed for help, and Barbara went to him. Now here am I; I scrambled up the old pear-tree trained against the wall. What is it, a Chaumontel or a Jargonelle? It can't be a Bon Chrétien, or it would not have borne me.'

Eve's face was white, her eyes were wide with terror, her hands behind her scrabbled at the wall, and tore the paper. 'Oh, what do you want? Pray, pray go!'

'I will come in at the window, I will caper and whistle, and scream and fiddle. I will jump on the bed and kick all the clothes this way, that way. I will throw your Sunday frock out of the window; I will smash the basin and water-bottle, and glass and jug. I will throw the mirror against the wall; I will tear down the blinds and curtains, and drive the curtain-pole through the windows; I will throw your candle into the heap of clothes and linen and curtain, and make a blaze which will burn the room and set the house flaming, unless you make me a solemn promise. I have a message for you from poor Martin. Poor Martin! his heart is breaking. He can think only of lovely Eve. As soon as the sun sets be on the Raven Rock to-morrow.'

I cannot. Do leave the window.'

Very well,' said the boy, 'in ten minutes the house

N

will be on fire. I am coming in; you run away. I shall lock you out, and before you have got help together the room will be in a blaze.'

'What do you want? I will promise anything to be rid of you.'

'Promise to be on the Raven Rock to-morrow evening.'

'Why must I be there?'

'Because I have a message to give you there.'

'Give it me now.'

'I cannot; it is too long. That sister of yours will come tumbling in on us with a Roley-poley, gammon and spinach, Heigh-ho! says Anthony Roley, oh!'

'Yes, yes! I will promise.'

Instantly he slipped his leg out, she saw only the hands on the bottom of the window. Then up came the boy's queer face again, that he might make grimaces at her and shake his fist, and point to candle, and bed, and garments, and curtains: and then, in a moment, he was gone.

Some minutes elapsed before Eve recovered courage to leave her place, shut her window, and take off the tawdry dress in which she had disguised herself.

She heard the voices of the servant maids returning along the lane. Soon after Barbara came upstairs. She found her sister sitting on the bed.

'What is it, Eve? You look white and frightened.'

Eve did not answer.

'What is the matter, dear? Have you been alarmed at anything?'

'Yes, Bab,' in a faint voice.

'Did you see anything from your window?'

'I think so.'

'I cannot understand,' said Barbara. 'I also fancied I saw a dark figure dart across the garden and leap the wall whilst I was reading to papa. I can't say, because there was a candle in our room.'

'Don't you think,' said Eve, in a faltering voice, 'it

may have been Joseph Woodman parting with Jane?' Eve's cheeks coloured as she said this; she was false with her sister.

Barbara shook her head, and went into her own room. 'He has gone,' she thought, 'because the house is watched, his whereabouts has been discovered. I am glad he is gone. It is best for himself, for Eve'—after a pause— 'and for me.'

CHAPTER XXVII.

POOR MARTIN.

Eve was uneasy all next day—at intervals—she could do nothing continuously—because of her promise. The re-collection that she had bound herself to meet Watt on the Raven Rock at sundown came on her repeatedly during the day, spoiling her happiness. She would not have scrupled to fail to keep her promise, but that the horrible boy would be sure to force himself upon her, and in revenge do some dreadful mischief. She was so much afraid of him, that she felt that to keep her appointment was the lesser evil.

As the sun declined her heart failed her, and just before the orb set in bronze and gold, she asked Jane, the house-maid, to accompany her through the fields to the Raven Rock.

Timid Eve dare not trust herself alone on the dangerous platform with that imp. He was capable of any devilry. He might scare her out of her wits.

Jane was a good-natured girl, and she readily obliged her young mistress. Jane Welsh's mother, who was a widow, lived not far from Morwell, in a cottage on the banks of the Tamar, higher up, where a slip of level meadow ran out from the cliffs, and the river made a loop round it.

As Eve walked through the fields towards the wood, and neared the trees and rocks, she began to think that she had made a mistake. It would not do for Jane to see Watt. She would talk about him, and Barbara would hear, and question her. If Barbara asked her why she had gone out at dusk to meet the boy, what answer could she make?

When Eve came to the gate into the wood, she stood still, and holding the gate half open, told Jane she might stay there, for she would go on by herself.

Jane was surprised.

'Please, Miss, I've nothing to take me back to the house.' Eve hastily protested that she did not want her to return: she was to remain at the gate—'And if I call—come on to me, Jane, not otherwise. I have a headache, and I want to be alone.'

'Very well, Miss.'

But Jane was puzzled, and said to herself, 'There's a lover, sure as eggs in April.'

Then Eve closed the gate between herself and Jane, and went on. Before disappearing into the shade of the trees, she looked back, and saw the maid where she had left her, plaiting grass.

A lover! A lover is the philosopher's stone that turns the sordid alloy of life into gold. The idea of a lover was the most natural solution of the caprice in Miss Eve's conduct. As every road leads to Rome, so in the servant-maid mind does every line of life lead to a sweetheart.

Jane, having settled that her young mistress had gone on to meet a lover, next questioned who that lover could be, and here she was utterly puzzled. Sure enough Miss Eve had been to a dance at the Cloberrys', but whom she had met there, and to whom lost her heart, that Jane did not know, and that also Jane was resolved to ascertain.

She noiselessly unhasped the gate, and stole along the path. The burnished brazen sky of evening shone between the tree trunks, but the foliage had lost its verdure in the gathering dusk. The honeysuckles poured forth their scent in waves. The air near the hedge and deep into the wood was honeyed with it. White and yellow speckled currant moths were flitting about the hedge. Jane stole along, stealthily, from tree to tree, fearful lest Eve should turn and catch her spying. A large Scotch pine cast a shadow under it like ink. On reaching that, Jane knew she could see the top of the Raven Rock.

As she thus advanced on tip-toe she heard a rustling, as of a bird in the tree overhead. Her heart stood still. Then, before she had time to recover herself, with a shrill laugh, a little black figure came tumbling down before her out of the tree, capered, leaped at her, threw his arms round her neck, and screamed into her face, 'Carry me! Carry me! Carry me!'

Then his arms relaxed, he dropped off, shrieking with laughter, and Jane fled, as fast as her limbs could bear her, back to the gate, through the gate and away over the meadows to Morwell House.

Eve had gone on to the platform of rock; she stood there irresolute, hoping that the detested boy would not appear, when she heard his laugh and shout, and the scream of Jane. She would have fainted with terror, had not at that moment a tall man stepped up to her and laid his hand on her arm. 'Do not be afraid, sweet fairy Eve! It is I—your poor slave Martin,—perfectly bewitched, drawn back by those loadstone eyes. Do not be frightened, Watt is merely giving a scare to the inquisitive servant.'

Eve was trembling violently. This was worse than meeting the ape of a boy. She had committed a gross indiscretion. What would Barbara say?—her father, if he heard of it, how vexed he would be!

'I must go back,' she said, with a feeble effort at dignity. 'This is too bad; I have been deceived.' Then she gave way to weakness, and burst into tears.

'No,' he said carelessly, 'you shall not go. I will not suffer you to escape now that I have a chance of seeing

you and speaking with you. To begin at the beginning—
I love you. There! you are all of a tremble. Sit down
and listen to what I have to say. You will not? Well,
consider. I run terrible risks by being here; I may say
that I place my life in your delicate hands.'

She looked up at him, still too frightened to speak, even
to comprehend his words.

'I do not know you!' she whispered, when she was
able to gather together the poor remnants of her strength.

'You remember me. I have your ring, and you have
mine. We are, in a manner, bound to each other. Be
patient, dear love; listen to me. I will tell you all my
story.'

He saw that she was in no condition to be pressed. If
he spoke of love she would make a desperate effort to
escape. Weak and giddy though she was, she would not
endure that from a man of whom she knew nothing. He
saw that. He knew he must give her time to recover from
her alarm, so he said, 'I wish, most beautiful fairy, you
would rest a few minutes on this piece of rock. I am a
poor, hunted, suffering, misinterpreted wretch, and I come
to tell you my story, only to entreat your sympathy and
your prayers. I will not say a rude word, I will not lay
a finger on you. All I ask is: listen to me. That cannot
hurt you. I am a beggar, a beggar whining at your feet,
not asking for more alms than a tear of pity. Give me
that, that only, and I go away relieved.'

She seemed somewhat reassured, and drew a long
breath.

'I had a sister of your name.'

She raised her head, and looked at him with surprise.

'It is an uncommon name. My poor sister is gone.
I suppose it is your name that has attracted me to you,
that induces me to open my heart to you. I mean to
confide to you my troubles. You say that you do not
know me. I will tell you all my story, and then, sweet
Eve, you will indeed know me, and, knowing me, will

shower tears of precious pity, that will infinitely console me.'

She was still trembling, but flattered, and relieved that he asked for nothing save sympathy. That of course she was at liberty to bestow on a deserving object. She was wholly inexperienced, easily deceived by flattery.

'Have I frightened you?' asked Martin. 'Am I so dreadful, so unsightly an object as to inspire you with aversion and terror?' He drew himself up and paused. Eve hastily looked at him. He was a strikingly handsome man, with dark hair, wonderful dark eyes, and finely chiselled features.

'I said that I put my life in your hands. I spoke the truth. You have but to betray me, and the police and the parish constables will come in a *posse* after me. I will stand here with folded arms to receive them; but mark my words, as soon as they set foot on this rock, I will fling myself over the edge and perish. If *you* sacrifice me, my life is not worth saving.'

'I will not betray you,' faltered Eve.

'I know it. You are too noble, too true, too heroic to be a traitress. I knew it when I came here and placed myself at your mercy.'

'But,' said Eve timidly, 'what have you done? You have taken my ring. Give it back to me, and I will not send the constables after you.'

'You have mine.'

'I will return it.'

'About that hereafter,' said Martin grandly, and he waved his hand. 'Now I answer your question, What have I done? I will tell you everything. It is a long story and a sad one. Certain persons come out badly in it whom I would spare. But it may not be otherwise. Self-defence is the first law of nature. You have, no doubt, heard a good deal about me, and not to my advantage. I have been prejudiced in your eyes by Jasper. He is narrow, does not make allowances, has never recovered the strait-

lacing father gave him as a child.   His conscience has not
expanded since infancy.'

Eve looked at Martin with astonishment.

' Mr. Jasper Babb has not said anything—'

' Oh, there ! ' interrupted Martin, ' you may spare your
sweet lips the fib.   I know better than that.   He grumbles
and mumbles about me to everyone who will open an ear
to his tales.   If he were not my brother——'

Now Eve interrupted him.   ' Mr. Jasper your brother ! '

' Of course he is.   Did he not tell you so ? '   He saw
that she had not known by the expression of her face, so,
with a laugh, he said, ' Oh dear, no !   Of course Jasper
was too grand and sanctimonious a man to confess to the
blot in the family.   I am that blot—look at me ! '

He showed his handsome figure and face by a theatrical
gesture and position.   ' Poor Martin is the blot, to which
Jasper will not confess, and yet—Martin survives this
neglect and disrespect.'

The overweening vanity, the mock humility, the assurance of the man passed unnoticed by Eve.   She breathed
freely when she heard that he was the brother of Jasper.
There could have been no harm in an interview with
Jasper, and consequently very little in one with his brother.
So she argued, and so she reconciled herself to the situation.   Now she traced a resemblance between the brothers
which had escaped her before ; they had the same large dark
expressive eyes, but Jasper's face was not so regular, his
features not so purely chiselled as those of Martin.   He
was broader built ; Martin had the perfect modelling of a
Greek statue.   There was also a more manly, self-confi-
dent bearing in Martin than in the elder brother, who
always appeared bowed as with some burden that oppressed
his spirits, and took from him self-assertion and buoyancy,
that even maimed his vigour of manhood.

' I dare say you have had a garbled version of my story,'
continued Martin, seating himself ; and Eve, without considering, seated herself also.   Martin let himself down

gracefully, and assumed a position where the evening light, still lingering in the sky, could irradiate his handsome face. 'That is why I have sought this interview. I desired to put myself right with you. No doubt you have heard that I got into trouble.'

She shook her head.

'Well, I did. I was unlucky. In fact, I could stay with my father no longer. I had already left him for a twelvemonth, but I came back, and, in Scriptural terms, such as he could understand, asked him to give me the portion of goods that fell to me. He refused, so I took it.'

'Took—took what?'

'My portion of goods, not in stock but in money. For my part,' said Martin, folding his arms, 'it has ever struck me that the Prodigal Son was far the nobler of the brothers. The eldest was a mean fellow, the second had his faults—I admit it—but he was a man of independence of action ; he would not stand being bullyragged by his father, so he went away. I got into difficulties over that matter. My father would not overlook it, made a fuss, and so on. My doctrine is : Let bygones be bygones, and accept what comes and don't kick. That my father could not see, and so I got locked up.'

'Locked up—where?'

'In a pill-box. I managed, however, to escape ; I am at large, and at your feet—entreating you to pity me.'

He suited the action to the word. In a moment he was gracefully kneeling before her on one knee, with his hand on his heart.

'Oh, Miss Eve,' he said, 'since I saw your face in the moonlight I have never forgotten it. Wherever I went it haunted me. I saw those great beautiful eyes looking timidly into mine ; by day they eclipsed the sun. Whatever I did I thought only of you. And now—what is it that I ask of you ? Nothing but forgiveness. The money—the portion of goods that fell to me—was yours. My father owed it to you. It was intended for you. But now, hear me, you noble, generous-spirited girl ; I have borrowed the money, it shall be returned—or its equivalent.   If you desire it, I will swear.'   He stood up and assumed an attitude.

'Oh, no !' said Eve ; ' you had my money ?'

'As surely as I had your ring.'

'Much in the same way,' she said, with a little sharpness.

'But I shall return one with the other. Trust me. Stand up ; look me in the face. Do I bear the appearance of a cheat, a thief, a robber ? Am I base, villanous ! No, I am nothing but a poor, foolish, prodigal lad, who has got into a scrape, but will get out of it again. You forgive me. Hark ! I hear someone calling.'

'It is Barbara. She is looking for me.'

'Then I disappear.'   He put his hand to his lips, wafted her a kiss, whispered ' When you look at the ring, remember poor—poor Martin,' and he slipped away among the bushes.

CHAPTER XXVIII.

FATHER AND SON.

BARBARA was mistaken.   Jasper had gone to Buckfastleigh, gone openly to his father's house, in the belief that his father was dying.   He knocked at the blotched and scaled door under the dilapidated portico, but received no answer. He tried the door. It was locked and barred.   Then he went round to the back, noting how untidy the garden was, how out of repair was the house ; and in the yard of the kitchen he found the deaf housekeeper. His first question, shouted into her ear, naturally was an inquiry after his father.   He learned to his surprise that the old man was not ill, but was then in the factory.   Thinking that his question had been misunderstood, he entered the house, went into his father's study, then up to his bedroom, and through the dirty window-panes saw the old man leaving the mill on his way back to the house.

What, then, had Watt meant by sending him to the old home on false tidings? The boy was indeed mischievous, but this was more than common mischief. He must have sent him on a fool's errand for some purpose of his own. That the boy wanted to hear news of his father was possible, but not probable. The only other alternative Jasper could suggest to explain Watt's conduct was the disquieting one that he wanted to be rid of Jasper from Morwell for some purpose of his own. What could that purpose be?

Jasper's blood coursed hot through his veins. He was angry. He was a forbearing man, ready always to find an excuse for a transgressor, but this was a transgression too malicious to be easily forgiven. Jasper determined, now that he was at home, to see his father, and then to return to the Jordans as quickly as he could. He had ridden his own horse, that horse must have a night's rest, but to-morrow he would return.

He was thus musing when Mr. Babb came in.

'You here!' said the old man. 'What has brought you to Buckfastleigh again? Want money, of course.' Then snappishly, 'You shan't get it.'

'I am come,' said his son, 'because I had received information that you were ill. Have you been unwell, father?'

'I—no! I'm never ill. No such luck for you. If I were ill and helpless, you might take the management, you think. If I were dead, that would be nuts to you.'

'My father, you wrong me. I left you because I would no longer live this wretched life, and because I hate your unforgiving temper.'

'Unforgiving!' sneered the old manufacturer. 'Martin was a thief, and he deserved his fate. Is not Brutus applauded because he condemned his own son? Is not

David held to be weak because he bade Joab spare Absalom?'

'We will not squeeze old crushed apples. No juice will run from them,' replied Jasper. 'The thing was done, and might have been forgiven. I would not have returned now had I not been told that you were dying.'

'Who told you that lie?'

'Walter.'

'He! He was ever a liar, a mocker, a blasphemer! How was he to know? I thank heaven he has not shown his jackanapes visage here since he left. I dying! I never was sounder. I am better in health and spirits since I am quit of my sons. They vexed my righteous soul every day with their ungodly deeds. So you supposed I was dying, and came here to see what meat could be picked off your father's bones?'

Jasper remembered Watt's sneer. It was clear whence the boy had gathered his mean views of men's motives.

'I'll trouble you to return whence you came,' said Ezekiel Babb. 'No blessing has rested on me since I brought the strange blood into the house. Now that all of you are gone—you, Eve number one, and Eve number two, Martin and Walter—I am well. The Son of Peace has returned to this house; I can read my Bible and do my accounts in quiet, without fears of what new bit of mischief or devilry my children have been up to, without any more squeaking of fiddles and singing of profane songs all over the house. Come now!'—the old man raised his bushy brows and flashed a cunning, menacing glance at his son—'come now! if you had found me dead—in Abraham's bosom—what would you have done? I know what Walter would have done: he would have capered up and down all over the house, fiddling like a devil, like a devil as he is.' He looked at Jasper again, inquisitively. Well, what would you have done?—fiddled too?'

'My father, as you desire to know, I will tell you. I

would at once have realised what I could, and have cleared off the debt to Mr. Jordan.'

'Well, you may do that when the day comes,' said the old manufacturer, shrugging his shoulders. 'It is nothing to me what you do with the mill and the house and the land after I am '—he turned up his eyes to the dirty ceiling—'where the wicked cease from fiddling and no thieves break in and steal. I am not going to pay the money twice over. My obligation ended when the money went out of this house. I did more than I was required. I chastised my own son for taking it. What was seven years on Dartmoor? A flea-bite. Under the old law the rebellious son was stoned till he died. I suppose, now, you are hungry. Call the old crab; kick her, pinch her, till she understands, and let her give you something to eat. There are some scraps, I know, of veal-pie and cold potatoes. I think, by the way, the veal-pie is done. Don't forget to ask a blessing before you fall-to on the cold potatoes.' Then he rubbed his forehead and said, 'Stay, I'll go and rouse the old toad myself; you stay here. You are the best of my children. All the rest were a bad lot—too much of the strange blood in them.'

Whilst Mr. Babb is rousing his old housekeeper to produce some food, we will say a few words of the past history of the Babb family.

Eve the first, Mr. Babb's wife, had led a miserable life. She did not run away from him: she remained and poured forth the fiery love of her heart upon her children, especially on her eldest, a daughter, Eve, to whom she talked of her old life—its freedom, its happiness, its attractions. She died of a broken spirit on the birth of her third son, Walter. Then Eve, the eldest, a beautiful girl, unable to endure the bad temper of her father, the depressing atmosphere of the house, and the cares of housekeeping imposed on her, ran away after a travelling band of actors.

Jasper, the eldest son, grew up to be grave and resigned. He was of use in the house, managing it as far as he was allowed, and helping his father in many ways. But the old man, who had grumbled at and insulted his wife whilst she was alive, could not keep his tongue from the subject that still rankled in his heart. This occasioned quarrels; the boy took his mother's side, and refused to hear his father's gibes at her memory. He was passionately attached to his next brother Martin. The mother had brought a warm, loving spirit into the family, and Jasper had inherited much of it. He stood as a screen between his brother and father, warding off from the former many a blow and angry reprimand. He did Martin's school tasks for him; he excused his faults; he admired him for his beauty, his spirit, his bearing, his lively talk. There was no lad, in his opinion, who could equal Martin; Watt was right when he said that Jasper had contributed to his ruin by humouring him, but Jasper humoured him because he loved him, and pitied him for the uncongeniality of his home. Martin displayed a talent for music, and there was an old musician at Ashburton, the organist of the parish church, who developed and cultivated his talent, and taught him both to play and sing. Jasper had also an instinctive love of music, and he also learned the violin and surpassed his brother, who had not the patience to master the first difficulties, and who preferred to sing.

The father, perhaps, saw in Martin a recrudescence of the old proclivities of his mother; he tried hard to interfere with his visits to the musician, and only made Martin more set on his studies with him. But the most implacable, incessant state of war was that which raged between the old father and his youngest son, Walter, or Watt as his brothers called him. This boy had no reverence in him. He scouted the authority of his father and of Jasper. He scoffed at everything the old man held sacred. He absolutely refused to go to the Baptist Chapel frequented by his father, he stopped his ears and made grimaces at his brothers and the servants during family worship, and the devotions were not unfrequently concluded with a rush of the old man at his youngest son and the administration of resounding clouts on the ears.

At last a quarrel broke out between them of so fierce a nature that Watt was expelled the house. Then Martin left to follow Watt, who had joined a travelling dramatic company. After a year, however, Martin returned, very thin and woe-begone, and tried to accommodate himself to home-life once more. But it was not possible; he had tasted of the sort of life that suited him—one rambling, desultory, artistic. He robbed his father's bureau and ran away.

Then it was that he was taken, and in the same week sent to the assizes, and condemned to seven years' penal labour in the convict establishment at Prince's Town. Thence he had escaped, assisted by Jasper and Watt, whilst the former was on his way to Morwell with the remnant of the money recovered from Martin.

The rest is known to the reader.

Whilst Jasper ate the mean meal provided for him, his father watched him.

'So,' said the old man, and the twinkle was in his cunning eyes, 'so you have hired yourself to Mr. Ignatius Jordan at Morwell as his steward?'

'Yes, father. I remain there as pledge to him that he shall be repaid, and I am doing there all I can to put the estate into good order. It has been shockingly neglected.'

'Who for?' asked Mr. Babb.

'I do not understand.'

'For whom are you thus working?'

'For Mr. Jordan, as you said!'

The manufacturer chuckled.

'Jasper,' said he, 'some men look on a pool and see nothing but water. I put my head in, open my eyes, and see what is at the bottom. That girl did not come here for nothing. I put my head under water and opened my eyes.'

'Well?' said Jasper, with an effort controlling his irritation.

'Well! I saw it all under the surface. I saw you. She came here because she was curious to see the factory and the house, and to know if all was as good as you had bragged about. I gave her a curt dismissal; I do not want a daughter-in-law thrusting her feet into my shoes till I cast them off for ever.'

Jasper started to his feet and upset his chair. He was very angry. 'You utterly wrong her,' he said. 'You open your eyes in mud, and see only dirt. Miss Jordan came here out of kindness towards me, whom she dislikes and despises in her heart.'

Mr. Babb chuckled.

'Well, I won't say that you have not acted wisely. Morwell will go to that girl, and it is a pretty property.'

'I beg your pardon, you are wrong. It is left to the second—Eve.'

'So, so! It goes to Eve! That is why the elder girl came here, to see if she could fit herself into Owlacombe.'

Jasper's face burnt, and the muscles of his head and neck quivered, but he said nothing. He dared not trust himself to speak. He had all his life practised self-control, but he never needed it more than at this moment.

'I see it all,' pursued the old man, his crafty face contracting with a grin; 'Mr. Jordan thought to provide for both his daughters. Buckfast mill and Owlacombe for the elder, Morwell for the younger—ha, ha! The elder to take you so as to get this pretty place. And she came to look at it and see if it suited her. Well! It is a pretty place —only,' he giggled, 'it ain't vacant and to be had just yet.'

Jasper took his hat; his face was red as blood, and his dark eyes flashed.

'Don't go,' said the old manufacturer; 'you did not see their little trap and walked into it, eh? One word of warning I must give you. Don't run after the younger ; Eve is your niece.'

'Father!'

'Ah! that surprises you, does it? It is true. Eve's mother was your sister. Did Mr. Jordan never tell you that?'

'Never!'

'It is true. Sit down again to the cold potatoes. You shall know all, but first ask a blessing.'

CHAPTER XXIX.

HUSH-MONEY.

'Yes,' said Mr. Babb, settling himself on a chair ; then finding he had sat on the tails of his coat, he rose, held a tail in each hand, and reseated himself between them ; 'yes.'

'Do you mean seriously to tell me that Mr. Jordan's second wife was my sister?'

'Well—in a way. That is, I don't mean your sister in a way, but his wife in a way.'

'I have heard nothing of this ; what do you mean?'

'I mean that he did not marry her.'

Jasper Babb's face darkened. 'I have been in his house and spoken to him, and not known that. What became of my sister?'

The old man fidgeted on his chair. It was not comfortable. 'I'm sure I don't know,' he said.

'Did she die?'

'No,' said Mr. Babb, 'she ran off with a play-actor.'

'Well—and after that?'

'After what? After the play-actor? I do not know, I have not heard of her since. I don't want to. Was not that enough?'

'And Mr. Jordan—does he know nothing?'

o

'I cannot tell. If you are curious to know you can ask.'

'This is very extraordinary. Why did not Mr. Jordan tell me the relationship? He knew who I was.'

The old man laughed, and Jasper shuddered at his laugh, there was something so base and brutal in it.

'He was not so proud of how he behaved to Eve as to care to boast of the connection. You might not have liked it, might have fizzed and gone pop.'

Jasper's brow was on fire, his eyebrows met, and a sombre sparkle was in his eye.

'You have made no effort to trace her?'

Mr. Babb shrugged his shoulders.

'Tell me,' said Jasper, leaning his elbow on the table, and putting his hand over his eyes to screen them from the light, and allow him to watch his father's face—'tell me everything, as you undertook. Tell me how my poor sister came to Morwell, and how she left it.'

'There is not much to tell,' answered the father; 'you know that she ran away from home after her mother's death; you were then nine or ten years old. She hated work, and lusted after the pomps and vanities of this wicked world. After a while I heard where she was, that she was ill, and had been taken into Morwell House to be nursed, and that there she remained after her recovery.'

'Strange,' mused Jasper; 'she fell ill and was taken to Morwell, and I—it was the same. Things repeat themselves; the world moves in a circle.'

'Everything repeats itself. As in Eve's case the sickness led up to marriage, or something like it, so will it be in your case. This is what Mr. Jordan and Eve did: they went into the little old chapel, and took each other's hands before the altar, and swore fidelity to each other; that was all. Mr. Jordan is a Catholic, and would not have the knot tied by a church parson, and Eve would not confess to her name, she had that sense of decency left in her. They satisfied their consciences but it was no legal mar-

riage. I believe he would have done what was right, but
she was perverse, and refused to give her name, and say
both who she was and whence she came.'

' Go on,' said Jasper.

' Well, then, about a year after this I heard where she
was, and I went after her to Morwell, but I did not go
openly—I had no wish to encounter Mr. Jordan. I tried
to persuade Eve to return with me to Buckfastleigh. Who
can lay to my charge that I am not a forgiving father?
Have I not given you cold potato, and would have furnished
you with veal pie if the old woman had not finished the
scraps? I saw Eve, and I told her my mind pretty freely,
both about her running away and about her connection
with Jordan. I will say this for her—she professed to be
sorry for what she had done, and desired my forgiveness.
That, I said, I would give her on one condition only, that
she forsook her husband and child, and came back to keep
house for me. I could not bring her to a decision, so I
appointed her a day, and said I would take her final answer
on that. But I was hindered going; I forget just now
what it was, but I couldn't go that day.'

' Well, father, what happened? '

' As I could not keep my appointment—I remember
now how it was, I was laid up with a grip of lumbago at
Tavistock—I sent one of the actors there, from whom I
had heard about her, with a message. I had the lumbago
in my back that badly that I was bent double. When I
was able to go, on the morrow, it was too late; she was
gone.'

' Gone! Whither? '

' Gone off with the play-actor,' answered Mr. Babb,
grimly. ' It runs in the blood.'

' You are sure of this? '

'Mr. Jordan told me so.'

' Did you not pursue her? '

' To what end? I had done my duty. I had tried my
utmost to recover my daughter, and when for the second

time she played me false, I wiped off the dust of my feet as a testimony against her.'

'She left her child?'

'Yes, she deserted her child as well as her husband—that is to say, Mr. Ignatius Jordan. She deserted the house that had sheltered her, to run after a homeless, bespangled, bepainted play-actor. I know all about it. The life at Morwell was too dull for her, it was duller there than at Buckfastleigh. Here she could see something of the world; she could watch the factory hands coming to their work and leaving it; but there she was as much out of the world as if she were in Lundy Isle. She had a hankering after the glitter and paint of this empty world.'

'I cannot believe this. I cannot believe that she would desert the man who befriended her, and forsake her child.'

'You say that because you did not know her. You know Martin; would he not do it? You know Watt; has he any scruples and strong domestic affections? She was like them; had in her veins the same boiling, giddy, wanton blood.'

Jasper knew but too well that Martin and Watt were unscrupulous, and followed pleasure regardless of the calls of duty. He had been too young when his sister left home to know anything of her character. It was possible that she had the same light and careless temperament as Martin.

'A horse that shies once will shy again,' said the old man. 'Eve ran away from home once, and she ran away from the second home. If she did not run away from home a third time it probably was that she had none to desert.'

'And Mr. Jordan knows nothing of her?'

'He lives too far from the stream of life to see the broken dead things that drift down it.'

Jasper considered. The flush of anger had faded from his brow; an expression of great sadness had succeeded.

His hand was over his brow, but he was no longer intent on his father's face ; his eyes rested on the table.

'I must find out something about my sister. It is too horrible to think of our sister, our only sister, as a lost, sunk, degraded thing.'

He thought of Mr. Jordan, of his strange manner, his abstracted look, his capricious temper. He did not believe that the master of Morwell was in his sound senses. He seemed to be a man whose mind had preyed on some great sorrow till all nerve had gone out of it. What was that sorrow ? Once Barbara had said to him, in excuse for some violence and rudeness in her father's conduct, that he had never got over the loss of Eve's mother.

'Mr. Jordan was not easy about his treatment of my daughter,' said old Babb. 'From what little I saw of him seventeen years ago I take him to be a weak-spirited man. He was in a sad take-on then at the loss of Eve, and having a baby thrown on his hands unweaned. He offered me the money I wanted to buy those fields for stretching the cloth. You may be sure when a man presses money on you, and is indifferent to interest, that he wants you to forgive him something. He desired me to look over his conduct to my daughter, and drop all inquiries. I dare say they had had words, and then she was ready in her passion to run away with the first vagabond who offered.'

Then Jasper removed his hand from his face, and laid one on the other upon the table. His face was now pale, and the muscles set. His eyes looked steadily and sternly at the mean old man, who averted his eyes from those of his son.

'What is this ? You took a bribe, father, to let the affair remain unsifted ! For the sake of a few acres of meadow you sacrificed your child ! '

'Fiddlesticks-ends,' said the manufacturer. 'I sacrificed nothing. What could I do ? If I ran after Eve and found her in some harlequin and columbine booth, could I force her to return ? She had made her bed, and must lie on it. What could I gain by stirring in the matter? Let sleeping dogs lie.'

'Father,' said Jasper, very gravely, 'the fact remains that you took money that looks to me very much like a bribe to shut your eyes.'

'Pshaw! pshaw! I had made up my mind. I was full of anger against Eve. I would not have taken her into my house had I met her. Fine scandals I should have had with her there! Better let her run and disappear in the mud, than come muddy into my parlour and besmirch all the furniture and me with it, and perhaps damage the business. These children of mine have eaten sour grapes, and the parent's teeth are set on edge. It all comes '—the old man brought his fist down on the table —'of my accursed folly in bringing strange blood into the house, and now the chastisement is on me. Are you come back to live with me, Jasper? Will you help me again in the mill?'

'Never again, father, never,' answered the young man, standing up. 'Never, after what I have just heard. I shall do what I can to find my poor sister, Eve Jordan's mother. It is a duty—a duty your neglect has left to me; a duty hard to take up after it has been laid aside for seventeen years; a duty betrayed for a sum of money.'

'Pshaw!' The old man put his hands in his pockets, and walked about the room. He was shrunk with age; his eagle profile was without beauty or dignity.

Jasper followed him with his eye, reproachfully, sorrowfully.

'Father,' he said, 'it seems to me as if that money was hush-money, and that you, by taking it, had brought the blood of your child on your own head.'

'Blood! Fiddlesticks! Blood! There is no blood in the case. If she chose to run, how was I to stop her? Blood, indeed! Red raddle!'

CHAPTER XXX.

BETRAYAL.

BARBARA came out on the platform of rock. Eve stood before her trembling, with downcast eyes, conscious of having done wrong, and of being put in a position from which it was difficult to escape.

Barbara had walked fast. She was hot and excited, and her temper was roused. She loved Eve dearly, but Eve tried her.

'Eve,' she said sharply, 'what is the meaning of this? Who has been here with you?'

The young girl hung her head.

'What is the meaning of this?' she repeated, and her tone of voice showed her irritation. Barbara had a temper.

Eve murmured an inarticulate reply.

'What is it? I cannot understand. Jane came tearing home with a rhodomontade about a boy jumping down on her from a tree, and I saw him just now at the gate making faces at me. He put his fingers into his mouth, hooted like an owl, and dived into the bushes. What is the meaning of this?'

Eve burst into tears, and hid her face on her sister's neck.

'Come, come,' said Barbara, somewhat mollified, 'I must be told all. Your giddiness is leading you into a hobble. Who was that on the rock with you? I caught a glimpse of a man as I passed the Scotch fir, and I thought the voice I heard was that of Jasper.'

The girl still cried, cried out of confusion, because she did not know how to answer her sister. She must not tell the truth; the secret had been confided to her. Poor Martin's safety must not be jeopardised by her. Barbara was so hot, impetuous, and frank, that she might let out about him, and so he might be arrested. What was she to say and do?

'Come back with me,' said Barbara, drawing her sister's hand through her arm. 'Now, then, Eve, there must be no secrets with me. You have no mother; I stand to you in the place of mother and sister in one. Was that Jasper?'

Eve's hand quivered on her sister's arm; in a faint voice she answered, 'Yes, Barbara.' Had Miss Jordan looked round she would have seen her sister's face crimson with shame. But Barbara turned her eyes away to the far-off pearly range of Cornish mountains, sighed, and said nothing.

The two girls walked together through the wood without speaking till they came to the gate, and there they entered the atmosphere of honeysuckle fragrance.

'Perhaps that boy thought he would scare me as he scared Jane,' said Barbara. 'He was mistaken. Who was he?'

'Jasper's brother,' answered Eve in a low tone. She was full of sorrow and humiliation at having told Barbara an untruth, her poor little soul was tossed with conflicting emotions, and Barbara felt her emotion through the little hand resting on her arm. Eve had joined her hands, so that as she walked she was completely linked to her dear elder sister.

Presently Eve said timidly, 'Bab, darling, it was not Mr. Jasper.'

'Who was the man then?'

'I cannot, I must not, tell.'

'That will do,' said Barbara decidedly; 'say no more about it, Eve; I know that you met Jasper Babb and no one else.'

'Well,' whispered Eve, 'don't be cross with me. I did not know he was there. I had no idea.'

'It *was* Mr. Babb?' asked Barbara, suddenly turning and looking steadily at her.

Here was an opportunity offered a poor, weak creature. Eve trembled, and after a moment's vacillation fell into the pitfall unconsciously dug for her by her sister. 'It was Mr. Babb, dear Barbara.'

Miss Jordan said no more, her bosom was heaving. Perhaps she could not speak. She was angry, troubled, distracted; angry at the gross imposition practised by Jasper in pretending to leave the place, whilst lurking about it to hold secret meetings with her sister; troubled she was because she feared that Eve had connived at his proceedings, and had lost her heart to him—troubled also because she could not tell to what this would lead; distracted she was, because she did not know what steps to take. Before she reached home she had made up her mind, and on reaching Morwell she acted on it with promptitude, leaving Eve to go to her room or stay below as suited her best.

She went direct to her father. He was sitting up, looking worse and distressed; his pale forehead was beaded with perspiration; his shaking hand clutched the table, then relaxed its hold, then clutched again.

'Are you feeling worse, papa?'

'No,' he answered, without looking at her, but with his dazed eyes directed through the window. 'No—only for black thoughts. They come flying to me. If you stand at evening under a great rock, as soon as the sun sets you see from all quarters the ravens flying towards it, uttering doleful cries, and they enter into the clefts and disappear for the night. The whole rock all night is alive with ravens. So is it with me. As my day declines the sorrows and black thoughts come back to lodge in me, and torment me with their clawing and pecking and croaking. There is no driving them away. They come back.'

'Dear papa,' said Barbara, 'I am afraid I must add to them. I have something very unpleasant to communicate.'

'I suppose,' said Mr. Jordan peevishly, 'you are out of coffee, or the lemons are mouldy, or the sheets have been torn on the thorn hedge. These matters do not trouble me.' He signed with his finger. 'They are like black spots in the air, but instead of floating they fly, and they all fly one way—towards me.'

'Father, I am afraid for Eve!'

'What?' His face was full of terror. 'What of her? What is there to fear? Is she ill?'

'It is, dearest papa, as I foresaw. She has set her heart on Mr. Jasper, and she meets him secretly. He asked leave of you yesterday to go home to Buckfastleigh; but he has not gone there. He has not left this neighbourhood. He is secreting himself somewhere, and this evening he met darling Eve on the Raven Rock, when he knew you were here ill, and I was in the house with you.'

'I cannot believe it,' said Mr. Jordan, with every token of distress, wiping his wet brow with his thin hands, clasping his hands, plucking at his waistcoat, biting his quivering lips.

'It is true, dearest papa. Eve took Jane with her as far as the gate, and there an ugly boy, who, Eve tells me, is Jasper's brother, scared the girl away. I hurried off to the Rock as soon as told of this, and I saw through an opening of the trees someone with Eve, and heard a voice like that of Mr. Jasper. When I charged Eve with having met him, she could not deny it.'

'What does he want? Why did he ask to leave?'

'I can put but one interpretation on his conduct. I have for some time suspected a growing attachment between him and Eve. I suppose he knows that you never would consent——'

'Never, never!' He clenched his hands, raised them over his head, uttered a cry, and dropped them.

'Do be careful, dear papa,' said Barbara. 'You forget your wound; you must not raise your right arm.'

'It cannot be! It cannot be! Never, never!' He

was intensely moved, and paid no heed to his daughter's caution. She caught his right hand, held it between her own firmly, and kissed it. 'My God!' cried the unhappy man. 'Spare me this! It cannot be! The black spots come thick as rain.' He waved his left hand as though warding off something. 'Not as rain—as bullets.'

'No, papa, as you say, it never, never can be.'

'Never!' he said eagerly, his wild eyes kindling with a lambent terror. 'There stands between them a barrier that must cut them off the one from the other for ever. But of that you know nothing.'

'It is so,' said Barbara; 'there does stand an impass-able barrier between them. I know more than you sup-pose, dear papa. Knowing what I do I have wondered at your permitting his presence in this house.'

'You know?' He looked at her, and pressed his brow. 'And Eve, does she know?'

'She knows nothing,' answered Barbara; 'I alone—that is, you and I together—alone know all about him. I found out when he first came here, and was ill.'

'From anything he said?'

'No—I found a bundle of his clothes.'

'I do not understand.'

'It came about this way. There was a roll on the saddle of his horse, and when I came to undo it, that I might put it away, I found that it was a convict suit.' Mr. Jordan stared. 'Yes!' continued Barbara, speaking quickly, anxious to get the miserable tale told. 'Yes, papa, I found the garments which betrayed him. When he came to himself I showed them to him, and asked if they were his. Afterwards I heard all the particulars: how he had robbed his own father of the money laid by to repay you an old loan, how his father had prosecuted him, and how he had been sent to prison; how also he had escaped from prison. It was as he was flying to the Tamar to cross it, and get as far as he could from pursuit, that he met with his accident, and remained here.'

'Merciful heaven!' exclaimed Mr. Jordan; 'you know all this, and never told me!'

'I told no one,' answered Barbara, 'because I promised him that I would not betray him, and even now I would have said nothing about it but that you tell me that you know it as well as I. No,' she added, after having drawn a long breath, 'no, not even after all the provocation he has given would I betray him.'

Mr. Jordan looked as one dazed.

'Where then are these clothes—this convict suit?'

'In the garret. I hid them there.'

'Let me see them. I cannot yet understand.'

Barbara left the room, and shortly returned with the bundle. She unfolded it, and spread the garments before her father. He rubbed his eyes, pressed his knuckles against his temples, and stared at them with astonishment.

'So, then, it was he—Jasper Babb—who stole Eve's money?'

'Yes, papa.'

'And he was taken and locked up for doing so—where?'

'In Prince's Town prison.'

'And he escaped?'

'Yes, papa. As I was on my way to Ashburton, I passed through Prince's Town, and thus heard of it.'

'Barbara! why did you keep this secret from me? If I had known it, I would have run and taken the news myself to the police and the warders, and have had him recaptured whilst he was ill in bed, unable to escape.'

It was now Barbara's turn to express surprise.

'But, dear papa, what do you mean? You have told me yourself that you knew all about Mr. Jasper.'

'I knew nothing of this. My God! How thick the black spots are, and how big and pointed!'

'Papa dear, what do you mean? You assured me you knew everything.'

'I knew nothing of this. I had not the least suspicion.'

'But, papa '—Barbara was sick with terror—' you told me that this stood as a bar between him and Eve ?'

'No—Barbara. I said that there was a barrier, but not this. Of this I was ignorant.'

The room swam round with Barbara. She uttered a faint cry, and put the back of her clenched hands against her mouth to choke another rising cry. 'I have betrayed him ! My God ! My God ! What have I done ?'

CHAPTER XXXI.

CALLED TO ACCOUNT.

'Go,' said Mr. Jordan, 'bring Eve to me.'

Barbara obeyed mechanically. She had betrayed Jasper. Her father would not spare him. The granite walls of Prince's Town prison rose before her, in the midst of a waste as bald as any in Greenland or Siberia. She called her sister, bade her go into her father's room, and then, standing in the hall, placed her elbows on the window ledge, and rested her brow and eyes in her palms. She was consigning Jasper back to that miserable jail. She was incensed against him. She knew that he was unworthy of her regard, that he had forfeited all right to her consideration, and yet—she pitied him. She could not bring herself to believe that he was utterly bad ; to send him again to prison was to ensure his complete ruin.

'Eve,' said Mr. Jordan, when his youngest daughter came timidly into the room, ' tell me, whom did you meet on the Raven Rock ?'

The girl hung her head and made no reply. She stood as a culprit before a judge, conscious that his case is hopeless.

'Eve,' he said again, ' I insist on knowing. Whom did you meet?'

She tried to speak, but something rose in her throat, and choked her. She raised her eyes timidly to her father, who had never, hitherto, spoken an angry word to her. Tears and entreaty were in her eyes, but the room was dark, night had fallen, and he could not see her face.

' Eve, tell me, was it Babb?'

She burst into a storm of sobs, and threw herself on her knees. 'O papa! sweetest, dearest papa! Do not ask me! I must not tell. I promised him not to say. It is as much as his life is worth. He says he never will be taken alive. If it were known that he was here the police would be after him. Papa dear!' she clasped and fondled, and kissed his hand, she bathed it in her tears, ' do not be angry with me. I can bear anything but that. I do love you so, dear, precious papa!'

'My darling,' he replied, 'I am not angry. I am troubled. I am on a rock and hold you in my arms, and the black sea is rising—I can feel it. Leave me alone, I am not myself.'

An hour later Barbara came in.

'What, papa—without a light?'

'Yes—it is dark everywhere, within as without. The black spots have run one into another and filled me. It will be better soon. When Jasper Babb shows his face again, he shall be given up.'

'O papa, let him escape this time. All we now want is to get him away from this place, away from Eve.'

'All we now want!' repeated Mr. Jordan. 'Let the man off who has beggared Eve!'

'Papa, Eve will be well provided for.'

'He has robbed her.'

'But, dear papa, consider. He has been your guest. He has worked for you, he has eaten at your table, partaken of your salt. When you were hurt, he carried you to your bed. He has been a devoted servant to you.'

'We are quits,' said Mr. Jordan. 'He was nursed when he was ill. That makes up for all the good he has done me. Then there is that other account which can never be made up.'

'I am sure, papa, he repents.'

'And tries to snatch away Eve, as he has snatched away her fortune?'

'Papa, there I think he may be excused. Consider how beautiful Eve is. It is quite impossible for a man to see her and not love her. I do not myself know what love is, but I have read about it, and I have fancied to myself what it is—a kind of madness that comes on one, and obscures the judgment. I do not believe that Mr. Jasper had any thought of Eve at first, but little by little she won him. You know, papa, how she has run after him, like a kitten; and so she has stolen his heart out of his breast before he knew what she was about. Then, after that, everything—honour, duty went. I dare say it is very hard for one who loves to think calmly and act conscientiously! Would you like the lights brought in, papa?'

He shook his head.

'You must not remain up longer than you can bear,' she said. She took a seat on a stool, and leaned her head on her hand, her elbow resting on her knee. 'Papa, whilst I have been waiting in the hall, I have turned the whole matter over and over in my mind. Papa, I suppose that Eve's mother was very, very beautiful?'

He sighed in the dark and put his hands together. The pale twilight through the window shone on them; they were white and ghost-like.

'Papa dear, I suppose that you saw her when she was ill every day, and got to love her. I dare say you struggled against the feeling, but your heart was too strong for your head and carried your resolutions away, just as I have seen a flood on the Tamar against the dam at Abbotswear; it has burst through all obstructions, and in a moment every trace of the dam has disappeared. You were under the

same roof with her. Then there came a great ache here'
—she touched her heart—'allowing you no rest. Well,
dear papa, I think it must have been so with Mr. Babb.
He saw our dear sweet Eve daily, and love for her swelled
in his heart; he formed the strongest resolutions, and
platted them with the toughest considerations, and stamped
and wedged them in with vigorous effort, but all was of no
avail—the flood rose and burst over it and carried all
away.'

Mr. Jordan was touched by the allusion to his dead or
lost wife, but not in the manner Barbara intended.

'I have heard,' continued Barbara, 'that Eve's mother
was brought to this house very ill, and that you cared for
her till she was recovered. Was it in this room? Was it
in this bed?'

She heard a low moan, and saw the white hands raised
in deprecation, or in prayer.

'Then you sat here and watched her; and when she
was in fever you suffered; when her breath came so faint
that you thought she was dying, your very soul stood on
tiptoe, agonised. When her eyes opened with reason in
them, your heart leaped. When she slept, you sat here
with your eyes on her face and could not withdraw them.
Perhaps you took her hand in the night, when she was
vexed with horrible dreams, and the pulse of your heart
sent its waves against her hot, tossing, troubled heart, and
little by little cooled that fire, and brought peace to that
unrest. Papa, I dare say that somehow thus it came
about that Eve got interested in Mr. Jasper and grew to
love him. I often let her take my place when he was ill.
You must excuse dearest Eve. It was my fault. I should
have been more cautious. But I thought nothing of it
then. I knew nothing of how love is sown, and throws up
its leaves, and spreads and fills the whole heart with a
tangle of roots.'

In this last half hour Barbara had drawn nearer to her
father than in all her previous life. For once she had

entered into his thoughts, roused old recollections, both sweet and bitter—inexpressibly sweet, unutterably bitter—and his heart was full of tears.

'Was Eve's mother as beautiful as our darling?'

'O yes, Barbara!' His voice shook, and he raised his white hands to cover his eyes. 'Even more beautiful.'

'And you loved her with all your heart?'

'I have never ceased to love her. It is that, Barbara, which'—he put his hands to his head, and she understood him—'which disturbed his brain.

'But,' he said, suddenly as waking from a dream, 'Barbara, how do you know all this? Who told you?'

She did not answer him, but she rose, knelt on the stool, put her arms round his neck, and kissed him. Her cheeks were wet.

'You are crying, Barbara.'

'I am thinking of your sorrows, dear papa.'

She was still kneeling on one knee, with her arms round her father. 'Poor papa! I want to know really what became of Eve's mother.'

The door was thrown open.

'Yes; that is what I have come to ask,' said Jasper, entering the room, holding a wax candle in each hand. He had intercepted the maid, Jane, with the candles, taken them from her, and as she opened the door entered, to hear Barbara's question. The girl turned, dropped one arm, but clung with the other to her father, who had just placed one of his hands on her head. Her eyes, from having been so long in the dark, were very large. She was pale, and her cheeks glistened with tears.

She was too astonished to recover herself at once, dazzled by the strong light; she could not see Jasper, but she knew his voice.

He put the candlesticks—they were of silver—on the table, shut the door behind him, and standing before Mr. Jordan with bowed head, his earnest eyes fixed on the old man's face, he said again, ' Yes, that is what I have come to ask. Where is Eve's mother ? '

No one spoke. Barbara recovered herself first; she rose from the stool, and stepped between her father and the steward.

' It is not you,' she said, ' who have a right to ask questions. It is we who have to call you to account.'

' For what, Miss Jordan ? ' He spoke to her with deference—a certain tone of reverence which never left him when addressing her.

' You must give an account of yourself,' she said.

' I am just returned from Buckfastleigh,' he answered.

' And, pray, how is your father who was dying ? ' she asked, with a curl of her lip and a quiver of contempt in her voice.

' He is well,' replied Jasper. ' I was deceived about his sickness. He has not been ill. I was sent on a fool's errand.'

' Then,' said Mr. Jordan, who had recovered himself, ' what about the money ? '

' The recovery of that is as distant as ever, but also as certain.'

' Mr. Jasper Babb,' exclaimed Ignatius Jordan, ' you have not been to Buckfastleigh at all. You have not seen your father; you have deceived me with—— '

Barbara hastily interrupted him, saying with beating heart, and with colour rising to her pale cheeks, ' I pray you, I pray you, say no more. We know very well that you have not left this neighbourhood.'

' I do not understand you, Miss Jordan. I am but just returned. My horse is not yet unsaddled.'

' Not another word,' exclaimed the girl, with pain in her voice. ' Not another word if you wish us to retain a particle of regard for you. I have pitied you, I have excused you but if you *lie*—I have said the word, I cannot withdraw it—I give you up.' Fire was in her heart, tears in her throat

'I will speak,' said Jasper. 'I value your regard, Miss Jordan, above everything that the world contains. I cannot tamely lose that. There has been a misapprehension. How it has arisen I do not know, but arisen it has, and dissipated it shall be. It is true, as I said, that I was deceived about my father's condition, wilfully, maliciously deceived. I rode yesterday to Buckfastleigh, and have but just returned. If my father had been dying you would not have seen me here so soon.'

'We cannot listen to this. We cannot endure this,' cried Barbara. 'Will you madden me, after all that has been done for you? It is cruel, cruel!' Then, unable to control the flood of tears that rose to her eyes, she left the room and the glare of candles.

Jasper approached Mr. Jordan. He had not lost his self-restraint. 'I do not comprehend this charge of falsehood brought against me. I can bring you a token that I have seen my father, a token you will not dispute. He has told me who your second wife was. She was my sister. Will you do me the justice to say that you believe me?'

'Yes,' answered the old man, faintly.

'May I recall Miss Jordan? I cannot endure that she should suppose me false.'

'If you will.'

'One word more. Do you wish our kinship to be known to her, or is it to be kept a secret, at least for a while?'

'Do not tell her.'

Then Jasper went out into the hall. Barbara was there, in the window, looking out into the dusk through the dull old glass of the lattice.

'Miss Jordan,' said he, 'I have ventured to ask you to return to your father, and receive his assurance that I spoke the truth.'

'But,' exclaimed Barbara, turning roughly upon him, 'you were on the Raven Rock with my sister at sunset,

and had your brother planted at the gate to watch against
intruders.'

'My brother?'

'Yes, a boy.'

'I do not understand you.'

'It is true. I saw him, I saw you. Eve confessed it.
What do you say to that?'

Jasper bit his thumb.

Barbara laughed bitterly.

'I know why you pretended to go away—because a
policeman was here on Sunday, and you were afraid. Take
care! I have betrayed you. Your secret is known. You
are not safe here.'

'Miss Jordan,' said the young man quietly, 'you are
mistaken. I did not meet your sister. I would not deceive you for all the world contains. I warn you that
Miss Eve is menaced, and I was sent out of the way lest
I should be here to protect her.'

Barbara gave a little contemptuous gasp.

'I cannot listen to you any longer,' she said angrily.
'Take my warning. Leave this place. It is no longer
safe. I tell you—I, yes, I have betrayed you.'

'I will not go,' said Jasper, 'I dare not. I have the
interest of your family too near my heart to leave.'

'You will not go!' exclaimed Barbara, trembling with
anger and scorn. 'I neither believe you, nor trust you.
I'—she set her teeth and said through them, with her
heart in her mouth—'Jasper, I *hate* you!'

CHAPTER XXXII.

WANDERING LIGHTS.

No sooner was Mr. Jordan left alone than his face became
ghastly, and his eyes were fixed with terror, as though he
saw before him some object of infinite horror. He put his

quivering thin hands on the elbows of his armchair and
let himself slide to his knees, then he raised his hollow
eyes to heaven, and clasped his hands and wrung them ;
his lips moved, but no vocal prayers issued from them.
He lifted his hands above his head, uttered a cry and fell
forward on his face upon the oak floor. Near his hand
was his stick with which he rapped against the wall or on
the floor when he needed assistance. He laid hold of this,
and tried to raise himself, but faintness came over him,
and he fell again and lost all consciousness.

When he recovered sufficiently to see what and who
were about him, he found that he had been lifted on to his
bed by Jasper and Barbara, and that Jane was in the
room. His motion with his hands, his strain to raise
himself, had disturbed the bandages and reopened his
wound, which was again bleeding, and indeed had soaked
through his clothes and stained the floor.

He said nothing, but his eyes watched and followed
Jasper with a mixture of hatred and fear in them.

'He irritates me,' he whispered to his daughter ; 'send
him out. I cannot endure to see him.'

Then Barbara made an excuse for dismissing Jasper.

When he was gone, Mr. Jordan's anxiety instead of
being allayed was increased. He touched his daughter,
and drew her ear to him, and whispered, 'Where is he
now ? What is he doing ? '

'I do not know, papa. He is probably in his room.'

'Go and see.'

'Papa dear, I cannot do that. Do you want him ? '

'Do *I* want him ? No, Barbara, but I do not choose
that he shall escape. Go and look if there is a light in
his window.'

She was about to send Jane, when her father impatiently insisted on her going herself. Wondering at his
caprice she obeyed.

No sooner was the door closed behind her, than the
old man signed Jane Welsh to come near him.

'Jane,' he said in a whisper, 'I want you to do something for me. No one must know about it. You have a sweetheart, I've heard, the policeman, Joseph Woodman, at Tavistock.'

The girl pulled at the ends of her apron, and looking down, said, 'Lawk! How folks do talk!'

'Is it true, Jane?'

'Well, sir, I won't deny us have been keeping company, and on Sunday went to a love-feast together.'

'That is well,' said Mr. Jordan earnestly, with his wild eyes gleaming. 'Quick, before my daughter comes. Stand nearer. No one must hear. Would you do Joseph a good turn and get him a sergeantry?'

'O please, sir!'

'Then run as fast as you can to Tavistock.'

'Please, sir, I durstn't. It be night and it's whisht¹ over the moor.'

'Then leave it, and I will send someone else, and you will lose your lover.'

'What do you want me to do, sir? I wouldn't have that neither.'

'Then run to Tavistock, and tell Joseph Woodman to communicate at once with the warder of the Prince's Town jail, and bid him bring sufficient men with him, and come here, and I will deliver into their hands a runaway convict, a man who broke out of jail not long ago.'

'Please, sir, where is he? Lawk, sir! What if he were on the moor as I went over it?'

'Never mind where he is. I will produce him at the right moment. Above all—Jane—remember this, not a word of what I have said to Mr. Jasper or to Miss Barbara. Go secretly, and go at once. Hush! Here she comes.'

Barbara entered. 'A light is in his window,' she said. Then her father laughed, and shut his hands.

'So,' he muttered, 'so I shall snap him.'

¹ Whisht = uncanny.

When her father was composed, and seemed inclined to sleep, Barbara left his room, and went out of the house. She needed to be by herself. Her bosom heaved. She had so much to think of, so many troubles had come upon her, the future was dark, the present uncertain.

If she were in the house she would not be able to enjoy that quiet for which she craved, in which to compose the tumult of her heart, and arrange her ideas. There she was sure to be disturbed : a maid would ask for a duster, or another bunch of candles ; the cook would send to announce that the chimney of the kitchen was out of order, the soot or mortar was falling down it ; the laundry-maid would ask for soap ; Eve would want to be amused. Every other minute she would have some distracting though trifling matter forced on her. She must be alone. Her heart yearned for it. She would not go to the Rock, the association with it was painful. It was other with the moor, Morwell Down, open to every air, without a tree behind which an imp might lurk and hoot and make mows.

Accordingly, without saying a word to anyone, Barbara stole along the lane to the moor.

That was a sweet summer night. The moon was not yet risen, the stars were in the sky, not many, for the heaven was not dark, but suffused with lost sunlight. To the east lay the range of Dartmoor mountains, rugged and grey ; to the west, peaked and black against silver, the Cornish tors. But all these heights on this night were scintillating with golden moving spots of fire. The time had come for what is locally called ' swaling,' that is, firing the whinbrakes. In places half a hill side was flaked with red flame, then it flared yellow, then died away. Clouds of smoke, tinged with fire reflection from below, rolled away before the wind. When the conflagration reached a dense and tall tree-like mass of gorse the flame rose in a column, or wavered like a golden tongue. Then, when the material was exhausted and no contiguous brake continued the fire, the conflagration ended, and left only a patch of dull glowing scarlet ember.

Barbara leaned against the last stone hedge which divided moor from field, and looked at the moving lights without thinking of the beauty and wildness of the spectacle. She was steeped in her own thoughts, and was never at any time keenly alive to the beautiful and the fantastic.

She thought of Jasper. She had lost all faith in him. He was false and deceitful. What could she believe about that meeting on the Raven Rock? He might have convinced her father that he was not there. He could not convince her. What was to be done? Would her father betray the man? He was ill now and could do nothing. Why was Jasper so obstinate as to refuse to leave? Why? Because he was infatuated with Eve.

On that very down it was that Jasper had been thrown and nearly killed. If only he had been killed outright. Why had she nursed him so carefully? Far better to have left him on the moor to die. How dare he aspire to Eve? The touch of his hand carried a taint. Her brain was dark, yet, like that landscape, full of wandering sparks of fire. She could not think clearly. She could not feel composedly. Those moving, wavering fires, now rushing up in sheaves of flame, now falling into a sullen glow burnt on the sides of solid mountains, but her fiery thoughts, that sent a blaze into her cheek and eye, and then died into a slow heat, moved over tossing billows of emotion. She put her hand to her head as if by grasping it she could bring her thoughts to a standstill; she pressed her hands against her bosom, as if by so doing she could fix her emotions. The stars in the serene sky burned steadily, ever of one brightness. Below, these wandering fires flared, glowed, and went out. Was it not a picture of the contrast between life on earth and life in the settled celestial habitations? Barbara was not a girl with much fancy, but some such a thought came into her mind, and might have taken form had not she at the moment seen a dark figure issue from the lane.

'Who goes there?' she called imperiously.

The figure stopped, and after a moment answered: 'Oh, Miss! you have a-given me a turn. It be me, Jane.'

'And pray,' said Barbara, 'what brings you here at night? Whither are you going?'

The girl hesitated, and groped in her mind for an excuse. Then she said: 'I want, miss, to go to Tavistock.'

'To Tavistock! It is too late. Go home to bed.'

'I must go, Miss Barbara. I'm sure I don't want to. I'm scared of my life, but the master have sent me, and what can I do? He've a-told me to go to Joseph Woodman.'

'It is impossible, at this time. It must not be.'

'But, Miss, I promised I'd go, and sure enough I don't half like it, over those downs at night, and nobody knows what one may meet. I wouldn't be caught by the Whish Hounds and Black Copplestone, not for'—the girl's imagination was limited, so she concluded, 'well, Miss, not for nothing.'

Barbara considered a moment, and then said, 'I have no fear. I will accompany you over the Down, till you come to habitations. I am not afraid of returning alone.'

'Thank you, Miss Barbara, you be wonderfully good.'

The girl was, indeed, very grateful for her company. She had had her nerves sorely shaken by the encounter with Watt, and now in the fulness of her thankfulness she confided to her mistress all that Mr. Jordan had said, concluding with her opinion that probably 'It was naught but a fancy of the Squire; he do have fancies at times. Howsomever, us must humour 'm.'

Jasper also had gone forth. In his breast also was trouble, and a sharp pain, that had come with a spasm when Barbara told him how she hated him.

But Jasper did not go to Morwell Down. He went towards the Raven Rock that lay on the farther side of the house. He also desired to be alone and under the calm sky. He was stifled by the air of a house, depressed by the ceiling.

The words of Barbara had wounded him rather than stung him. She had not only told him that she hated him, but had given the best proof of her sincerity by betraying him. Suspecting him of carrying on an unworthy intrigue with Eve, she had sacrificed him to save her sister. He could not blame her, her first duty was towards Eve. One comfort he had that, though Barbara had betrayed him, she did not seek his punishment, she sought only his banishment from Morwell.

Once—just once—he had half opened her heart, looked in, and fancied he had discovered a tender regard for him lurking in its bottom. Since then Barbara had sought every opportunity of disabusing his mind of such an idea. And now, this night, she had poured out her heart at his feet, and shown him hatred, not love.

Jasper's life had been one of self-denial. There had been little joy in it. Anxieties had beset him from early childhood; solicitude for his brother, care not to offend his father. By nature he had a very loving heart, but he had grown up with none to love save his brother, who had cruelly abused his love. A joyous manhood never ensues on a joyless boyhood. Jasper was always sensible of an inner sadness, even when he was happy. His brightest joys were painted on a sombre background, but then, how much brighter they seemed by the contrast—alas, only, that they were so few! The circumstances of his rearing had driven him in upon himself, so that he lived an inner life, which he shared with no one, and which was unperceived by all. Now, as he stood on the Rock, with an ache at his heart, Jasper uncovered his head, and looked into the softly lighted vault, set with a few faint stars. As he stood thus with his hands folded over his hat, and looked westward at the clear, cold, silvery sky behind and over the Cornish moors, an unutterable yearning strained his heart. He said no word, he thought no thought. He simply stood uncovered under the summer night sky, and from his heart his pain exhaled.

Did he surmise that at that same time Barbara was standing on the moor, also looking away beyond the horizon, also suffering, yearning, without knowing for what she longed? No, he had no thought of that.

And as both thus stood far removed in body, but one in sincerity, suffering, fidelity, there shot athwart the vault of heaven a brilliant dazzling star.

Mr. Coyshe at his window, smoking, said: 'By Ginger! a meteor!'

But was it not an angel bearing the dazzling chalice of the sangreal from highest heaven, from the region of the still stars, down to this world of flickering, fading, wandering fires, to minister therewith balm to two distressed spirits?

CHAPTER XXXIII.

THE OWLS.

BARBARA had been interrupted in her meditations, so was Jasper. As he stood lost in a painful dream, but with a dew from heaven falling on his parched soul, suddenly he was startled out of his abstraction by a laugh and an exclamation at his elbow.

'Well, Jasper, composing verses to the weak-eyed Leah or the blue-orbed Rachel?'

'What brings you here, Watt?' asked Jasper, disguising his annoyance.

'Or, my sanctimonious fox, are you waiting here for one of the silly geese to run to you?'

'You have come here bent on mischief,' said Jasper, disdaining to notice his jokes.

The evening, the still scene, the solitary platform raised

so high above the land beyond, had seemed holy, soothing as a church, and now, at once, with the sound of Walter's voice, the feeling was gone, all seemed desecrated.

'Watt,' said Jasper, sternly, 'you sent me away to Buckfastleigh by a lie. Why did you do that? It is utterly false that my father is ill and dying.'

'Is it so? Then I dreamed it, Jasper. Morning dreams come true, folks say. There, my brother, you are a good, forgiving fellow. You will pardon me. The fact is that Martin and I wanted to know how matters went at home. I did not care to go myself, Martin could not go, so—I sent you, my good simpleton.'

'You told me a lie.'

'If I had told you the truth you would not have gone. What was that we were taught at school? "Magna est veritas, et prævalebit." I don't believe it; experience tells me the contrary. Long live lies; they win the day all the world over.'

'What brings you here?'

'Have I not told you? I desired to see you and to have news of my father. You have been quick about it, Jasper. I could scarce believe my eyes when I saw you riding home.'

'You have been watching?'

'Of course I have. My eyes are keen. Nothing escapes them.'

'Walter, this will not do. I am not deceived; you did not come here for the purpose you say. You want something else, what is it?'

The boy laughed, snapped his fingers, and began to dance, whistling a tune, on the rock; approaching, then backing from Jasper.

'Oh, you clever old Jasper!' he laughed, 'now you begin to see—like the puppy pitched into the water-butt, who opened his eyes when too late.'

Jasper folded his arms. He said nothing, but waited till the boy's mad pranks came to an end. At last Watt, seeing that he could not provoke his brother, desisted, and came to him with affected humility.

'There, Jasper—Saint Jasper, I mean—I will be quiet and go through my catechism.'

'Then tell me why you are here.'

'Well, now, you shall hear our scheme. Martin and I thought that you had better patch up your little quarrel with father, and then we knew we should have a good friend at his ear to prompt forgiveness, and so, perhaps, as his conscience stirred, his purse-strings might relax, and you would be able to send us a trifle in money. Is not this reasonable?'

Yes, there could be no denying it, this was reasonable and consistent with the characters of the two, who would value their father's favour only by what it would profit them. Nevertheless Jasper was unsatisfied. Watt was so false, so unscrupulous, that his word never could be trusted.

Jasper considered for a few minutes, then he asked, 'Where is Martin—is he here?'

'Here!' jeered the boy, 'Martin here, indeed! not he. He is in safe quarters. Where he is I will blab to no one, not even to you. He sends me out from his ark of refuge as the dove, or rather as the raven, to bring him news of the world from which he is secluded.'

'Walter, answer me this. Who met Miss Eve this evening on this very rock? Answer me truly. More depends on this than you are aware of.'

'Miss Eve! What do you mean? My sister who is dead and gone? I do not relish the company of ghosts.'

'You know whom I mean. This is miserable evasion. I mean the younger of the daughters of Mr. Jordan. She was here at sundown this evening and someone was with her. I conjure you by all that you hold sacred——'

'I hold nothing sacred,' said the boy.

'I conjure you most solemnly to tell me the whole truth, as brother to brother.'

'Well, then—as brother to brother – I did.'

'For what purpose, Watt?'

'My dear Jasper, can we live on air? Here am I hopping about the woods, roosting in the branches, and there is poor Martin mewed up in his ark. I must find food for him and myself. You know that I have made the acquaintance of the young lady who, oddly enough, bears the name of our dear departed mother and sister. I have appealed to her compassion, and held out my hat for money. I offered to dance on my head, to turn a wheel all round the edge of this cliff, in jeopardy of my life for half a guinea, and she gave me the money to prevent me from risking broken bones.'

'Oh, Watt, you should not have done this!'

'We must live. We must have money.'

'But, Watt, where is all that which was taken from my pocket?'

'Gone,' answered the boy. 'Gone as the snow before south-west wind. Nothing melts like money, not even snow, no, nor butter, no, nor a girl's heart.' Then with a sly laugh, 'Jasper, where does old addle-brains keep his strong box?'

'Walter!' exclaimed Jasper, indignantly.

'Ah!' laughed the boy, 'if I knew where it was I would creep to it by a mouse hole, and put my little finger into the lock, and when I turned that, open flies the box.'

'Walter, forbear. You are a wicked boy.'

'I confess it. I glory in it. Father always said I was predestined to ——'

'Be silent,' ordered Jasper, angrily; 'you are insufferable.'

'There, do not ruffle your feathers over a joke. Have you some money to give me now?'

'Watt,' said Jasper, very sternly, 'answer me frankly, if you can. I warn you.' He laid his hand on the boy's arm. 'A great deal depends on your giving me a truthful answer. Is Martin anywhere hereabouts? I fear he is, in spite of your assurances, for where you are he is not often far away. The jackal and the lion hunt together.'

'He is not here. Good-bye, old brother Grave-airs.' Then he ran away, but before he had gone far turned and hooted like an owl, and ran on, and was lost in the gloom of the woods, but still as he ran hooted at intervals, and owls answered his cry from the rocks, and flitted ghost-like about in the dusk, seeking their brother who called them and mocked at them.

Now that he was again alone, Jasper in vain sought to rally his thoughts and recover his former frame of mind. But that was not possible. Accordingly he turned homewards.

He was very tired. He had had two long days' ride, and had slept little if at all the previous night. Though recovered after his accident he was not perfectly vigorous, and the two hard days and broken rest had greatly tired him. On reaching Morwell he did not take a light, but cast himself, in his clothes, on his bed, and fell into a heavy sleep.

Barbara walked quietly back after having parted with Jane. She hoped that Jasper had on second thoughts taken the prudent course of escaping. It was inconceivable that he should remain and allow himself to be retaken. She was puzzled how to explain his conduct. Then all at once she remembered that she had left the convict suit in her father's room ; she had forgotten to remove it. She quickened her pace and arrived breathless at Morwell.

She entered her father's apartment on tiptoe. She stood still and listened. A night-light burned on the floor, and the enclosing iron pierced with round holes cast circles of light about the walls. The candle was a rushlight of feeble illuminating power.

Barbara could see her father lying, apparently asleep, in bed, with his pale thin hands out, hanging down, clasped, as if in prayer ; one of the spots of light danced over the finger tips and nails. She heard him breathe, as in sleep.

Then she stepped across the room to where she had cast the suit of clothes. They lay in a grey heap, with the spots of light avoiding them, dancing above them, but not falling on them.

Barbara stooped to pick them up.

'Stay, Barbara,' said her father. 'I hear you. I see what you are doing. I know your purpose. Leave those things where they lie.'

'O papa! dear papa, suffer me to put them away.'

'Let them lie there, where I can see them.'

'But, papa, what will the maids think when they come in? Besides it is untidy to let them litter about the floor.'

He made an impatient gesture with his hand.

'May I not, at least, fold them and lay them on the chair?'

'You may not touch them at all,' he said in a tone of irritation. She knew his temper too well to oppose him further.

'Good night, dear papa. I suppose Eve is gone to bed?'

'Yes; go also.'

She was obliged, most reluctantly, to leave the room. She ascended the stairs, and entered her own sleeping apartment. From this a door communicated with that of her sister. She opened this door and with her light entered and crossed it.

Eve had gone to bed, and thrown all her clothes about on the floor. Barbara had some difficulty in picking her way among the scattered articles. When she came to the bedside, she stood, and held her candle aloft, and let the light fall over the sleeping girl.

How lovely she was, with her golden hair in confusion on the pillow! She was lying with her cheek on one rosy palm, and the other hand was out of bed, on the white sheet—and see! upon the finger, Barbara recognised the turquoise ring. Eve did not venture to wear this by day.

At night, in her room, she had thrust the golden hoop over her finger, and had gone to sleep without removing it.

Barbara stooped, and kissed her sister's cheek. Eve did not awake, but smiled in slumber; a dimple formed at the corner of her mouth.

Then Barbara went to her own room, opened her desk, and the secret drawer, and looked at the bunch of dry roses. They were very yellow now, utterly withered and worthless. The girl took them, stooped her face to them—was it to discover if any scent lingered in the faded leaves? Then she closed the drawer and desk again, with a sigh.

Was Barbara insensible to what is beautiful, inappreciative of the poetry of life? Surely not. She had been forced by circumstances to be practical, to devote her whole thought to the duties of the house and estate; she had said to herself that she had no leisure to think of those things that make life graceful; but through her strong, direct, and genuine nature ran a 'Leitmotif' of sweet, pure melody, kept under and obscured by the jar and jangle of domestic cares and worries, but never lost. There is no nature, however vulgar, that is deficient in its musical phrase, not always quite original and unique, and only the careless listener marks it not. The patient, attentive ear suspects its presence first, listens for it, recognises it, and at last appreciates it.

In poor faithful Barbara now the sweet melody, somewhat sad, was rising, becoming articulate, asserting itself above all other sounds and adventitious strains—but, alas! there was no ear to listen to it.

Barbara went to her window and opened it.

'How the owls are hooting to-night!' she said. 'They, like myself, are full of unrest. To-whit! To-whoo!'

CHAPTER XXXIV.

THE DOVES.

BARBARA had no thought of going to bed. She could not have slept had she gone. There was a clock in the tower, a noisy clock that made its pulsations heard through the quadrangle, and this clock struck twelve. By this time Jane had roused the young policeman, and he was collecting men to assist him in the capture. Perhaps they were already on their way,—or were they waiting for the arrival of warders from Prince's Town? Those warders were more dangerous men than the constables, for they were armed with short guns, and prepared to fire should their game attempt to break away.

She looked across the court at Jasper's window. No light was in it. Was he there, asleep? or had he taken her advice and gone? She could not endure the thought of his capture, the self-reproach of having betrayed him was more than she could bear. Barbara, usually so collected and cool, was now nervous and hot.

More light was in the sky than had been when she was on the down. The moon was rising over the roof. She could not see it, but she saw the reflection in Jasper's window, like flakes of silver.

What should she do? Her distress became insupportable, and she felt she must be doing something to relieve her mind. The only thing open to her was to make another attempt to recover the prison suit. If she could destroy that, it would be putting out of the way one piece of evidence against him—a poor piece, still *a* piece. She was not sure that it would avail him anything, but it was worth risking her father's anger on the chance.

She descended the stairs once more to her father's room. The door was ajar, with a feeble yellow streak

issuing from it. She looked in cautiously. Then with
the tread of a thief she entered and passed through a maze
of quivering bezants of dull light. She stooped, but, as
she touched the garments, heard her father's voice, and
started upright. He was speaking in his sleep—'*De profundis clamavi ad te;*' then he tossed and moaned, and
put up his hand and held it shaking in the air. '*Si
iniquitates*'—he seemed troubled in his sleep, unable to
catch the sequence of words, and repeated '*Si iniquitates
observaveris,*' and lay still on his pillow again; whilst
Barbara stood watching him, with her finger to her lip,
afraid to move, afraid of the consequences, should he wake
and see her in her disobedience.

Then he mumbled, and she heard him pulling at his
sheet. '*Out of love, out of the deeps of love, I have sinned.*'
Then suddenly he cried out, '*Si iniquitates observaveris,
Domine, quis sustinebit?*'—he had the sentence complete,
or nearly so, and it appeased him. Barbara heard him
sigh, she stole to his side, bowed over his ear, and said,
'*Apud te propitiatio est: speravit anima mea in Domino.*'
Whether he heard or not she did not know; he breathed
thenceforth evenly in sleep, and the expression of distress
left his face.

Then Barbara took up the bundle of clothes and softly
withdrew. She was risking something for Jasper—the
loss of her father's regard. She had recently drawn
nearer to his heart than ever before, and he had allowed
her to cling round his neck and kiss him. Yet now she
deliberately disobeyed him. He would be very angry next
morning.

When she was in the hall she turned over in her mind
what was best to be done with the clothes. She could
not hide them in the house. Her father would insist
on their reproduction. They must be destroyed. She
could not burn them: the fire in the kitchen was out.
The only way she could think of getting rid of them
was to carry them to the Raven Rock and throw them

over the precipice. This, accordingly, she did. She left the house, and in the moonlight walked through the fields and wood to the crag and hurled the bundle over the edge.

Now that this piece of evidence against Jasper was removed, it was expedient that he should escape without further delay—if he were still at Morwell.

Barbara had a little money of her own. When she unlocked her desk and looked at the withered flowers, she drew from it her purse, that contained her savings. There were several pounds in it. She drew the knitted silk purse from her pocket, and, standing in the moonlight, counted the sovereigns in her hand. She was standing before the gatehouse near the old trees, hidden by their shadow. She looked up at Jasper's other window—that which commanded the entrance and was turned from the moon. Was he there? How could she communicate with him, give him the money, and send him off? Then the grating clock in the tower tolled one. Time was passing, danger drew on apace. Something must be done. Barbara picked up some pebbles and threw them at Jasper's window, but her aim was bad or her arm shook, and they scattered without touching the glass.

All at once she heard feet—a trampling in the lane—and she saw also that lights were burning on the down. The lights were merely gorse blazes, for Morwell Moor was being 'swaled,' and the flames were creeping on; and the trampling was of young colts and bullocks that fed on the down, which were escaping before the fires; but to Barbara's nervous fear the lights and the tramp betokened the approach of a body of men to capture Jasper Babb. Then, without any other thought but to save him, she ran up the stair, struck at his door, threw it open, and entered. He started from his bed, on which he had cast himself fully dressed, and from dead weariness had dropped asleep.

'For God's dear sake,' said Barbara, 'come away!

They are after you; they are close to the house. Here is money—take it, and go by the garden.'

She stood in the door, holding it, trembling in all her limbs, and the door she held rattled.

He came straight towards her.

'Miss Jordan!' he exclaimed. 'Oh, Miss Jordan I shall never forgive myself. Go down into the garden—I will follow at once. I will speak to you; I will tell you all.'

'I do not wish you to speak. I insist on your going.'

He came to her, took her hand from the door, and led her down the stairs. As they came out into the gateway they heard the tramp of many feet, and a rush of young cattle debouched from the lane upon the open space before the gate.

Barbara was not one to cry, but she shivered and shrank before her eyes told her what a mistake she had made.

'Here,' she said, 'I give you my purse. Go!'

'No,' answered Jasper. 'There is no occasion for me to go. I have acted wrongly, but I did it for the best. You see, there is no occasion for fear. These ponies have been frightened by the flames, and have come through the moor-gate, which has been left open. I must see that they do not enter the court and do mischief.'

'Never mind about the cattle, I pray you. Go! Take this money; it is mine. I freely give it you. Go!'

'Why are you so anxious about me if you hate me?' asked Jasper. 'Surely it would gratify hate to see me handcuffed and carried off!'

'No, I do not hate you—that is, not so much as to desire that. I have but one desire concerning you—that we should never see your face again.'

'Miss Jordan, I shall not be taken.'

She flared up with rage, disappointment, shame. 'How dare you!' she cried. 'How dare you stand here and set me at naught, when I have done so much for you

—when I have even ventured to rouse you in the depth
of night! My God! you are enough to madden me. I
will not have the shame come on this house of having
you taken here. Yes—I recall my words—I do hate
you.'

She wrung her hands; Jasper caught them and held
them between his own.

'Miss Barbara, I have deceived you. Be calm.'

'I know only too well that you have deceived me—all
of us,' she said passionately. 'Let go my hands.'

'You misunderstand me. I shall not be taken, for I
am not pursued. I never took your sister's money. I
have never been in jail.'

She plucked her hands away.

'I do not comprehend.'

'Nevertheless, what I say is simple. You have supposed me to be a thief and an escaped convict. I am
neither.'

Barbara shook her head impatiently.

'I have allowed you to think it for reasons of my own.
But now you must be undeceived.'

The young cattle were galloping about in front, kick-
ing, snorting, trying the hedges. Jasper left Barbara for
a while that he might drive them into a field where they
could do no harm. She remained under the great gate
in the shadow, bewildered, hoping that what he now said
was true, yet not daring to believe his words.

Presently he returned to her. He had purposely left
her that she might have time to compose herself. When
he returned she was calm and stern.

'You cannot blind me with your falsehoods,' she said.
'I know that Mr. Ezekiel Babb was robbed by his
own son. I know the prison suit was yours. You confessed it when I showed it you on your return to consciousness: perhaps before you were aware how seriously you
committed yourself. I know that you were in jail at
Prince's Town, and that you escaped.'

'Well, Miss Jordan, what you say is partly true, and partly incorrect.'

'Are you not Mr. Babb's son?' she asked imperiously. He bowed; he was courtly in manner.

'Was not his son found guilty of robbing him?'

He bowed again.

'Was he not imprisoned for so doing?'

'He was so.'

'Did he not escape from prison?'

'He did.'

'And yet,' exclaimed Barbara angrily, 'you dare to say with one breath that you are innocent, whilst with the next you confess your guilt! Like the satyr in the fable, I would drive you from my presence, you blower of true and false!'

He caught her hands again and held her firmly, whilst he drew her out of the shadow of the archway into the moonlight of the court.

'Do you give it up?' he asked; and, by the moon, the sickle moon, on his pale face, she saw him smile. By that same moon he saw the frown on her brow. 'Miss Barbara, I am not Ezekiel Babb's *only* son!'

Her heart stood still; then the blood rushed through her veins like the tidal bore in the Severn. The whole of the sky seemed full of daylight. She saw all now clearly. Her pride, her anger fell from her as the chains fell from Peter when the angel touched him.

'No, Miss Jordan, I am guiltless in this matter— guiltless in everything except in having deceived you.'

'God forgive you!' she said in a low tone as her eyes fell and tears rushed to them. She did not draw her hands from his. She was too much dazed to know that he held them. 'God forgive you!—you have made me suffer very much!'

She did not see how his large earnest eyes were fixed upon her, how he was struggling with his own heart to refrain from speaking out what he felt; but had she met

his eye then in the moonlight, there would have been no
need of words, only a quiver of the lips, and they would
have been clasped in each other's arms.

She did not look up; she was studying, through a
veil of tears, some white stones that caught the moonlight.

'This is not the time for me to tell you the whole sad
tale,' he went on. 'I have acted as I thought my duty
pointed out—my duty to a brother.'

'Yes,' said Barbara, 'you have a brother—that strange
boy.'

A laugh, jeering and shrill, close in their ears. From
behind the great yew appeared the shoulders and face of
the impish Walter.

'Oh, the pious, the proper Jasper! Oh, ho, ho!
What frail men these saints are who read their Bibles
to weak-eyed Leahs and blooming Rachels, and make
love to both!

He pointed jeeringly at them with his long fingers.

'I set the down on fire for a little fun. I drove the
ponies along this lane; and see, I have disturbed a pair
of ring-doves as well. I won't hoot any more; but—
coo! coo! coo!' He ran away, but stopped every now
and then and sent back to them his insulting imitations of
the call of wood-pigeons—'Coo! coo! coo!'

CHAPTER XXXV.

THE ALARM BELL.

NEXT morning Barbara entered the hall after having seen
about the duties of the house, ordered dinner, weighed out
spices and groats, made the under-servant do the work of
Jane, who was absent; she moved about her usual duties
with her usual precision and order, but without her usual
composure,

When she came into the hall on her way to her father's room, she found Eve there engaged and hard at work on some engrossing occupation.

'Oh, Bab! do come and see how bright and beautiful I am making this,' said the girl in overflowing spirits and pride. 'I found it in the chest in the garret, and I am furbishing it up.' She held out a sort of necklace or oriental carcanet, composed of chains of gold beads and bezants. 'It was so dull when I found it, and now it shines like pure gold!' Her innocent, childish face was illumined with delight. 'I am become really industrious.'

'Yes, dear; hard at work doing nothing.'

'I should like to wear this,' she sighed.

That she had deceived her sister, that she had given her occasion to be anxious about her, had quite passed from her mind, occupied only with glittering toys.

Barbara hesitated at her father's door. She knew that a painful scene awaited her. He was certain to be angry and reproach her for having disobeyed him. But her heart was relieved. She believed in the innocence of Jasper. Strengthened by this faith, she was bold to confront her father.

She tapped at the door and entered.

She saw at once that he had heard her voice without, and was expecting her. There was anger in his strange eyes, and a hectic colour in his hollow cheeks. He was partly dressed, and sat on the side of the bed. In his hand he held the stick with which he was wont to rap when he needed assistance.

'Where are the clothes that lay on the floor last night?' was his salutation, pointing with the stick to the spot whence Barbara had gathered them up.

'They are gone, papa; I have taken them away.'

She looked him firmly in the face with her honest eyes, unwincing. He, however, was unable to meet her steadfast gaze. His eyes flickered and fell. His mouth was drawn and set with a hard, cruel expression, such as his face rarely wore ; a look which sometimes formed, but was as quickly effaced by a wave of weakness. Now, however, the expression was fixed.

'I forbade you to touch them. Did you hear me ? '

'Yes, dear papa, I have disobeyed you, and I am sorry to have offended you ; but I cannot say that I repent having taken the clothes away. I found them, and I had a right to remove them.'

'Bring them here immediately.'

'I cannot do so. I have destroyed them.'

'You have dared to do that ! ' His eyes began to kindle and the colour left his cheeks, which became white as chalk. Barbara saw that he had lost command over himself. His feeble reason was overwhelmed by passion.

'Papa,' she said, in her calmest tones, 'I have never disobeyed you before. Only on this one occasion my conscience——'

'Conscience!' he cried. 'I have a conscience in a thornbush, and yours is asleep in feathers. You have dared to creep in here like a thief in the night and steal from me what I ordered you to leave.'

He was playing with his stick, clutching it in the middle and turning it. With his other hand he clutched and twisted and almost tore the sheets. Barbara believed that he would strike her, but when he said ' Come here,' she approached him, looking him full in the face without shrinking.

She knew that he was not responsible for what he did, yet she did not hesitate about obeying his command to approach. She had disobeyed him in the night in a matter concerning another, to save that other ; she would not disobey now to save herself.

His face was ugly with unreasoning fury, and his eyes wilder than she had seen them before. He held up the stick.

'Papa,' she said, 'not your right arm, or you will reopen the wound.'

Her calmness impressed him. He changed the stick into his left hand, and, gathering up the sheet into a knot, thrust it into his mouth and bit into it.

Was the moment come that Barbara had long dreaded? And was she to be the one on whom his madness first displayed itself?

'Papa,' she said, 'I will take any punishment you think fit, but, pray, do not strike me, I cannot bear that—not for my own sake, but for yours.'

He paid no attention to her remonstrance, but raised the stick, holding it by the ferule.

Steadily looking into his sparkling eyes, Barbara repeated the words he had muttered and cried in his sleep, '*De profundis clamavi ad te, Domine. Si iniquitates observaveris, quis sustinebit?*'

Then, as in a dissolving view on a sheet one scene changes into another, so in his wild eyes the expression of rage shifted to one of fear; he dropped the stick, and Jasper, who at that moment entered, took it and laid it beyond his reach.

Mr. Jordan fell back on his pillow and moaned, and put his hands over his brow, and beat his temples with his palms. He would not look at his daughter again, but peevishly turned his face away.

Now Barbara's strength deserted her; she felt as if the floor under her feet were rolling and as if the walls of the room were contracting upon her.

'I must have air,' she said. Jasper caught her arm and led her through the hall into the garden.

Eve, alarmed to see her sister so colourless, ran to support her on the other side, and overwhelmed her with inconsiderate attentions.

'You must allow her time to recover herself,' said Jasper. 'Miss Jordan has been up a good part of the night. The horses on the down were driven on the premises by the fire and alarmed her and made her rise. She will be well directly.'

'I am already recovered,' said Barbara, with affected cheerfulness. 'The room was close. I should like to be left a little bit in the sun and air, by myself, and to myself.'

Eve readily ran back to her burnishing of the gold beads and bezants, and Jasper heard Mr. Jordan calling him, so he went to his room. He found the sick gentleman with clouded brow and closed lips, and eyes that gave him furtive glances but could not look at him steadily.

'Jasper Babb,' said Mr. Jordan, 'I do not wish you to leave the house or its immediate precincts to-day. Jane has not returned, Eve is unreliable, and Barbara overstrained.'

'Yes, sir, I will do as you wish.'

'On no account leave. Send Miss Jordan to me when she is better.'

When, about half-an-hour after, Barbara entered the room, she went direct to her father to kiss him, but he repelled her.

'What did you mean,' he asked, without looking at her, 'by those words of the Psalm?'

'Oh, papa! I thought to soothe you. You are fond of the *De Profundis*—you murmur it in your sleep.'

'You used the words significantly. What are the deeds I have done amiss for which you reproach me?'

'We all need pardon—some for one thing, some for another. And, dearest papa, we all need to say '*Apud te propitiatio est: speravit anima mea in Domino.*'

'*Propitiatio!*' repeated Mr. Jordan, and resumed his customary trick of brushing his forehead with his hand as though to sweep cobwebs from it which fell over and clouded his eyes. 'For what? Say out plainly of what you accuse me. I am prepared for the worst. I cannot endure these covert stabs. You are always watching me. You are ever casting innuendos. You cut and pierce me worse than the scythe. That gashed my body, but you drive your sharp words into my soul.'

'My dear papa, you are mistaken.'

'I am not mistaken. Your looks and words have meaning. Speak out.'

'I accuse you of nothing, darling papa, but of being perhaps just a little unjust to me.'

She soon saw that her presence was irritating him, her protestations unavailing to disabuse his mind of the prejudice that had taken hold of it, and so, with a sigh, she left him.

Jane Welsh did not return all day. This was strange. She had promised Barbara to return the first thing in the morning. She was to sleep in Tavistock, where she had a sister, married.

Barbara went about her work, but with abstracted mind, and without her usual energy.

She was not quite satisfied. She tried to believe in Jasper's innocence, and yet doubts would rise in her mind in spite of her efforts to keep them under.

Whom had Eve met on the Raven Rock? Jasper had denied that he was the person: who, then, could it have been? The only other conceivable person was Mr. Coyshe, and Barbara at once dismissed that idea. Eve would never make a mystery of meeting Doctor Squash, as she called him.

At last, as evening drew on, Jane arrived. Barbara met her at the door and remonstrated with her.

'Please, miss, I could not help myself. I found Joseph Woodman last night, and he said he must send for the warders to identify the prisoner. Then, miss, he said I was to wait till he had got the warders and some constables, and when they was ready to come on I might come too, but not before. I slept at my sister's last night.'

'Where are the men now?'

'They are about the house—some behind hedges, some in the wood, some on the down.'

Barbara shuddered.

' Please miss, they have guns. And, miss, I were to
come on and tell the master that all was ready, and if he
would let them know where the man was they'd trap
him.'

' There is no man here but Mr. Babb.'

Jane's face fell.

' Lawk, miss! If Joseph thought us had been making
games of he, I believe he'd never marry me—and after
going to a Love Feast with him, too! 'Twould be serious
that, surely.'

' Joseph has taken a long time coming.'

' Joseph takes things leisurely, miss—'tis his nature.
Us have been courting time out o' mind; and, please,
miss, if the man were here, then the master was to give
the signal by pulling the alarm-bell. Then the police and
warders would close in on the house and take him.'

Barbara was as pale now as when nearly fainting in
the morning. This was not the old Barbara with hale
cheeks, hearty eyes, and ripe lips, tall and firm, and
decided in all her movements. No! This was not at all
the old Barbara.

' Well, Miss Jordan, what is troubling you?' asked
Jasper. ' The house is surrounded. Men are stationed
about it. No one can leave it without being challenged.'

' Yes,' said Barbara quickly. ' By the Abbot's Well
there runs a path down between laurels, then over a stile
into the wood. It is still possible—will you go?'

' You do not trust me?'

' I wish to—but——'

' Will you do one thing more for me?'

She looked timidly at him.

' Peal the alarm-bell.'

CHAPTER XXXVI.

CONFESSIONS.

As the bell clanged Mr. Jordan came out of his door. He had been ordered to remain quiet and take no exercise; but now, leaning on his stick and holding the door jamb, he came forth.

'What is this?' he asked, and Jasper put his hand to the rope to arrest the upward cast. 'Why are you ringing, Barbara? Who told you to do so?'

'I bade her ring,' said Jasper, 'to call these,' he pointed to the door.

Several constables were visible; foremost came Joseph and a prison warder.

'Take him!' cried Mr. Jordan: 'arrest the fellow. Here he is—he is unarmed.'

'What! Mr. Jasper!' asked Joseph. Among the servants and labourers the young steward was only known as Mr. Jasper. 'Why, sir, this is—this is—Mr. Jasper!'

'This is the man,' said Ignatius Jordan, clinging to the door-jamb and pointing excitedly with his stick,—'this is the man who robbed his own father of money that was mine. This is the man who was locked up in jail and broke out, and, by the mercy and justice of Heaven, was cast at my door.'

'I beg your pardon, sir,' said Joseph, 'I don't understand. This is your steward, Mr. Jasper.'

'Take him, handcuff him before my eyes. This is the fellow you have been in search of; I deliver him up.'

'But, sir,' said the warder, 'you are wrong. This is not our escaped convict.'

'He is, I tell you I know he is.'

'I am sorry to differ from you, sir, but this is not he. I know which is which. Why, this chap's hair have never been cut. If he'd been with us he'd have a head like a mole's back.'

'Not he!' cried Mr. Jordan frantically. 'I say to you this *is* Jasper Babb.'

'Well, sir,' said the warder, 'sorry to differ, sir, but our man ain't Jasper at all—he's Martin.'

Then Joseph turned his light blue eyes round in quest of Jane. 'I'll roast her! I'll eat her,' he muttered, 'at the next Love Feast.'

The men went away much disappointed, grumbling, swearing, ill-appeased by a glass of cider each; Jane sulked in the kitchen, and said to Barbara, 'This day month, please, miss.'

Mr. Jordan, confounded, disappointed, crept back to his room and cast himself on his bed.

The only person in the house who could have helped them out of their disappointment was Eve, who knew something of the story of Martin, and knew, moreover, or strongly suspected, that he was not very far off. But no one thought of consulting Eve.

When all the party of constables was gone, Barbara stood in the garden, and Jasper came to her.

'You will tell me all now?' she said, looking at him with eyes full of thankfulness and trust.

'Yes, Miss Jordan, everything. It is due to you. May I sit here by you on the garden seat?'

She seated herself, with a smile, and made room for him, drawing her skirts to her.

The ten-week stocks, purple and white, in a bed under the window filled the air with perfume; but a sweeter perfume than ten-week stocks, to Barbara, charged the atmosphere — the perfume of perfect confidence. Was Barbara plain? Who could think that must have no love for beauty of expression. She had none of her sister's loveliness, but then Eve had none of hers. Each had a charm of her own,—Eve the charm of exquisite physical perfection, Barbara that of intelligence and sweet faith and complete self-devotion streaming out of eye and mouth—indeed, out of every feature. Which is lovelier—the lantern, or the light within? There was little of soul and character in frivolous Eve.

When Jasper seated himself beside Miss Jordan neither spoke for full ten minutes. She folded her hands on her lap. Perhaps their souls were, like the ten-week stocks, exhaling sweetness.

'Dear Miss Jordan,' said Jasper, 'how pleasantly the thrushes are singing!'

'Yes,' she replied, 'but I want to hear your story—I can always listen to the thrushes.'

He was silent after this for several minutes. She did not further press him. She knew he would tell her all when he had rallied his courage to do so. They heard Eve upstairs in her room lightly singing a favourite air from 'Don Giovanni.'

'It is due to you,' said Jasper at last. 'I will hide nothing from you, and I know your kind heart will bear with me if I am somewhat long.'

She looked round, smiled, just raised her fingers on her lap and let them fall again.

When Jasper saw that smile he thought he had never seen a sweeter sight. And yet people said that Barbara was plain!

'Miss Jordan, as you have heard, my brother Martin took the money. Poor Martin! Poor, dear Martin! His is a broken life, and it was so full of promise!'

'Did you love Martin very dearly?'

'I *do* love him dearly. I have pitied him so deeply. He has had a hard childhood. I will tell you all, and your good kind soul will pity, not condemn him. You have no conception what a bright handsome lad he was. I love to think of him as he was—guileless, brimming with spirits. Unfortunately for us, our father had the idea that he could mould his children's character into whatever shape he desired, and he had resolved to make

R

of Martin a Baptist minister, so he began to write on his
tender heart the hard tenets of Calvinism, with an iron
pen dipped in gall. When my brother and I played
together we were happy—happy as butterflies in the sun.
When we heard our father's voice or saw him, we ran
away and hid behind bushes. He interfered with our pursuits, he sneered at our musical tastes, he tried to stop our
practising on the violin. We were overburdened with
religion, had texts rammed into us as they ram groats
down the throats of Strasburg geese. Our livers became
diseased like these same geese—our moral livers. Poor
Martin could least endure this education : it drove him
desperate. He did what was wrong through sheer provocation. By nature he is good. He has a high spirit, and
that led him into revolt.'

'I have seen your brother Martin,' said Barbara.
'When you were brought insensible to this house he was
with you.'

'What did you think of him?' asked Jasper, with
pride in his tone.

'I did not see his face, he never removed his hat.'

'Has he not a pleasant voice! and he is so grand and
generous in his demeanour!'

Barbara said nothing. Jasper waited, expecting some
word of praise.

'Tell me candidly what you thought of him,' said
Jasper.

'I do not like to do so. I did form an opinion of him,
but—it was not favourable.'

'You saw him for too short a time to be able to judge,'
said the young man. 'It never does to condemn a man
off-hand without knowing his circumstances. Do you
know, Miss Jordan, that saying of St. Paul about premature judgments? He bids us not judge men, for the
Great Day will reveal the secrets of all hearts, and then—
what is his conclusion? "All men will be covered with
confusion and be condemned of men and angels"? · Not

so—"Then shall every man have praise of the Lord." Their motives will show better than their deeds.'

'How sweetly the thrushes are singing!' said Barbara now; then—'So also Eve may be misunderstood.'

'Oh, Miss Jordan! when I consider what Martin might have become in better hands, with more gentle and sympathetic treatment, it makes my heart bleed. I assure you my boyhood was spent in battling with the fatal influences that surrounded him. At last matters came to a head. Our father wanted to send Martin away to be trained for a preacher, and Martin took the journey money provided him, and joined a company of players. He had a good voice, and had been fairly taught to sing. Whether he had any dramatic talent I can hardly say. After an absence of a twelvemonth or more he returned. He was out of his place, and professed penitence. I dare say he really was sorry. He remained a while at home, but could not get on with our father, who was determined to have his way with Martin, and Martin was equally resolved not to become a Dissenting minister. To me it was amazing that my father should persevere, because it was obvious that Martin had no vocation for the pastorate; but my father is a determined man. Having made up his mind that Martin was to be a preacher, he would not be moved from it. In our village a couple of young men resolved to go to America. They were friends of Martin, and persuaded him to join them. He asked my father to give him a fit-out and let him go. But no—the old gentleman was not to be turned from his purpose. Then a temptation came in poor Martin's way, and he yielded to it in a thoughtless moment, or, perhaps, when greatly excited by an altercation with his father. He took the money and ran away.'

'He did not go to America?'.

'No, Miss Jordan. He rejoined the same dramatic company with which he had been connected before. That was how he was caught.'

'And the money?'

'Some of it was recovered, but what he had done with most of it no one knows; the poor thriftless lad least of all. I dare say he gave away pounds right and left to all who made out a case of need to him.'

Then these two, sitting in the garden perfumed with stocks, heard Eve calling Barbara.

'It is nothing,' said Barbara; 'Eve is tired of polishing her spangles, and so wants me. I cannot go to her now: I must hear the end of your story.'

'I was on my way to this place,' Jasper continued, 'when I had to pass through Prince's Town. I found my other brother there, Walter, who is also devoted to our poor Martin; Walter had found means of communicating with his brother, and had contrived plans of escape. He had a horse in readiness, and one day, when the prisoners were cutting turf on the moor, his comrades built a turf-stack round Martin, and the warders did not discover that he was missing till he had made off. Walter persuaded me to remain a day or two in the place to assist in carrying out the escape, which was successfully executed. We got away off Dartmoor, avoided Tavistock, and lost ourselves on these downs, but were making for the Tamar, that we might cross into Cornwall by bridge or ferry, or by swimming our horses; and then we thought to reach Polperro and send Martin out of the kingdom in any ship that sailed.'

'Why did you not tell me this at once, when you came to our house?' asked Barbara, with a little of her old sharpness.

'Because I did not know you then, Miss Jordan; I could not be sure that you might be trusted.'

She shook her head. 'Oh, Mr. Jasper! I am not trustworthy. I did betray what I believed to be your secret.'

'Your very trustiness made you a traitor,' he answered courteously. 'Your first duty was to your sister.'

'Why did you allow me to suppose that you were the criminal?'

'You had found the prison clothes, and at first I sought to screen my brother. I did not know where Martin was; I wished to give him ample time for escape by diverting suspicion to myself.'

'But afterwards? You ought, later, to have undeceived me,' she said, with a shake in her voice, and a little accent of reproach.

'I shrank from doing that. I thought when you visited Buckfastleigh you would have found out the whole story; but my father was reticent, and you came away without having learned the truth. Perhaps it was pride, perhaps a lingering uneasiness about Martin, perhaps I felt that I could not tell of my dear brother's fall and disgrace. You were cold, and kept me at a distance——'

Then, greatly agitated, Barbara started up.

'Oh, Mr. Jasper!' she said with quivering voice, 'what cruel words I have spoken to you—to you so generous, so true, so self-sacrificing! You never can forgive me; and yet from the depth of my heart I desire your pardon. Oh, Jasper! Mr.'—a sob broke the thread of her words—'Mr. Jasper, when you were ill and unconscious, I studied your face hour after hour, trying to read the evil story of your life there, and all I read was pure, and noble, and true. How can I make you amends for the wrong I have done you!'

As she stood, humbled, with heaving bosom and throat choking—Eve came with skips and laugh along the gravel walk. 'I have found you!' she exclaimed, and clapped her hands.

'And I—and I——' gasped Barbara—'I have found how I may reward the best of men. There! there!' she said, clasping Eve's hand and drawing her towards Jasper. 'Take her! I have stood between you too long; but, on my honour, only because I thought you unworthy of her.'

She put Eve's hand in that of Jasper, then before

either had recovered from the surprise occasioned by her words and action, she walked back into the house, gravely, with erect head, dignified as ever.

CHAPTER XXXVII.

THE PIPE OF PEACE.

BARBARA went to her room. She ran up the stairs: her stateliness was gone when she was out of sight. She bolted her door, threw herself on her knees beside her bed, and buried her face in the counterpane.

'I am so happy!' she said; but her happiness can hardly have been complete, for the bed vibrated under her weight—shook so much that it shook down a bunch of crimson carnations she had stuck under a sacred picture at the head of the bed, and the red flowers fell about her dark hair, and strewed themselves on the counterpane round her head. She did not see them. She did not feel them.

If she had been really and thoroughly happy when at last she rose from her knees, her cheeks would not have shone with tears, nor would her handkerchief have been so wet that she hung it out of her window to dry it, and took another from her drawer.

Then she went to her glass and brushed her hair, which was somewhat ruffled, and she dipped her face in the basin.

After that she was more herself. She unlocked her desk and from it took a small box tied round with red ribbon. Within this box was a shagreen case, and in this case a handsome rosewood pipe, mounted in silver.

This pipe had belonged to her uncle, and it was one of the little items that had come to her. Indeed, in the division of family relics, she had chosen this. Her cousins had teased her, and asked whether it was intended for her future husband. She had made no other reply than that she fancied it, and so she had kept it. When she selected it, she had thought of Jasper. He smoked occasionally. Possibly, she thought she might some day give it him, when he had proved himself to be truly repentant.

Now he was clear from all guilt, she must make him the present—a token of complete reconciliation. She dusted the pretty bowl with her clean pocket-handkerchief, and looked for the lion and head to make sure that the mounting was real silver. Then she took another look at herself in the glass, and came downstairs, carrying the calumet of peace enclosed in its case.

She found Jasper sitting with Eve on the bench where she had left them. They at once made way for her. He rose, and refused to sit till she had taken his place.

'Mr. Jasper,' she said, and she had regained entire self-command, 'this is a proud and happy day for all of us—for you, for Eve, and for me. I have been revolving in my mind how to mark it and what memorial of it to give to you as a pledge of peace established, misunderstandings done away. I have been turning over my desk as well as my mind, and have found what is suitable. My uncle won this at a shooting-match. He was a first-rate shot.'

'And the prize,' said Jasper, 'has fallen into hands that make very bad shots.'

'What do you mean? Oh!' Barbara laughed and coloured. 'You led me into that mistake about yourself.'

'This is the bad shot I mean,' said Jasper: 'you have brought Miss Eve here to me, and neither does Eve want me, nor do I her.'

Barbara opened her eyes very wide. 'Have you quarrelled?' she inquired, turning to see the faces of Jasper and her sister. Both were smiling with a malicious humour.

'Not at all. We are excellent friends.'

'You do not love Eve?'

'I like Eve, I love someone else.'

The colour rushed into Barbara's face, and then as suddenly deserted it. What did he mean? A sensation of
vast happiness overspread her, and then ebbed away.
Perhaps he loved someone at Buckfastleigh. She, plain,
downright Barbara—what was she for such a man as Jasper had approved himself? She quickly recovered herself,
and said, ' We were talking about the pipe.'

' Quite so,' answered Jasper. ' Let us return to the
pipe. You give it me—your uncle's prize pipe?'

' Yes, heartily. I have kept it in my desk unused, as it
has been preserved since my uncle's death; but you must
use it; and I hope the tobacco will taste nice through it.'

' Miss Jordan,' said Jasper, ' you have shown me such
high honour, that I feel bound to honour the gift in a
special manner. I can only worthily do so by promising
to smoke out of no other pipe so long as this remains entire, and should an accident befall it, to smoke out of no
other not replaced by your kind self.'

Eve clapped her hands.

' A rash promise,' said Barbara. ' You are at liberty
to recall it. If I were to die, and the pipe were broken,
you would be bound to abjure smoking.'

' If you were to die, dear Miss Jordan, I should bury
the pipe in your grave, and something far more precious
than that.'

' What?'

' Can you ask?' He looked her in the eyes, and again
her colour came, deep as the carnations that had strewed
her head.

' There, there!' he said, ' we will not talk of graves,
and broken pipes, and buried hearts; we will get the pipe
to work at once, if the ladies do not object.'

' I will run for the tinder-box,' said Eve eagerly.

' I have my amadou and steel with me, and tobacco,'
Jasper observed; ' and mind, Miss Barbara is to consecrate
the pipe for ever by drawing out of it the first whiff of
smoke.'

Barbara laughed. She would do that. Her heart was wonderfully light, and clear of clouds as that sweet still evening sky.

The pipe was loaded; Eve ran off to the kitchen to fetch a stick out of the fire with glowing end, because, she said, 'she did not like the smell of the burning amadou.'

Jasper handed the pipe to Barbara, who, with an effort to be demure, took it.

'Are you ready?' asked Jasper, who was whirling the stick, making a fiery ring in the air.

Barbara had put the pipe between her lips, precisely in the middle of her mouth.

'No, that will not do,' said the young man; 'put the pipe in the side of your mouth. Where it is now I cannot light it without burning the tip of your nose.'

Barbara put her little finger into the bowl to assure herself that it was full. Eve was on her knees at her sister's feet, her elbows on her lap, looking up amused and delighted. Barbara kept her neck and back erect, and her chin high in the air. A smile was on her face, but no tremor in her lip. Eve burst into a fit of laughter. 'Oh, Bab, you look so unspeakably droll!' But Barbara did not laugh and let go the pipe. Her hands were down on the bench, one on each side of her. She might have been sitting in a dentist's chair to have a tooth drawn. She was a little afraid of the consequences; nevertheless, she had undertaken to smoke, and smoke she would—one whiff, no more.

'Ready?' asked Jasper.

She could not answer, because her lips grasped the pipe with all the muscular force of which they were capable. She replied by gravely and slowly bowing her head.

'This is our calumet of peace, is it not, Miss Jordan? A lasting peace never to be broken—never?'

She replied again only by a serious bow, head and pipe going down and coming up again.

'Ready?' Jasper brought the red-hot coal in contact

with the tobacco in the bowl. The glow kindled Barbara's face. She drew a long, a conscientiously long, breath. Then her brows went up in query.

'Is it alight?' asked Eve, interpreting the question.

'Wait a moment——Yes,' answered Jasper.

Then a long spiral of white smoke, like a jet of steam from a kettle that is boiling, issued from Barbara's lips, and rose in a perfect white ring. Her eyes followed the ring.

At that moment—bang! and again—bang!—the discharge of firearms.

The pipe fell into her lap.

'What is that?' asked Eve, springing to her feet. They all hurried out of the garden, and stood in front of the house, looking up and down the lane.

'Stay here and I will see,' said Jasper. 'There may be poachers near.'

'In pity do not leave us, or I shall die of fear,' cried Eve.

The darkness had deepened. A few stars were visible. Voices were audible, and the tread of men in the lane. Then human figures were visible. It was too dark at first to distinguish who they were, and the suspense was great.

As, however, they drew nearer, Jasper and the girls saw that the party consisted of Joseph, the warder, and a couple of constables, leading a prisoner.

'We have got him,' said Joseph Woodman, 'the right man at last.'

'Whom have you got?' asked Barbara.

'Whom!—why, the escaped felon, Martin Babb.'

A cry. Eve had fainted.

CHAPTER XXXVIII.

TAKEN !

WE must go back in time, something like an hour and a half or two hours, and follow the police and warders after they left Morwell, to understand how it happened that Martin fell into their hands. They had retired sulky and grumbling. They had been brought a long way, the two warders a very long way, for nothing. When they reached the down, one of the warders observed that he was darned if he had not turned his ankle on the rough stones of the lane. The other said he reckoned they had been shabbily treated, and it was not his ankle but his stomach had been turned by a glass of cider sent down into emptiness. Some cold beef and bread was what he wanted. Whereat he was snapped at by the other, who advised him to kill one of the bullocks on the moor and make his meal on that.

'Hearken,' said Joseph; 'brothers, an idea has struck me. We have not captured the man, and so we shan't have the reward.'

'Has it taken you half an hour to discover that?'

'Yes,' answered Joseph simply. 'Thinking and digesting are much the same. I ain't a caterpillar that can eat and digest at once.'

'I wish I'd had another glass of cider,' said one of the constables, 'but these folk seemed in a mighty haste to get rid of us.'

'There is the "Hare and Hounds" at Goatadon,' said Joseph.

'That is a long bit out of the road,' remonstrated the constable.

'What is time to us police!' answered Joseph. 'It is made to be killed, like a flea.'

'And hops away as fast,' said another.

'Let us get back to Tavistock,' said a warder.

'Oh, if you wish it,' answered Joseph; 'only it *do* seem a cruel pity.'

'What is a pity?'

'Why, that you should ha' come so far and not seen the greatest wonder of the world.'

'What may that be?'

'The fat woman,' answered Joseph Woodman. 'The landlady of the "Hare and Hounds." You might as well go to Egypt and not see the pyramids, or to Rome and not see the Pope, or to London and not see the Tower.'

'I don't make any account of fat women,' said the warder, who had turned his ankle.

'But this,' argued Joseph, 'is a regular marvel. She's the fattest woman out of a caravan—I believe the fattest in England; I dare say the very fattest in the known world. What there be in the stars I can't say.'

'Now,' said the warder, who had turned his stomach, 'what do *you* call fat?' He was in a captious mood.

'What do I call fat?' repeated Joseph; 'why, that woman. Brother, if you and I were to stretch our arms at the farthest, taking hold of each other with one hand, we couldn't compass her and take hold with the other.'

'I don't believe it,' said the warder emphatically.

''Tain't possible a mortal could be so big,' said the other warder.

'I swear it,' said Joseph with great earnestness.

'There is never a woman in the world,' said the warder with the bad ankle, 'whose waist I couldn't encircle, and I've tried lots.'

'But I tell you this woman is out of the common altogether.'

'Have you ever tried?' sneered the warder with the bad stomach.

'No, but I've measured her with my eye.'

'The eye is easy deceived as to distances and dimensions. Why, Lord bless you! I've seen in a fog a sheep on the moor look as big as a hippopotamus.'

'But the landlady is not on the moor nor in a fog,' persisted Joseph. 'I bet you half-a-guinea, laid out in drink, that 'tis as I say.'

'Done!' said both warders. 'Done!' said the constables, and turning to their right, they went off to the 'Hare and Hounds,' two miles out of their way, to see the fat woman and test her dimensions.

Now this change in the destination of the party led to the capture of Martin, and to the wounding of the warder who complained of his stomach.

The party reached the little tavern—a poor country inn built where roads crossed—a wretched house, tarred over its stone face as protection against the driving rains. They entered, and the hostess cheerfully consented to having her girth tested. She was accustomed to it. Her fatness was part of her stock-in-trade : it drew customers to the 'Hare and Hounds' who otherwise would have gone on to Beer Alston, where was a pretty and pert maid.

Whilst the officers were refreshing themselves, and one warder had removed his boot to examine his ankle, the door of the room where they sat was opened and Martin came in, followed by Watt. His eyes were dazzled, as the room was strongly lighted, and he did not at first observe who were eating and drinking there. It was in this lonely inn that he and Walter were staying and believed themselves quite safe. A few miners were the only persons they met there.

As Martin stood in the doorway looking at the party, whilst his eyes accustomed themselves to the light, one of the warders started up. 'That is he! Take him! Our man!'

Instantly all sprang to their feet except Joseph, who was leisurely in all his movements, and the warder with bare foot, without considering fully what he did, threw his boot at Martin's head.

Martin turned at once and ran, and the men dashed out of the inn after him, both warders catching up their guns, and he who was bootless running, forgetful of his ankle, with bare foot.

The night was light enough for Martin to be seen, with the boy running beside him, across the moor. The fires were still flickering and glowing; the gorse had been burnt and so no bushes could be utilised as a screen. His only chance of escape was to reach the woods, and he ran for Morwell.

But Martin, knowing that there were fire-arms among his pursuers, dared not run in a direct line; he swerved from side to side, and dodged, to make it difficult for them to take aim. This gave great facilities to the warder who had both boots on, and who was a wiry, long-legged fellow, to gain on Martin.

' Halt ! ' shouted he, ' halt, or I fire ! '

Then Martin turned abruptly and discharged a pistol at him. The man staggered, but before he fell he fired at Martin, but missed.

Almost immediately Martin saw some black figures in front of him, and stood, hesitating what to do. The figures were those of boys who were spreading the fires among the furze bushes, but he thought that his course was intercepted by his pursuers. Before he had decided where to run he was surrounded and disarmed.

The warder was so seriously hurt that he was at once placed on a gate and carried on the shoulders of four of the constables to Beer Alston, to be examined by Mr. Coyshe and the ball extracted. This left only three to guard the prisoner, one of whom was the warder who had sprained his ankle, and had been running with that foot bare, and who was now not in a condition to go much farther.

' There is nothing for it,' said Joseph, who was highly elated, ' but for us to go on to Morwell. We must lock the chap up there. In that old house there are scores of strong places where the monks were imprisoned. To-morrow we can take him to Tavistock.' Joseph did not say that Jane Welsh was at Morwell; this consideration, doubtless, had something to do with determining the arrangement. On reaching Morwell, which they did almost at once, for Martin had been captured on the down near the entrance to the lane, the first inquiry was for a safe place where the prisoner might be bestowed.

Jane, hearing the noise, and, above all, the loved voice of Joseph, ran out.

'Jane,' said the policeman, 'where can we lock the rascal up for the night?'

She considered for a moment, and then suggested the corn-chamber. That was over the cellar, the walls lined with slate, and the floor also of slate. It had a stout oak door studded with nails, and access was had to it from the quadrangle, up a flight of stone steps. There was no window to it. 'I'll go ask Miss Barbara for the key,' she said. 'There is nothing in it now but some old onions. But'—she paused—'if he be locked up there all night, he'll smell awful of onions in the morning.'

Reassured that this was of no importance, Jane went to her mistress for the key. Barbara came out and listened to the arrangement, to which she gave her consent, coldly. The warder could now only limp. She was shocked to hear of the other having been shot.

A lack of hospitality had been shown when the constables and warders came first, through inadvertence, not intentionally. Now that they desired to remain the night at Morwell and guard there the prisoner, Barbara gave orders that they should be made comfortable in the hall. One would have to keep guard outside the door where Martin was confined, the other two would spend the night in the hall, the window of which commanded the court and the stairs that led to the corn-chamber. 'I won't have the men in the kitchen,' said Barbara, 'or the maids will lose their heads and nothing will be done.' Besides, the kitchen was out of the way of the corn-chamber.

'We shall want the key of the corn-store,' said Joseph, 'if we may have it, miss.'

'Why not stow the fellow in the cellar?' asked a constable.

'For two reasons,' answered Joseph. 'First, because he would drink the cider; and second, because—no offence meant, miss—we hope that the maids 'll be going to and fro to the cellar with the pitcher pretty often.'

Joseph was courting the maid of the house, and therefore thought it well to hint to Barbara what was expected of the house to show that it was free and open.

The corn-room was unlocked, a light obtained, and it was thoroughly explored. It was floored with large slabs of slate, and the walls were lined six feet high with slate, as a protection against rats and mice. Joseph progged the walls above that. All sound, not a window. He examined the door: it was of two-inch oak plank, and the hinges of stout iron. In the corner of the room was a heap of onions that had not been used the preceding winter. A bundle of straw was procured and thrown down.

'Lie there, you dog, you murderous dog!' said one of the men, casting Martin from him. 'Move at your peril!'

'Ah!' said the lame warder, 'I only wish you would make another attempt to escape that I might give you a leaden breakfast.' He limped badly. In running he had cut his bare foot and it bled, and he had trodden on the prickles of the gorse, which had made it very painful.

'There's a heap of onions for your pillow,' said Joseph. 'Folks say they are mighty helpful to sleep—' this was spoken satirically; then with a moral air—'But, sure enough, there's no sleeping, even on an onion pillow, without a good conscience.'

As the men were to spend the night without sleep—

one out of doors, to be relieved guard by the other, the lame warder alone excused the duty, as he was unable to walk—Barbara ordered a fire to be lighted in the great hall. The nights were not cold, but damp; the sky was clear, and the dew fell heavily. It would, moreover, be cheerful for the men to sit over a wood fire through the long night, and take naps by it if they so liked. Supper was produced and laid on the oak table by Jane, who ogled Joseph every time she entered and left the hall

She placed a jug on the table. Joseph went after her.

' You are a dear maid,' he said, ' but one jug don't go far. You must mind the character of the house and maintain it. I see cold mutton. It is good, but chops are better. This ain't an inn. It's a gentleman's house. I see cheese. Ain't there anywhere a tart and cream? Mr. Jordan is not a farmer: he's a squire. I'd not have it said of me I was courting a young person in an inferior situation.'

The fire was made up with a faggot. It blazed merrily. Joseph sat before it with his legs outspread, smiling at the flames; he had his hands on his knees. After having run hard and got hot he felt chilled, and the fire was grateful. Moreover, his hint had been taken. Two jugs stood on the table, and hot chops and potatoes had been served. He had eaten well, he had drunk well. All at once he laughed.

' What is the joke, Joe? '

' I've an idea, brother. If t'other warder dies I shall not have to pay the half-guinea because I lost my bet. He was so confounded long in the arm. That will be prime! And—we shall share the reward without him! Beautiful! '

' Umph! Has it taken you all this time to find that out? I saw it the moment the shot struck. That's why I ran on with a bad foot.'

CHAPTER XXXIX.

GONE!

NEITHER Jasper, Barbara, nor Eve appeared. Mr. Jordan was excited, and had to be told what had taken place, and this had to be done by Jasper. Barbara was with her sister. Eve had recovered, and had confessed everything. Now all was clear to the eyes of Barbara. The meeting on the Raven Rock had been the one inexplicable point, and now that was explained. Eve hid nothing from her sister; she told her about the first meeting with Martin, his taking the ring, then about the giving of the turquoise ring, finally about the meeting on the Rock. The story was disquieting. Eve had been very foolish. The only satisfaction to Barbara was the thought that the cause of uneasiness was removed, and about to be put beyond the power of doing further mischief. Eve would never see Martin again. She had seen so little of him that he could have produced on her heart but a light and transient impression. The romance of the affair had been the main charm with Eve.

When Jasper left the squire's room, after a scene that had been painful, Barbara came to him and said, 'I know everything now. Eve met your brother Martin on the Raven Rock. He has been trying to win her affections. In this also you have been wrongly accused by me.' Then with a faint laugh, but with a timid entreating look, 'I can do no more than confess now, I have such a heavy burden of amends to make.'

'Will it be a burden, Barbara?'

She put her hand lightly on his arm.

'No, Jasper—a delight.'

He stooped and kissed her hand. Little or nothing

had passed between them, yet they understood each other.

'Hist! for shame!' said a sharp voice through the garden window. She looked and saw the queer face of Watt.

'That is too cruel, Jasp love-making when our poor Martin is in danger! I did not expect it of you.'

Barbara was confused. The boy's face could ill be discerned, as there was no candle in the room, and all the light, such as there was—a silvery summer twilight— flowed in at the window, and was intercepted by his head.

'Selfish, Jasp! and you, miss—if you are going to enter the family, you should begin to consider other members than Jasper,' continued the boy. All his usual mockery was gone from his voice, which expressed alarm and anxiety. 'There lies poor Martin in a stone box, on a little straw, without a mouthful, and his keepers are given what they like!'

'Oh, Jasper!' said Barbara with a start, 'I am so ashamed of myself. I forgot to provide for him.'

'You have not considered, I presume, what will become of poor Martin. In self-defence he shot at a warder, and whether he wounded or killed him I cannot say. Poor Martin! Seven years will be spread into fourteen, perhaps twenty-one. What will he be when he comes out of prison! What shall I do all these years without him!'

'Walter,' said Jasper, going to the window, and speaking in a subdued voice, 'what can be done? I am sorry enough for him, but I can do nothing.'

'Oh, you will not try.'

'Tell me, what can I do?'

'There! let *her*,' he pointed to Barbara, 'let her come over here and speak with me. Everything now depends on her.'

'On me!' exclaimed Barbara.

'Ah, on you. But do not shout. I can hear if you

whisper. Miss, that poor fellow in the stone box is Jasper's brother. If you care at all for Jasper, you will not interfere. I do not ask you to move a finger to help Martin : I ask you only not to stand in others' way.'

'What do you mean?'

'Go into the hall, you and Jasper, instead of standing sighing and billing here. Allow me to be there also. There are two more men arrived—two of those who carried the winged snipe away. That makes four inside and one outside ; but one is lamed and without his boot. Feed them all well. Don't spare cider ; and give them spirits-and-water. Help to amuse them.'

'For what end?'

'That is no concern of yours. For what end! Hospitality, the most ancient of virtues. Above all, do not interfere with the other one.'

'What other one?'

'You know—Miss Eve,' whispered the boy. 'Let the maidens in, the housemaid certainly ; she has a sweetheart among them, and the others will make pickings.'

Then, without waiting for an answer, the queer boy ran along the gravel path and leaped the dwarf wall into the stable yard, which lay at a lower level.

'What does he mean?' asked Barbara.

'He means,' said Jasper, 'that he is going to make an attempt to get poor Martin off.'

'But how can he?'

'That I do not know.'

'And whether we ought to assist in such a venture I do not know,' said Barbara thoughtfully.

'Nor do I,' said Jasper ; 'my heart says one thing, my head the other.'

'We will follow our hearts,' said Barbara vehemently, and caught his hands and pressed them. 'Jasper, he is your brother ; with me that is a chief consideration. Come into the hall ; we will give the men some music.'

Jasper and Barbara went to the hall, and found that

the warder had his foot bandaged in a chair, and seemed to be in great pain. He was swearing at the constables who had come from Beer Alston for not having called at the 'Hare and Hounds' on their way for his boot. He tried to induce one of them to go back for it; but the sight of the fire, the jugs of cider, the plates heaped with cake, made them unwilling again to leave the house.

'We ain't a-going without our supper,' was their retort. 'You are comfortable enough here, with plenty to eat and to drink.'

'But,' complained the man, 'I can't go for my boot myself, don't you see?' But see they would not. Jane had forgotten all her duties about the house in the excitement of having her Joseph there. She had stolen into the hall, and got her policeman into a corner.

'When is it your turn to keep guard, Joe?' she asked.

'Not for another hour,' he replied. 'I wish I hadn't to go out at all.'

'Oh, Joe, I'll go and keep guard with you!'

Also the cook stole in with a bowl and a sponge, and a strong savour of vinegar. She had come to bathe the warder's foot, unsolicited, moved only by a desire to do good, doubtless. Also the under-housemaid's beady eyes were visible at the door looking in to see if more fuel were required for the fire.

Clearly, there was no need for Barbara to summon her maids. As a dead camel in the desert attracts all the vultures within a hundred miles, so the presence of these men in the hall drew to them all the young women in the house.

When they saw their mistress enter, they exhibited some hesitation. Barbara, however, gave them a nod, and more was not needed to encourage them to stay.

'Jane,' said Barbara, 'here is the key. Fetch a couple of bottles of Jamaica rum, or one of rum and one of brandy. Patience,' to the under-housemaid, 'bring hot water, sugar, tumblers, and spoons.'

A thrill of delight passed through the hearts of the men, and their eyes sparkled.

Then in at the door came the boy with his violin, fiddling, capering, dancing, making faces. In a moment he sprang on the table, seated himself, and began to play some of the pretty 'Don Giovanni' dance music.

He signed to Barbara with his bow, and pointed to the piano in the parlour, the door of which was open. She understood him and went in, lit the candles, and took a 'Don Giovanni' which her sister had bought, and practised with Jasper. Then he signed to his brother, and Jasper also took down his violin, tuned it, and began to play.

'Let us bring the piano into the hall,' said Barbara, and the men started to fulfil her wish. Four of them conveyed it from the parlour. At the same time the rum and hot water appeared, the spoons clinked in the glasses. Patience, the under-housemaid, threw a faggot on the fire.

'What is that?' exclaimed the lame warder, pointing through the window.

It was only the guard, who had extended his march to the hall and put his face to the glass to look in at the brew of rum-and-water, and the comfortable party about the fire. 'Go back on your beat, you scoundrel!' shouted the warder, menacing the constable with his fist. Then the face disappeared; but every time the sentinel reached the hall window, he applied his nose to the pane and stared in thirstily at the grog that steamed and ran down the throats of his comrades, and cursed the duty that kept him without in the falling dew. His appearance at intervals at the glass, where the fire and candlelight illumined his face, was like that of a fish rising to the surface of a pond to breathe.

'Is your time come yet outside, Joe dear?' whispered Jane.

'Hope not,' growled Joseph, helping himself freely to rum; putting his hand round the tumbler, so that none might observe how high the spirit stood in the glass before he added the water.

'Oh, Joe duckie, don't say that. I'll go and keep you company on the stone steps: we'll sit there in the moonlight all alone, as sweet as anything.'

'You couldn't ekal this grog.' answered the unromantic Joseph, 'if you was ever so sweet. I've put in four lumps of double-refined.'

'You've a sweet tooth, Joe,' said Jane.

'Shall I bathe your poor suffering foot again?' asked the cook, casting languishing eyes at the warder.

'By-and-by, when the liquor is exhausted,' answered the warder.

'Would you like a little more hot water to the spirit?' said Patience, who was setting—as it is termed in dance phraseology—at the youngest of the constables.

'No, miss, but I'd trouble you for a little more spirit,' he answered, 'to qualify the hot water.'

Then the scullery-maid, who had also found her way in, blocked the other constable in the corner, and offered to sugar his rum. He was a married man, middle-aged, and with a huge disfiguring mole on his nose; but there was no one else for the damsel to ogle and address, so she fixed upon him.

All at once, whilst this by-play was going on, under cover of the music, the door from the staircase opened, and in sprang Eve, with her tambourine, dressed in the red-and-yellow costume she had found in the garret, and wearing her burnished necklace of bezants. Barbara withdrew her hands from the piano in dismay, and flushed with shame.

'Eve!' she exclaimed, 'go back! How can you!' But the boy from the table beckoned again to her, pointing to the piano, and her fingers; Eve skipped up to her and whispered, 'Let me alone, for Jasper's sake,' then bounded into the middle of the hall, and rattled her tambourine and clinked its jingles.

The men applauded, and tossed off their rum-and-water; then, having finished the rum, mixed themselves eagerly hot jorums of brandy.

The face was at the window, with the nose flat and white against the glass, like a dab of putty.

Barbara's forehead darkened, and she drew her lips together. Her conscience was not satisfied. She suspected that this behaviour of Eve was what Walter had alluded to when he begged her not to interfere. Walter had seen Eve, and planned it with her. Was she right, Barbara asked herself, in what she was doing to help a criminal to escape?

The money he had taken was theirs—Eve's; and if Eve chose to forgive him and release him from his punishment, why should she object? Martin was the brother of Jasper, and for Jasper's sake she must go on with what she had begun.

So she put her fingers on the keys again, and at once Watt and Jasper resumed their instruments. They played the music in 'Don Giovanni,' in the last act, where the banquet is interrupted by the arrival of the statue. Barbara knew that Eve was dancing alone in the middle of the floor before these men, before him also who ought to be pacing up and down in front of the corn-chamber; but she would not turn her head over her shoulder to look at her, and her brow burnt, and her cheeks, usually pale, flamed. As for Eve, she was supremely happy; the applause of the lookers-on encouraged her. Her movements were graceful, her beauty radiant. She looked like Zerlina on the boards.

Suddenly the boy dropped his bow, and before anyone could arrest his hand, or indeed had a suspicion of mischief, he threw a canister of gunpowder into the blazing fire. Instantly there was an explosion. The logs were flung about the floor, Eve and the maids screamed, the piano and violins were hushed, doors were burst open, panes of glass broken and fell clinking, and every candle was extinguished. Fortunately the hall floor was of slate.

The men were the first to recover themselves—all, that is, but the warder, who shrieked and swore because a red-hot cinder had alighted on his bad foot.

The logs were thrust together again upon the hearth, and a flame sprang up.

No one was hurt, but in the doorway, white, with wild eyes, stood Mr. Jordan, signing with his hand, but unable to speak.

'Oh, papa! dear papa!' exclaimed Barbara, running to him, 'do go back to bed. No one is hurt. We have had a fright, that is all.'

'Fools!' cried the old man, brandishing his stick. 'He is gone! I saw him—he ran past my window.'

CHAPTER XL.

ANOTHER SACRIFICE.

WATT was no longer in the hall. Whither he had gone none knew; how he had gone none knew. The man in the quadrangle was too alarmed by the glass panes being blown out in his face, to see whether the boy had passed that way. But, indeed, no one now gave thought to Watt; the men ran to the corn-chamber to examine it. A lantern was lighted, the door examined and found to be locked. It was unfastened, and Joseph and the rest entered. The light penetrated every corner, fell on the straw and the onion-heap. Martin Babb was not there.

'May I be darned!' exclaimed Joseph, holding the lantern over his head. 'I looked at the walls, at the floor, at the door: I never thought of the roof, and it is by the roof he has got away.'

Indeed, the corn-chamber was unceiled. Martin,

possibly assisted, had reached the rafters, thence had crept along the roof in the attics, and had entered the room that belonged to the girls, and descended from the window by the old Jargonelle pear.

Then the constables and Joseph turned on the sentinel, and heaped abuse upon him for not having warned them of what was going on. It was in vain for him to protest that from the outside he could not detect what was in process of execution under the roof. Blame must attach to someone, and he was one against four.

Their tempers were not the more placable when it was seen that the bottle of brandy had been upset and was empty, the precious spirit having expended itself on the floor.

Then the question was mooted whether the fugitive should not be pursued at once, but the production by Barbara of another bottle of rum decided them not to do so, but await the arrival of morning. Suddenly it occurred to Joseph that the blame attached, not to any of those present, who had done their utmost, but to the warder who had been shot, and so had detached two of their number, and had reduced the body so considerably by this fatality as to incapacitate them from drawing a cordon round the house and watching it from every side. If that warder were to die, then the whole blame might be shovelled upon him along with the earth into his grave.

The search was recommenced next day, but was ineffectual. In which direction Martin had gone could not be found. Absolutely no traces of him could be discovered.

Presently Mr. Coyshe arrived, in a state of great excitement. He had attended the wounded man, and had heard an account of the capture; on his way to Morwell the rumour reached him that the man had broken away again. Mr. Coyshe had, as he put it, an inquiring mind. He thirsted for knowledge, whether of scientific or of social interest. Indeed, he took a lively interest in other people's affairs. So he came on foot, as hard as he could walk, to Morwell, to learn all particulars, and at the same time pay a professional visit to Mr. Jordan.

Barbara at once asked Mr. Coyshe into the parlour; she wanted to have a word with him before he saw her father.

Barbara was very uneasy about Eve, whose frivolity, lack of ballast, and want—as she feared—of proper self-respect might lead her into mischief. How could her sister have been so foolish as to dress up and dance last evening before a parcel of common constables! To Barbara such conduct was inconceivable. She herself was dignified and stiff with her inferiors, and would as soon have thought of acting before them as Eve had done as of jumping over the moon. She did not consider how her own love and that of her father had fostered caprice and vanity in the young girl, till she craved for notice and admiration. Barbara thought over all that Eve had told her: how she had lost her mother's ring, how she had received the ring of turquoise, how she had met Martin on the Rock platform. Every incident proclaimed to her mind the instability, the lack of self-respect, in her sister. The girl needed to be watched and put into firmer hands. She and her father had spoiled her. Now that the mischief was done she saw it.

What better step could be taken to rectify the mistake than that of bringing Mr. Coyshe to an engagement with Eve?

She was a straightforward, even blunt, girl, and when she had an aim in view went to her work at once. So, without beating about the bush, she said to the young doctor—

'Mr. Coyshe, you did me the honour the other day of confiding to me your attachment to Eve. I have been considering it, and I want to know whether you intend at once to speak to her. I told my father your wishes, and he is, I believe, not indisposed to forward them.'

'I am delighted to hear it,' said the surgeon; 'I would like above everything to have the matter settled, but Miss Eve never gives me a chance of speaking to her alone.'

'She is shy,' said Barbara; then, thinking that this was not exactly true, she corrected herself; 'that is to say—she, as a young girl, shrinks from what she expects is coming from you. Can you wonder?'

'I don't see it. I'm not an ogre.'

'Girls have feelings which, perhaps, men cannot comprehend,' said Barbara.

'I do not wish to be precipitate,' observed the young surgeon. 'I'll take a chair, please, and then I can explain to you fully my circumstances and my difficulties.' He suited his action to his word, and graciously signed to Barbara to sit on the sofa near his chair. Then he put his hat between his feet, calmly took off his gloves and threw them into his hat.

'I hate precipitation,' said Mr. Coyshe. 'Let us thoroughly understand each other. I am a poor man. Excuse me, Miss Jordan, if I talk in a practical manner. You are long and clear headed, so—but I need not tell you that—so am I. We can comprehend each other, and for a moment lay aside that veil of romance and poetry which invests an engagement.'

Barbara bowed.

'An atmosphere surrounds a matrimonial alliance; let us puff it away for a moment and look at the bare facts. Seen from a poetic standpoint, marriage is the union of two loving hearts, the rapture of two souls discovering each other. From the sober ground of common sense it means two loaves of bread a day instead of one, a milliner's bill at the end of the year in addition to that of the tailor, two tons of coals where one had sufficed. I need not tell you, being a prudent person, that when I am out for the day my fire is not lighted. If I had a wife of course a fire would have to burn all day. I may almost say that matrimony means three tons of coal instead of one, and *you* know how costly coals come here.'

'But, Mr. Coyshe——'

'Excuse me,' he said, 'I may be plain, but I am truthful. I am putting matters before you in the way in which I am forced to view them myself. When an ordinary individual looks on a beautiful woman he sees only her beauty. I see more ; I anatomise her mentally, and follow the bones, and nerves, and veins, and muscles. So with this lovely matrimonial prospect. I see its charms, but I see also what lies beneath, the anatomy, so to speak, and that means increased coal, butcher's, baker's bills, three times the washing, additional milliners' accounts.'

'You know, Mr. Coyshe,' said Barbara, a little startled at the way he put matters, 'you know that eventually Morwell comes to Eve.'

'My dear Miss Jordan, if a man walks in stocking soles, expecting his father-in-law's shoes, he is likely to go limpingly. How am I to live so long as Mr. Jordan lives ? I know I should flourish after his death—but in the mean time—there is the rub. I'd marry Eve to-morrow but for the expense.'

'Is there not something sordid——' began Barbara

'I will not allow you to finish a sentence, Miss Jordan, which your good sense will reproach you for uttering. I saw at a fair a booth with outside a picture of a mermaid combing her golden hair, and with the face of an angel. I paid twopence and went inside, to behold a seal flopping in a tub of dirty water. All the great events of life— birth, marriage, death—are idealised by poets, as that disgusting seal was idealised on the canvas by the artist : horrible things in themselves but inevitable, and therefore to be faced as well as we may. I need not have gone in and seen that seal, but I was deluded to do so by the ideal picture.'

'Surely,' exclaimed Barbara laughing, 'you put marriage in a false light ? '

' Not a bit. In almost every case it is as is described, a delusion and a horrible disenchantment. It shall not be so with me, so I picture it in all its real features. If you do not understand me the fault lies with you. Even the blessed sun cannot illumine a room when the panes of the window are dull. I am a poor man, and a poor man must look at matters from what you are pleased to speak of as a sordid point of view. There are plants I have seen suspended in windows said to live on air. They are all pendulous. Now I am not disposed to become a drooping plant. Live on air I cannot. There is enough earth in my pot for my own roots, but for my own alone.'

' I see,' said Barbara, laughing, but a little irritated. ' You are ready enough to marry, but have not the means on which to marry.'

' Exactly,' answered Mr. Coyshe. ' I have a magnificent future before me, but I am like a man swimming, who sees the land but does not touch as much as would blacken his nails. Lord bless you ! ' said Mr. Coyshe, ' I support a wife on what I get at Beer Alston ! Lord bless me ! ' he stood up and sat down again, ' you might as well expect a cock to lay eggs.'

Barbara bit her lips. ' I should not have thought you so practical,' she said.

' I am forced to be so. It is the fate of poor men to have to count their coppers. Then there is another matter. If I were married, well, of course, it is possible that I might be the founder of a happy family. In the South Sea Islands the natives send their parents periodically up trees and then shake the trunks. If the old people hold on they are reprieved, if they fall they are eaten. We eat our parents in England also, and don't wait till they are old and leathery. We begin with them when we are babes, and never leave off till nothing is left of them to devour. We feed on their energies, consume their substance, their time, their brains, their hearts piecemeal.'

' Well ! '

'Well,' repeated Mr. Coyshe, 'if I am to be eaten I must have flesh on my bones for the coming Coyshes to eat.'

'You need not be alarmed as to the prospect,' said Barbara gravely. 'I have been left a few hundred pounds by my aunt, they bring in about fifty pounds a year. I will make it over to my sister.'

'You see for yourself,' said Mr. Coyshe, 'that Eve is not a young lady who can be made into a sort of house-keeper. She is too dainty for that. Turnips may be tossed about, but not apricots.'

'Yes,' said Barbara, 'I and my sister are quite different.'

'You will not repent of this determination?' asked Mr. Coyshe. 'I suppose it would not be asking you too much just to drop me a letter with the expression of your intention stated in it? I confess to a weakness for black and white. The memory is so treacherous, and I find it very like an adhesive chest plaster—it sticks only on that side which applies to self.'

'Mr. Coyshe,' said Barbara, 'shall we go in and see papa? You shall be satisfied. My memory will not play me false. My whole heart is wrapped up in dear Eve, and the great ambition of my life is to see her happy. Come, then, we will go to papa.'

CHAPTER XLI.

ANOTHER MISTAKE.

BARBARA saw Mr. Coyshe into her father's room, and then went upstairs to Eve, caught her by the arm, and drew her into her own room. Barbara had now completely made up her mind that her sister was to become Mrs. Coyshe. Eve was a child, never would be other, never capable of deciding reasonably for herself. Those who loved her,

those who had care of her must decide for her. Barbara
and her father had grievously erred hitherto in humouring all Eve's caprices, now they must be peremptory with
her, and arrange for her what was best, and force her to
accept the provision made for her.

What are love matches but miserable disappointments?
Not quite so bad as pictured by Mr. Coyshe. The reality
would not differ from the ideal as thoroughly as the seal
from the painted mermaid; but there was truth in what
he said. A love match was entered into by two young
people who have idealised each other, and before the first
week is out of the honeymoon they find the ideal shat-
tered, and a very prosaic reality standing in its place.
Then follow disappointment, discontent, rebellion. Far
better the foreign system of parents choosing partners for
their children; they are best able to discover the real
qualities of the suitor because they study them dispas-
sionately, and they know the characters of their daughters.
Who can love a child more than a parent, and therefore
who is better qualified to match her suitably?

So Barbara argued with herself. Certainly Eve must
not be left to select her husband. She was a creature of
impulse, without a grain of common-sense in her whole
nature.

Barbara drew Eve down beside her on the sofa at the
foot of her bed, and put her arm round her waist. Eve
was pouting, and had red eyes; for her sister had scolded
her that morning sharply for her conduct the preceding
night, and her father had been excited, and for the first
time in his life had spoken angrily to her, and bidden her
cast off and never resume the costume in which she had
dressed and bedizened herself.

Eve had retired to her room in a sulk, and in a rebellious frame of mind. She cried and called herself an ill-
treated girl, and was overcome with immense pity for the
hardships she had to undergo among people who could not
understand and would not humour her.

Eve's lips were screwed up, and her brow as nearly contracted into a frown as it could be, and her sweet cheeks were kindled with fiery temper-spots.

'Eve dear,' said Barbara, 'Mr. Coyshe is come.'

Eve made no answer, her lips took another screw, and her brows contracted a little more.

'Eve, he is closeted now with papa, and I know he has come to ask for the hand of the dearest little girl in the whole world.'

'Stuff!' said Eve peevishly. .

'Not stuff at all,' argued Barbara, 'nor'—intercepting another exclamation—'no, dear, nor fiddlesticks. He has been talking to me in the parlour. He is sincerely attached to you. He is an odd man, and views things in quite a different way from others, but I think I made out that he wanted you to be his wife.'

'Barbara,' said Eve, with great emphasis, 'nothing in the world would induce me to submit to be called Mrs. Squash.'

'My dear, if the name is the only objection, I think he will not mind changing it. Indeed, it is only proper that he should. As he and you will have Morwell, it is of course right that a Jordan should be here, and—to please the Duke and you—he will, I feel sure, gladly assume our name. I agree with you that, though Coyshe is not a bad name, it is not a pretty one. It lends itself to corruption.'

'Babb is worse,' said Eve, still sulky.

'Yes, darling, Babb is ugly, and it is the pet name you give me, as short for Barbara. I have often told you that I do not like it.'

'You never said a word against it till Jasper came.'

'Well, dear, I may not have done so. When he did settle here, and we knew his name, it was not, of course, seemly to call me by it. That is to say,' said Barbara, colouring, 'it led to confusion—in calling for me, for instance, he might have thought you were addressing him.'

'Not at all,' said Eve, still filled with a perverse spirit.

T

'I never called him Babb at all, I always called him Jasper.' Then she took up her little apron and pulled at the embroidered ends, and twisted and tortured them into horns. 'It would be queer, sister, if you were to marry Jasper, you would become double Babb.'

'Don't,' exclaimed Barbara, bridling; 'this is unworthy of you, Eve; you are trying to turn your arms against me, when I am attacking you.'

'May I not defend myself?'

Then Barbara drew her arm tighter round her sister, kissed her pretty neck under the delicate shell-like ear, and said, 'Sweetest! we never fight. I never would raise a hand against you. I would run a pair of scissors into my own heart rather than snip a corner off this dear little ear. There, no more fencing even with wadded foils. We were talking of Mr. Coyshe.'

Eve shrugged her shoulders.

'*Revenons à nos moutons*,' she said, 'though I cannot say old Coyshe is a sheep; he strikes me rather as a jackdaw.'

'Old Coyshe! how can you exaggerate so, Eve! He is not more than five or six-and-twenty.'

'He is wise and learned enough to be regarded as old. I hate wise and learned men.'

'What is there that you do not hate which is not light and frivolous?' asked Barbara a little pettishly. 'You have no serious interests in anything.'

'I have no interests in anything here,' said Eve, 'because there is nothing here to interest me. I do not care for turnips and mangold, and what are the pigs and poultry to me? Can I be enthusiastic over draining? Can the price of bark make my pulses dance? No, Barbie (Bab you object to), I am sick of a country life in a poky corner of the most out-of-the-way county in England except Cornwall. Really, Barbie, I believe I would marry any man who would take me to London, and let me go to the theatre and to balls, and concerts and shows. Why, Barbara!

I'd rather travel round the country in a caravan and dance on a tight-rope than be moped up here in Morwell, **an old** fusty, mouldering monk's cell.'

'My dear Eve!'

Barbara was so shocked, she could say no more.

'I am in earnest. Papa is ill, and that makes the place more dull than ever. Jasper was some fun, he played the violin, and taught me music, but now you have meddled, and deprived me of that amusement; I am sick of the monotony here. It is only a shade better than Lanherne convent, and you know papa took me away from that; I fell ill with the restraint.'

'You have no restraint here.'

'No—but I have nothing to interest me. I feel always as if I was hungry for something I could not get. Why should I have "Don Giovanni," and "Figaro," and the "Barber of Seville" on my music-stand, and strum at them? I want to see them, and hear them alive, acting, singing, particularly amid lights and scenery, and in proper costume. I cannot bear this dull existence any longer. If Doctor Squash will take me to a theatre or an opera I'll marry him, just for that alone—that is my last word.'

Barbara was accustomed to hear Eve talk extravagantly, and had not been accustomed to lay much weight on what she said; but this was spoken so vehemently, and was so prodigiously extravagant, that Barbara could only loosen her hold of her sister, draw back to the far end of the sofa, and stare at her dismayedly. In her present state of distress about Eve she thought more seriously of Eve's words than they deserved. Eve was angry, discontented, and said what came uppermost, so as to annoy her sister.

'Eve dear,' said Barbara gravely, 'I pray you not to talk in this manner, as if you had said good-bye to all right principle and sound sense. Mr. Coyshe is downstairs. We must decide on an answer, and that a definite one.'

'*We!*' repeated Eve; 'I suppose it concerns me only.'

'What concerns you concerns me; you know that very well, Eve.'

'I am not at liberty, I suppose, to choose for myself?'

'You are a dear good girl, who will elect what is most pleasing to your father and sister, and promises greatest happiness to yourself.'

Eve sat pouting and playing with the ends of her apron. Then she took one end which she had twisted into a horn, and put it between her pearly teeth, whilst she looked furtively and mischievously at her sister, who sat with her hands on her lap, tapping the floor with her feet.

'Barbie!' said Eve slily.

'Well, dear!'

'Do lend me your pocket-handkerchief. I have been crying and made mine wet. Papa was so cross and you scolded me so sharply.'

Barbara, without looking at her sister, held out her handkerchief to her. Eve took it, pulled it out by the two ends, twirled it round, folded, knotted it, worked diligently at it, got it into the compact shape she desired, laid it in her arms, with the fingers under it, and then, without Barbara seeing what she was about—'Hist!' said Eve, and away shot the white rabbit she had manufactured into Barbara's lap. Then she burst into a merry laugh. The clouds had rolled away. The sun was shining.

'How can you! How can you be so childish!' burst from Barbara, as she started up, and let the white rabbit fall at her feet. 'Here we are,' said Barbara, with some anger, 'here we are discussing your future, and deciding your happiness or sorrow, and you—you are making white rabbits! You really, Eve, are no better than a child. You are not fit to choose for yourself. Come along with me. We must go down. Papa and I will settle for you as is best. You want a master who will bring you into order, and, if possible, force you to think.'

CHAPTER XLII.

ENGAGED.

IF a comparison were made between the results of well and ill considered ventures, which would prove the most uniformly successful? Not certainly those undertakings which have been most carefully weighed and prudently determined on. Just as frequently the rash and precipitate venture is crowned with success as that which has been wisely considered; and just as often the latter proves a failure, and falsifies every expectation. Nature, Fate, whatever it be that rules our destinies, rules them crookedly, and, with mischief, upsets all our calculations. We build our card-houses, and she fillips a marble into them and brings them down. Why do we invariably stop every hole except that by which the sea rolls through our dyke? Why do we always forget to lock the stable door till the nag has been stolen?

The old myth is false which tells of Prometheus as bound and torn and devoured by the eagle; Pro-metheus is free and unrent, it is Epi-metheus who is in chains, and writhing, and looks back on the irrevocable past, and curses itself and is corroded with remorse.

What is the fate of Forethought but to be flouted by capricious Destiny, to be ever proved a fool and blind, to be shown that it were just as well had it never existed?

Eve hung back as Barbara led her to her father's door. Mr. Coysho was in there, and though she had said she would take him she did not mean it. She certainly did not want to have to make her decision then. Her face became a little pale, some of the bright colour had gone from it when her temper subsided and she had begun to play at making rabbits. Now more left her cheeks, and she held back as Barbara tried to draw her on. But Barbara was very determined, and though Eve was wayward, she would not take the trouble to be obstinate. 'I can but say no,' she said to herself, 'if the creature does ask me.' Then she whispered into Barbara's ear, 'Bab, I won't have a scene before all the parish.'

'All the parish, dear!' remonstrated the elder, 'there is no one there but papa and the doctor; and if the latter means to speak he will ask to have a word with you in private, and you can go into the drawing-room.'

'But I don't want to see him.'

Barbara threw open the door.

Mr. Jordan was propped up in his bed on pillows. He was much worse, and a feverish fire burned in his eyes and cheeks. He saw Eve at once and called her to him.

Then her ill-humour returned, she pouted and looked away from Mr. Coyshe so as not to see him. He bowed and smiled, and pushed forward extending his hand, but she brushed past with her eyes fixed on her father. She was angry with Barbara for having brought her down.

'Eve,' said Mr. Jordan, 'I am very ill. The doctor has warned me that I have been much hurt by what has happened. It was your doing, Eve. You were foolish last night. You forgot what was proper to your station. Your want of consideration is the cause of my being so much worse, and of that scoundrel's escape.'

'O papa, I am very sorry I hurt you, but as for his getting off—I am glad! He had stolen my money, so I have a right to forgive him, and that I do freely.'

'Eve!' exclaimed her father, 'you do not know what you say. Come nearer to me, child.'

'If I am to be scolded, papa,' said Eve, sullenly, 'I'd like not to have it done in public.' She looked round the room, everywhere but at Mr. Coyshe. Her sister watched her anxiously.

'Eve,' said the old man, 'I am very ill and am not likely to be strong again. I cannot be always with you. I am not any more capable to act as your protector, and

Barbara has the cares of the house, and lacks the authority to govern and lead you.'

'I don't want any governing and leading, papa,' said Eve, studying the bed cover. 'Papa,' after a moment, 'whilst you lie in bed, don't you think all those little tufts on the counterpane look like poplars? I often do, and imagine gardens and walks and pleasure-grounds among them.'

'Eve,' said her father, 'I am not going to be put off what I have to say by such poor artifices as this. I am going to send you back to Lanherne.'

'Lanherne!' echoed Eve, springing back. 'I can't go there, papa; indeed I can't. It is dull enough here, but it is ten thousand times duller there. I have just said so to Barbara. I can't go, I won't go to Lanherne. I don't see why I should be forced. I'm not going to be a nun. My education has been completed under Barbara. I know where Cape Guardafui is, and the Straits of Malacca, and the Coromandel Coast. I know Mangnall's questions and answers right through—that is, I know the questions and some of the answers. I can read "Télémaque." What more is wanted of any girl? I don't desire any more learning. I hate Lanherne. I fell ill last time I was there. Those nuns look like hobgoblins, and not like angels. I shall run away. Besides, it was eternally semolina pudding there, and, papa, I hate semolina. Always semolina on fast days, and the puddings sometimes burnt. There now, my education *is* incomplete. I do not know whence semolina comes. Is it vegetable, papa? Mr. Coyshe, you are scientific, tell us the whole history of the production of this detestable article of commerce.'

'Semolina ——' began Mr. Coyshe.

'Never mind about semolina,' interrupted Barbara, who saw through her sister's tricks. 'We will turn up the word in the encyclopædia afterwards. We are considering Lanherne now.'

'I don't mind the large-grained semolina so much,'

said Eve, with a face of childlike simplicity; 'that is
almost as good as tapioca.'

Her father caught her wrist and drew her hand upon
the bed. He clutched it so tightly that she exclaimed that
he hurt her.

'Eve,' he said, 'it is necessary for you to go.

Her face became dull and stubborn again.

'Is Mr. Coyshe here to examine my chest, and see if I
am strong enough to endure confinement? Because I was
the means, according to you, papa, of poor—of the
prisoner escaping last night, therefore I am to be sent to
prison myself to-morrow.'

'I am not sending you to prison,' said her father,
'I am placing you under wise and pious guardians. You
are not to be trusted alone any more. Barbara has
been——'

'There! there!' exclaimed Eve, flashing an angry
glance at her sister, and bursting into tears; 'was there
ever a poor girl so badly treated? I am scolded, and
threatened with jail. My sister, who should love me and
take my part, is my chief tormentor, and instigates you,
papa, against me. She is rightly called Barbara—she is a
savage. I know so much Latin as to understand that.'

Barbara touched Mr. Coyshe, and signed to him to
leave the room with her.

Eve watched them out of the room with satisfaction.
She could manage her father, she thought, if left alone with
him. But her father was thoroughly alarmed. He had
been told that she had met Martin on the rock. Barbara
had told him this to exculpate Jasper. Her conduct on the
preceding night had, moreover, filled him with uneasiness.

'Papa,' said Eve, looking at her little foot and shoe,
'don't you think Mr. Coyshe's ears stick out very much?
I suppose his mother was not particular with him to put
them under the rim of his cap.'

'I have not noticed.'

'And, papa, what eager, staring eyes he has got! I think he straps his cravat too tight.'

'Possibly.'

'Do you know, dear papa, there is a little hole just over the mantelshelf in my room, and the other day I saw something hanging down from it. I thought it was a bit of string, and I went up to it and pulled it. Then there came a little squeak, and I screamed. What do you suppose I had laid hold of? It was a mouse's tail. Was that not an odd thing, papa, for the wee mouse to sit in its run and let its tail hang down outside?'

'Yes, very odd.'

'Papa, how did all those beautiful things come into the house which I found in the chest upstairs? And why were you so cross with me for putting them on?'

The old man's face changed at once, the wild look came back into his eye, and his hand which clasped her wrist clutched it so convulsively, that she felt his nails cut her tender skin.

'Eve!' he said, and his voice quivered, 'never touch them again. Never speak of them again. My God!' he put his hand to his brow and wiped the drops which suddenly started over it, 'my God! I fear, I fear for her.'

Then he turned his agitated face eagerly to her, and said—

'Eve! you must take him. I wish it. I shall have no peace till I know you are in his hands. He is so wise and so assured. I cannot die and leave you alone. I wake up in the night bathed in a sweat of fear, thinking of you, fearing for you. I imagine all sorts of things. Do you not wish to go to Lanherne? Then take Mr. Coyshe. He will make you a good husband. I shall be at ease when you are provided for. I cannot die—and I believe I am nearer death than you or Barbara, or even the doctor, sup- poses—I cannot die, and leave you here alone, unprotected. O Eve! if you love me do as I ask. You must either go to Lanherne or take Mr. Coyshe. It must be one or the other. What is that?' he asked suddenly, drawing back in the bed, and staring wildly at her, and pointing at her forehead with a white quivering finger. 'What is there? A stain—a spot. One of my black spots, very big. No, it is red. It is blood! It came there when I was wounded by the scythe, and every now and then it breaks out again. I see it now.'

'Papa!' said Eve, shuddering, 'don't point at me in that way, and look so strange; you frighten me. There is nothing there. Barbie washed it off long ago.'

Then he wavered in his bed, passing one hand over the other, as washing—'It cannot wash off,' he said, despairingly. 'It eats its way in, farther, farther, till it reaches the very core of the heart, and then——' he cast himself back and moaned.

'It was very odd of the mouse,' said Eve, 'to sit with her little back to the room, looking into the dark, and her tail hanging out into the chamber.' She thought to divert her father's thoughts from his fancies.

'Eve!' he said in a hoarse voice, and turned sharply round on her, 'let me see your mother's ring again. To-day you shall put it on. Hitherto you have worn it hung round your neck. To-day you shall bear it on your finger, in token that you are engaged.'

'Oh, papa, dear! I don't——'

'Which is it to be, Lanherne or Mr. Coyshe?'

'I won't indeed go to Lanherne.'

'Very well; then you will take Mr. Coyshe. He will make you happy. He will not always live here; he talks of a practice in London. He tells me that he has found favour with the Duke. If he goes to London——'

'Oh, papa! Is he really going to London?'

'Yes, child!'

'Where all the theatres are! Oh, papa! I should like to live in a town, I do not like being mewed up in the country. Will he have a carriage?'

'I suppose so.'

'Oh, papa! and a tiger in buttons and a gold band?'

'I do not know.'

'I am sure he will, papa! I'd rather have that than go to Lanherne.'

Mr. Jordan knocked with his stick against the wall. Eve was frightened.

'Papa, don't be too hasty. I only meant that I hate Lanherne!'

In fact, she was alarmed by his mention of the ring, and following her usual simple tactics had diverted the current of his thoughts into another direction.

Barbara and Mr. Coyshe came in.

'She consents,' said Mr. Jordan. 'Eve, give him your hand. Where is the ring?'

She drew back.

'I want the ring,' he said again, impatiently.

'Papa, I have not got it—that is—I have mislaid it.'

'What!' he exclaimed, trying to sit up, and becoming excited. 'The ring—not lost! Mislaid! It must be found. I will have it. Your mother's ring! I will never, never forgive if that is lost. Produce it at once.'

'I cannot, papa. I don't know—— O—Mr. Coyshe, quick, give me your hand. There! I consent. Do not be excited, dear papa. I'll find the ring to-morrow.'

CHAPTER XLIII.

IN A MINE.

Eve had no sooner consented to take Mr. Coyshe, just to save herself the inconvenience of being questioned about the lost ring, than she ran out of the room, and to escape further importunity ran over the fields towards the wood. She had scarcely gone three steps from the house before she regretted what she had done. She did not care for Mr. Coyshe. She laughed at his peculiarities. She did not be-

lieve, like her father and sister, in his cleverness. But she
saw that his ears and eyes were unduly prominent, and she
was alive to the ridiculous. Mr. Coyshe was more to her
fancy than most of the young men of the neighbourhood,
who talked of nothing but sport, and who would grow with
advancing age to talk of sport and rates, and beyond rates
would not grow. Eve was not fond of hunting. Barbara
rarely went after the hounds, Eve never. She did not love
horse exercise ; she preferred sauntering in the woods and
lanes, gathering autumn-tinted blackberry leaves, to a run
over the downs after a fox. Perhaps hunting required too
much exertion for her : Eve did not care for exertion. She
made dolls' clothes still, at the age of seventeen ; she
played on the piano and sang ; she collected leaves and
flowers for posies. That was all Eve cared to do. Whatever she did she did it listlessly, because nothing thoroughly
interested her. Yet she felt that there might be things
which were not to be encountered at Morwell that would
stir her heart and make her pulses bound. In a word, she
had an artistic nature, and the world in which she moved
was a narrow and inartistic world. Her proper faculties
were unevoked. Her true nature slept.

The hoot of an owl, followed by a queer little face peeping at her from behind a pine. She did not at once re-
cognise Watt, as her mind was occupied with her engagement to Mr. Coyshe.

Now at the very moment Watt showed himself her
freakish mind had swerved from a position of disgust at
her engagement, into one of semi-content with it. Mr.
Coyshe was going to London, and there she would be free
to enjoy herself after her own fashion, in seeing plays,
hearing operas, going to all the sights of the great town,
in a life of restless pleasure-seeking, and that was exactly
what Eve desired.

Watt looked woe-begone. He crept from behind the
tree. His impudence and merriment had deserted him.
Tears came into his eyes as he spoke.

'Are they all gone?' he asked, looking cautiously about.

'Whom do you mean?'

'The police.'

'Yes, they have left Morwell. I do not know whither. Whether they are searching for your brother or have given up the search I cannot say. What keeps you here?'

'O Miss Eve! poor Martin is not far off. It would not do for him to run far. He is in hiding at no great distance, and—he has nothing to eat.'

'Where is he? What can I do?' asked Eve, frightened.

'He is in an old mine. He will not be discovered there. Even if the constables found the entrance, which is improbable, they would not take him, for he would retreat into one of the side passages and escape by an airhole in another part of the wood.'

'I will try what I can do. I dare say I might smuggle some food away from the house and put it behind the hedge, whence you could fetch it.'

'That is not enough. He must get away.'

'There is Jasper's horse still with us. I will ask Jasper, and you can have that.'

'No,' answered the boy, 'that will not do. We must not take the road this time. We must try the water.'

'We have a boat,' said Eve, 'but papa would never allow it to be used.'

'Your papa will know nothing about it, nor the prudent Barbara, nor the solemn Jasper. You can get the key and let us have the boat.'

'I will do what I can, but'—as a sudden thought struck her—'Martin must let me have my ring again. I want it so much. My father has been asking for it.'

'How selfish you are!' exclaimed the boy reproachfully. 'Thinking of your own little troubles when a vast danger menaces our dear Martin. Come with me. You must see Martin and ask him yourself for that ring. I dare not speak of it; he values that ring above everything. You must plead for it yourself with that pretty mouth and those speaking eyes.'

'I must not; indeed I must not!'

'Why not? You will not be missed. No one will harm you. You should see the poor fellow, to what he is reduced by love for you. Yes, come and see him. He would never have been here, he would have been far away in safety, but he had the desire to see you again.'

'Indeed, I cannot accompany you.'

'Then you must do without the ring.'

'I want my ring again vastly. My father is cross because I have not got it, and I have promised to show it him. How can I keep my promise unless it be restored to me?'

'Come, come!' said the boy impatiently. 'Whilst you are talking you might have got half-way to his den.'

'I will only just speak to him,' said Eve, 'two words, and then run home.'

'To be sure. That will be ample—two words,' sneered the boy, and led the way.

The old mine adit was below the rocks near the river, and at no great distance from the old landing-place, where Jasper had recently constructed a boathouse. The ground about the entrance was thickly strewn with dead leaves, mixed with greenish shale thrown out of the copper mine, and so poisonous that no grass had been able to grow over it, though the mine had probably not been worked for a century or even more. But the mouth of the adit was now completely overgrown with brambles and fringed with ferns. The dogwood, now in flower, had thickly clambered near the entrance wherever the earth was not impregnated with copper and arsenic.

Eve shrank from the black entrance and hung back, but the boy caught her by the arm and insisted on her coming with him. She surmounted some broken masses of rock that had fallen before the entrance, and brushed aside the dogwood and briars. The air struck chill and damp against her brow as she passed out of the sun under the stony arch.

The rock was lichened. White-green fungoid growths hung down in streamers; the floor was dry, though water dripped from the sides and nourished beds of velvet moss as far in as the light penetrated. So much rubble covered the bottom of the adit, that the water filtered through it and passed by a subterranean channel to the river.

After taking a few steps forward, Eve saw Martin half sitting, half lying on a bed of fern and heather; the grey light from the entrance fell on his face. It was pale and drawn; but he brightened up when he saw Eve, and he started to his knee to salute her.

'I cannot stand upright in this cursed hole,' he said, 'but at this moment it matters not. On my knee I do homage to my queen.' He seized her hand and pressed his lips to it.

'Here you see me,' he said, 'doomed to shiver in this pit, catching my death of rheumatism.'

'You will surely soon get away,' said Eve. 'I am very sorry for you. I must go home, I may not stay.'

'What! leave me now that you have appeared as a sunbeam, shining into this abyss to glorify it! Oh, no— stay a few minutes, and then I shall remain and dream of the time you were here. Look at my companions.' He pointed to the roof, where curious lumps like compacted cobwebs hung down. 'These are bats, asleep during the day. When night falls they will begin to stir and shake their wings, and scream, and fly out. Shall I have to sleep in this den, with the hideous creatures crying and flapping about my head?'

'Oh, that will be dreadful! But surely you will leave this when night comes on?'

'Yes, if you will help me to get away.'

'I will furnish you with the key to the boathouse. I will hide it somewhere, and then your brother can find it.'

'That will not satisfy me. You must bring the key here.'

'Why? I cannot do that.'

'Indeed you must; I cannot live without another glimpse of your sweet face. Peter was released by an angel. It shall be the same with Martin.'

'I will bring you the key,' said Eve nervously, 'if you will give me back my ring.'

'Your ring!' exclaimed Martin; 'never! Go—call the myrmidons of justice and deliver me into their hands.'

'I would not do that for the world,' said Eve with tears in her eyes; 'I will do everything that I can to help you. Indeed, last night, I got into dreadful trouble by dressing up and playing my tambourine and dancing to attract the attention of the men, whilst you were escaping from the corn-chamber. Papa was very angry and excited, and Barbara was simply—dreadful. I have been scolded and made most unhappy. Do, in pity, give me up the ring. My papa has asked for it. You have already got me into another trouble, because I had not the ring. I was obliged to promise to marry Doctor Coyshe just to pacify papa, he was so excited about the ring.'

'What! engaged yourself to another?'

'I was forced into it, to-day, I tell you—because I had not got the ring. Give it me. I want to get out of my engagement, and I cannot without that.'

'And I—it is not enough that I should be hunted as a hare—my heart must be broken! Walter! where are you? Come here and listen to me. Never trust a woman. Curse the whole sex for its falseness and its selfishness. There is no constancy in this world.' And he sighed and looked reproachfully at Eve. 'After all I have endured and suffered—for you.'

Eve's tears flowed. Martin's attitude, tone of voice, were pathetic and moved her. 'I am very sorry,' she said, 'but—I never gave you the ring. You snatched it

from me. You are unknown to me, I am nothing to you,
and you are—you are——'

'Yes, speak out the bitter truth. I am a thief, a runaway convict, a murderer. Use every offensive epithet
that occurs in your vocabulary. Give a dog a bad name
and hang him. I ought to have known the sex better
than to have trusted you. But I loved, I was blinded by
passion. I saw an angel face, and blue eyes that promised a heaven of tenderness and truth. I saw, I loved,
I trusted—and here I am, a poor castaway ship, lying
ready to be broken up and plundered by wreckers. O the
cruel, faithless sex! We men, with our royal trust, our
splendid self-sacrifice, become a ready prey ; and when we
are down, the laughing heartless tyrants dance over us.
When the lion was sick the ass came and kicked him. It
was the last indignity the royal beast could endure, he
laid his head between his paws and his heart brake. Leave
me—leave me to die.'

'O Martin!' said Eve, quite overcome by his great-
ness, and the vastness of his devotion, 'I have never hurt
you, never offended you. You are like my papa, and have
fancies.'

'I have fancies. Yes, you are right, terribly right. I
have had my fancies. I have lived in a delusion. I believed in the honesty of those eyes. I trusted your word——'

'I never gave you a word.'

'Do not interrupt me. I *did* suppose that your heart
had surrendered to me. The delusion is over. The heart
belongs to a vulgar village apothecary. That heart which
I so treasured ——' his voice shook and broke, and Eve
sobbed. 'Who brought the police upon me?' he went on.
'It was you, whom I loved and trusted, you who possess
an innocent face and a heart full of guile. And here I lie,
your victim, in a living grave your cruel hands have
scooped out for me in the rock.'

'O—indeed, this mine was dug hundreds of years ago.'

He turned a reproachful look at her, 'Why do you

interrupt me? I speak metaphorically. You brought me
to this, and if you have a spark of good feeling in your
breast you will get me away from here.'

'I will bring you the key as soon as the sun sets.'

'That is right. I accept the token of penitence with
gladness, and hope for day in the heart where the light
dawns.'

'I must go—I really must go,' she said.

He bowed grandly to her, with his hand on his heart.

'Come,' said Watt. 'I will help you over these rubbish heaps. You have had your two words.'

'O stay!' exclaimed Eve, 'my ring! I came for that
and I have not got it. I must indeed, indeed have it.'

'Eve,' said Martin, 'I have been disappointed, and
have spoken sharply of the sex. But I am not the man
to harbour mistrust. Deceived I have been, and perhaps
am now laying myself open to fresh disappointment. I
cannot say. I cannot go against my nature, which is
frank and trustful. There—take your ring. Come back
to me this evening with it and the key, and prove to
me that all women are not false, that all confidence placed
in them is not misplaced.'

CHAPTER XLIV.

TUCKERS.

BARBARA sat in the little oak parlour, a pretty room that
opened out of the hall; indeed it had originally been a
portion of the hall, which was constructed like a letter
L. The hall extended to the roof, but the branch at right
angles was not half the height. It was ceiled about ten
feet from the floor, and instead of being, like the hall,
paved with slate, had oak boards. The window looked
into the garden. Mr. Jordan's father had knocked away
the granite mullions, and put in a sash-window, out of

keeping with the room and house, but agreeable to the
taste of the period, and admitting more light. A panelled
division cut the room off from the hall. Barbara and Eve
could not agree about the adornment of this apartment.
On the walls were a couple of oil paintings, and Barbara
supplemented them with framed and glazed mezzotints.
She could not be made by her sister to see the incon-
gruity of engravings and oil paintings hanging side by
side on dark oak panels. On the chimney-piece was a
French ormolu clock, which was Eve's detestation. It
was badly designed and unsuitable for the room. So was
the banner-screen of a poodle resting on a red cushion;
so were the bugle mats on the table; so were the antima-
cassars on all the arm-chairs and over the back of the
sofa; so were some drawing-room chairs purchased by
Barbara, with curved legs, and rails that were falling out
periodically. Barbara thought these chairs handsome,
Eve detestable. The chimney-piece ornaments, the vases
of pale green glass illuminated with flowers, were also
objects of aversion to one sister and admiration to the
other. Eve at one time refused to make posies for the
vases in the parlour, and was always protesting against
some new introduction by her sister, which violated the
principles of taste.

'I don't like to live in a dingy old hall like this,' Eve
would say; 'but I like a place to be fitted up in keeping
with its character.'

Barbara was now seated in this debatable ground. Eve
was out somewhere, and she was alone and engaged with
her needle. Her father, in the next room, was dozing.
Then to the open window came Jasper, leaned his arms
on the sill—the sash was up—and looked in at Barbara.

'Hard at work as usual?' he said.

She smiled and nodded, and looked at him, holding
her needle up, with a long white thread in it.

'On what engaged I dare not ask,' said Jasper.

'You may know,' she said, laughing. 'Sewing in

tuckers. I always sew tuckers on Saturdays, both for
myself and for Eve.'

' And, pray, what are tuckers ? '

' Tuckers '—she hesitated to find a suitable description,
' tuckers are—well, tuckers.' She took a neck of a dress
which she had finished and put it round her throat. 'Now
you see. Now you understand. Tuckers are the garnishing, like parsley to a dish.'

' And compliments to speech. So you do Eve's as well
as your own.'

'O dear, yes ; Eve cannot be trusted. She would forget all about them and wear dirty tuckers.'

' But she worked hard enough burnishing the brass
necklace.'

' O yes, that shone ! tuckers are simply—clean.'

' My Lady Eve should have a lady's-maid.'

' Not whilst I am with her. I do all that is needful
for her. When she marries she must have one, as she is
helpless.'

' You think Eve will marry ? '

' O yes ! It is all settled. She has consented.'

He was a little surprised. This had come about very
suddenly, and Eve was young.

' I am glad you are here,' said Barbara, ' only you have
taken an unfair advantage of me.'

· I Barbara ? '

' Yes, Jasper, you.' She looked up into his face with
a heightened colour. He had never called her by her
plain Christian name before, nor had she thus addressed
him, but their hearts understood each other, and a formal
title would have been an affectation on either side.

' I will tell you why,' said the girl ; ' so do not put on
such a puzzled expression. I want to speak to you
seriously about a matter that—that—well, Jasper, that
makes me wish you had your face in the light and mine in
the shade. Where you stand the glare of the sky is behind
you, and you can see every change in my face, and that

unnerves me. Either you shall come in here, take my
place at the tuckers, and let me talk to you through the
window, or else I shall move my chair close to the window,
and sit with my back to it, and we can talk without watching each other's face.'

'Do that, Barbara. I cannot venture on the tuckers.'

So, laughing nervously, and with her colour changing
in her cheeks, and her lips twitching, she drew her chair
close to the window, and seated herself, not exactly with
her back to it, but sideways, and turned her face from it.

The ground outside was higher than the floor of the
parlour, so that Jasper stood above her, and looked down
somewhat, not much, on her head, her dark hair so neat
and glossy, and smoothly parted. He stooped to the
mignonette bed and gathered some of the fragrant delicate
little trusses of colourless flowers, and with a slight apology
thrust two or three among her dark hair.

'Putting in tuckers,' he said. 'Garnishing the sweetest
of heads with the plant that to my mind best symbolises
Barbara.'

'Don't,' she exclaimed, shaking her head, but not
shaking the sprigs out of her hair. 'You are taking un-
warrantable liberties, Mr. Jasper.'

'I will take no more.' He folded his arms on the sill.
She did not see, but she felt, the flood of love that poured
over her bowed head from his eyes. She worked very hard
fastening off a thread at the end of a tucker.

'I also,' said Jasper, 'have been desirous of a word
with you, Barbara.'

She turned, looked up in his face, then bent her head
again over her work. The flies, among them a great blue-
bottle, were humming in the window; the latter bounced
against the glass, and was too stupid to come down and go
out at the open sash.

'We understand each other,' said Jasper, in a low voice,
as pleasant and soft as the murmur of the flies. 'There
are songs without words, and there is speech without

voice : what I have thought and felt you know, though I have not told you anything, and I think I know also what you think and feel. Now, however, it is as well that we should come to plain words.'

'Yes, Jasper, I think so as well, that is why I have come over here with my tuckers.'

'We know each other's heart,' he said, stooping in over her head and the garnishing of mignonette, and speaking as low as a whisper, not really in a whisper but in his natural warm, rich voice. 'There is this, dear Barbara, about me. My name, my family, are dishonoured by the thoughtless, wrongful act of my poor brother. I dare not ask you to share that name with me, not only on this ground, but also because I am absolutely penniless. A great wrong has been done to your father and sister by us, and it does not become me to ask the greatest and richest of gifts from your family. Hereafter I may inherit my father's mill at Buckfastleigh. When I do I will, as I have undertaken, fully repay the debt to your sister, but till I can do that I may not ask for more. You are, and must be, to me a far-off, unapproachable star, to whom I look up, whom I shall ever love and stretch my hands towards.'

'I am not a star at all,' said Barbara, 'and as for being far off and unapproachable, you are talking nonsense, and you do not mean it or you would not have stuck bits of mignonette in my hair. I do not understand rhodomontade.'

Jasper laughed. He liked her downright, plain way. 'I am quoting a thought from " Preciosa,"' he said.

'I know nothing of " Preciosa," save that it is something Eve strums.'

'Well—divest what I have said of all exaggeration of simile, you understand what I mean.'

'And I want you to understand my position exactly, Jasper,' she said. 'I also am penniless. The money my aunt left me I have made over to Eve because she could

not marry Mr. Coyshe without something present, as well
as a prospect of something to come.'

' What ! sewn your poor little legacy in as a tucker to
her wedding gown ? '

' Mr. Coyshe wants to go to London, he is lost here ;
and Eve would be happy in a great city, she mopes in the
country. So I have consented to this arrangement. I do
not want the money as I live here with my father, and it
is a real necessity for Eve and Mr. Coyshe. You see—I
could not do other.'

' And when your father dies, Morwell also passes to
Eve. What is left for you ? '

' Oh, I shall do very well. Mr. Coyshe and Eve would
never endure to live here. By the time dear papa is called
away Mr. Coyshe will have made himself a name, be a
physician, and rolling in money. Perhaps he and Eve
may like to run here for their short holiday and breathe
our pure air, but otherwise they will not occupy the place,
and I thought I might live on here and manage for them.
Then '—she turned her cheek and Jasper saw a glitter on
the long dark lash, but at the same time the dimple of a
smile on her cheek—' then, dear friend '—she put up her
hand on the sill, and he caught it—' then, dear friend,
perhaps you will not mind helping me. Then probably your
little trouble will be over.' She was silent, thinking, and
he saw the dimple go out of her smooth cheek, and the
sparkling drop fall from the lash on that cheek. ' All is
in God's hand,' she said. ' We do wrong to look forward ;
I shall be happy to leave it so, and wait and trust.'

Then he put the other hand which did not clasp hers
under her chin, and tried to raise her face, but he could
only reach her brow with his lips and kiss it. He said not
one word.

' You do not answer,' she said.

' I cannot,' he replied.

Then the door was thrown open and Eve entered,
flushed, and holding up her finger.

'Look, Bab!—look, dear! I have my ring again. Now I can shake off that doctor.'

'O Eve!' gasped Barbara; 'the ring! where did you get it?' She turned sharply to Jasper. 'She has seen him—your brother Martin—again.'

Eve was, for a moment, confused, but only for a moment. She recovered herself and said merrily, 'Why, Barbie dear, however did you get that crown of mignonette in your hair? You never stuck it there yourself. You would not dream of such a thing; besides, your arm is not long enough to reach the flower-bed. Jasper! confess you have been doing this.' She clasped her hands and danced. 'O what fun!' she exclaimed: 'but really it is a shame of me interfering when Barbara is so busy with the tuckers, and Jasper in garnishing Barbara's head.' Then she bounded out of the room, leaving her sister in confusion.

CHAPTER XLV.

DUCK AND GREEN PEAS.

EVE might evade an explanation by turning the defence into an attack when first surprised, but she was unable to resist a determined onslaught, and when Barbara followed her and parried all her feints, and brought her to close quarters, Eve was driven to admit that she had seen Martin, who was in concealment in the wood, and that she had undertaken to furnish him with food and the boat-house key. Jasper was taken into consultation, and promised to seek his brother and provide for him what was necessary, but neither he nor Barbara could induce her to remain at home and not revisit the fugitive.

'I know that Jasper will not find the place without me,' she said. 'Watt only discovered it by his prowling about as a weasel. I must go with Mr. Jasper, but I promise you, Barbie, it shall be for the last time.' There was reason in her argument, and Barbara was forced to acquiesce.

Accordingly in the evening, not before, the two set out for the mine, Eve carrying some provisions in a basket. Jasper was much annoyed that his brother was still in the neighbourhood, and still causing trouble to the sisters at Morwell.

Eve had shown her father the ring. The old man was satisfied ; he took it, looked hard at it, slipped it on his little finger, and would not surrender it again. Eve must explain this to Martin if he redemanded the ring, which he was like enough to do.

Neither she nor Jasper spoke much to each other on the way ; he had his thoughts occupied, and she was not easy in her mind. As they approached the part of the wood where the mine shaft was, she began to sing the song in 'Don Giovanni,' *Là ci darem,* as a signal to Watt that friends drew nigh through the bushes. On entering the adit they found Martin in an ill humour. He had been without food for many hours, and was moreover suffering from an attack of rheumatism.

'I said as much this morning, Eve,' he growled. 'I knew this hateful hole would make me ill, and here I am in agonies. Oh, it is of no use your bringing me the key of the boat ; *I* can't go on the water with knives running into my back, and, what is more, I can't stick in this hateful burrow. How many hours on the water down to Plymouth ? I can't even think of it ; I should have rheumatic fever. I'd rather be back in jail—there I suppose they would give me hot-bottles and blankets. And this, too, when I had prepared such a treat for Eve. Curse it ! I'm always thinking of others, and getting into pickles myself accordingly.'

'Why, pray, what were you scheming to do for Miss Eve ? ' asked Jasper.

'O, the company I was with for a bit is at Plymouth, and are performing Weber's new piece, " Preciosa," and I thought I'd like to show it to her—and then the manager, Justice Barret, knows about her mother. When I told him of my escape, and leaving you at Morwell, he said that he had left one of his company there named Eve. I thought it would be a pleasure to the young lady to meet him, and hear what he had to tell of her mother.'

'And you intended to carry Eve off with you?'

'I intended to persuade her to accompany me. Perhaps she will do so still, when I am better.'

Jasper was angry, and spoke sharply to his brother. Martin turned on his bed of fern and heather, and groaning, put his hands over his ears.

'Come,' said he, 'Watt, give me food. I can't stand scolding on an empty stomach, and with aches in my bones.'

He was impervious to argument; remonstrance he resented. Jasper took the basket from Eve, and gave him what he required. He groaned and cried out as Watt raised him in his arms. Martin looked at Eve, appealing for sympathy. He was a martyr, a guiltless sufferer, and not spared even by his brother.

'I think, Martin,' said Jasper, 'that if you were well wrapped in blankets you might still go in the boat.'

'You seem vastly eager to be rid of me,' answered Martin peevishly, 'but, I tell you, I will not go. I'm not going to jeopardise my life on the river in the fogs and heavy dews to relieve you from anxiety. How utterly and unreasonably selfish you are! If there be one vice which is despicable, it is selfishness. I repeat, I won't go, and I won't stay in this hole. You must find some safe and warm place in which to stow me. I throw all responsibilities on you. I wish I had never escaped from jail—I have been sinking ever since I left it. There I had a dry cell and food. From that I went to the corn-chamber at Morwell, which was dry—but, faugh! how it stank of onions! Now I have this damp dungeon that smells of mould. Watt and you got me out of prison, and got me away from the warders and constables, so you must provide for me now. I have nothing more to do with it. If you take a responsibility on you, my doctrine is, go through with it; don't take it up and drop it half finished. What news of that fellow I shot? Is he dead?'

'No—wounded, but not dangerously.'

'There, then, why should I fear? I was comfortable in jail. I had my meals regularly there, and was not subjected to damp. I trust my country would have cared for me better than my brothers, who give me at one time onions for a pillow, and at another heather for a bed.'

'My dear Martin,' said Jasper, 'I think if you try you can walk up the road; there is a woodman's hut among the trees near the Raven Rock, but concealed in the coppice. It is warm and dry, and no one will visit it whilst the leaves are on the trees. The workmen keep their tools there, and their dinners, when shredding in winter or rending in spring. You will be as safe there as here, and so much nearer Morwell that we shall be able easily to furnish you with necessaries till you are better, and can escape to Plymouth.'

'I'm not sure that it is wise for me to try to get to Plymouth. The police will be on the look-out for me there, and they will not dream that I have stuck here—this is the last place where they would suppose I stayed. Besides, I have no money. No; I will wait till the company move away from the county, and I will rejoin it at Bridgewater, or Taunton, or Dorchester. Justice Barret is a worthy fellow; a travelling company can't always command such abilities as mine, so the accommodation is mutual.'

Martin was assisted out of the mine. He groaned, cried out, and made many signs of distress; he really was suffering, but he made the most of his suffering. Jasper stood on one side of him. He would not hear of Walter sustaining him on the other side; he must have Eve as his support, and he could only support himself on her by putting his arm over her shoulders. No objections raised by Jasper were of avail. Watt was not tall enough. Watt's steps were irregular. Watt was required to go on ahead and see that no one was in the way. Martin was certainly a very handsome man. He wore a broad-brimmed hat, and fair long hair; his eyes were dark and large, his features regular, his complexion pale and interesting. Seeing that Jasper looked at his hair with surprise, he laughed, and leaning his head towards him whispered, 'Those rascals at Prince's Town cropped me like a Puritan. I wear a theatrical wig before the sex, till my hair grows again.'

Then leaning heavily on Eve, he bent his head to her ear, and made a complimentary remark which brought the colour into her cheek.

'Jasper,' said he, turning his head again to his brother, 'mind this, I cannot put up with cyder; I am racked with rheumatism, and I must have generous drink. I suppose your father's cellar is well stocked?' He addressed Eve. 'You will see that the poor invalid is not starved, and has not his vitals wrung with vinegar. I have seen ducks about Morwell; what do you say to duck with onion stuffing for dinner to-morrow—and tawny port, eh? I'll let you both into another confidence. I am not going to lie on bracken. By hook or by crook you must contrive to bring me out a feather bed. If I've not one, and a bolster and pillow and blankets—by George and the dragon! I'll give myself up to the beaks.'

Then he moaned, and squeezed Eve's shoulder.

'Green peas,' he said when the paroxysm was over. 'Duck and green peas; I shall dine off that to-morrow—and tell the cook not to forget the mint. Also some carrot sliced, boiled, then fried in Devonshire cream, with a little shallot cut very fine and toasted, sprinkled on top. 'Sweetheart,' aside to Eve into her ear, 'you shall come and have a snack with me. Remember, it is an invitation. We will not have old solemn face with us as a mar-fun, shall we?'

The woodman's hut when reached after a slow ascent was found to be small, warm, and in good condition. It was so low that a man could not stand upright in it, but it was sufficiently long to allow him to lie his length therein. The sides were of wattled oak branches, compacted with heather and moss, and the roof was of turf. The floor was dry, deep bedded in fern.

'It is a dog's kennel,' said the dissatisfied Martin; 'or rather it is not so good as that. It is the sort of place made for swans and geese and ducks beside a pond, for shelter when they lay their eggs. It really is humiliating that I should have to bury my head in a sort of water-fowl's sty.'

Eve promised that Martin should have whatever he desired. Jasper had, naturally, a delicacy in offering anything beyond his own services, though he knew he could rely on Barbara.

When they had seen the exhausted and anguished martyr gracefully reposing on the bracken bed, to rest after his painful walk, and had already left, they were recalled by his voice shouting to Jasper, regardless of every consideration that should have kept him quiet, 'Don't be a fool, Jasper, and shake the bottle. If you break the crust I won't drink it.' And again the call came, 'Mind the green peas.'

As Jasper and Eve walked back to Morwell neither spoke much, but on reaching the last gate, Eve said—

'O, dear Mr. Jasper, do help me to persuade Barbie to let me go! I have made up my mind; I must and will see the play and hear all that the manager can tell me about my mother.'

'I will go to Plymouth, Miss Eve. I must see this Mr. Justice Barret, and I will learn every particular for you.'

'That is not enough. I want to see a play. I have never been to a theatre in all my life.'

'I will see what your sister says.'

'I am obstinate. I shall go, whether she says yes or no.'

'To-morrow is Sunday,' said Jasper, 'when no theatre is open.'

'Besides,' added Eve, 'there is poor Martin's duck and green peas to-morrow.'

'And crusted port. If we go, it must be Monday.'

CHAPTER XLVI.

'PRECIOSA.'

Eve had lost something of her light-heartedness; in spite of herself she was made to think, and grave alternatives were forced upon her for decision. The careless girl was dragged in opposite directions by two men, equally selfish and conceited, the one prosaic and clever, the other æsthetic but ungifted; each actuated by the coarsest self-seeking, neither regarding the happiness of the child. Martin had a passionate fancy for her, and had formed some fantastic scheme of turning her into a singer and an actress; and Mr. Coyshe thought of pushing his way in town by the aid of her money.

Eve was without any strength of character, but she had obstinacy, and where her pleasure was concerned she could be very obstinate. Hitherto she had not been required to act with independence. She had submitted in most things to the will of her father and sister, but then their will had been to give her pleasure and save her annoyance. She had learned always to get her own way by an exhibition of peevishness if crossed.

Now she had completely set her heart on going to Plymouth. She was desirous to know something about her mother, as her father might not be questioned concerning her; and she burned with eagerness to see a play. It would be hard to say which motive predominated. One alone might have been beaten down by Barbara's opposition, but two plaited in and out together made so tough a string that it could not be broken. Barbara did what she could, but her utmost was unavailing. Eve had sufficient shrewdness to insist on her desire to see and converse with a friend of her mother, and to say as little as possible about her other motive. Barbara could appreciate one, she would see no force in the other.

Eve carried her point. Barbara consented to her going under the escort of Jasper. They were to ride to Beer Ferris and thence take boat. They were not to stay in Plymouth, but return the same way. The tide was favourable; they would probably be home by three o'clock in the morning, and Barbara would sit up for them. It was important that Mr. Jordan should know nothing of the expedition, which would greatly excite him. As for Martin, she would provide for him, though she could not undertake to find him duck and green peas and crusted port every day.

One further arrangement was made. Eve was engaged to Mr. Coyshe, therefore the young doctor was to be invited to join Eve and Jasper at Beer Alston, and accompany her to Plymouth. A note was despatched to him to prepare him, and to ask him to have a boat in readiness, and to allow of the horses being put in his stables.

Thus, everything was settled, if not absolutely in accordance with Eve's wishes—she objected to the company of the doctor—yet sufficiently so to make her happy. Her happiness became greater as the time approached for her departure, and when she left she was in as joyful a mood as any in which Barbara had ever seen her.

Everything went well. The weather was fine, and the air and landscape pleasant; not that Eve regarded either as she rode to Beer Alston. There the tiresome surgeon joined her and Jasper, and insisted on giving them refreshments. Eve was impatient to be on her way again, and was hardly civil in her refusal; but the harness of self-conceit was too dense over the doctor's breast for him to receive a wound from her light words.

In due course Plymouth was reached, and, as there was time to spare, Eve, by her sister's directions, went to a convent, where were some nuns of their acquaintance, and stayed there till fetched by the two young men to go with them to the theatre. Jasper had written before and secured tickets.

At last Eve sat in a theatre—the ambition, the dream of her youth was gratified. She occupied a stall between Jasper and Mr. Coyshe, a place that commanded the house, but was also conspicuous.

Eve sat looking speechlessly about her, lost in astonishment at the novelty of all that surrounded her; the decorations of white and gold, the crimson curtains, the chandelier of glittering glass-drops, the crowd of well-dressed ladies, the tuning of the instruments of the orchestra, the glare of light, were to her an experience so novel that she felt she would have been content to come all the way for that alone. That she herself was an object of notice, that opera-glasses were turned upon her, never occurred to her. Fond as she was of admiration, she was too engrossed in admiring to think that she was admired.

A hush. The conductor had taken his place and raised his wand. Eve was startled by the sudden lull, and the lowering of the lights.

Then the wand fell, and the overture began. 'Preciosa' had been performed in London the previous season for the first time, and now, out of season, it was taken to the provinces. The house was very full. A military orchestra played.

Eve knew the overture arranged for the piano, for Jasper had introduced her to it; she had admired it; but what was a piano arrangement to a full orchestra? Her eye sparkled, a brilliant colour rushed into her cheek. This was something more beautiful than she could have conceived. The girl's soul was full of musical appreciation, and she had been kept for seventeen years away from the proper element in which she could live.

Then the curtain rose, and disclosed the garden of Don Carcamo at Madrid. Eve could hardly repress an exclamation of astonishment. She saw a terrace with marble statues, and a fountain of water playing, the crystal drops sparkling as they fell. Umbrageous trees on both sides threw their foliage overhead and met, forming a succession of bowery arches. Roses and oleanders bloomed at the sides. Beyond the terrace extended a distant landscape of rolling woodland and corn fields threaded by a blue winding river. Far away in the remote distance rose a range of snow-clad mountains.

Eve held up her hands, drew a long breath and sighed, not out of sadness, but out of ecstasy of delight.

Don Fernando de Azevedo, in black velvet and lace, was taking leave of Don Carcamo, and informing him that he would have left Madrid some days ago had he not been induced to stay and see Preciosa, the gipsy girl about whom the town was talking. Then entered Alonzo, the son of Don Carcamo, enthusiastic over the beauty, talent, and virtue of the maiden.

Eve listened with eager eyes and ears, she lost not a word, she missed not a motion. Everything she saw was real to her. This was true Spain, yonder was the Sierra Nevada. For aught she considered, these were true hidalgoes. She forgot she was in a theatre, she forgot everything, her own existence, in her absorption. Only one thought obtruded itself on her connecting the real with the fictitious. Martin ought to have stood there as Alonzo, in that becoming costume.

Then the orchestra played softly, sweetly—she knew the air, drew another deep inspiration, her flush deepened. Over the stage swept a crowd of gentlemen and ladies, and a motley throng singing in chorus. Then came in gipsies with tambourines and castanets, and through the midst of them Preciosa in a crimson velvet bodice and saffron skirt, wearing a necklace of gold chains and coins.

Eve put her hands over her mouth to check the cry of

astonishment ; the dress—she knew it—it was that she
had found in the chest. It was that, or one most similar.

Eve hardly breathed as Preciosa told the fortunes of
Don Carcamo and Don Fernando. She saw the love of
Alonzo kindled, and Alonzo she had identified with Martin.
She—she herself was Preciosa. Had she not worn that
dress, rattled that tambourine, danced the same steps?
The curtain fell ; the first act was over, and the hum of
voices rose. But Eve heard nothing. Mr. Coyshe endeavoured to engage her in conversation, but in vain. She
was in a trance, lifted above the earth in ecstasy. She was
Preciosa, she lived under a Spanish sun. This was her
world, this real life. No other world was possible hence-
forth, no other life endurable. She had passed out of a
condition of surprise ; nothing could surprise her more,
she had risen out of a sphere where surprise was possible
into one where music, light, colour, marvel were the proper
atmosphere.

The most prodigious marvels occur in dreams and excite no astonishment. Eve had passed into ecstatic dream.

The curtain rose, and the scene was forest, with rocks,
and the full moon shining out of the dark blue sky, silver-
ing the trunks of the trees and the mossy stones. A gipsy
camp ; the gipsies sang a chorus with echo. The captain
smote with hammer on a stone and bade his men prepare
for a journey to Valencia. The gipsies dispersed, and then
Preciosa appeared, entering from the far background, with
the moonlight falling on her, subduing to low tones her
crimson and yellow, holding a guitar in her hands. She
seated herself on a rock, and the moonbeams played about
her as she sang and accompanied herself on her instrument.

> Lone am I, yet am not lonely,
>   For I see thee, loved and true,
> Round me flits thy form, thine only,
>   Moonlit gliding o'er the dew.

> Wander where I may, or tarry,
>   Hangs my heart alone on thee,
> Ever in my breast I carry
>   Thoughts that burn and torture me.

Unattainable and peerless
　In my heaven a constant star,
Heart o'erflowing, eyes all tearless,
　Gaze I on thee from afar.

The exquisite melody, the pathos of the scene, the poetry of the words, were more than Eve could bear, and tears rolled down her cheeks. Mr. Coyshe looked round in surprise; he heard her sob, and asked if she were tired or unwell. No! she sobbed out of excess of happiness. The combined beauty of scene and song oppressed her heart with pain, the pain of delight greater than the heart could contain.

Eve saw Alonzo come, disguised as a hunter, having abandoned his father, his rank, his prospects, for love of Preciosa. Was not this like Martin?—Martin the heroic, the self-sacrificing man who rushed into peril that he might be at her feet—Martin, now laid up with rheumatism for her sake.

She saw the gipsies assemble, their tents were taken down, bales were collected, all was prepared for departure. Alonzo was taken into the band and fellowship was sworn.

The moon had set, but see—what is this? A red light smites betwixt the trees and kindles the trunks orange and scarlet, the rocks are also flushed, and simultaneously with a burst, joyous, triumphant, the whole band sing the chorus of salutation to the rising sun. Preciosa is exalted on a litter and is borne on the shoulders of the gipsies. The light brightens, the red blaze pervades, transforms the entire scene, bathes every actor in fire; the glorious song swells and thrills every heart, and suddenly, when it seemed to Eve that she could bear no more, the curtain fell. She sprang to her feet, unconscious of everything but what she had seen and heard, and the whole house rose with her and roared its applause and craved for more.

It is unnecessary for us to follow Eve's emotions through the entire drama, and to narrate the plot, to say how that the gipsies arrive at the castle of Don Fernando where he is celebrating his silver wedding, how his son Eugenio, by an impertinence offered to Preciosa, exasperates the disguised Alonzo into striking him, and is arrested, how Preciosa intercedes, and how it is discovered that she is the daughter of Don Fernando, stolen seventeen years before. The reader may possibly know the drama; if he does not, his loss is not much; it is a drama of little merit and no originality, which would never have lived had not Weber furnished it with a few scraps of incomparably beautiful music.

The curtain fell, the orchestra departed, the boxes were emptying. All those in the stalls around Eve were in movement. She gave a long sigh and woke out of her dream, looked round at Jasper, then at Mr. Coyshe, and smiled; her eyes were dazed, she was not fully awake.

'Very decent performance,' said the surgeon, 'but we shall see something better in London.'

'Well, Eve,' said Jasper, 'are you ready? I will ask for the manager, and then we must be pushing home.'

'Home!' repeated Eve, and repeated it questioningly.

'Yes,' answered Jasper, 'have you forgotten the row up the river and the ride before us?'

She put her hand to her head.

'Oh, Jasper,' she said, 'I feel as if I were at home now—here, where I ought always to have been, and was going again into banishment.'

CHAPTER XLVII.

NOAH'S ARK.

JASPER left Eve with Mr. Coyshe whilst he went in quest of the manager. He had written to Mr. Justice Barret as soon as it was decided that the visit was to be made, so as to prepare him for an interview, but there had not been

time for a reply. The surgeon was to order a supper at
the inn. A few minutes later Jasper came to them. He
had seen the manager, who was then engaged, but re-
quested that they would shortly see him in his rooms at
the inn. Time was precious, the little party had a journey
before them. They therefore hastily ate their meal, and
when Eve was ready, Jasper accompanied her to the apart-
ments occupied by the manager. Mr. Coyshe was left over
the half-consumed supper, by no means disposed, as it had
to be paid for, to allow so much of it to depart uneaten.

Jasper knocked at the door indicated as that to the
rooms occupied by the manager and his family, and on
opening it was met by a combination of noises that bewildered, and of odours that suffocated.

'Come in, I am glad to see you,' said a voice; 'Justice
sent word I was to expect and detain you.'

The manager's wife came forward to receive the visitors.

She was a pretty young woman, with very light frizzled
hair, cut short—a head like that of the 'curly-headed-plough-
boy.' Eve could hardly believe her eyes, this was the real
Preciosa, who on the stage had worn dark flowing hair.
The face was good-humoured, simple, but not clean, for
the paint and powder had been imperfectly washed off. It
adhered at the corners of the eyes and round the nostrils.
Also a ring of white powder lingered on her neck and at
the roots of her hair on her brow.

'Come in,' she said, with a kindly smile that made
pleasant dimples in her cheeks, 'but take care where you
walk. This is my parrot, a splendid bird, look at his green
back and scarlet wing. Awake, old Poll?'

'Does your mother know you're out?' answered the
parrot hoarsely, with the hard eyes fixed on Eve.

The girl turned cold and drew back.

'Look at my Tom,' said Mrs. Justice Barret, 'how he
races round his cage.' She pointed to a squirrel tearing
inanely up the wires of a revolving drum in which he was

confined. ' That is the way in which he greets my return
from the theatre. Mind the cradle! Excuse my dress, I
have been attending to baby.' She rocked vigorously.
' Slyboots, he knows when I come back without opening
his peepers. Sucking your thumb vigorously, are you? I
could eat it—I could eat you, you are sweet as barley-
sugar.' The enthusiastic mother dived with both arms
into the cradle, brought out the child, and hugged it till it
screamed.

' What is Jacko about, I wonder,' said the ex-Preciosa;
' do observe him, sitting in the corner as demure as an old
woman during a sermon. I'll warrant he's been at more
mischief. What do you suppose I have found him out in ?
I was knitting a stocking for Justice, and when the time
came for me to go to the theatre I put the half-finished
stocking with the ball of worsted down in the bed, I mistrusted Jacko. As I dare not leave him in this room with
baby, I locked him into the sleeping apartment. Will you
believe me ? he found what I had concealed. He plunged
into the bed and discovered the stocking and unravelled
the whole; not only so, but he has left his hair on the
sheets, and whatever Justice will say to me and to Jacko I
do not know. Never mind, if he is cross I'll survive it.
Now Jacko, how often have I told you not to bite off the
end of your tail ? The poor fellow is out of health, and
we must not be hard on him.'

The monkey blinked his eyes, and rubbed his nose.
He knew that his delinquencies were being expatiated
on.

' You have not seen all my family yet,' said Mrs.
Barret. ' There is a box of white mice under the bed in the
next room. The darlings are so tame that they will nestle
in my bosom. Do you believe me ? I went once to the
theatre, quite forgetting one was there, till I came to dress,
I mean undress, and then it tumbled out; I missed my
leads that evening, I was distracted lest the mouse should
get away. I told the prompter to keep him till I could

reclaim the rascal. Come in, dears! Come in!' This
was shouted, and a boy and girl burst in at the door.

'My only darlings, these three,' said Mrs. Barret,
pointing to the children and the babe. 'They've been
having some supper. Did you see them on the stage?
They were gipsies. Be quick and slip out of your clothes,
pets, and tumble into bed. Never mind your prayers to-
night. I have visitors, and cannot attend to you. Say
them twice over to-morrow morning instead. What?
Hungry still? Here, Jacko! surrender that crust, and
Polly must give up her lump of sugar; bite evenly between
you.' Then turning to her guests, with her pleasant face
all smiles, 'I love animals! I have been denied a large
family, I have only three, but then—I've not been married
six years. One must love. What would the world be
without love? We are made to love. Do you agree with
me, Jacko, you mischievous little pig? Now—no biting,
Polly! You snapping also?'

Then, to her visitors, 'Take a chair—that is—take
two.'

To her children, 'What, is this manners? Your hat,
Bill, and your frock, Philadelphia, and heaven knows what
other rags of clothes on the only available chairs.' She
swept the children's garments upon the floor, and kicked
them under the table.

'Now then,' to the guests, 'sit down and be comfortable. Justice will be here directly. Barret don't much
like all these animals, but Lord bless your souls! I can't
do without them. My canary died,' she sniffled and wiped
nose and eyes on the back of her hand. 'He got poisoned
by the monkey, I suspect, who fed him on scraps of green
paper picked off the wall. One must love! But it comes
expensive. They make us pay damages wherever we stay.
They charge things to our darlings I swear they never did.
The manager is as meek as Moses, and he bears like a
miller's ass. Here he comes—I know his sweet step.
Don't look at me. I'll sit with my back to you, baby is

fidgety.' Then entered the manager, Mr. Justice Barret, a quiet man with a pasty face.

'That's him,' exclaimed the wife, 'I said so. I knew his step. I adore him. He is a genius. I love him—even his pimples. One must love. Now—don't mind me.' The good-natured creature carried off her baby into a corner, and seated herself with it on a stool : the monkey followed her, knowing that he was not appreciated by the manager, and seated himself beside her, also with his back to the company, and was engrossed in her proceedings with the baby.

Mr. Justice Barret had a bald head, he was twice his wife's age, had a very smooth face shining with soap. His hands were delicate and clean. He wore polished boots, and white cravat, and a well-brushed black frock-coat. How he managed in a menagerie of children and animals to keep himself tidy was a wonder to the company.

'O Barret dear!' exclaimed his lady, looking over her shoulder, and the monkey turned its head at the same time. 'I've had a jolly row with the landlady over that sheet to which I set fire.'

'My dear,' said the manager, 'how often have I urged you not to learn your part on the bed with the candle by your side or in your hand? You will set fire to your precious self some day.'

'About the sheet, Barret,' continued his wife; 'I've paid for it, and have torn it into four. It will make pocket-handkerchiefs for you, dear.'

'Rather large?' asked the manager deferentially

'Rather, but that don't matter. Last longer before coming to the wash, and so save money in the end.'

The manager was now at length able to reach and shake hands with Eve and Jasper.

'Bless me, my dear child,' he said to the former, 'you remind me wonderfully of your mother. How is she? I should like to see her again. A sad pity she ever gave up the profession. She had the instincts of an artiste in her,

but no training, horribly amateurish ; that, however, would
rub off.'

'She is dead,' answered Eve. 'Did you not know
that ? '

'Dead!' exclaimed the manager. 'Poor soul! so
sweet, so simple, so right-minded. Dead, dead ! Ah me !
the angels go to heaven and the sinners are left. Did
she remain with your father, or go home to her own
parents ? '

'I thought,' said Eve, much agitated, ' that you could
have told me concerning her.'

'I !' Mr. Justice Barret opened his eyes wide. ' I I '

'My dear ! ' called Mrs. Barret, ' will you be so good as
to throw me over my apron. I am dressing baby for the
night, and heaven alone knows where his little night-shirt
is. I'll tie him up in this apron.' 'Does your mother
know you're out ? ' asked the parrot with its head on one
side, looking at Eve.

'I think,' said Jasper, ' it would be advisable for me to
have a private talk with you, Mr. Barret, if you do not
mind walking with me in the square, and then Miss Eve
Jordan can see you after. Our time is precious.'

'By all means,' answered the manager, ' if Miss Jordan
will remain with my wife.'

'O yes,' said Eve, looking at the parrot ; she was alarmed
at the bird.

'Do not be afraid of Poll,' said Mr. Barret. Then to
his wife, ' Sophie! I don't think it wise to tie up baby as
you propose. He might be throttled. We are going out.
Look for the night dress, and let me have the apron again
for Polly.'

At once the article required rushed like a rocket through
the air, and struck the manager on the breast.

'There,' said he, ' I will cover Polly, and she will go
to sleep and talk no more.'

Then the manager and Jasper went out.

'Now,' said the latter, ' in few words I beg you to tell

me what you know about the wife of Mr. Jordan of Mor-well. She was my sister.'

'Indeed !—and your name ? I forget what you wrote.'

'My name is Babb, but that matters nothing.'

'I never knew that of your sister. She would not tell whence she came or who she was.'

'From your words just now,' said Jasper, 'I gather that you are unaware that she eloped from Morwell with an actor. I could not speak of this before her daughter.'

'Eloped with an actor !' repeated the manager. 'If she did, it was after I knew her. Excuse me, I cannot be-lieve it. She may have gone home to her father ; he wanted her to return to him.'

'You know that ?'

'Of course I do. He came to me, when I was at Tavi-stock, and learned from me where she was. He went to Morwell to see her once or twice, to induce her to return to him.'

'You must be very explicit,' said Jasper gravely. 'My sister never came home. Neither my father nor I know to this day what became of her.'

'Then she must have remained at Morwell. Her daughter says she is dead.'

'She did not remain at Morwell. She disappeared.'

'This is very extraordinary. I will tell you all I know, but that is not much. She was not with us very long. She fell ill as we were on our way from Plymouth to Launceston, and we were obliged to leave her at Morwell, the nearest house, that is some eighteen or nineteen years ago. She never rejoined us. After a year, or a year and a half, we were at Tavistock, on our way to Plymouth, from Exeter by Okehampton, and there her father met us, and I told him what had become of her. I know that I walked out one day to Morwell and saw her. I believe her father had several interviews with her, then something occurred which prevented his meeting her as he had en-gaged, and he asked me to see her again and explain his absence. I believe her union with the gentleman at Morwell was not quite regular, but of that I know nothing for certain. Anyhow, her father disapproved and would not meet Mr., what was his name?—O, Jordan. He saw his daughter in private, on some rock that stands above the Tamar. There also I met her, by his direction. She was very decided not to leave her child and husband, though sorry to offend and disobey her father. That is all I know —yes!—I recall the day—Midsummer Eve, June the twenty-third. I never saw her again.'

'But are you not aware that my father went to Morwell on the next day, Midsummer Day, and was told that Eve had eloped with you?'

'With me!' the manager stood still. 'With me! Nonsense!'

'On the twenty-fourth she was gone.'

Mr. Barret shook his head. 'I cannot understand.'

'One word more,' said Jasper. 'You will see Miss Eve Jordan. Do not tell her that I am her uncle. Do not cast a doubt on her mother's death. Speak to her only in praise of her mother as you knew her.'

'This is puzzling indeed,' said the manager. 'We have had a party with us, an amateur, a walking character, who talked of Morwell as if he knew it, and I told him about the Miss Eve we had left there and her marriage to the squire. I may have said, "If ever you go there again, remember me to the lady, supposing her alive, and tell me if the child be as beautiful as I remember her mother."'

'There is but one man,' said Jasper, 'who holds the key to the mystery, and he must be forced to disclose.'

CHAPTER XLVIII.

IN PART.

MR. JORDAN knew more of what went on than Barbara
suspected. Jane Welsh attended to him a good deal, and
she took a mean delight in spying into the actions of her
young mistresses, and making herself acquainted with
everything that went on in the house and on the estate.
In this she was encouraged by Mr. Jordan, who listened to
what she told him and became excited and suspicious ; and
the fact of exciting his suspicions was encouragement to
the maid. The vulgar mind hungers for notoriety, and
the girl was flattered by finding that what she hinted
stirred the crazy mind of the old man. He was a man
prone to suspicion, and to suspect those nearest to him.
The recent events at Morwell had made him mistrust his
own children. He could not suppose that Martin Babb
had escaped without their connivance. It was a triumph
to the base mind of Jane to stand closer in her master's
confidence than his own children, and she used her best
endeavours to thrust herself further in by aggravating his
suspicions.

Barbara was not at ease in her own mind, she was
particularly annoyed to hear that Martin was still in the
neighbourhood, on their land ; naturally frank, she was
impatient of the constraint laid on her. She heartily desired that the time would come when concealments might
end. She acknowledged the necessity for concealment, but
resented it, and could not quite forgive Jasper for having
forced it upon her. She even chilled in her manner towards him, when told that Martin was still a charge. The
fact that she was obliged to think of and succour a man
with whom she was not in sympathy, reacted on her relations with Jasper, and produced constraint.

That Jane watched her and Jasper, Barbara did not suspect. Honourable herself, she could not believe that another would act dishonourably. She under-valued Jane's abilities. She knew her to be a common-minded girl, fond of talking, but she made no allowance for that natural inquisitiveness which is the seedleaf of intelligence. The savage who cannot count beyond the fingers of one hand is a master of cunning. There is this difference between men and beasts. The latter bite and destroy the weakly of their race; men attack, rend, and trample on the noblest of their species.

Mr. Jordan knew that Jasper and Eve had gone together for a long journey, and that Barbara sat up awaiting their return. He had been left unconsulted, he was uninformed by his daughters, and was very angry. He waited all next day, expecting something to be said on the subject to him, but not a word was spoken.

The weather now changed. The brilliant summer days had suffered an eclipse. The sky was overcast with grey cloud, and cold north-west winds came from the Atlantic, and made the leaves of beech and oak shiver. On the front of heaven, on the face of earth, was written Ichabod—the glory is departed. What poetry is to the mind, that the sun is to nature. The sun was withdrawn, and the hard light was colourless, prosaic. There was nowhere beauty any more. Two chilly damp days had transformed all. Mr. Jordan shivered in his room. The days seemed to have shortened by a leap.

Mr. Jordan, out of perversity, because Barbara had advised his remaining in, had walked into the garden, and after shivering there a few minutes had returned to his room, out of humour with his daughter because he felt she was in the right in the counsel she gave.

Then Jane came to him, with mischief in her eyes, breathless. 'Please, master,' she said in low tones, looking about her to make sure she was not overheard. 'What do y' think, now! Mr. Jasper have agone to the wood, carrying a blanket. What can he want that for, I'd like to know. He's not thinking of sleeping there, I reckon.'

'Go after him, Jane,' said Mr. Jordan. 'You are a good girl, more faithful than my own flesh and blood. Do not allow him to see that he is followed.'

The girl nodded knowingly, and went out.

'Now,' said Mr. Jordan to himself, 'I'll come to the bottom of this plot at last. My own children have turned against me. I will let them see that I can counter-plot. Though I be sick and feeble and old, I will show that I am master still in my own house. Who is there?'

Mr. Coyshe entered, bland and fresh, rubbing his hands. 'Well, Jordan,' said he—he had become familiar in his address since his engagement—' how are you? And my fairy Eve, how is she? None the worse for her junket?'

'Junket!' repeated the old man. 'What junket?'

'Bless your soul!' said the surgeon airily. 'Of course you think only of curdled milk. I don't allude to that local dish—or rather bowl—I mean Eve's expedition to Plymouth t'other night.'

'Eve—Plymouth!'

'Of course. Did you not know? Have I betrayed a secret? Lord bless me, why should it be kept a secret? She enjoyed herself famously. Knows no better, and thought the performance was perfection. I have seen Kemble, and Kean, and Vestris. But for a provincial theatre it was well enough.'

'You went with her to the theatre?'

'Yes, I and Mr. Jasper. But don't fancy she went only out of love of amusement. She went to see the manager, a Mr. Justice Thing-a-majig.'

'Barret?'

'That's the man, because he had known her mother.'

Mr. Jordan's face changed, and his eyes stared. He put up his hands as though waving away something that hung before him.

'And Jasper?'

'Oh, Jasper was with her. They left me to eat my supper in comfort. I can't afford to spoil my digestion, and I'm particularly fond of crab. You cannot eat crab in a scramble and do it justice.'

'Did Jasper see the manager?' Mr. Jordan's voice was hollow. His hands, which he held deprecatingly before him, quivered. He had his elbows on the arms of his chair.

'Oh, yes, of course he did. Don't you understand? He went with Eve whilst I finished the crab. It was really a shame; they neither of them half cleaned out their claws, they were in such a hurry. "Preciosa" was not amiss, but I preferred crab. One can get plays better elsewhere, but crab nowhere of superior quality.'

Mr. Jordan began to pick at the horse-hair of his chair arm. There was a hole in the cover and his thin white nervous fingers plucked at the stuffing, and pulled it out, and twisted it and threw it down, and plucked again.

'What—what did Jasper hear?' he asked falteringly.

'How can I tell, Jordan? I was not with them. I tell you, I was eating my supper quietly, and chewing every mouthful. I cannot bolt my food. It is bad—unprincipled to do so.'

'They told you nothing?'

'I made no inquiries, and no information was volunteered.'

A slight noise behind him made Coyshe turn. Eve was in the doorway. 'Here she is to answer for herself,' said the surgeon. 'Eve, my love, your father is curious about your excursion to Plymouth, and wants to know all you heard from the manager.

'Oh, papa! I ought to have told you!' stammered Eve.

'What did he say?' asked the old man, half-impatiently, half fearfully.

'Look here, governor,' said the surgeon; 'it strikes

me that you are not acting straight with the girl, and as
she is about to become my wife, I'll stand up for her and
say what is fitting. I cannot see the fun of forcing her
to run away a day's journey to pick up a few scraps of
information about her mother, when you keep locked up
in your own head all that she wants to know. I can understand and make allowance for you not liking to tell her
everything, if things were not as is reported—quite
ecclesiastically square between you and the lady. But
Eve is no longer a child. I intend her to become my
wife, and sooner or later she must know all. Make a
clean breast and tell everything.'

'Yes,' said Jasper entering, 'the advice is good.'

'You come also!' exclaimed the old man, firing up
and pointing with trembling fingers to the intruder; '*you*
come—*you* who have led my children into disobedience?
My own daughters are in league against me. As for this
girl, Eve, whom I have loved, who has been to me as the
apple of my eye, she is false to me.'

'Oh, papa! dear papa!' pleaded Eve with tears, 'do
not say this. It is not true.'

'Not true? Why do you practise concealment from
me? Why do you carry about with you a ring which Mr.
Coyshe never gave you? Produce it, I have been told
about it. You have left it on your table and it has been
seen, a ring with a turquoise forget-me-not. Who gave
you that? Answer me if you dare. What is the meaning of these runnings to and fro into the woods, to the
rocks?' The old man worked himself into wildness and
want of consideration for his child, and for Coyshe to whom
she was engaged. 'Listen to me, you,' he turned to the
surgeon, holding forth his stick which he had caught up;
'u shall judge between us. This girl, this daughter of
'ie, has met again and again in secret a man whom I
:e, a man who robbed his own father of money that
pu'longed to me, a man who has been a jail-bird, an
h:scaped felon. Is not this so? Eve, deny it if you can.'

'Father!' began Eve, trembling, you are ill, you are excited.'

'Answer me!' he shouted so loud as to make all start, striking at the same time the floor with his stick, 'have you not met him in secret?'

She hung her head and sobbed.

'You aided that man in making his escape when he was in the hands of the police. I brought the police upon him, and you worked to deliver him. Answer me. Was it not so?'

She faintly murmured, 'Yes.'

This had been but a conjecture of Mr. Jordan. He was emboldened to proceed, but now Jasper stood forward, grave, collected, facing the white, wild old man. 'Mr. Jordan,' he said, 'that man of whom you speak is my brother. I am to blame, not Miss Eve. Actively neither I nor—most assuredly—your daughter assisted in his escape; but I will not deny that I was aware he meditated evasion, and he effected it, not through active assistance given him, but because his guards were careless, and because I did not indicate to them the means whereby he was certain to get away, and which I saw and they overlooked.'

'Stand aside,' shouted the angry old man. He loved Eve more than he loved anyone else, and as is so often the case when the mind is unhinged, his suspicion and wrath were chiefly directed against his best beloved. He struck at Jasper with his stick, to drive him on one side, and he shrieked with fury to Eve, who cowered and shrank from him. 'You have met this felon, and you love him. That is why I have had such difficulty with you to get your consent to Mr. Coyshe. Is it not so? Come, answer.'

'I like poor Martin,' sobbed Eve. 'I forgive him for taking my money; it was not his fault.'

'See there! she confesses all. 'Who gave you that ring with the blue stones of which I have been told? It did not belong to your mother. Mr. Coyshe never gave

Y

it you. Answer me at once or I will throw my stick at you. Who gave you that ring?'

The surgeon, in his sublime self-conceit, not for a moment supposing that any other man had been preferred to himself, thinking that Mr. Jordan was off his head, turned to Eve and said in a low voice, 'Humour him. It is safest. Say what he wishes you to say.'

'Martin gave me the ring,' she answered, trembling.

'How came you one time to be without your mother's ring? How came you at another to be possessed of it? Explain that.'

Eve threw herself on her knees with a cry.

'Oh, papa! dear papa! ask me no more questions.'

'Listen all to me,' said Mr. Jordan, in a loud hard voice. He rose from his chair, resting a hand on each arm, and heaving himself into an upright position. His face was livid, his eyes burned like coals, his hair bristled on his head, as though electrified. He came forward, walking with feet wide apart, and with his hands uplifted, and stood over Eve still kneeling, gazing up at him with terror.

'Listen to me, all of you. I know more than any of you suppose. I spy where you are secret. That man who robbed me of my money has lurked in this neighbourhood to rob me of my child. Shall I tell you who he is, this felon, who stole from his father? He is her mother's brother, Eve's uncle.'

Eve stared with blank eyes into his face, Martin— her uncle! She uttered a cry and covered her eyes.

CHAPTER XLIX.

THE OLD GUN.

Mr. Jordan was alone in his room. Evening had set in, the room was not only chilly, it was dark. He sat in his leather-backed leather-armed chair with his stick in his hands,—in both hands, held across him, and now and then he put the stick up to his mouth and gnawed at it in the middle. At others he made a sudden movement, slipping his hand down to the ferule and striking in the air with the handle at the black spots which floated in the darkness, of a blackness most intense. He was teased by them, and by his inability to strike them aside. His stick went through them, as through ink, and they closed again when cut, and drifted on through his circle of vision un-hurt, undisturbed.

Mr. Coyshe was gone; he had ordered the old man to be left as much in quiet as might be, and he had taken a boy from the farm with him on a horse, to bring back a soothing draught which he promised to send. Mr. Jordan had complained of sleeplessness, his nerves were evidently in a high and perilous state of tension. Before he left, Mr. Coyshe had said to Barbara, ' Keep an eye on your father, there is irritation somewhere. He talks in an un-reasoning manner. I will send him something to compose him, and call again to-morrow. In the meantime,' he coughed, ' I—I—would not allow him to shave himself.'

Barbara's blood curdled. ' You do not think—' She was unable to finish her sentence.'

' Do as I say, and do not allow him to suppose himself watched.'

Now Barbara acted with unfortunate indiscretion. Knowing that her father was suspicious of her, and com-plained of her observing him, knowing also that his sus-picions extended to Jasper whom he disliked, knowing also that he had taken a liking for Jane, she bade Jane remain about her father, and not allow him to be many minutes unwatched.

Jane immediately went to the old gentleman, and told him the instructions given her. ' And—please your honour,' she crept close to him, ' I've seen him. He is on the Raven Rock. He has lighted a fire and is warming himself. I think it be the very man that was took here,

Y 2

but I can't say for certain, as I didn't see the face of him
as was took, nor of him on the Rock, but they be both
men, and much about a height.'

'Jane! Is Joseph anywhere about?'

'No sir,—not nigher than Tavistock.'

'Go to him immediately. Bid him collect what men
he can, and surround the fellow and secure him.'

'But, your honour! Miss Barbara said I was to watch
you as a cat watches a mouse.'

'Who is master here, I or she? I order you to go;
and if she is angry I will protect you against her. I am
to be watched, am I? By my own children? By my
servant? This is more than I can bear. The whole
world is conspiring against me. How can I trust anyone
—even Jane? How can I say that the police were not
bribed before to let him go? And they may be bribed
again. Trust none but thyself,' he muttered, and stood
up.

'Please, master,' said Jane, 'you may be certain I will
do what you want. I'm not like some folks, as is un-
natural to their very parents. Why, sir! what do y'
think? As I were a coming in, who should run by me,
looking the pictur' of fear, but Miss Eve. And where do
y' think her runned? Why, sir—I watched her, and her
went as fast as a leaping hare over the fields towards the
Raven Rock—to where he be. Well, I'm sure I'd not do
that. I don't mind a-going to love feasts in chapel with
Joseph, but I wouldn't go seeking him in a wood. Some
folks have too much self-respect for that, I reckon.' She
muttered this looking up at the old man, uncertain how he
would take it.

'Go,' said he. 'Leave me—go at once.'

Presently Barbara came in, and found her father
alone.

'What, no one with you, papa?'

'No—I want to be alone. Do you grudge me quiet?
Must I live under a microscope? Must I have everything

I do marked, every word noted? Why do you peer in
here? Am I an escaped felon to be guarded? Am I
likely to break out? Will you leave me? I tell you I do
not want you here. I desire solitude. I have had you
and Coyshe and Eve jabbering here till my head spins and
my temples are bursting. Leave me alone.' Then, with
the craftiness of incipient derangement, he said, 'I have
had two—three bad nights, and want sleep. I was dozing
in my chair when Jane came in to light a fire. I sent her
out. Then, when I was nodding off again, I heard cook
or Jasper tramping through the hall. That roused me,
and now when I hoped to compose myself again, you thrust
yourself upon me; are you all in a league to drive me
mad, by forbidding me sleep? That is how Hopkins, the
witch-finder, got the poor wretches to confess. He would
not suffer them to sleep, and at last, in sheer madness and
hunger for rest, they confessed whatever was desired of
them. You want to force something out of me. That is
why you will not let me sleep.'

'Papa dear, I shall be so glad if you can sleep. I promise you shall be left quite alone for an hour.'

'O an hour! limited to sixty minutes.'

'Dear papa, till you rap on the wall, to intimate that
you are awake.'

'You will not pry and peer?'

'No one shall come near you. I will forbid everyone
the hall, lest a step on the pavement should disturb you.'

'What are you doing there?'

'Taking away your razor, papa.'

Then he burst into a shrill, bitter laugh—a laugh that
shivered through her heart. He said nothing, but remained
chuckling in his chair.

'I dare say Jasper will sharpen them for you, papa, he
is very kind,' said Barbara, ashamed of her dissimulation.
So it came about that the old half-crazy squire was left in
the gathering gloom entirely alone and unguarded. Nothing
could do him more good than a refreshing sleep, Barbara

argued, and went away to her own room, where she lit a candle, drew down her blind, and set herself to needle-work.

She had done what she could. The pantry adjoined the room of her father. Jane would hear if he knocked or called. She did not know that Jane was gone.

Ignatius Jordan sat in the armchair, biting at his stick, or beating in the air with it at the blots which troubled his vision. These black spots took various shapes; some-times they were bats, sometimes falling leaves. Then it appeared to him as if a fluid that was black but with a crimson glow in it as of a subdued hidden fire was running and dripped from ledge to ledge—invisible ledges they were—in the air before him. He put his stick out to touch the stream, and then it ran along the stick and flowed on his hand and he uttered a cry, because it burned him. He held his hand up open before him, and thought the palm was black, but with glowing red veins inter-secting the blackness, and he touched the lines with the finger of his left hand.

'The line of Venus,' he said, 'strong at the source, fiery and broken by that cross cut—the line of life—long, thin, twisted, tortured, nowhere smooth, and here—What is this?—the end.'

Then he looked at the index finger of his left hand, the finger that had traced the lines, and it seemed to be alight or smouldering with red fire.

He heard a strange sound at the window, a sound shrill and unearthly, close as in his ear, and yet certainly not in the room. He held his breath and looked round. He could see nothing through the glass but the grey evening sky, no face looking in and crying at the window. What was it? As he looked it was repeated. In his excited condition of mind he did not seek for a natural explanation. It was a spirit call urging him on. It was silent. Then again repeated. Had he lighted the candle and examined the glass he would have seen a large snail crawling up the pane, creating the sound by the vibration of the glass as it drew itself along.

Then Mr. Jordan rose out of his chair, and looking cautiously from side to side and timorously at the window whence the shrill sound continued, he unlocked a cupboard in the panelling and drew from it powder and shot.

Barbara had taken away his razors. She feared lest he should do himself an injury; but though he was weary of his life, he had no thought of hastening his departure from it. His mind was set with deadly resolution of hate on Martin—Martin, that man who had robbed him, who escaped from him as often as he was taken. Everyone was in league to favour Martin. No one was to be trusted to punish him. He must make sure that the man did not escape this time. This time he would rely on no one but himself. He crossed the room with soft step, opened the door, and entered the hall. There he stood looking about him. He could hear a distant noise of servants talking in the kitchen, but no one was near, no eye observed him. Barbara, true to her promise, was upstairs, believing him asleep. The hall was dark, but not so dark that he could not distinguish what he sought. Some one passed with a light outside, a maid going to the wash-house. The light struck through the transomed window of the hall, painting a black cross against the wall opposite, a black cross that travelled quickly and fell on the old man, creeping along to the fire-place, holding the wall. He remembered the Midsummer Day seventeen years ago when he had stood there against that wall with arms extended in the blaze of the setting sun as a crucified figure against the black shadow of the cross. His life had been one long crucifixion ever since, and his cross a shadow. Then he stood on a hall chair and took down from its crooks an old gun.

'Seventeen years ago,' he muttered. 'My God! it failed not then, may it not fail me now!'

CHAPTER L.

BY THE FIRE.

MARTIN was weary of the woodman's hut, as he was before weary of the mine. Watt had hard work to pacify him. His rheumatism was better. Neither Jasper nor Walter could decide how far the attack was real and how far simulated. Probably he really suffered, and exaggerated his sufferings to provoke sympathy.

Whilst the weather was summery he endured his captivity, for he could lie in the sun on a hot rock and smoke or whistle, with his hands in his pockets, and Martin loved to lounge and be idle ; but when the weather changed, he became restive, ill-humoured, and dissatisfied. What aggravated his discontent was a visit from Barbara, whom he found it impossible to impress with admiration for his manly beauty and pity for his sorrows.

'That girl is a beast,' he said to Walter, when she was gone. 'I really could hardly be civil to her. A perfect Caliban, devoid of taste and feeling. Upon my word some of our fellow-beings are without humanity. I could see through that person at a glance. She is made up of selfishness. If there be one quality most repulsive to me, that is it— selfishness. I do not believe the creature cast a thought upon me, my wants, my sufferings, my peril. Watt, if she shows her ugly face here again, stand against the door, and say, "Not at home."'

'Dear Martin, we will go as soon as you are well enough to leave.'

'Whither are we to go ? I cannot join old Barret and his wife and monkeys and babies and walking-sticks of actors, as long as he is in the county. I would go to Bristol or Bath or Cheltenham if I had money, but these miserly Jordans will not find me any. They want to drive

me away without first lining my pocket. I know what was
meant by those cold slabs of mutton, to-day. It meant, go
away. I wait till they give me money.'

'Dear Martin, you must not be inconsiderate.'

'I glory in it. What harm comes of it? It is your
long-headed, prudent prophets who get into scrapes and
can't get out of them again. I never calculate; I act on
impulse, and that always brings me right.'

'Not always, Martin, or you would not be here.'

'O, yes, even here. When the impulse comes on me to
go, I shall go, and you will find I go at the right time. If
that Miss Jordan comes here again with her glum ugly
mug, I shall be off. Or Jasper, looking as if the end of
the world were come. I can't stand that. See how
cleverly I got away from Prince's Town.'

'I helped you, Martin.'

'I do not pretend that I did all myself. I did escape,
and a brilliantly executed manœuvre it was. I thought I
was caught in a cleft stick when I dropped on the party of
beaks at the "Hare and Hounds," but see how splendidly
I got away. I do believe, Watt, I've missed my calling,
and ought to have been a general in the British army.'

'But, dear Martin, generals have to scheme other
things beside running away.'

'None of your impudence, you jackanapes. I tell you
I do *not* scheme. I act on the spur of the moment. If I
had lain awake a week planning I could have done nothing
better. The inspiration comes to me the moment I require
it. Your vulgar man always does the wrong thing when
an emergency arises. By heaven, Watt! this is a dog's
life I am leading, and not worth living. I am shivering.
The damp worms into one's bones. I shall go out on the
Rock.'

'O, Martin, stay here. It is warmer in this hut. A
cold wind blows.'

'It is midwinter here, and can't be more Siberia-like
out there. I am sick of the smell of dry leaves. I am

tired of looking at withered sticks. The monotony of this place is unendurable. I wish I were back in prison.'

'I will play my violin to amuse you,' said the boy

'Curse your fiddle, I do not want to have that squeaking in my ears; besides, it is sure to be out of tune with the damp, and screw up as you may, before you have gone five bars it is flat again. Why has Eve not been here to tell me of what she saw in Plymouth?'

'My dear Martin, you must consider. She dare not come here. You cannot keep open house, and send round cards of invitation, with " Mr. Martin Babb at home." '

'I don't care. I shall go on the Rock, and have a fire.'

'A fire!' exclaimed Watt, aghast.

'Why not? I am cold, and my rheumatism is worse. I won't have rheumatic fever for you or all the Jordans and Jaspers in Devonshire.'

'I entreat you, be cautious. Remember you are in hiding. You have already been twice caught.'

'Because on both occasions I ran into the hands of the police. The first time I attempted no concealment. I did not think my father would have been such a—such a pig as to send them after me. I'll tell you what, my boy, there is no generosity and honour anywhere. They are like the wise teeth that come, not to be used, but to go, and go painfully.' Then he burst out of the hut, and groaning and cursing scrambled through the coppice to the Raven Rock.

Walter knew too well that when his brother had resolved on anything, however outrageous, it was in vain for him to attempt dissuasion. He therefore accompanied him up the steep slope and through the bushes, lending him a hand, and drawing the boughs back before him, till he reached the platform of rock.

The signs of autumn were apparent everywhere. Two days before they had not been visible. The bird-cherry was turning; the leaves of the dog-wood were royal purple,

and those at the extremity of the branches were carmine.
Here and there umbelliferous plants had turned white ; all
the sap was withdrawn, they were bleached at the prospect
of the coming decay of nature. The heather had donned its
pale flowers ; but there was no brightness in the purples and
pinks, they were the purples and pinks not of sunflush, but
of chill. A scent of death pervaded the air. The foxgloves had flowered up their long spires to the very top,
and only at the very top did a feeble bell or two bloom whilst
the seeds ripened below. No butterflies, no moths even
were about. The next hot day the scarlet admirals would
be out, but now they hung with folded wings downwards,
exhibiting pepper and salt and no bright colour under the
leaves, waiting and shivering.

‘Everything is doleful,’ said Martin, standing on the
platform and looking round. ‘Only one thing lacks to
make the misery abject, and that is rain. If the clouds
drop, and the water leaks into my den, I’ll give myself up,
and secure a dry cell somewhere—then Jasper and the
Jordans may make the best of it. I’m not going to become a confirmed invalid to save Jasper’s pride, and help
on his suit to that dragon of Wantley. If he thinks it
against his interest that I should be in gaol, I’ll go back
there. I’m not eager to have that heap of superciliousness
as a sister-in-law, Walter, so collect sticks and fern that
I may have a fire.’

‘Martin, do not insist on this ; the light and smoke
will be seen.’

‘Who is there to see ? This rock is only visible from
Cornwall, and there is no bridge over the Tamar for some
miles up the river. Who will care to make a journey of
some hours to ask why a fire has been kindled on the Raven
Rock ? Look behind, the trees screen this terrace, no one
at Morwell will see. The hills and rocks fold on the river
and hide us from all habitable land. Do not oppose me ;
I will have a fire.’

‘O, Martin,’ said the boy, ‘you throw on me all the

responsibility of caring for your safety, and you make my task a hard one by your thoughtlessness.'

'I am so unselfish,' said Martin gravely. 'I never do consider myself. I can't help it, such is my nature.'

Walter reluctantly complied with his brother's wish. The boy had lost his liveliness. The mischief and audacity were driven out of him by the responsibility that weighed on him.

Abundance of fuel was to be had. The summer had been hot, and little rain had fallen. Wood had been cut the previous winter, and bundles of faggots lay about, that had not been removed and stacked.

Before long the fire was blazing, and Martin crouched at it warming his hands and knees. His face relaxed whilst that of Walter became lined with anxiety. As he was thus seated, Jasper came on him carrying a blanket. He was dismayed at what his brother had done, and reproached him.

Martin shrugged his shoulders. 'It is very well for you in a dry house, on a feather bed and between blankets, but very ill for poor me, condemned to live like a wild beast. You should have felt my hands before I had a fire to thaw them at, they were like the cold mutton I had for my dinner.'

'Martin, you must put that fire out. You have acted with extreme indiscretion.'

'Spare me your reproaches; I know I am indiscreet. It is my nature, as it lies in the nature of a lion to be noble, and of a dog to be true.'

'Really,' said Jasper, hotly, disturbed out of his usual equanimity by the folly of his brother, 'really, Martin, you are most aggravating. You put me to great straits to help you, and strain to the utmost my relations to the Jordan family. I do all I can—more than I ought—for you, and you wantonly provoke danger. Who but you would have had the temerity to return to this neighbourhood after your escape and my accident! Then—why do you remain here?

I cannot believe in your illness. Your lack of common consideration is the cause of incessant annoyance to your friends. That fire shall go out.' He went to it resolutely, and kicked it apart, and threw some of the flaming oak sticks over the edge of the precipice.

'I hope you are satisfied now,' said Martin sulkily. 'You have spoiled my pleasure, robbed me of my only comfort, and have gained only this—that I wash my hands of you, and will leave this place to-night. I will no longer remain near you—inhuman, unbrotherly as you are.'

'I am very glad to hear that you are going,' answered Jasper. 'You shall have my horse. That horse is my own, and he will carry you away. Send Walter for it when you like. I will see that the stable-door is open, and the saddle and bridle handy. The horse is in a stable near the first gate, away from the house, and can be taken unobserved.'

'You are mightily anxious to be rid of me,' sneered Martin. 'And this is a brother!'

'I had brought you a blanket off my own bed, because I supposed you were cold.'

'I will not have it,' said Martin sharply. 'If you shiver for want of your blanket I shall be blamed. Your heart will overflow with gall against poor me. Keep your blanket to curl up in yourself. I shall leave to-night. I have too much proper pride to stay where I am not wanted, with a brother who begrudges me a scrap of fire.'

Jasper held out his hand. 'I must go back at once,' he said. 'If you leave to-night it may be years before we meet again. Come, Martin, you know me better than your words imply. Do not take it ill that I have destroyed your fire. I think only of your safety. Give me your hand, brother ; your interest lies at my heart.'

Martin would not touch the proffered hand, he folded his arms and turned away. Jasper looked at him, long and sadly, but Martin would not relent, and he left.

'Get the embers together again,' ordered Martin.

' Under the Scottish fir are lots of cones full of resin ; pile them on the fire, and make a big blaze. Let Jasper see it. I will show him that I am not going to be beaten by his insolence.'

' He may have been rough, but he was right,' said Watt.

' Oh ! you also turn against me ! A viper I have cherished in my bosom ! '

The boy sighed ; he dare no longer refuse, and he sorrowfully gathered the scattered fire together, fanned the embers, applied to them bits of dry fern, then fir cones, and soon a brilliant jet of yellow flame leaped aloft.

Martin raised himself to his full height that the fire might illuminate him from head to foot, and so he stood, with his arms folded, thinking what a fine fellow he was, and regretting that no appreciative eye was there to see him.

' What a splendid creature man is ! ' said he to himself or Walter. ' So great in himself ; and yet, how little and mean he becomes through selfishness ! I pity Jasper— from my heart I pity him. I am not angry—only sorry.'

CHAPTER LI.

A SHOT.

' OF all things I could have desired—the best ! ' exclaimed Martin Babb as Eve came from the cover of the wood upon the rocky floor. She was out of breath, and could not speak. She put both hands on her breast to control her breathing and quiet her throbbing heart.

Martin drew one foot over the other, poising it on the toe, and allowed the yellow firelight to play over his handsome face and fine form. The appreciative eye was there. ' Lovelier than ever ! ' exclaimed Martin. ' Preciosa come to the forest to Alonzo, not Alonzo to Preciosa.

> The forest green !
> Where warm the summer sheen ;
>   And echo calls,
>   And calls—through leafy halls.
> Hurrah for the life 'neath the greenwood tree !
> My horn and my dogs and my gun for me!
>   Trarah ! Trarah ! Trarah !'

He sang the first verse of the gipsy chorus with rich tones. He had a beautiful voice, and he knew it.

The song had given her time to obtain breath, and she said, 'Oh, Martin, you must go—you must indeed ! '

'Why, my Preciosa ? '

'My father knows all—how, I cannot conjecture, but he does know, and he will not spare you.'

'My sweet flower,' said Martin, not in the least alarmed, ' the old gentleman cannot hurt me. He cannot himself fetch the dogs of justice and set them on me; and he cannot send for them without your consent. There is plenty of time for me to give them the slip. All is arranged. To-night I leave on Jasper's horse, which he is good enough to lend me.'

'You do not know my father. He is not alone—Mr. Coyshe is with him. I cannot answer for what he may do.'

'Hah ! ' said Martin, ' I see ! Jealousy may spur him on. He knows that we are rivals. Watt, be off with you after the horse. Perhaps it would be better if I were to depart. I would not spare that pill-compounding Coyshe were he in my power, and I cannot expect him to spare me.' He spoke, and his action was stagy, calculated to impress Eve.

'My dear Walter,' said Martin, ' go to Morwell some other way than the direct path ; workmen may be about—the hour is not so late.'

The boy did not wait for further orders.

'You need not fear for me,' said the escaped convict. ' Even if that despicable roll-pill set off to collect men, I would escape him. I have but to leave this spot, and I am safe I presume not one of my pursuers will be mounted.'

' Why have you a fire here ? '

' The fire matters nothing,' said Martin grandly ; ' indeed '—he collected more fircones and threw them on— ' indeed, if the form of the hare is to be discovered, let it be discovered warm. The hunters will search the immediate neighbourhood, and the hare will be flying far, far away.'

' You know best, of course ; but it seems to me very dangerous.'

' I laugh at danger ! ' exclaimed Martin, throwing a faggot on the flames. ' I disport in danger as the seamew in the storm.' He unfolded his arms and waved them over the fire as a bird flapping its wings.

' And now,' he went on, ' I leave you—*you*—to that blood-letter. Why do I trouble myself about my own worthless existence, when you are about to fall a prey to his ravening jaw ? No, Eve, that must never be.'

' Martin,' said Eve, ' I must really go home. I only ran here to warn you to be off, and to tell you something. My father has just said that my mother was your sister.'

He looked at her in silence for some moments in real astonishment—so real that he dropped his affected attitude and expression of face.

' Can this be possible ! '

' He declared before Mr. Coyshe and me that it was so.'

' You have the same name as my lost sister,' said Martin. ' Her I hardly remember. She ran away from home when I was very young, and what became of her we never heard. If my father knew, he was silent about his knowledge. I am sure Jasper did not know.'

' And Mr. Barret, the manager, did not know either,' added Eve. ' When my mother was with him she bore a feigned name, and said nothing about her parents, nor told where was her home.'

Then Martin recovered himself and laughed.

' Why, Eve,' said he, ' if this extraordinary story be

true, I am your uncle and natural protector. This has
settled the matter. You shall never have that bolus-maker,
leech-applier, Coyshe. I forbid it. I shall stand between
you and the altar of sacrifice. I extend my wing, and you
take refuge under it. I throw my mantle over you and
assure you of my protection. The situation is really—
really quite dramatic.'

' Do not stand so near the edge of the precipice,' pleaded
Eve.

' I always stand on the verge of precipices, but never
go over,' he answered. 'I speak metaphorically. Now,
Eve, the way is clear. You shall run away from home as
did your mother, and you shall run away with me. Remember, I am your natural protector.'

'I cannot—I cannot indeed.' Eve shrank back.

' I swear you shall,' said Martin impetuously. ' It may
seem strange that I, who am in personal danger myself,
should consider you : but such is my nature—I never
regard self when I can do an heroic action. I say, Eve,
you shall go with me. I am a man with a, governing will,
to which all must stoop. You have trifled with the doctor
and with me. I hate that man though I have never seen
him. I would he were here and I would send him, spectacles and all——'

' He does not wear spectacles.'

' Do not interrupt. I speak symbolically. Spectacles
and all, I repeat, with his bottles of leeches, and pestle and
mortar, and pills and lotions, over the edge of this precipice
into perdition. Good heavens ! if I leave and you remain,
I shall be coming back—I cannot keep away. If I escape,
it must be with you or not at all. You have a horse of
your own : you shall ride with me. You have a purse :
fill it and bring it in your pocket. Diamonds, silver spoons
—anything.'

She was too frightened to know what to say. He,
coward and bully as he was, saw his advantage, and assumed the tone of bluster. ' Do you understand me ? I

will not be trifled with. The thing is settled : you come with me.'

'I cannot—indeed I cannot,' said Eve despairingly.

'You little fool! Think of what you saw in the theatre. That is the proper sphere for you, as it is for me. You were born to live on the stage. I am glad you have told me what became of my sister. The artistic instinct is in us. The fire of genius is in our hearts. You cannot drag out life in such a hole as this : you must come into the world. It was so with your mother. Whose example can you follow better than that of a mother ?'

'My father would——'

'Your father will not be surprised. What is born in the bone comes out in the flesh. If your mother was an actress—you must be one also. Compare yourself with your half-sister. Is there soul in that mass of common-place ? Is there fire in that cake ? Her mother, you may be certain, was a pudding—a common vulgar suet-pudding. We beings of Genius belong to another world, and we must live in that world or perish. It is settled. You ride with me to-night. I shall introduce you to the world of art, and you will soon be its most brilliant star.'

'Hark!' exclaimed Eve, starting. 'I heard something stir.'

Both were silent, and listened. They stood opposite each other, near the edge of the precipice. The darkness had closed in rapidly. The cloudy sky cut off the last light of day. Far, far below, the river cast up at one sweep a steely light, but for the most part of its course it was lost in the inky murkiness of the shadows of mountain, forest, and rock.

Away at a distance of several miles, on the side of the dark dome of Hingston Hill, a red star was glimmering— the light from a miner's or moorman's cabin. The fire that flickered on the platform cast flashes of gold on the nearest oak boughs, but was unable to illumine the gulf of darkness that yawned under the forest trees.

Martin stood facing the wood, with his back to the abyss, and the light irradiated his handsome features. Eve timidly looked at him, and thought how noble he seemed.

' Was it the sound of a horse's hoof you heard ? ' asked Martin. ' Walter is coming with Jasper's horse.'

' I thought a bush moved,' answered Eve, ' and that I heard a click.'

' It is nothing,' said Martin, ' nothing but an attempt on your part to evade the force of my argument, to divert the current of my speech. You women squirm like eels. There is no holding you save by running a stick through your gills. Mind you, I have decided your destiny. It will be my pride to make a great actress of you. What applause you will gain ! What a life of merriment you will lead ! I shall take a pride in the thought that I have snatched you away from under the nose of that doctor. Pshaw ! '—he paused—' pshaw ! I do not believe that story about your mother being my sister. Whether she were or not matters nothing. You, like myself, have a soul, and a soul that cannot live on a farmyard dungheap. What is that ! I hear a foot on the bracken. Can it be Watt ? '

He was silent, listening. He began to feel uneasy. Then from behind the wood came the shrill clangour of a bell.

' Something has happened,' said Eve, in great terror. ' That is the alarm bell of our house.'

' My God !' cried Martin, ' what is Watt about ! He ought to have been here.' In spite of his former swagger he became uneasy. ' Curse him, for a dawdle ! am I going to stick here till taken because he is lazy ? That bell is ringing still.' It was pealing loud and fast. ' I shall leave this rock. If I were taken again I should never escape more. Seven years ! seven years in prison—why, the best part of my life would be gone, and you—I should see you no more. When I came forth you would be Mrs. Sawbones.

I swear by God that shall not be. Eve! I will not have
it. If I get off, you shall follow me. Hark! I hear the
tramp of the horse.'

He threw up his hands and uttered a shout of joy. He
ran forward to the fire, and stood by it, with the full glare
of the blazing fircones on his eager face.

'Eve! joy, joy! here comes help. I will make you
mount behind me. We will ride away together. Come,
we must meet Watt at the gate.'

A crack, a flash.

Martin staggered back, and put his hand to his breast.
Eve fell to her knees in speechless terror.

'Come here,' he said hoarsely, and grasped her arm.
'It is too late: I am struck, I am done for.'

A shout, and a man was seen plunging through the
bushes.

'Eve!' said Martin, 'I will not lose you.' He dragged
her two paces in his arms. All power of resistance was
gone from her. 'That doctor shall not have you—I'll
spoil that at least.' He stooped, kissed her lips and cheek
and brow and eyes, and in a moment flung himself, with
her in his arms, over the edge of the precipice into the
black abyss.

CHAPTER LII.

THE WHOLE.

A MOMENT later, only a moment later, and a moment too
late, Mr. Jordan reached the platform, having beaten the
branches aside, regardless of the leaves that lashed his face
and the brambles that tore his hands. Then, when he saw
that he was too late, he uttered a cry of despair. He flung
his gun from him, and it went over the edge and fell where
it was never found again. Then he raised his arms over
his head and clasped them, and brought them down on his

hair—he wore no hat ; and at the same time his knees
gave way, and he fell fainting on his face, with his arms
extended : the wound in his side had reopened, and the
blood burst forth and ran in a red rill towards the fire.

A few minutes later Jasper came up. Watt was at the
gate with the horse. They had heard the shot, and Jasper had run on. He was followed quickly by Walter, who
had fastened up the horse, unable to endure the suspense.

' Mr. Jordan is shot,' gasped Jasper, ' Martin has shot
him. Help me. I must staunch the wound.'

' Not I,' answered the boy ; ' I care nothing for him. I
must find Martin. Where is he ? Gone to the hut ? There
is no time to be lost. I must find him—that cursed bell is
ringing.'

Without another thought for the prostrate man, Walter
plunged into the coppice, and ran down the steep slope towards the woodcutter's hovel. It did not occur to Jasper
that the shot he had heard proceeded from the squire's
gun. He knew that Martin was armed. He supposed that
he had seen the old man emerge from the wood, and, supposing him to be one of his pursuers, had fired at him and
made his escape. He knew nothing of Eve's visit to the
Raven Rock and interview with his brother.

He turned the insensible man over on his back and discovered, to his relief, that he was not dead. He tore open
his shirt and found that he was unwounded by any bullet,
but that the old self-inflicted wound in his side had opened
and was bleeding freely. He knew how to deal with this.
He took the old man's shirt and tore it to form a bandage,
and passed it round him and stopped temporarily the ebbing tide. He heard Walter calling Martin in the wood.
It was clear that he had not found his brother in the hut.
Now Jasper understood why the alarm-bell was ringing.
Barbara had discovered that her father had left the house,
and, in fear for the consequences, was summoning the
workmen from their cottages to assist in finding him.

Watt reappeared in great agitation, and, without casting a look at the insensible man, said, 'He is not there, he may be back in the mine. He may have unlocked the boathouse and be rowing over the Tamar, or down—no—the tide is out, he cannot get down.' Then away he went again into the wood.

Mr. Jordan lay long insensible. He had lost much blood. Jasper knelt by him. All was now still. The bell was no longer pealing. No step could be heard. The bats flitted about the rock ; the fire-embers snapped. The wind sighed and piped among the trees. The fire had communicated itself to some dry grass, and a tuft flamed up, then a little spluttering flame crept along from grass haulm and twig to a tuft of heather, which it kindled, and which flared up. Jasper, kneeling by Mr. Jordan, watched the progress of the fire without paying it much attention. In moments of anxiety trifles catch the eye. He dare not leave the old man. He waited till those who had been summoned by the bell came that way.

Presently Ignatius Jordan opened his eyes. 'Eve !' he said, and his dim eyes searched the feebly-illuminated platform. Then he laid his head back again on the moss and was unconscious or lost in dream—Jasper could not decide which. Jasper went to the fire and threw on some wood and collected more. The stronger the flame the more likely to attract the notice of the searchers. He trod out the fire where it stole, snakelike, along the withered grass that sprouted out of the cracks in the surface of the rock. He went to the edge of the precipice, and listened in hopes of hearing something, he hardly knew what—a sound that might tell him Walter had found his brother. He heard nothing—no dip of oars, no rattle of a chain, from the depths and darkness below. He returned to Mr. Jordan, and saw that he was conscious and recognised him. The old man signed to him to draw near.

'The end is at hand. The blood has nearly all run out. Both are smitten—both the guilty and the guiltless.'

Jasper supposed he was wandering in his mind.

'I will tell you all,' said the old man. 'You are her brother, and ought to know.'

'You are speaking of my lost sister Eve!' said Jasper eagerly. Not a suspicion crossed his mind that anything had happened to the girl.

'I shall soon rejoin her, and the other as well. I would not speak before because of my child. I could not bear that she should look with horror on her father. Now it matters not. She has followed her mother. The need for silence is taken away. Wait! I must gather my strength, I cannot speak for long.'

Then from the depths of darkness below the rock, came the hoot of an owl. Jasper knew that it was Watt's signal to Martin—that he was searching for him still. No answering hoot came.

'You went to Plymouth. You saw the manager who had known my Eve. What did he say?'

'He told me very little.'

'Did he tell you where she was?'

'No. He saw her for the last time on this rock. He had been sent here by her father, who was unable to keep his appointment.'

'Go on.'

'That is all. She refused to desert you and her child. It is false that she ran away with an actor.'

'Who said she had? Not I—not I. Her own father, her own father—not I.'

'Then what became of her? Mr. Barret told me he had been to see her here at Morwell once or twice whilst the company was at Tavistock, and found her happy. After that my father came and tried to induce her to return to Buckfastleigh with him.'

Mr. Jordan put out his white thin hand and laid it on Jasper's wrist.

'You need say no more. The end is come, and I will tell you all. I knew that one of the actors came out and saw her—not once only, but twice—and then her father

came, and she met him in secret, here in the wood, on this
rock. I did not know that he whom she met was her
father. I supposed she was still meeting the actor privately. I was jealous. I loved Eve. Oh, my God! my
God!'—he put his hands against his temples—'when
have I ceased to love her?'

He did not speak for some moments. Again from the
depths, but more distant, came the to-whoo of the owl.
Mr. Jordan removed his hands from his brow and laid
them flat at his side on the rock.

'I was but a country gentleman, with humble pursuits
—a silent man, who did not care for society—and I knew
that I could not compare with the witty attractive men of
the world. I knew that Morwell was a solitary place, and
that there were few neighbours. I believed that Eve was
unhappy here : I thought she was pining to go back to the
merry life she had led with the players. I thought she was
weary of me, and I was jealous—jealous and suspicious. I
watched her, and when I found that she was meeting someone in secret here on this rock, and that she tried to hide
from me especially that she was doing this, then I went
mad—mad with disappointed love, mad with jealousy. I
knew she intended to run away from me.' He made a sign
with his hand that he could say no more.

Jasper was greatly moved. At length the mystery was
being revealed. The signs of insanity in the old man had
disappeared. He spoke with emotion, as was natural,
but not irrationally. The fact of being able to tell what
had long been consuming his mind relieved it, and perhaps
the blood he had lost reduced the fever which had produced
hallucination.

Jasper said in as quiet a voice as he could command,
'My sister loved you and her child, and had no mind to
leave you. She was grateful to you for your kindness
to her. Unfortunately her early life was not a happy one.
My father treated her with harshness and lack of
sympathy. He drove her, by his treatment, from home.

Now, Mr. Jordan, I can well believe that in a fit of jealousy and unreasoning passion you drove my poor sister away from Morwell—you were not legally married, and could do so. God forgive you! She did not desert you: you expelled her. Now I desire to know what became of her. Whither did she go? If she be still alive, I must find her.'

'She is not alive,' said Mr. Jordan.

Then a great horror came over Jasper, and he shrank away. 'You did not drive her in a fit of desperation to—to self-destruction?'

Mr. Jordan's earnest eyes were fixed on the dark night sky. He muttered — the words were hardly audible— *Si iniquitates observaveris, Domine : Domine, quis sustinebit?*

Jasper did not catch what he said, and thinking it was something addressed to him, he stooped over Mr. Jordan and said, 'What became of her? How did she die? Where is she buried?'

The old man raised himself on one arm and tried to sit up, and looked at Jasper with quivering lips; then held his arm over the rock as, pointing to the abyss, 'Here!' he whispered, and fell back on the moss.

Jasper saw that he had again become unconscious. He feared lest life—or reason—should desert him before he had told the whole story.

It was some time before the squire was able to speak. When consciousness returned he bent his face to Jasper, and there was not that flicker and wildness in his eyes which Jasper had observed at other times, and which had made him uneasy. Mr. Jordan looked intently and steadily at Jasper.

'She did not run away from me. I did not drive her from my house as you think. It can avail nothing to conceal the truth longer. I did not wish that Eve, my child, should know it; but now—it matters no more. My fears are over. I have nothing more to disturb me.

I care for no one else. I saw my wife on this rock meet the actor, I watched them. They did not know that I was spying. I could not hear much of what they said; I caught only snatches of sentences and stray words. I thought he was urging her to go with him.'

'No,' interrupted Jasper, 'it was not so. He advised her not to return with her father, but to remain with you.'

'Was it so? I was fevered with love and jealousy. I heard his last words—she was to be there on the morrow, Midsummer Day, and then to give the final decision. If I had had my gun I would have shot him there, but I was unarmed. All that night I was restless. I could not sleep; I was as one in a death agony. I thought that Eve was going to desert me for another. And when on the morrow, Midsummer Day, she went at the appointed hour to the Raven Rock, I followed her. She had taken her child—she had made up her mind—she was going. Then I took down my gun and loaded it.'

Jasper's heart stood still. Now for the first time he began to see and fear what was coming. This was worse than he had anticipated.

'I crept along behind a hedge, till I reached the wood. Then I stole through the gate under the trees. I came beneath the great Scotch pine'—he pointed in the direction. 'She had her child with her. She had made up her mind —so I thought—to leave me, and take with her the babe. That she could not leave. Now I see she took it only that she might show the little thing to her father. I watched her on the rock. She kissed the babe and soothed it, and fondled it, and sang to it. She had a sweet voice. I was watching—there—and I had my gun in my hands. The man was not come. I saw rise up before me the life my Eve would lead; I saw how she would sink, how the man would desert her, and she would fall lower; and my child, what would become of my child? Then she turned and looked in my direction. She was listening for the step of her lover. She stooped, and laid the child on the moss, where I lie now. I suppose it opened its eyes, and she began to sing and dance to it, snapping her fingers as though playing castanets. My heart flared within me, my hand shook, and God knows how it was—I do not. I cannot say how it came about, but in one moment the gun was discharged and she fell. I did not mean to kill her when I loaded it, but I did mean to kill the man, the seducer. But whether I did it purposely then, or my finger acted without my will, I cannot say. All is dark to me when I look back—dark as is the darkness over the edge of this rock.'

Jasper could not speak. He stood and looked with horror on the wounded, wretched man.

'I buried her,' said Mr. Jordan, 'in the old copper-mine—long deserted, and only known to me—and there she lies. That is the whole.'

Then he covered his eyes and said no more.

CHAPTER LIII.

BY LANTERN-LIGHT.

WHEN Barbara had finished her needlework, the wonder which had for some time been obtruding itself upon her—what had become of Eve—became prominent, and awoke a fear in her lest she should have run off into the wood to Martin. She did not wish to think that Eve would do such a thing; but, if she were not in the house, and neither her step nor her voice announced her presence, where was she? Eve was never able to amuse herself, by herself, for long. She must be with someone—with a maid if no one else were available. She had no resources in herself. If she were with Jasper, it did not matter; but Barbara hardly thought Eve was with him.

She laid aside her needlework, looked into her sister's room, without expecting to see Eve there, then descended and sought Jane, to inquire whether her father had given signs of being awake by knocking. Jane, however, was not in the pantry nor in the kitchen. Jane had not been seen for some time. Then Barbara very softly stole through the hall and tapped at her father's door. No answer. She opened it and looked in. The room was quite dark. She stood still and listened. She did not hear her father breathe. In some surprise, but hardly yet in alarm, she went for a candle, and returned with it to the room Mr. Jordan occupied. To her amazement and alarm, she found it empty. She ran into the parlour—no one was there. She sought through the house and garden, and stables—not a sign of her father anywhere, and, strangely enough, not of Eve, or of Jane either. Jasper, likewise, had not been seen for some time. Then, in her distress, Barbara rang the alarm-bell, long, hastily, and strongly. When, after the lapse of some while spent in fruitless search, Barbara arrived at the Raven Rock, she was not alone—two or three of the farm labourers and Joseph the policeman were with her. Jane had found her sweetheart on his way to Morwell to visit her. The light of the fire on the Rock, illumining the air above the trees, had attracted the notice of one of the workmen, and now the entire party came on to the Rock as Mr. Jordan had finished his confession, and Jasper, sick at heart, horror-stricken, stood back, speechless, not able to speak.

Barbara uttered a cry of dismay when she saw her father, and threw herself on her knees at his side. He made a sign to her to keep back, he did not want her; he beckoned to Jasper.

'One word more,' he said in a low tone. 'My hours are nearly over. Lay us all three together—my wife, my child, and me.'

'Papa,' said Barbara, 'what do you mean? what is the matter?'

He paid no attention to her. 'I have told you where *she* lies. When you have recovered my poor child——'

' What child ? ' asked Jasper.

' Eve ; what other ? '

Jasper did not understand, and supposed he was wandering.

' He—your brother—leaped off the precipice with her in his arms.'

' Papa ! ' cried Barbara.

' She is dead—dashed to pieces—and he too.

Barbara looked at Jasper, then, in terror ran to the edge. Nothing whatever could be seen. That platform of rock might be the end of the world, a cliff jutting forth into infinite space and descending into infinite abysses of blackness. She leaned over and called, but received no answer. Jasper could hardly believe in the truth of what had been said. Turning to the policeman and servants, he spoke sternly : ' Mr. Jordan must be removed at once. Let him be lifted very carefully and carried into the house. He has lain here already unsuccoured too long.'

' I will not be removed,' said the old man ; ' leave me here, I shall take no further harm. Go—seek for the body of my poor Eve.'

' John Westlake,' called Barbara to one of the men, ' give me the lantern at once.' The man was carrying one. Then, distracted between fear for her sister and anxiety about her father, she ran back to Mr. Jordan to know how he was.

' You need be in no immediate anxiety about him,' said Jasper. ' It is true that his wound has opened and bled, but I have tightly bandaged it again.'

Joseph, the policeman, stood by helpless, staring blankly about him and scratching his ear.

Then Barbara noticed a blanket lying in a heap on the rock—the blanket Jasper had brought to his brother, but which had been refused. She caught it up at once and tore it into shreds, knotted the ends together, took the lantern from the man Westlake, and let the light down the face of the crag. The lantern was of tin and horn, and through the sides but a dull light was thrown. She could see nothing—the lantern caught in ivy and heather bushes and turned on one side ; the candle-flame scorched the horn.

'I can see nothing,' she said despairingly. 'What shall I do ! '

Suddenly she grasped Jasper's hand, as he knelt by her, looking down.

'Do you hear ? '

A faint moan was audible. Was it a human voice, or was a bough swayed and groaning in the wind ?

All crowded to the edge and held their breath. Mr. Jordan was disregarded in the immediate interest attaching to the fate of Eve.

No other sound was heard.

Jasper ran and gathered fir and oak branches and grass, bound them into a faggot, set it on fire, and threw it over the edge, so that it might fall wide of the Rock and illumine its face. There was a glare for a moment, but the faggot went down too swiftly to be of any avail.

Then Walter, whom none had hitherto observed, pushed through, and, without saying a word to anyone, kicked off his shoes and went over the edge.

'Let him go,' said Jasper as one of the men endeavoured to stay him ; 'the boy can climb like a squirrel. Let him take the lantern, Barbara, that he may see where to plant his foot and what to hold.' Then he took the blanket rope from her hand, raised the light, and slowly lowered it again beside the descending boy.

Watt went down nimbly yet cautiously, clinging to ivy and tufts of grass, feeling every projection, and trying with his foot before trusting his weight to it. He did not hurry himself. He did not regard those who watched his advance. His descent was in zigzags. He crept along ledges, found a cleft or a step of stone, or a tuft of heather, cr a stem of ivy. All at once he grasped the lantern.

'I see something! Oh, Jasper, what can it be!'
gasped Barbara.

'Be careful,' he said; 'do not overbalance yourself.'

I have found *her*,' shouted Watt; 'only her—not
him.'

'God be praised!' whispered Barbara.

'Is she alive?' called Jasper.

'I do not know, I do not care. Martin is not here.'

'Now,' said Jasper, 'come on, you men—that is, all
but one. We must go below; not over the cliff, but round
through the coppice. We can find our way to the lantern.
The boy must be at the bottom. She has fallen,' he addressed Barbara now, 'she has fallen, I trust, among
bushes of oak which have broken the force of the fall. Do
not be discouraged. Trust in God. Stay here and pray.'

'Oh, Jasper, I cannot! I must go with you.'

'You cannot. You must not. The coppice and brambles would tear your clothes and hands and face. The
scramble is difficult by day and dangerous by night. You
must remain here by your father. Trust me. I will do
all in my power for poor Eve. We cannot bring her up
the way we descend. We must force our way laterally into
a path. You remain by your father, and let a man run
for another or two more lanterns.'

Then Jasper went down by way of the wood with the
men scrambling, falling, bursting through the brakes;
some cursing when slashed across the face by an oak bough
or torn through cloth and skin by a braid of bramble. They
were quite invisible to Barbara, and to each other. They
went downward: fast they could not go, fearing at every
moment to fall over a face of rock; groping, struggling as
with snakes, in the coils of wood; slipping, falling, scrambling to their feet again, calling each other, becoming
bewildered, losing their direction. The lantern that Watt
held was quite invisible to them, buried above their heads
in the densest undergrowth. The only man of them who
came unhurt out of the coppice was Joseph, who, fearing

for his face and hands and uniform, unwilling that he should appear lacerated and disfigured before Jane, instead of finding his way down through the brush, descended leisurely by the path or road that made a long circuit to the water's edge, and then ascended by the same road again to the place whence he had started.

Jasper, who had more intelligence than the rest, had taken his bearings, before starting, by the red star on the side of Hingston Hill, that shone out of a miner's hut window. This he was able always to see, and by it to steer his course; so that eventually he reached the spot where was Watt with the lantern.

'Where is she? What are you doing?' he asked breathlessly. His hands were torn and bleeding, his face bruised.

'Oh, I do not know. I left her. I want to find Martin—he cannot be far off.'

The boy was scrambling on a slope of fallen rubble.

'I insist, Watt: tell me. Give me the lantern at once.'

'I will not. She is up there. You can make out the ledge against the sky, and by the light of the fire above; but Martin—whither is he gone?'

Then away farther down went the boy with his lantern. Instead of following him, Jasper climbed up the rubble slope to the ledge. His eyes had become accustomed to the dark. He distinguished the fluttering end of a white or light-coloured dress. Then he swung himself up upon the ledge, and saw, by the faint light that still lingered in the sky, the figure of a woman—of Eve—lying on one side, with the hands clinging to a broken branch of ivy. A thick bed of heather was on this ledge—so thick that it had prevented Eve from rolling off it when she had fallen into the bush.

He stooped over her. He felt her heart, he put his ear to her mouth. Immediately he called up to Barbara, 'She is alive, but insensible.'

Then he put his hands to his mouth and shouted to the men who had started with him.

He was startled by seeing Watt with the lantern close to him: the light was on the boy's face. It was agitated with fear, rage, and distress. His eyes were full of tears, sweat poured from his brow.

'Why do you shout?' he said, and shook his fist in Jasper's face. 'Have you no care for Martin? I cannot find him yet, but he is near. Be silent, and do not bring the men here. If he is alive I will get him away in the boat. If he is dead——' then his sobs burst forth. 'Martin! poor Martin! where can he be! Do not call: let no one come here. Oh, Martin, Martin!' and away went the boy down again. 'Why is *she* fallen here and found at once, and *he* is lost! Oh, Martin—poor Martin!' the edge of the rock came in the way of the light, and Jasper saw no more of the boy and the lantern.

Unrestrained by what his youngest brother had said, Jasper called repeatedly, till at last the men gathered where he was. Then, with difficulty Eve was moved from where she lay and received in the arms of the men below. She moaned and cried out with pain, but did not recover consciousness.

Watt was travelling about farther down with his dull light, sometimes obscured, sometimes visible. One of the men shouted to him to bring the lantern up, but his call was disregarded, and next moment Watt and his lantern were forgotten, as another came down the face of the cliff, lowered by Barbara.

Then the men moved away with their burden, and one went before with the light exploring the way. Barbara above knelt at the edge of the rock and prayed, and as she prayed her tears fell over her cheeks.

At length the little cluster of men appeared with their light through the trees, approaching the Rock from the wood; they had reached the path and were coming along it. Jasper took the lantern and led the way.

A A

'Lay her here,' he said, 'near her father, where there is moss, till we can get a couple of gates.' Then, suddenly, as the men were about to obey him, he uttered an exclamation of horror. He had put the lantern down beside Mr. Jordan.

'Stand back,' he said to Barbara, who was coming up, ' stand back, I pray you ! '

But there was no need for her to stand back: she had seen what he would have hidden from her. In the darkness and loneliness, unobserved, Mr. Jordan had torn away his bandages, and his blood had deluged the turf. It had ceased to flow now—for he was dead.

CHAPTER LIV.

ANOTHER LOAD.

THE sad procession moved to Morwell out of the wood, preceded by the man Westlake, mounted on Jasper's horse, riding hard for the doctor. Then came a stable-boy with the lantern, and after the light two gates—first, that on which was laid the dead body of Mr. Jordan ; then another, followed closely by Barbara, on which lay Eve breathing, but now not even moaning. As the procession was half through the first field the bell of the house tolled. Westlake had communicated the news to the servant-maids, and one of them at once went to the bell.

Lagging behind all came Joseph Woodman, the policeman. The King of France in the ballad marched up a hill, and then marched down again, having accomplished nothing. Joseph had reversed the process : he had leisurely marched down the hill, and then more leisurely marched up it again ; but the result was the same as that attained by the King of France.

On reaching Morwell Jasper said in a low voice to the men, 'You must return with me: there is another to be sought for. Who saw the boy with the lantern last? He may have found him by this time.'

Then Joseph said slowly, 'As I was down by the boat-house I saw something.'

'What did you see?'

'I saw up on the hill-side a lantern travelling this way, then that way, so'—he made a zigzag indication in the air with his finger. 'It went very slow. It went, so to speak, like a drop o' rain on a window-pane, that goes this way, then it goes a little more that way, then it goes quite contrary, to the other side. Then it changes its direction once again and it goes a little faster.'

'I wish you would go faster,' said Jasper impatiently. 'What did you see at last?'

'I'm getting into it, but I must go my own pace,' said Joseph with unruffled composure. 'You understand me, brothers—I'm not speaking of a drop o' rain on a window-glass, but of a lantern-light on the hill-side—and bless you, that hill-side was like a black wall rising up on my right hand into the very sky. Well then, the light it travelled like a drop o' rain on a glass—first to this side, then to that. You've seen drops o' rain how they travel'—he appealed to all who listened. 'And I reckon you know how that all to once like the drop, after having travelled first this road, then that road, in a queer contrary fashion, and very slow, all to once like, as I said, down it runs like a winking of the eye and is gone. So exactly was it with thicky (that) there light. It rambled about on the face of the blackness: first it crawled this way, then it crept that; always, brothers, going a little lower and then—to once—whish!—I saw it shoot like a falling star—I mean a raindrop—and I saw it no more.'

'And then?'

'Why—and then I came back the same road I went down.'

'You did not go into the bushes in search?'

' How should I ? ' answered Joseph, ' I'd my best uniform on. I'd come out courting, not thief-catching.'

' And you know nothing further ? '

' How should I ? Didn't I say I went back up the road
same way as I'd come down ? I warn't bound to get my
new cloth coat and trousers tore all abroad by brimbles,
not for nobody. I know my duty better than that. The
county pays for 'em.'

Directed by this poor indication, Jasper led the men
back into the wood and down the woodman's truck
road, that led by a long sweep to the bottom of the
cliffs.

The search was for a long time ineffectual ; but at
length, at the foot of a rock, they came on the object of
their quest—the body of Martin—among fragments of
fallen crag, and over it, clinging to his brother with
one arm, the hand passed through the ring of a battered
lantern, was Walter. The light was extinguished in the
lantern and the light was beaten out of the brothers.
Jasper looked into the poor boy's face—a scornful smile
still lingered on the lips.

Apparently he had discovered his brother's body and
then had tried to drag it away down the steep slope towards the old mine, in the hopes of hiding there and finding that Martin was stunned, not dead ; but in the darkness he had stumbled over another precipice or slidden
down a run of shale and been shot with his burden over a
rock. Again the sad procession was formed. The two
gates that had been already used were put in requisition a
second time, and the bodies of Martin and Watt were
carried to Morwell and laid in the hall, side by side, and
he who carried a light placed it at their head.

Mr. Coyshe had arrived. For three of those brought
in no medical aid was of avail.

Barbara, always practical and self-possessed, had
ordered the cook to prepare supper for the men. Then the
two dead brothers were left where they had been laid, with

the dull lantern burning at their head, and the hungry searchers went to the kitchen to refresh.

Joseph ensconced himself by the fire, and Jane drew close to him.

'I reckon,' said the policeman, 'I'll have some hot grog.' Then he slid his arm round Jane's waist and said, 'In the midst of death we are in life. Is that really, now, giblet pie? The cold joint I don't fancy '—he gave Jane a smack on the cheek. 'Jane, I'll have a good help of the giblet pie, please, and the workmen can finish the cold veal. I like my grog hot and strong and with three lumps of double-refined sugar. You'll take a sip first, Jane, and I'll drink where your honeyed lips have a-sipped. When you come to consider it in a proper spirit '—he drew Jane closer to his side—' there's a deal of truth in Scriptur'. In the midst of death we *are* in life. Why, Jane, we shall enjoy ourselves this evening as much as if we were at a love-feast. I've a sweet tooth, Jane—a very sweet tooth.'

CHAPTER LV.

WHAT EVERY FOOL KNOWS.

JASPER stood on the staircase waiting. Then he heard a step descend. There was no light: the maids, in the excitement and confusion, had forgotten their duties. No lamp on the staircase, none in the hall. Only in the latter the dull glimmer of the horn lantern that irradiated but did not illumine the faces of two who were dead. The oak door at the foot of the stairs was ajar, and a feeble light from this lantern penetrated to the staircase. The window admitted some greyness from the overcast sky.

'Tell me, Barbara,' he said, 'what is the doctor's report?'

Jasper!' Then Barbara's strength gave way, and

she burst into a flood of tears. He put his arm round her, and she rested her head on his breast and cried herself out. She needed this relief. She had kept control over herself by the strength of her will. There was no one in the house to think for her, to arrange anything ; she had the care of everything on her, beside her great sorrow for her father, and fear for Eve. As for the servant girls, they were more trouble than help. *Men* were in the kitchen ; that sufficed to turn their heads and make them leave undone all they ought to have done, and do just those things they ought not to do. At this moment, after the strain, the presence of a sympathetic heart opened the fountain of her tears and broke down her self-restraint.

Jasper did not interrupt her, though he was anxious to know the result of Mr. Coyshe's examination. He waited patiently, with the weeping girl in his arms, till she looked up and said, ' Thank you, dear friend, for letting me cry here : it has done me good.'

' Now, Barbara, tell me all.'

' Jasper, the doctor says that Eve will live.'

' God's name be praised for that ! '

' But he says that she will be nothing but a poor cripple all her days.'

' Then we must take care of her.'

' Yes, Jasper, I will devote my life to her.'

' *We* will, Barbara.'

She took his hand and pressed it between both hers.

' But,' she said hesitatingly, ' what if Mr. Coyshe——' She did not finish the sentence.

' Wait till Mr. Coyshe claims her.'

' He is engaged to her, so of course he will, the more readily now that she is such a poor crushed worm.'

Jasper said nothing. He knew Mr. Coyshe better than Barbara, perhaps. He had taken his measure when he went with him over the farm after the signing of the will.

' This place is hers by her father's will,' said Jasper ;

'and, should the surgeon draw back, she will need you and me to look after her interests.'

'Yes,' said Barbara, 'she will need us both.'

Then she withdrew her hands and returned upstairs.

A few days later Mr. Coyshe took occasion to clear the ground. He explained to Barbara that his engagement must be considered at an end. He was very sorry, but he must look out for his own interests, as he had neither parent alive to look out for them for him. It would be quite impossible for him to get on with a wife who was a cripple.

'You are premature, Mr. Coyshe,' said Miss Jordan stiffly. 'If you had waited till my sister were able to speak and act, she would have, herself, released you.'

'Exactly,' said the unabashed surgeon; 'but I am so considerate of the feelings of the lady, that I spare her the trouble.'

And now let us spread the golden wings of fancy, and fly the scenes of sorrow—but fly, not in space, but in time; measure not miles, but months.

It is autumn, far on into September, and Michaelmas has brought with it the last days of summer. Not this the autumn that we saw coming on, with the turning dogwood and bird-cherry, but another.

In the garden the colchicum has raised its pale lilac flowers. The Michaelmas daisy is surrounded by the humming-bird moth with transparent wings, but wings that vibrate so fast that they can only be seen as a quiver of light. The mountain ash is hung with clusters of clear crimson berries, and the redbreasts and finches are about it, tearing improvidently at the store, thoughtless of the coming winter, and strewing the soil with wasted coral.

Eve is seated in the sun outside the house, in the garden, and on her knees is a baby—Barbara's child, and yet Eve's also, for if Barbara gave it life, Eve gave it a name. Before her sister Barbara kneels, now just restored from her confinement, a little pale and large in eye, looking up at her sister and then down at the child. Jasper stands by contemplating the pretty group.

'Eve,' said Barbara in a low tremulous voice, 'I have had for some months on my heart a great fear lest, when my little one came, I should love it with all my heart, and rob you. I had the same fear before I married Jasper, lest he should snatch some of my love away from the dear suffering sister who needs all. But now I have no such fear any more, for love, I find, is a great mystery—it is infinitely divisible, yet ever complete. It is like'—she lowered her voice reverently—' it is like what we Catholics believe about the body of our Lord, the very Sacrament of Love. That is in Heaven and in every church. It is on every altar, and in every communicant, entire. I thought once that when I had a husband, and then a little child, love would suffer diminution—that I could not share love without lessening the portion of each. But it is not so. I love my baby with my whole undivided heart ; I love you, my sister, equally with my whole undivided heart ; and I love my husband also,' she turned and smiled at Jasper, 'with my very whole and undivided heart. It is a great mystery, but love is divine, and divine things are perceived and believed by the heart, though beyond the reason.'

'So,' said Eve, smiling, and with her blue eyes filling, ' my dear, dear Barbara, once so prosaic and so practical, is becoming an idealist and poetical.'

'Wherever unselfish love reigns, there is poetry,' said Jasper ; 'the sweetest of the songs of life is the song of self-sacrificing love. Barbara never was prosaic. She was always an idealist ; but, my dear Eve, the heart needs culture to see and distinguish true poetry from false sentiment. That you lacked at one time. That you have now. I once knew a little girl, light of heart, and loving only self, with no earnest purpose, blown about by every caprice. Now I see a change—a change from base element to a divine presence. I see a sweet face as of old, but I see something in it, new-born; a soul full of self-reproach and passionate love; a heart that is innocent as of old, but yet that has learned a great deal, and all good, through suffering. I see a life that was once purposeless now instinct with purpose—the purpose to live for duty, in self-sacrifice, and not for pleasure. My dear Eve, the great and solemn priest Pain has laid his hands on you and broken you, and held you up to Heaven, and you are not what you were, and yet—and yet are the same.'

Eve could not speak. She put her arms round her sister's neck, and clung to her, and the tears flowed from both their eyes, and fell upon the tiny Eve lying on the knees of the elder Eve.

But though they were clasped over the child, no shadow fell on its little face. The baby laughed.

.　　.　　.　　.　　.　　.　　.

Some years ago—the author cannot at the moment say how many, nor does it matter—he paid a visit to Morwell, and saw the sad havoc that had been wrought to the venerable hunting-lodge of the Abbots of Tavistock. The old hall had disappeared, a floor had been put across it, and it had been converted into an upper and lower story of rooms. One wing had been transformed into a range of model cottages for labourers. The house of the Jordans was now a farm.

The author asked if he might see the remains of antiquity within the house.

An old woman who had answered his knock and ring, replied, ' There are none—all have been swept away.'

' But,' said he, ' in my childhood I remember that the place was full of interest; and by the way, what has become of the good people who lived here? I have been in another part of the country, and indeed a great deal abroad.'

' Do you mean Mr. Jasper ? '

' No : Jasper, no—the name began with J.'

'The old Squire Jordan your honour means, no doubt. He be dead ages ago. Mr. Jasper married Miss Jordan—Miss Barbara we called her. When Miss Eve died, they went away to Buckfastleigh, where they had a house and a factory. There was a queer matter about the old squire's death—did you never hear of that, sir?'

'I heard something; but I was very young then.'

'My Joseph could tell you all about it better than I.'

'Who is your Joseph?'

'Well, sir, I'm ashamed to say it, but he's my sweetheart, who's been a-courting of me these fifty years.'

'Not married yet?'

'He's a slow man is Joseph. I reckon he'd 'a' spoken out if he d been able at last, but the paralysis took 'm in the legs. He put off and off—and I encouraged him all I could; but he always was a slow man.'

'Where is he now?'

'Oh, he's with his married sister. He sits in a chair, and when I can I run to 'm and take him some backy or barley-sugar. He's vastly fond o' sucking sticks o' barley-sugar. Gentlefolks as come here sometimes give me a shilling, and I lay that out on getting Joseph what he likes. He always had a sweet tooth.'

'Then you love him still?'

The old woman looked at me with surprise. Her hand and head shook.

'Of course I does: love is eternal—every fool knows that.'

THE END.

PRINTED BY
SPOTTISWOODE AND CO., NEW-STREET SQUARE
LONDON

ALPHABETICAL CATALOGUE OF BOOKS

IN

GENERAL LITERATURE AND FICTION

PUBLISHED BY

CHATTO & WINDUS

III ST. MARTIN'S LANE, CHARING CROSS

Telegrams
Bookstore, London

LONDON, W.C.

Telephone No.
3524 Central

ADAMS (W. DAVENPORT).—
A Dictionary of the Drama: A Guide to the Plays, Playwrights, Players, and Playhouses of the United Kingdom and America, from the Earliest Times to the Present. Vol. I. (A to G). Demy 8vo, cloth 10s. 6d. net.—Vol. II., completing the Work, is in preparation.

À KEMPIS (THOMAS).—Of the Imitation of Christ, as translated from the Latin by RICHARD WHYTFORD in 1556; re-edited into modern English by WILFRID RAYNAL, O.S.B. With Illustrations in colour and line by W. RUSSELL FLINT. Large crown 8vo, cloth, 7s. 6d. net; EDITION DE LUXE, small 4to, printed on pure rag paper, parchment, 15s. net; pigskin with clasps, 25s. net.

ALDEN (W. L.). — Drewitt's Dream. Crown 8vo, cloth, 6s.

ALLEN (GRANT), Books by.
Post-Prandial Philosophy. Crown 8vo, art linen, 3s. 6d.

Crown 8vo, cloth, 3s. 6d. each; post 8vo, illustrated boards, 2s. each.
Babylon. With 12 Illustrations.
Strange Stories.
The Beckoning Hand.
For Maimie's Sake.
Philistia. | **In all Shades.**
The Devil's Die.
This Mortal Coil.
The Tents of Shem.
The Great Taboo.
Dumaresq's Daughter.
Under Sealed Orders.
The Duchess of Powysland.
Blood Royal.
Ivan Greet's Masterpiece.
The Scallywag. With 24 Illustrations.
At Market Value.

The Tents of Shem. POPULAR EDITION, medium 8vo, 6d.
Babylon. CHEAP EDITION, post 8vo, cloth, 1s. net.

ANDERSON (MARY).—Othello's Occupation. Crown 8vo, cloth, 3s. 6d.

ANTROBUS (C. L.), Novels by.
Crown 8vo, cloth, 6s. each.
Quality Corner. | **Wildersmoor**
The Wine of Finvarra.

ALEXANDER (Mrs.), Novels by.
Crown 8vo, cloth 3s. 6d. each; post 8vo, picture boards, 2s. each.
Valerie's Fate. | **Mona's Choice.**
A Life Interest. | **Woman's Wit.**

Crown 8vo, cloth, 3s. 6d. each.
The Cost of her Pride.
A Golden Autumn.
Barbara, Lady's Maid & Peeress.
Mrs. Crichton's Creditor.
A Missing Hero.
A Fight with Fate.
The Step-mother.

Blind Fate. Post 8vo, picture boards, 2s.

ALMAZ (E. F.).—Copper under the Gold. Crown 8vo, cloth, 3s. 6d.

AMERICAN FARMER, LETTERS FROM AN. By J. H. St. JOHN CRÈVECOEUR, with Prefatory Note by W. P. TRENT, and Introduction by LUDWIG LEWISOHN. Demy 8vo, cloth, 6s. net.

APPLETON (G. W.), Novels by.
Rash Conclusions. Cr. 8vo, cl., 3s. 6d.
The Lady in Sables. Cr. 8vo, cl., 6s.

ARNOLD (E. L.), Stories by.
The Wonderful Adventures of Phra the Phœnician. Crown 8vo, cloth, with 12 Illusts. by H. M. PAGET, 3s. 6d.; post 8vo, illustrated boards, 2s.
The Constable of St. Nicholas. With a Frontispiece. Crown 8vo, cloth, 3s. 6d.; picture cloth, flat back, 2s.

ART and LETTERS LIBRARY (The). Large crown 8vo. Each volume with 8 Coloured Plates, and 24 in Half-tone. Buckram, 7s. 6d. net per vol. EDITION DE LUXE, small 4to, with 5 additl. plates, printed on pure rag paper, parchment, 15s. net per vol.; vellum, 20s. net per vol.; morocco, 30s. net per vol.
Stories of the Italian Artists from Vasari. Collected and arranged by E. L. SEELEY.
Artists of the Italian Renaissance: their Stories as set forth by Vasari, Ridolfi, Lanzi, and the Chroniclers. Collected and arranged by E. L. SEELEY.
Stories of the Flemish and Dutch Artists, from the Time of the Van Eycks to the End of the Seventeenth Century, drawn from Contemporary Records. Collected and arranged by VICTOR REYNOLDS.

ART & LETTERS LIBRARY—*contd.*

Stories of the English Artists, from Vandyck to Turner (1600-1851), drawn from Contemporary Records. Collected and arranged by RANDALL DAVIES and CECIL HUNT.

Stories of the French Artists, from Clouet to Ingres, drawn from Contemporary Records. Collected and arranged by P. M. TURNER and C. H. COLLINS BAKER.

Stories of the Spanish Artists until Goya. Drawn from Contemporary Records. Collected and arranged by LUIS CARRENO. [*Preparing.*

The Little Flowers of S. Francis of Assisi: Trans. by Prof. T. W. ARNOLD.

Large crown 8vo, cloth, 7s. 6d. net each ; parchment, 10s. 6d. net each.

Women of Florence. By Prof. ISIDORO DEL LUNGO. Translated by MARY G. STEEGMANN. With Introduction by Dr. GUIDO BIAGI, 2 Coloured Plates and 24 in Half-tone.

The Master of Game: The Oldest English Book on Hunting. By EDWARD, Second Duke of York. Edited by W. A. and F. BAILLIE-GROHMAN. With Introduction by THEODORE ROOSEVELT, Photogravure Frontispiece, and 23 full-page Illustrations after Illuminations.

ARTEMUS WARD'S Works. Crown 8vo, cloth, with Portrait, 3s. 6d.; post 8vo, illustrated boards, 2s.

ARTIST (The Mind of the): Thoughts and Sayings of Artists on their Art. Collected and arranged by Mrs. LAURENCE BINYON. With 8 full-page Plates. Fcap.8vo. cloth,gilt top, 3s.6d.net.

ASHTON (JOHN).—Social Life in the Reign of Queen Anne. With 85 Illustrations. Crown 8vo, cloth, 3s. 6d.

AUGUSTINE (Saint), The Confessions of, as translated by Dr. E. B. PUSEY. Edited by TEMPLE SCOTT, with an Introduction by Mrs. MEYNELL. With 11 Plates in four colours and 1 in four colours and gold, by MAXWELL ARMFIELD. Large cr. 8vo, cloth, 7s. 6d. net. Also an EDITION DE LUXE. cr. 4to, pure rag paper,with the plates mtd.,parchment, 15s. net; pigskin with clasps, 25s. net.

AUSTEN (JANE), The Works of: The ST. MARTIN'S ILLUSTRATED EDITION, in Ten Volumes, each Illustrated with Ten Reproductions after Water-colours by A. WALLIS MILLS. With Bibliographical and Biographical Notes by R. BRIMLEY JOHNSON. Post 8vo, cloth, 3s. 6d. net per vol. The Novels are arranged in the following order. Vols. I. and II., PRIDE AND PREJUDICE; Vols. III. and IV., SENSE AND SENSIBILITY; Vol. V., NORTHANGER ABBEY; Vol. VI., PERSUASION; Vols. VII. and VIII., EMMA ; Vols. IX. and X., MANSFIELD PARK.

AUTHORS for the POCKET. Mostly compiled by A. H. HYATT. 16mo, cloth, 2s. net each ; leather, 3s. net each.

The Pocket R. L. S.
The Pocket Thackeray.
The Pocket Charles Dickens.
The Pocket Richard Jefferies.
The Pocket George MacDonald.
The Pocket Emerson.
The Pocket Thomas Hardy.
The Pocket George Eliot.
The Pocket Charles Kingsley.
The Pocket Ruskin.
The Pocket Lord Beaconsfield.
The Flower of the Mind.

BACTERIA, Yeast Fungi, and Allied Species, A Synopsis of. By W. B. GROVE, B.A. With 87 Illustrations. Crown 8vo, cloth, 3s. 6d.

BALLADS and LYRICS of LOVE, selected from PERCY'S 'Reliques.' Edited with an Introduction by F. SIDGWICK. With 10 Plates in Colour after BYAM SHAW, R.I. Large fcap. 4to, cloth, 6s. net ; LARGE PAPER EDITION, parchment, 12s. 6d. net.

Legendary Ballads, selected from PERCY'S 'Reliques.' Edited with an Introduction by F. SIDGWICK. With 10 Plates in Colour after BYAM SHAW, R.I. Large fcap. 4to, cloth, 6s. net ; LARGE PAPER EDITION, parchment, 12s. 6d. net.

BARDSLEY (Rev. C. W.).— English Surnames: Their Sources and Significations. Cr. 8vo, cloth, 7s. 6d.

BARGAIN BOOK (The).—By C. E. JERNINGHAM. With a Photogravure Frontispiece. Demy 8vo, cloth, 10s. 6d. net. [*Preparing.*

BARING-GOULD (S.), Novels by. Crown 8vo, cloth, 3s. 6d. each ; post 8vo, illustrated boards, 2s. each ; POPULAR EDITIONS, medium 8vo, 6d. each.
Red Spider. | **Eve.**

BARKER (ELSA).—The Son of Mary Bethel. Crown 8vo, cloth, 6s.

BARR (AMELIA E.).—Love will Venture in. Cr. 8vo, cloth, 3s. 6d.

BARR (ROBERT), Stories by. Crown 8vo, cloth, 3s. 6d. each.
In a Steamer Chair. With 2 Illusts.
From Whose Bourne, &c. With 47 Illustrations by HAL HURST and others.
Revenge! With 12 Illustrations by LANCELOT SPEED and others.
A Woman Intervenes.
A Prince of Good Fellows. With 15 Illustrations by E. J. SULLIVAN.
The Speculations of John Steele.
The Unchanging East.

BARRETT (FRANK), Novels by. Post 8vo, illust. bds., 2s. ea.; cl., 2s. 6d. ea.
The Sin of Olga Zassoulich.
Little Lady Linton.
Honest Davie. | **Found Guilty**

BARRETT (FRANK), Novels by—*cont.*
Post 8vo, illus., bds., 2s. ea.; cl., 2s. 6d.ea.
John Ford; and His Helpmate.
A Recoiling Vengeance.
Lieut. Barnabas.

Cr. 8vo, cloth, 3s. 6d. each; post 8vo, illust.
boards, 2s. each; cloth limp, 2s. 6d. each.
For Love and Honour.
Between Life and Death.
Fettered for Life.
A Missing Witness. With 8 Illustrations by W. H. MARGETSON.
The Woman of the Iron Bracelets.
The Harding Scandal.
A Prodigal's Progress.
Folly Morrison.
Under a Strange Mask. With 19 Illustrations by E. F. BREWTNALL.
Was She Justified?
The Obliging Husband. With Coloured Frontispiece.

Crown 8vo, cloth, 6s. each.
Lady Judas.
The Error of Her Ways.

Fettered for Life. POPULAR EDITION, medium 8vo, 6d.

BARRINGTON (MICHAEL).—
The Knight of the Golden Sword.
Crown 8vo, cloth, 6s.

BASKERVILLE (JOHN): A
Memoir. By RALPH STRAUS and R. K.
DENT. With 13 Plates. Large quarto,
buckram, 21s. net.

BATH (The) in Diseases of the
Skin. by J. L. MILTON. Post 8vo, 1s.;
cloth, 1s. 6d.

BEACONSFIELD, LORD. ByT.
P. O'CONNOR, M.P. Crown 8vo, cloth, 5s.

BECHSTEIN(LUDWIG), and the
Brothers GRIMM.—As Pretty as
Seven, and other Stories. With 98
Illustrations by RICHTER. Square 8vo,
cloth, 6s. 6d.; gilt edges, 7s. 6d.

BENNETT (ARNOLD), Novels
by. Crown 8vo, cloth, 6s. each.
Leonora. | A Great Man.
Teresa of Watling Street. With 8
Illustrations by FRANK GILLETT.
Tales of the Five Towns.
Hugo.
Sacred and Profane Love. Crown
8vo, cloth, 6s.; CHEAP EDITION, with
picture cover in 3 colours, 1s. net.

Crown 8vo, cloth, 3s. 6d. each.
Anna of the Five Towns.
The Gates of Wrath.
The Ghost. | The City of Pleasure.

The Grand Babylon Hotel. Crown
8vo, cloth, 3s. 6d.; POPULAR EDITION,
medium 8vo, 6d.

BENNETT (W. C.).—Songs for
Sailors. Post 8vo, cloth, 2s.

BESANT and RICE, Novels by.
Cr. 8vo, cloth, 3s. 6d. each; post 8vo,
illust. bds. 2s. each; cl. limp, 2s. 6d. each.
Ready-Money Mortiboy.
The Golden Butterfly.
My Little Girl
With Harp and Crown.
This Son of Vulcan.
The Monks of Thelema.
By Celia's Arbour.
The Chaplain of the Fleet.
The Seamy Side.
The Case of Mr. Lucraft.
'Twas in Trafalgar's Bay.
The Ten Years' Tenant.

BESANT (Sir WALTER),
Novels by. Crown 8vo, cloth, 3s. 6d.
each; post 8vo, illustrated boards, 2s.
each; cloth limp, 2s. 6d. each.
All Sorts and Conditions of Men.
With 12 Illustrations by FRED. BARNARD.
The Captain's Room, &c.
All in a Garden Fair. With 6 Illustrations by HARRY FURNISS.
Dorothy Forster. With Frontispiece.
Uncle Jack, and other Stories.
Children of Gibeon.
The World Went Very Well Then.
With 12 Illustrations by A. FORESTIER.
Herr Paulus.
The Bell of St. Paul's.
For Faith and Freedom. With
Illusts. by A. FORESTIER and F. WADDY.
To Call Her Mine, &c. With 9 Illustrations by A. FORESTIER.
The Holy Rose, &c. With Frontispiece.
Armorel of Lyonesse. With 12 Illustrations by F. BARNARD.
St. Katherine's by the Tower.
With 12 Illustrations by C. GREEN.
Verbena Camellia Stephanotis.
The Ivory Gate.
The Rebel Queen.
Beyond the Dreams of Avarice.
With 12 Illustrations by W. H. HYDE.
In Deacon's Orders, &c. With Frontis.
The Revolt of Man.
The Master Craftsman.
The City of Refuge.

Crown 8vo, cloth 3s. 6d. each.
A Fountain Sealed.
The Changeling.
The Fourth Generation.
The Orange Girl. With 8 Illustrations
by F. PEGRAM.
The Alabaster Box.
The Lady of Lynn. With 12 Illustrations by G. DEMAIN-HAMMOND.
No Other Way. With 12 Illustrations
by C. D. WARD.

Crown 8vo, picture cloth, flat back, 2s. each.
St. Katherine's by the Tower.
The Rebel Queen.

LARGE TYPE, FINE PAPER EDITIONS, pott
8vo, cloth, gilt top, 2s. net each; leather,
gilt edges, 3s. net each.
London.
Westminster.
Jerusalem. (In collaboration with Prof.
E. H. PALMER.)

BESANT (Sir Walter)—*continued.*
FINE PAPER EDITIONS, pott 8vo, 2s. net ea.
Sir Richard Whittington.
Gaspard de Coligny.
All Sorts and Conditions of Men.
POPULAR EDITIONS, medium 8vo, 6*d.* each
All Sorts and Conditions of Men.
The Golden Butterfly.
Ready-Money Mortiboy.
By Celia's Arbour.
The Chaplain of the Fleet.
The Monks of Thelema.
The Orange Girl.
For Faith and Freedom.
Children of Gibeon.
DorothyForster. | **No Other Way.**
Demy 8vo, cloth, 7*s. 6d.* each.
London. With 125 Illustrations.
Westminster. With Etching by F. S.
WALKER, and 130 Illustrations.
South London. With Etching by F. S.
WALKER, and 118 Illustrations.
East London. With Etching by F. S.
WALKER, and 56 Illustrations by PHIL
MAY, L. RAVEN HILL, and J. PENNELL.
Crown 8vo, buckram, 6*s.* each.
As We Are and As We May Be.
Essays and Historiettes.
The Eulogy of Richard Jefferies.
Crown 8vo, cloth, 3*s. 6d.* each.
Fifty Years Ago. With 144 Illusts.
The Charm, and other Drawing-room
Plays. With 50 Illustrations by CHRIS
HAMMOND, &c.
Art of Fiction. Fcap. 8vo, cloth, 1*s.* net.

BIBLIOTHECA ROMANICA: A

series of the Classics of the Romance
(French, Italian, Spanish, and Portu-
guese) Languages: the Original Text,
with, where necessary, Notes and Introductions in the language of the Text.
Small 8vo, single parts, 8*d.* net per
vol.; cloth, single parts, 1*s.* net per vol.
Where two or more units are bound in one
volume (indicated by numbers against
the title) the price in wrapper remains 8d.
per unit, *i.e.*, two numbers cost 1*s. 4d.*;
three cost 2*s.*; four cost 2*s. 8d.* In the
cloth binding the additional cost is 4*d*
for the first, and 1*d.* for each succeeding
unit: *i.e.*, one unit costs 1*s.*; two cost
1*s. 9d.*; three cost 2*s. 6d.*; four cost 3*s. 3d.*

1. **Molière:** Le Misanthrope.
2. **Molière:** Les Femmes savantes.
3. **Corneille:** Le Cid.
4. **Descartes:** Discours de la mé-
thode.
5-6. **Dante:** Divina Commedia I.:
Inferno.
7. **Boccaccio:** Decameron: Prima
giornata.
8. **Calderon:** La vida es sueño.
9. **Restif de la Bretonne:** L'an
2000.
10. **Camões:** Os Lusiadas: Canto I., II.
11. **Racine:** Athalie.
12-15. **Petrarca:** Rerum vulgarium
fragmenta.
16-17. **Dante:** Divina Commedia II.:
Purgatorio,

BIBLIOTHECA ROMANICA—*continued.*
18-20. **Tillier:** Mon oncle Benjamin.
21-22. **Boccaccio:** Decameron: Seconda
giornata.
23-24. **Beaumarchais:** Le Barbier de
Séville.
25. **Camões:** Os Lusiadas: Canto III.
IV.
26-28. **Alfred de Musset:** Comédies et
Proverbes: La Nuit vénitienne;
André del Sarto; Les Caprices de
Marianne; Fantasio; On ne badine
pas avec l'amour.
29. **Corneille:** Horace.
30-31. **Dante:** Divina Commedia III.:
Paradiso.
32-34. **Prevost:** Manon Lescaut.
35-36. **Œuvres de Maître François
Villon.**
37-39. **Guillem de Castro:** Las Moce-
dades del Cid, I., II.
40. **Dante:** La Vita Nuova.
41-44. **Cervantes:** Cinco Novelas ejem-
plares.
45. **Camões:** Os Lusiadas: Canto V.,
VI., VII.
46. **Molière:** L'Avare.
47. **Petrarca:** I Trionfi.
48-49. **Boccaccio:** Decameron: Terza
giornata.
50. **Corneille:** Cinna.
51-52 **Camões:** Os Lusiadas: Canto VIII.,
IX., X.
53-54. **La Chanson de Roland.**
55-58 **Alfred de Musset:** Premières
Poésies.
59. **Boccaccio:** Decameron: Quarta
giornata.
60-61. **Maistre Pierre Pathelin:**
Farce du XV* siècle.
62-63. **Giacomo Leopardi:** Canti.
64-65. **Chateaubriand:** Atala.
66. **Boccaccio:** Decameron, Quinta
giornata.
67-70. **Blaise Pascal:** Les Provinciales

BIERCE (AMBROSE).—In the

Midst of Life. Crown 8vo, cloth, 3*s. 6d.*:
post 8vo, illustrated boards, 2*s.*; Cheap
Edition, picture cover, 1*s.* net.

BINDLOSS (HAROLD), Novels by.

Crown 8vo, cloth, 6*s.* each.
The Concession-Hunters.
The Mistress of Bonaventure.
Daventry's Daughter.

A Sower of Wheat. Cr. 8vo, cl., 3*s. 6d.*
Ainslie's Ju-ju. Crown 8vo, cloth,
3*s. 6d.*; picture cloth, flat back, 2*s.*

BLAKE (WILLIAM): A Critical

Study by A. C. SWINBURNE. With a
Portrait. Crown 8vo, buckram, 6*s.* net.

BOCCACCIO.—The Decameron.

With a Portrait. Pott 8vo, cloth, gilt
top, 2*s.* net; leather, gilt edges, 3*s.* net.

BODKIN (McD., K.C.), Books by. Crown 8vo, cloth, 3s. 6d. each.
Dora Myrl, the Lady Detective.
Shillelagh and Shamrock.
Patsev the Omadaun.

BORENIUS (TANCRED).—The Painters of Vicenza. With 15 Full-page Plates. Demy 8vo, cloth, 7s. 6d. net.

BOURGET (PAUL).—A Living Lie. Translated by JOHN DE VILLIERS. Crown 8vo, cloth, 3s. 6d.; Cheap Edition, picture cover, 1s. net.

BOYLE (F.), Works by. Post 8vo, illustrated boards, 2s. each.
Chronicles of No-Man's Land.
Camp Notes. | Savage Life.

BRAND (JOHN).—Observations on Popular Antiquities. With the Additions of Sir HENRY ELLIS. Crown 8vo, cloth, 3s. 6d.

BRAYSHAW (J. DODSWORTH). —Slum Silhouettes: Stories of London Life. Crown 8vo, cloth, 3s. 6d.

BREWER'S (Rev. Dr.) Diction- aries. Crown 8vo, cloth, 3s. 6d. each.
The Reader's Handbook of Famous Names in Fiction, Allusions, References, Proverbs, Plots, Stories, and Poems.
A Dictionary of Miracles: Imitative, Realistic, and Dogmatic.

BREWSTER (Sir DAVID), Works by. Post 8vo, cloth, 4s. 6d. each.
More Worlds than One: Creed of Philosopher, Hope of Christian. Plates.
The Martyrs of Science: GALILEO, TYCHO BRAHE, and KEPLER.
Letters on Natural Magic. With numerous Illustrations.

BRIDGE CATECHISM. By R. H. BRYDGES. Fcap. 8vo, cloth, 2s. 6d. net.

BRIDGE (J. S. C.).—From Island to Empire: A History of the Expansion of England by Force of Arms. With Introduction by Adm. Sir CYPRIAN BRIDGE. Maps and Plans. Large crown 8vo, cloth, 6s. net.

BRIGHT (FLORENCE).—A Girl Capitalist. Crown 8vo, cloth 6s.

BROWNING'S (ROBT.) POEMS. Pippa Passes; and Men and Women. With 10 Plates in Colour after ELEANOR F. BRICKDALE. Large fcap. 4to, cloth, 6s. net; LARGE PAPER EDITION, parchment, 12s. 6d. net.
Dramatis Personæ; and Dramatic Romances and Lyrics. With 10 Plates in Colour after E. F. BRICKDALE. Large fcap. 4to, cloth, 6s. net; LARGE PAPER EDITION, parchment, 12s. 6d. net.

BRYDEN (H. A.).—An Exiled Scot. With Frontispiece by J. S. CROMPTON, R.I. Crown 8vo, cloth, 3s. 6d.

BRYDGES (HAROLD). — Uncle Sam at Home. With 91 Illusts. Post 8vo, illust. boards 2s.; cloth limp, 2s. 6d.

BUCHANAN (ROBERT), Poems and Novels by.
The Complete Poetical Works of Robert Buchanan. 2 Vols., crown 8vo, buckram, with Portrait Frontispiece to each volume, 12s.

Crown 8vo, cloth, 3s. 6d. each; post 8vo, illustrated boards, 2s. each.
The Shadow of the Sword.
A Child of Nature.
God and the Man. With 11 Illustrations by F. BARNARD.
Lady Kilpatrick.
The Martyrdom of Madeline.
Love Me for Ever.
Annan Water. | Foxglove Manor.
The New Abelard. | Rachel Dene.
Matt: A Story of a Caravan.
The Master of the Mine.
The Heir of Linne.
Woman and the Man.

Crown 8vo, cloth, 3s. 6d. each.
Red and White Heather.
Andromeda.

POPULAR EDITIONS, medium 8vo, 6d. each.
The Shadow of the Sword.
God and the Man.
Foxglove Manor.
The Shadow of the Sword. LARGE TYPE, FINE PAPER EDITION. Pott 8vo, cloth, gilt top, 2s. net; leather, gilt edges, 3s. net.
The Charlatan. By ROBERT BUCHANAN and HENRY MURRAY. Crown 8vo, cloth, with Frontispiece by T. H. ROBINSON, 3s. 6d.; post 8vo, illustrated boards, 2s.

BURGESS (GELETT) and WILL IRWIN.—The Picaroons: A San Francisco Night's Entertainment. Crown 8vo, cloth, 3s. 6d.

BURTON (ROBERT). — The Anatomy of Melancholy. With a Photogravure Frontispiece. Demy 8vo, cloth, 7s. 6d.

CAINE (HALL), Novels by. Crown 8vo, cloth, 3s. 6d. each; post 8vo, illustrated boards, 2s. each; cloth limp, 2s. 6d. each.
The Shadow of a Crime.
A Son of Hagar. | The Deemster.
Also LIBRARY EDITIONS of the three novels, crown 8vo, cloth, 6s. each; CHEAP POPULAR EDITIONS, medium 8vo, portrait cover, 6d. each; and the FINE PAPER EDITION of The Deemster, pott 8vo, cloth, gilt top, 2s. net; leather, gilt edges, 3s. net.

CAMERON (V. LOVETT).—The Cruise of the 'Black Prince' Privateer. Cr. 8vo, cloth, with 2 Illustrations by P. MACNAB, 3s. 6d.; post 8vo, picture boards, 2s.

CAMPBELL (A. GODRIC). — Fleur-de-Camp: a Daughter of France. Crown 8vo, cloth, 6s.

CAMPING IN THE FOREST. With Illustrations in Colour and Line by MARGARET CLAYTON. Fcap. 4to, cloth, 3s. 6d. net.

CARLYLE (THOMAS).—On the Choice of Books. Post 8vo, cloth, 1s. 6d.

CARROLL (LEWIS), Books by. Alice in Wonderland. With 12 Coloured and many Line Illustrations by MILLICENT SOWERBY. Large crown 8vo, cloth gilt, 5s. net. Feeding the Mind. With a Preface by W. H. DRAPER. Post 8vo, boards, 1s. net; leather, 2s. net.

CARRUTH (HAYDEN).—The Ad- ventures of Jones. With 17 Illusts. Fcap. 8vo picture cover, 1s.; cloth, 1s. 6d.

CHAPMAN'S (GEORGE) Works. Vol. I., Plays Complete, including the Doubtful Ones.—Vol. II., Poems and Minor Translations, with Essay by A. C. SWINBURNE.—Vol. III., Translations of the Iliad and Odyssey. Three Vols. crown 8vo, cloth, 3s. 6d. each.

CHATFIELD-TAYLOR (H. C.)— Fame's Pathway. Cr. 8vo, cloth, 6s.

CHAUCER for Children: A Gol- den Key. By Mrs. H. R. HAWEIS. With 8 Coloured Plates and 30 Woodcuts. Crown 4to, cloth, 3s. 6d. Chaucer for Schools. With the Story of his Times and his Work. By Mrs. H. R. HAWEIS. Demy 8vo, cloth, 2s. 6d. The Prologue to the Canterbury Tales. Printed in black letter upon hand-made paper, with Illustrations by AMBROSE DUDLEY. Fcap. 4to, decorated cloth, red top, 2s. 6d. net.

CHESNEY (WEATHERBY), Novels by. Crown 8vo, cloth, 3s. 6d. each. The Cable-man. The Romance of a Queen. The Claimant. Crown 8vo, cloth, 6s.

CHESS, The Laws and Practice of; with an Analysis of the Openings. By HOWARD STAUNTON. Edited by R. B. WORMALD. Crown 8vo, cloth, 5s. The Minor Tactics of Chess: A Treatise on the Deployment of the Forces in obedience to Strategic Principle. By F. K. YOUNG and E. C. HOWELL. Fcap. 8vo, cloth, 2s. 6d. The Hastings Chess Tournament. The Authorised Account of the 230 Games played Aug.-Sept., 1895. With Annotations by PILLSBURY, LASKER, TARRASCH, STEINITZ, SCHIFFERS, TEICHMANN, BARDELEBEN, BLACKBURNE, GUNSBERG, TINSLEY, MASON, and ALBIN; Biographical Sketches, and 22 Portraits. Edited by H. F. CHESHIRE. Crown 8vo, cloth, 5s.

CHILD-LOVER'S CALENDAR, 1909. With Coloured Illusts. by AMELIA M. BOWERLEY. 16mo, picture bds, 1s. net.

CLARE (AUSTIN), Stories by. By the Rise of the River. Crown 8vo, cloth, 3s. 6d. Crown 8vo, cloth, 6s. each. The Tideway. Randal of Randalholme.

CLODD (EDWARD). — Myths and Dreams. Crown 8vo, cloth, 3s. 6d.

CLIVE (Mrs. ARCHER), Novels by. Post 8vo, cloth, 3s. 6d. each; illustrated boards, 2s. each. Paul Ferroll. Why Paul Ferroll Killed his Wife.

COBBAN (J. MACLAREN), Novels by. The Cure of Souls. Post 8vo, Illustrated boards, 2s. The Red Sultan. Crown 8vo, cloth, 3s. 6d.; post 8vo, Illustrated boards, 2s. The Burden of Isabel. Crown 8vo, cloth, 3s. 6d.

COLLINS (J. CHURTON, M.A.). —Jonathan Swift. Cr. 8vo, cl., 3s. 6d.

COLLINS (MORTIMER and FRANCES), Novels by. Cr. 8vo, cl., 3s. 6d. each; post 8vo, illustd. bds., 2s. each. From Midnight to Midnight. You Play me False. Blacksmith and Scholar. The Village Comedy. Frances. Post 8vo, illustrated boards, 2s. each. Transmigration. A Fight with Fortune. Sweet Anne Page. Sweet and Twenty.

COLOUR-BOOKS: Topographi- cal. Large fcap. 4to, cloth, 20s. net each. *Switzerland: The Country and its People. By CLARENCE ROOK. With 56 Illustrations in Three Colours by Mrs. JAMES JARDINE, and 24 in Two Tints. *The Face of China. Written and Illus. in Colour and Line by E. G. KEMP. *The Colour of Rome. By OLAVE M. POTTER. With Introduction by DOUGLAS SLADEN, and Illustrations in Three Colours and Sepia by YOSHIO MARKINO. *The Colour of London. By Rev. W. J. LOFTIE, F.S.A. With Introduction by M. H. SPIELMANN, F.S.A., and Illustrations in Three Colours and Sepia by YOSHIO MARKINO. *The Colour of Paris. By MM. LES ACADÉMICIENS GONCOURT. Edited by LUCIEN DESCAVES. With Introduction by L. BÉNÉDITE. Translated by M. D. FROST. Illustrated in Three Colours and Sepia, with an Essay, by YOSHIO MARKINO. *Cairo, Jerusalem, and Damascus. By D. S. MARGOLIOUTH, Litt.D. With Illustrations in Three Colours by W. S. S. TYRWHITT, R.B.A., and REGINALD BARRATT, A.R.W.S.

COLOUR-BOOKS—*continued.*

The Rhine. By H. J. MACKINDER. With Illustrations in Three Colours by Mrs. JAMES JARDINE, and Two Maps.

***Assisi of St. Francis.** By Mrs. ROBERT GOFF. With Introduction by J. KERR LAWSON, Illustrations in Three Colours by Colonel R. GOFF, and Reproductions of the chief Franciscan Paintings.

***Devon; its Moorlands, Streams, and Coasts.** By Lady ROSALIND NORTHCOTE. With Illustrations in Three Colours by F. J. WIDGERY.

The Greater Abbeys of England. By Right Rev. ABBOT GASQUET. With 60 Illustrations in Three Colours by WARWICK GOBLE.

Large foolscap 4to, cloth, 10s. 6d. net each.

***Venice.** By BERYL DE SÉLINCOURT and MAY STURGE-HENDERSON. With 30 Illustrations in Three Colours by REGINALD BARRATT, A.R.W.S.

Lisbon and Cintra: with some Account of other Cities and Sites in Portugal. By A. C. INCHBOLD. With 30 Illustrations In Three Colours by STANLEY INCHBOLD.

From the Thames to the Seine. By CHARLES PEARS. With 40 Illustrations in Three Colours and Sepia. Large fcap. 4to, cloth, 12s. 6d. net. [*Preparing.*

From the North Foreland to Penzance. By CLIVE HOLLAND. With numerous Illustrations in Three Colours by MAURICE RANDALL. Large fcap. 4to, cloth, 12s. 6d. net.

In the Abruzzi: The Country and the People. By ANNE MACDONELL. With 12 Illustrations in Three Colours by AMY ATKINSON. Large crown 8vo, cl., 6s. net.

The Barbarians of Morocco. By COUNT STERNBERG, translated by ETHEL PECK. With 12 Illustrations in Three Colours by DOUGLAS FOX PITT, R.I. Large crown 8vo, cloth, 6s. net.

₀ SPECIAL COPIES *on pure rag paper of these marked* * *may be had.*

COLLINS (WILKIE), Novels by.
Cr. 8vo, cl., 3s. 6d. each ; post 8vo, picture boards, 2s. each ; cl. limp, 2s. 6d. each.
Antonina. | Basil. | Hide and Seek
The Woman in White.
The Moonstone. | Man and Wife.
The Dead Secret. | After Dark.
The Queen of Hearts.
No Name | My Miscellanies.
Armadale. | Poor Miss Finch
Miss or Mrs.? | The Black Robe.
The New Magdalen.
Frozen Deep. | A Rogue's Life.
The Law and the Lady.
The Two Destinies.
The Haunted Hotel.
The Fallen Leaves.
Jezebel's Daughter.
Heart and Science. | 'I Say No.'
The Evil Genius. | Little Novels.
The Legacy of Cain. | Blind Love.

COLLINS (WILKIE)—*continued.*
POPULAR EDITIONS, medium 8vo, 6d. each.
Antonina.
The Woman in White.
The Law and the Lady.
Moonstone. | The New Magdalen.
The Dead Secret. | No Name.
Man and Wife | Armadale.
The Haunted Hotel, &c.
The Woman in White. LARGE TYPE, FINE PAPER EDITION. Pott 8vo, cloth, gilt top, 2s. net : leather, gilt edges, 3s. net.
The Frozen Deep. LARGE TYPE EDIT. Fcap. 8vo, cl., 1s. net ; leather, 1s. 6d. net.

COLQUHOUN (M. J.).—Every Inch a Soldier. Crown 8vo, cloth, 3s. 6d.; post 8vo, Illustrated boards, 2s.

COLT-BREAKING, Hints on. By W. M. HUTCHISON. Cr. 8vo, cl., 3s. 6d.

COLTON (ARTHUR). — The Belted Seas. Crown 8vo, cloth, 3s. 6d.

COMPENSATION ACT (THE), 1906: Who pays, to whom, to what, and when it is applicable. By A. CLEMENT EDWARDS, M.P. Crown 8vo, 1s. net; cloth, 1s. 6d. net.

COMPTON (HERBERT), Novels by.
The Inimitable Mrs. Massingham. Crown 8vo, cloth, 3s. 6d.; POPULAR EDITION, medium 8vo, 6d.

Crown 8vo, cloth, 6s. each.
The Wilful Way.
The Queen can do no Wrong.
To Defeat the Ends of Justice.

COOPER (E. H.), Novels by.
Crown 8vo, cloth, 3s. 6d. each.
Geoffory Hamilton.
The Marquis and Pamela.

CORNISH (J. F.).—Sour Grapes. Crown 8vo, cloth, 6s.

CORNWALL.—Popular Romances of the West of England: The Drolls, Traditions, and Superstitions of Old Cornwall. Collected by ROBERT HUNT, F.R.S. With two Plates by GEORGE CRUIKSHANK. Cr. 8vo, cl., 7s. 6d.

COURT (The) of the Tuileries, 1852 to 1870. By LE PETIT HOMME ROUGE. With a Frontispiece. Crown 8vo, cloth, 7s. 6d. net.

CRADDOCK (C. EGBERT), by.
The Prophet of the Great Smoky Mountains. Crown 8vo, cloth, 3s. 6d.; post 8vo, illustrated boards, 2s.

Crown 8vo, cloth, 3s. 6d. each.
His Vanished Star. | The Windfall.

CRESSWELL (HENRY). — A Lady of Misrule. Crown 8vo, cloth, 6s.

CRIM (MATT).—Adventures of a Fair Rebel. Crown 8vo, cloth, 3s. 6d.; post 8vo, illustrated boards, 2s.

CROCKETT (S. R.) and others.—
Tales of our Coast. By S. R.
CROCKETT, GILBERT PARKER, HAROLD
FREDERIC, 'Q.,' and W. CLARK RUSSELL.
With 13 Illustrations by FRANK BRANG-
WYN. Crown 8vo, cloth, 3s. 6d.

CROKER (Mrs. B. M.), Novels
by. Crown 8vo, cloth, 3s. 6d. each;
post 8vo, illustrated boards, 2s. each;
cloth limp, 2s. 6d. each.
Pretty Miss Neville.
A Bird of Passage. | Mr. Jervis.
Diana Barrington.
Two Masters. | Interference.
A Family Likeness.
A Third Person. | Proper Pride.
Village Tales & Jungle Tragedies.
The Real Lady Hilda.
Married or Single?
In the Kingdom of Kerry.
Miss Balmaine's Past.
Jason. | Beyond the Pale.
Terence. With 6 Illusts. by S. PAGET.
The Cat's-paw. With 12 Illustrations
by FRED PEGRAM.
The Spanish Necklace. With 8
Illusts. by F. PEGRAM.—Also a Cheap Ed.,
without Illusts., picture cover, 1s. net.

Crown 8vo, cloth, 3s. 6d. each; post 8vo,
cloth limp, 2s. 6d. each.
Infatuation. | Some One Else.
'To Let.' Post 8vo, picture boards, 2s.;
cloth limp, 2s. 6d.

POPULAR EDITIONS, medium 8vo. 6d. each.
Proper Pride. | The Cat's-paw.
Diana Barrington.
Pretty Miss Neville.
A Bird of Passage.
Beyond the Pale.
A Family Likeness.
Miss Balmaine's Past.

CROSS (M. B.).—A Question of
Means. Crown 8vo, cloth, 6s.

CRUIKSHANK'S COMIC AL-
MANACK. Complete in TWO SERIES.
The FIRST from 1835 to 1843; the
SECOND, from 1844 to 1853. A Gathering
of the Best Humour of THACKERAY,
HOOD, ALBERT SMITH, &c. With nu-
merous Steel Engravings and Woodcuts
by CRUIKSHANK, LANDELLS, &c. Two
Vols., crown 8vo, cloth, 7s. 6d. each.

CUMMING (C. F. GORDON),
Works by. Demy 8vo, cloth, 6s. each.
In the Hebrides. With 24 Illustrations
In the Himalayas and on the
Indian Plains. With 42 Illustrations
Two Happy Years in Ceylon.
With 28 Illustrations.
Via Cornwall to Egypt. Frontis.

CUSSANS (JOHN E.).—A Hand-
book of Heraldry; including instructions for Tracing Pedigrees, Deciphering
Ancient MSS., &c. With 408 Woodcuts
and 2 Colrd. Plates. Crown 8vo, cloth, 6s

DANBY (FRANK).—A Coquette
In Crape. Foolscap 8vo, cloth, 1s. net.

DAUDET (ALPHONSE).—The
Evangelist; or, Port Salvation.
Cr. 8vo, cloth, 3s. 6d.; post 8vo, bds., 2s.

DAVENANT (FRANCIS).—Hints
for Parents on Choice of Profession
for their Sons. Crown 8vo, 1s. 6d

DAVIDSON (H. C.).—Mr. Sad-
ler's Daughters. Cr. 8vo, cloth, 3s. 6d.

DAVIES (Dr. N. E. YORKE-),
Works by. Cr. 8vo, 1s. ea.; cl. 1s. 6d. ea.
One Thousand Medical Maxims
and Surgical Hints.
Nursery Hints: A Mother's Guide.
The Dietetic Cure of Obesity
(Foods for the Fat). With Chapters
on the Treatment of Gout by Diet.
Aids to Long Life. Crown 8vo, 2s.;
cloth, 2s. 6d.
Wine and Health: How to enjoy
both. Crown 8vo, cloth, 1s. 6d.

DEAKIN (DOROTHEA), Stories
by. Crown 8vo, cloth, 3s. 6d. each.
The Poet and the Pierrot.
The Princess & the Kitchen-maid.

DEFOE (DANIEL). — Robinson
Crusoe. With 37 Illusts. by GEORGE
CRUIKSHANK. LARGE TYPE, FINE PAPER
EDITION. Pott 8vo, cloth, gilt top, 2s. net;
leather, gilt edges, 3s. net.

DE MILLE (JAMES).—A Strange
Manuscript found in a Copper
Cylinder. Crown 8vo, cloth, with 19
Illustrations by GILBERT GAUL, 3s. 6d.;
post 8vo, illustrated boards, 2s.

DEVONSHIRE SCENERY, The
History of. By ARTHUR W. CLAYDEN,
M.A. With Illus. Demy 8vo, cl., 10s. 6d. net.
Devon: Its Moorlands, Streams,
and Coasts. By Lady ROSALIND
NORTHCOTE. With Illustrations in Three
Colours by F. J. WIDGERY. Large fcap.
4to, cloth, 20s. net

DEWAR (T. R.). — A Ramble
Round the Globe. With 220 Illustrations. Crown 8vo, cloth, 7s. 6d.

DICKENS (CHARLES), The
Speeches of. Edited and Annotated
by R. H. SHEPHERD. With a Portrait.
Pott 8vo, cloth, 2s. net; leather, 3s. net.
The Pocket Charles Dickens: being
Favourite Passages chosen by ALFRED
H. HYATT. 16mo, cloth, gilt top, 2s. net;
leather, gilt top, 3s. net.

DICTIONARIES.
The Reader's Handbook of
Famous Names in Fiction,
Allusions, References, Pro-
verbs, Plots, Stories, and Poems.
By Rev. E. C. BREWER, LL.D. Crown
8vo, cloth, 3s. 6d.
A Dictionary of Miracles,
Imitative, Realistic, and Dogmatic. By
Rev. E. C. BREWER, LL.D. Crown 8vo,
cloth, 3s. 6d.

DICTIONARIES—*continued.*

Familiar Allusions. By WILLIAM A. and CHARLES G. WHEELER. Demy 8vo, cloth, 7s. 6d. net.

Familiar Short Sayings of Great Men. With Historical and Explanatory Notes by SAMUEL A. BENT, A.M. Crown 8vo, cloth, 7s. 6d.

The Slang Dictionary: Etymological, Historical, and Anecdotal. Crown 8vo, cloth, 6s. 6d.

Words, Facts, and Phrases: A Dictionary of Curious, Quaint, and Out-of-the-Way Matters By ELIEZER EDWARDS. Crown 8vo, cloth, 3s. 6d

DIXON (WILLMOTT).—Novels by. Crown 8vo, cloth, 6s. each.
The Rogue of Rye.
King Hal—of Heronsea.

DOBSON (AUSTIN), Works by. Crown 8vo, buckram, 6s. each.
Four Frenchwomen. With Four Portraits.
Eighteenth Century Vignettes. In Three Series, each 6s.; also FINE-PAPER EDITIONS of the THREE SERIES, pott 8vo, cloth, 2s. net each; leather, 3s. net each.
A Paladin of Philanthropy, and other Papers. With 2 Illustrations.
Side-walk Studies. With 5 Illusts.

DONOVAN (DICK), Detective Stories by. Post 8vo, illustrated boards, 2s. each; cloth, 2s. 6d. each.
Caught at Last.
In the Grip of the Law.
Link by Link.
From Information Received.
Suspicion Aroused.
Riddles Read.
Chronicles of Michael Danevitch. Crown 8vo, cl., 3s. 6d. each; picture cl., flat back, 2s. each; post 8vo, illustrated boards, 2s. each; cloth limp, 2s. 6d. each.
The Man from Manchester.
The Mystery of Jamaica Terrace. Crown 8vo, cloth, 3s. 6d. each.
Deacon Brodie; or, Behind the Mask.
Tyler Tatlock, Private Detective. Cr. 8vo, cl., 3s. 6d. ea.; pict. cl., flat bk. 2s. ea.
The Records of Vincent Trill.
Tales of Terror. Crown 8vo, cloth, 3s. 6d. each; post 8vo, illustrated boards, 2s. each; cloth limp, 2s. 6d. each
Tracked to Doom.
A Detective's Triumphs.
Tracked and Taken.
Who Poisoned Hetty Duncan? Crown 8vo, picture cloth, flat back, 2s. each; post 8vo, illustrated boards, 2s. each; cloth limp, 2s. 6d. each.
Wanted! | **The Man-Hunter.**
Dark Deeds. Crown 8vo, cloth limp, 2s. 6d.; picture cloth, flat back, 2s.

DOWLING (RICHARD). — Old Corcoran's Money. Cr. 8vo, cl., 3s. 6d.

DOYLE (A. CONAN).—The Firm of Girdlestone. Crown 8vo, cloth, 3s. 6d.

DRAMATISTS, THE OLD. Edited by Col. CUNNINGHAM. Cr. 8vo, cloth, with Portraits, 3s. 6d. per Vol.

Ben Jonson's Works. With Notes, Critical and Explanatory, and a Biographical Memoir by WILLIAM GIFFORD. Three Vols.

Chapman's Works. Three Vols. Vol. I. contains the Plays complete; Vol. II., Poems and Minor Translations, with an Essay by A. C. SWINBURNE; Vol. III., Translations of the Iliad and Odyssey.

Marlowe's Works. One Vol.

Massinger's Plays. From GIFFORD'S Text. One Vol.

DUMPY BOOKS (The) for Children. Roy. 32mo, cloth, 1s. net ea.
1. **The Flamp, The Ameliorator, and The School-boy's Apprentice.** By E. V. LUCAS.
2. **Mrs. Turner's Cautionary Stories.**
3. **The Bad Family.** By Mrs. FENWICK.
4. **The Story of Little Black Sambo.** By HELEN BANNERMAN. Illustrated in colours.
5. **The Bountiful Lady.** By THOMAS COBB.
7. **A Flower Book.** Illustrated in colours by NELLIE BENSON.
8. **The Pink Knight.** By J. R. MONSELL. Illustrated in colours.
9. **The Little Clown.** By THOMAS COBB.
10. **A Horse Book.** By MARY TOURTEL. Illustrated in colours.
11. **Little People:** an Alphabet. By HENRY MAYER and T. W. H. CROSLAND. Illustrated in colours.
12. **A Dog Book.** By ETHEL DICKNELL. With Pictures in colours by CARTON MOORE PARK.
13. **The Adventures of Samuel and Selina.** By JEAN C. ARCHER. Illustrated in colours.
14. **The Little Girl Lost.** By ELEANOR RAPER.
15. **Dollies.** By RICHARD HUNTER. Illustrated in colours by RUTH COBB.
16. **The Bad Mrs. Ginger.** By HONOR C. APPLETON. Illustrated in colours.
17. **Peter Piper's Practical Principles.** Illustrated in colours.
18. **Little White Barbara.** By ELEANOR MARCH. Illustrated in colours.
20. **Towlocks and his Wooden Horse.** By ALICE M. APPLETON. Illus. in colours by HONOR C. APPLETON.
21. **Three Little Foxes.** By MARY TOURTEL. Illustrated in colours.
22. **The Old Man's Bag.** By T. W. H. CROSLAND. Illus. by J. R. MONSELL.
23. **Three Little Goblins.** By M. G. TAGGART. Illustrated in colours.
25. **More Dollies.** By RICHARD HUNTER. Illus. in colours by RUTH COBB.

DUMPY BOOKS—*continued*.

26. Little Yellow Wang-lo. By M. C. BELL. Illustrated in colours.

28. The Sooty Man. By E. B. MACKINNON and EDEN COYBEE. Illus.

30. Rosalina. Illustrated in colours by JEAN C. ARCHER.

31. Sammy and the Snarlywink. Illustrated in colours by LENA and NORMAN AULT.

33. Irene's Christmas Party. By RICHARD HUNTER. Ills. by RUTH COBB.

34. The Little Soldier Book. By JESSIE POPE. Illustrated in colours by HENRY MAYER.

35. The Dutch Doll's Ditties. By C. AUBREY MOORE.

36. Ten Little Nigger Boys. By NORA CASE.

37. Humpty Dumpty's Little Son. By HELEN R. CROSS.

38. Simple Simon. By HELEN R. CROSS. Illustrated in colours.

39. The Little Frenchman. By EDEN COYBEE. Illustrated in colours by K. J. FRICERO.

40. The Potato Book. By LILY SCHOFIELD. Illustrated in colours.

DUNCAN (SARA JEANNETTE), Books by. Cr. 8vo, cloth, 7s. 6d. each.
A Social Departure. With 111 Illustrations by F. H. TOWNSEND.
An American Girl in London. With 80 Illustrations by F. H. TOWNSEND.
The Simple Adventures of a Memsahib. With 37 Illustrations.

Crown 8vo, cloth, 3s. 6d. each.
A Daughter of To-Day.
Vernon's Aunt. With 47 Illustrations.

DUTT (ROMESH C.).—England and India: Progress during One Hundred Years. Crown 8vo, cloth, 2s.

DYSON (EDWARD). — In the Roaring Fifties. Crown 8vo, cloth, 6s.

EDWARDES (Mrs. ANNIE), Novels by.
A Point of Honour. Post 8vo, illustrated boards, 2s.
Archie Lovell. Crown 8vo, cloth, 3s. 6d.; post 8vo, illustrated boards, 2s.
A Plaster Saint. Cr. 8vo, cloth, 3s. 6d.

EDWARDS (ELIEZER).— Words, Facts, and Phrases: A Dictionary of Curious, Quaint, and Out-of-the-Way Matters. Crown 8vo, cloth, 3s. 6d.

EGERTON (Rev. J. C.).— Sussex Folk and Sussex Ways. With Four Illusts. Crown 8vo, cloth, 5s.

EGGLESTON (EDWARD).— Roxy. Post 8vo, illustrated boards, 2s.

ENGLISHMAN (An) in Paris: Recollections of Louis Philippe and the Empire. Crown 8vo, cloth, 3s. 6d.

EPISTOLÆ OBSCURORUM Virorum (1515-1517). Latin Text, with Translation, Introduction, Notes, &c., by F. G. STOKES. Royal 8vo, buckram, 25s. net.

EVERYMAN: A Morality. Printed on pure rag paper, with Illustrations by AMBROSE DUDLEY. Fcap. 4to, decorated cloth, red top, 2s. 6d. net.

EYES, Our: How to Preserve Them. By JOHN BROWNING. Crown 8vo, cloth, 1s.

FAIRY TALES FROM TUSCANY. By ISABELLA M. ANDERTON. Square 16mo, cloth, with Frontispiece. 1s. net.

FAMILIAR ALLUSIONS: Miscellaneous Information, including Celebrated Statues, Paintings, Palaces, Country Seats, Ruins, Churches, Ships, Streets, Clubs, Natural Curiosities, &c. By W. A. and C. G. WHEELER. Demy 8vo, cloth, 7s. 6d. net.

FAMILIAR SHORT SAYINGS of Great Men. By S. A. BENT, A.M. Crown 8vo, cloth, 7s. 6d.

FARADAY (MICHAEL), Works by. Post 8vo, cloth, 4s. 6d. each.
The Chemical History of a Candle: Lectures delivered before a Juvenile Audience. Edited by WILLIAM CROOKES, F.C.S. With numerous Illusts.
On the Various Forces of Nature, and their Relations to each other. Edited by WILLIAM CROOKES, F.C.S. With Illustrations.

FARRAR (F. W., D.D.).—Ruskin as a Religious Teacher. Square 16mo, cloth, with Frontispiece, 1s. net.

FARRER (J. ANSON).—War: Three Essays. Crown 8vo, cloth, 1s. 6d.

FENN (G. MANVILLE), Novels by. Crown 8vo, cloth, 3s. 6d. each; post 8vo, illustrated boards, 2s. each.
The New Mistress.
Witness to the Deed.
The Tiger Lily.
The White Virgin.

Crown 8vo, cloth, 3s. 6d. each.
A Woman Worth Winning.
Cursed by a Fortune.
The Case of Ailsa Gray.
Commodore Junk.
Black Blood. | **In Jeopardy.**
Double Cunning.
A Fluttered Dovecote.
King of the Castle.
The Master of the Ceremonies.
The Story of Antony Grace.
The Man with a Shadow.
One Maid's Mischief.
This Man's Wife.
The Bag of Diamonds, and Three Bits of Paste.
Running Amok.

FENN (G. MANVILLE)—*continued.*
Crown 8vo, cloth, 6s. each.

Black Shadows.
The Cankerworm.
So Like a Woman.

A Crimson Crime. Crown 8vo, cloth,
3s. 6d.; picture cloth, flat back, 2s.

FICTION, a Catalogue of, with
Descriptions and Reviews of nearly
TWELVE HUNDRED NOVELS, will be
sent free by CHATTO & WINDUS upon
application.

FIREWORK - MAKING, The
Complete Art of; or, The Pyrotechnist's
Treasury. By THOMAS KENTISH. With
267 Illustrations. Cr. 8vo, cloth, 3s. 6d.

FISHER (ARTHUR O.), Novels
by. Crown 8vo, cloth, 6s. each.
Withyford. With Coloured Frontispiece by G. D. ARMOUR, and 5 Plates in
sepia by R. H. BUXTON.
The Land of Silent Feet. With a
Frontispiece by G. D. ARMOUR.

FITZGERALD (PERCY), by.
Fatal Zero. Crown 8vo, cloth, 3s. 6d.;
post 8vo, illustrated boards, 2s.

Post 8vo, Illustrated boards, 2s. each.
Bella Donna. | **Polly.**
The Lady of Brantome.
Never Forgotten.
The Second Mrs. Tillotson.
Seventy-five Brooke Street.

FLAMMARION (CAMILLE).—
Popular Astronomy. Translated
by J. ELLARD GORE, F.R.A.S. With Three
Plates and 288 Illustrations. A NEW
EDITION, with an Appendix giving the
results of Recent Discoveries. Medium
8vo, cloth, 10s. 6d.

FLORENCE PRESS BOOKS.—
For information as to this important
Series, printed from a new type designed
by HERBERT P. HORNE, now first
engraved, see special Prospectus.

FORBES (Hon. Mrs. WALTER).
—**Dumb.** Crown 8vo cloth, 3s. 6d.

FRANCILLON (R. E.), Novels
by. Crown 8vo, cloth, 3s. 6d. each; post
8vo, illustrated boards, 2s. each.
One by One | **A Real Queen.**
A Dog and his Shadow.
Ropes of Sand. With Illustrations.

Post 8vo, Illustrated boards, 2s. each.
Romances of the Law.
King or Knave? | **Olympia.**

Jack Doyle's Daughter. Crown 8vo,
cloth, 3s. 6d.

FRANCO - BRITISH EXHIBI-
TION Illustrated Review (The),
1908. A Complete Souvenir of the Exhibition. Profusely illustrated. Edited
by F. G. DUMAS. Large folio, pictorial
cover, 6s. net; cloth, 7s. 6d. net. Also
the EDITION DE LUXE, printed on fine art
paper and in a special binding, 10s 6d net.

FREDERIC (HAROLD), Novels
by. Post 8vo, cloth, 3s. 6d. each;
illustrated boards, 2s. each.
Seth's Brother's Wife.
The Lawton Girl.

FREEMAN (R. AUSTIN).—John
Thorndyke's Cases. Illustrated by H.
M. BROCK, and from Photographs.
Crown 8vo, cloth, 3s. 6d. net.

FRY'S (HERBERT) Royal
Guide to the London Charities.
Edited by JOHN LANE. Published
Annually. Crown 8vo, cloth, 1s. 6d.

GARDENING BOOKS. Post 8vo,
1s. each; cloth, 1s. 6d. each.
**A Year's Work in Garden and
Greenhouse.** By GEORGE GLENNY.
Household Horticulture. By TOM
and JANE JERROLD. Illustrated.
The Garden that Paid the Rent.
By TOM JERROLD.
Our Kitchen Garden. By TOM
JERROLD. Post 8vo, cloth, 1s net.
**Sir William Temple upon the
Gardens of Epicurus;** together
with other XVIIth Century Garden
Essays. Edited with Notes and Introduc-
tion, by A. FORBES SIEVEKING, F.S.A.
With 6 Illustrations. Small 8vo, cloth
or boards, 1s. 6d. net; quarter vellum,
2s. 6d. net; three-quarter vellum, 5s. net.

GAULOT (PAUL), Books by.
The Red Shirts: A Tale of 'The
Terror.' Translated by JOHN DE VIL-
LIERS. Crown 8vo, cloth, with Frontis-
piece by STANLEY WOOD, 3s. 6d.; picture
cloth, flat back, 2s.

Crown 8vo, cloth, 6s. each.
Love and Lovers of the Past.
Translated by C. LAROCHE, M.A.
A Conspiracy under the Terror.
Translated by C. LAROCHE, M.A. With
Illustrations and Facsimiles.

GERMAN POPULAR STORIES.
Collected by the Brothers GRIMM and
Translated by EDGAR TAYLOR. With
Introduction by JOHN RUSKIN, and 22
Steel Plates after GEORGE CRUIKSHANK.
Square 8vo, cloth gilt, 6s.

GIBBON (CHARLES), Novels
by. Crown 8vo, cloth, 3s. 6d. each;
post 8vo, Illustrated boards, 2s. each.
Robin Gray.
The Golden Shaft.
The Flower of the Forest.
The Braes of Yarrow.
Of High Degree.
Queen of the Meadow.

GIBBON (CHARLES)—*continued.*
Post 8vo, illustrated boards, 2s. each.
For Lack of Gold.
What Will the World Say?
For the King. | **A Hard Knot.**
In Pastures Green.
In Love and War.
A Heart's Problem.
By Mead and Stream.
Fancy Free. | **Loving a Dream.**
In Honour Bound.
Heart's Delight. | **Blood-Money.**
The Dead Heart. Post 8vo, illustrated boards, 2s.; POPULAR EDITION, medium 8vo, 6d.

GERARD (DOROTHEA).—A
Queen of Curds and Cream. Crown 8vo, cloth, 3s. 6d.

GIBNEY (SOMERVILLE). —
Sentenced! Crown 8vo, cloth, 1s. 6d.

GIBSON (L. S.), Novels by.
Crown 8vo, cloth, 6s. each.
The Freemasons. | **Burnt Spices.**
Ships of Desire
The Freemasons. Cheap Edition, picture cover, 1s. net.

GILBERT (WILLIAM).—James
Duke, Costermonger. Post 8vo, illustrated boards, 2s.

GILBERT'S (W. S.) Original
Plays. In 3 Series. FINE-PAPER EDITION, Pott 8vo, cloth, gilt top, 2s. net each; leather, gilt edges, 3s. net each.
The FIRST SERIES contains: The Wicked World — Pygmalion and Galatea — Charity—The Princess—The Palace of Truth—Trial by Jury—Iolanthe.
The SECOND SERIES contains: Broken Hearts — Engaged — Sweethearts — Gretchen — Dan'l Druce—Tom Cobb —H.M.S. 'Pinafore'—The Sorcerer—The Pirates of Penzance.
The THIRD SERIES contains: Comedy and Tragedy — Foggerty's Fairy — Rosencrantz and Guildenstern—Patience—Princess Ida—The Mikado—Ruddigore—The Yeomen of the Guard—The Gondoliers--The Mountebanks—Utopia.
Eight Original Comic Operas
written by W. S. GILBERT. Two Series, demy 8vo, cloth, 2s. 6d. net each.
The FIRST SERIES contains: The Sorcerer —H.M.S. 'Pinafore'—The Pirates of Penzance—Iolanthe—Patience—Princess Ida—The Mikado—Trial by Jury.
The SECOND SERIES contains: The Gondoliers—The Grand Duke—The Yeomen of the Guard—His Excellency—Utopia, Limited—Ruddigore—The Mountebanks—Haste to the Wedding.
The Gilbert and Sullivan Birthday Book: Quotations for Every Day in the Year. Compiled by A. WATSON. Royal 16mo, cloth, 2s. 6d.

GISSING (ALGERNON), Novels
by. Crown 8vo, cloth, gilt top, 6s. each.
A Secret of the North Sea.

GISSING (ALGERNON)—*continued.*
Crown 8vo, cloth 6s. each.
Knitters in the Sun.
The Wealth of Mallerstang.
An Angel's Portion.
Baliol Garth.
The Dreams of Simon Usher.
Crown 8vo, cloth, 3s. 6d.

GLANVILLE (ERNEST), Novels
by. Crown 8vo, cloth, 3s. 6d. each; post 8vo, illustrated boards, 2s. each.
The Lost Heiress. With 2 Illustrations by HUME NISBET.
The Fossicker: A Romance of Mashonaland. Two Illusts. by HUME NISBET.
A Fair Colonist. With Frontispiece.
Crown 8vo, cloth, 3s. 6d. each.
The Golden Rock. With Frontispiece by STANLEY WOOD.
Tales from the Veld. With 12 Illusts.
Max Thornton. With 8 Illustrations by J. S. CROMPTON, R.I.

GLENNY (GEORGE).—A Year's
Work in Garden and Greenhouse: Practical Advice as to Flower, Fruit, and Frame Garden. Post 8vo, 1s.; cl., 1s. 6d.

GODWIN (WILLIAM). — Lives
of the Necromancers. Post 8vo, cl., 2s.

GOLDEN TREASURY of
Thought, The: A Dictionary of Quotations from the Best Authors. By THEODORE TAYLOR. Cr. 8vo, cl., 3s. 6d.

GOODMAN (E. J.)—The Fate of
Herbert Wayne. Cr. 8vo cl., 3s. 6d.

GORDON (SAMUEL). — The
Ferry of Fate: a Tale of Russian Jewry. Crown 8vo, cloth, 6s.

GORE (J. ELLARD, F.R.A.S.).—
Astronomical Curiosities. With two illustrations. Crown 8vo, cloth, 6s. net.

GRACE (ALFRED A.).—Tales
of a Dying Race. Cr. 8vo, cl., 3s. 6d.

GREEKS AND ROMANS, The
Life of the, described from Antique Monuments. By ERNST GUHL and W. KONER. Edited by Dr. F. HUEFFER. With 545 Illusts. Demy 8vo, cl., 7s. 6d.

GREEN (ANNA KATHARINE),
Novels by. Crown 8vo, cloth, 6s. each.
The Millionaire Baby.
The Woman in the Alcove.
The Amethyst Box. Crown 8vo, cloth, 3s. 6d.

GREENWOOD (JAMES).—The
Prisoner in the Dock. Crown 8vo, cloth, 3s. 6d.

GREY (Sir GEORGE). — The
Romance of a Proconsul. By JAMES MILNE. Crown 8vo, buckram 6s.

GRIFFITH (CECIL).—Corinthia
Marazion. Crown 8vo, cloth 3s. 6d.

GRIFFITHS (Major A.).—No. 99,
and Blue Blood. Crown 8vo, cloth, 2s.

GUNTER (A. CLAVERING).—A Florida Enchantment. Crown 8vo, cloth, 3s. 6d.

GUTTENBERG (VIOLET), Novels by. Crown 8vo, cloth, 6s. each.
Neither Jew nor Greek.
The Power of the Palmist.

GYP. — CLOCLO. Translated by NORA M. STATHAM. Cr. 8vo, cl., 3s. 6d.

HABBERTON (JOHN).—Helen's Babies. With Coloured Frontispiece and 60 Illustrations by EVA ROOS. Fcap. 4to, cloth, 6s.

HAIR, The: Its Treatment in Health, Weakness, and Disease. Translated from the German of Dr. J. PINCUS. Crown 8vo, 1s. : cloth, 1s. 6d.

HAKE (Dr. T. GORDON), Poems by. Crown 8vo, cloth, 6s. each.
New Symbols.
Legends of the Morrow.
The Serpent Play.
Maiden Ecstasy. Small 4to, cloth, 8s.

HALL (Mrs. S. C.).—Sketches of Irish Character. With Illustrations on Steel and Wood by CRUIKSHANK, MACLISE, GILBERT, and HARVEY. Demy 8vo, cloth, 7s. 6d.

HALL (OWEN), Novels by. The Track of a Storm. Crown 8vo, picture cloth, flat back, 2s.
Jetsam. Crown 8vo, cloth, 3s. 6d.
Crown 8vo, cloth, 6s. each.
Eureka. | Hernando.

HALLIDAY (ANDREW).— Every-day Papers. Post 8vo, illustrated boards, 2s.

HAMILTON (COSMO), Stories by.
The Glamour of the Impossible; and Through a Keyhole. Crown 8vo, cloth 3s. 6d.
Crown 8vo, cloth 6s. each.
Nature's Vagabond, &c.
Plain Brown.

HANDWRITING, The Philo- sophy of. With over 100 Facsimiles. By DON FELIX DE SALAMANCA. Post 8vo, half-cloth, 2s. 6d.

HARDY (IZA DUFFUS), Novels by. Crown 8vo, cloth, 6s. each.
The Lesser Evil.
Man, Woman, and Fate.
A Butterfly.

HARDY (THOMAS). — Under the Greenwood Tree. Post 8vo, cloth, 3s. 6d.; illustrated boards, 2s.; cloth limp, 2s. 6d. Also the FINE PAPER EDITION, pott 8vo, cloth, gilt top, 2s. net; leather, gilt edges, 3s. net; and the CHEAP EDITION medium 8vo, 6d.

HARKINS (E. F.).—The Schem- ers. Crown 8vo, cloth, 6s.

HARRIS (JOEL CHANDLER), Books by.
Uncle Remus. With 9 Coloured and 50 other Illustrations by J. A. SHEPHERD. Pott 4to cloth, gilt top, 6s.
Nights with Uncle Remus. With 8 Coloured and 50 other Illustrations by J. A. SHEPHERD. Imperial 16mo, cloth, 6s.

HARTE'S (BRET) Collected Works. LIBRARY EDITION, in Ten Volumes, crown 8vo, cloth, 6s. each.
Vol. I. COMPLETE POETICAL AND DRAMATIC WORKS. With Port.
" II. THE LUCK OF ROARING CAMP— BOHEMIAN PAPERS—AMERICAN LEGENDS.
" III. TALES OF THE ARGONAUTS— EASTERN SKETCHES.
" IV. GABRIEL CONROY.
" V. STORIES — CONDENSED NOVELS.
" VI. TALES OF THE PACIFIC SLOPE.
" VII. TALES OF THE PACIFIC SLOPE—II. With Portrait by JOHN PETTIE.
" VIII. TALES OF PINE AND CYPRESS.
" IX. BUCKEYE AND CHAPPAREL.
" X. TALES OF TRAIL AND TOWN.

Bret Harte's Choice Works in Prose and Verse. With Portrait and 40 Illustrations. Crown 8vo, cloth, 3s. 6d.
Bret Harte's Poetical Works, including SOME LATER VERSES. Crown 8vo, buckram, 4s. 6d.
In a Hollow of the Hills. Crown 8vo, picture cloth, flat back, 2s.
Condensed Novels. (Two Series in One Volume.) Pott 8vo, cloth, gilt top, 2s. net; leather, gilt edges, 3s. net.

Crown 8vo, cloth, 6s. each.
On the Old Trail.
Under the Redwoods.
From Sandhill to Pine.
Stories in Light and Shadow.
Mr. Jack Hamlin's Mediation.
Trent's Trust.

Crown 8vo, cloth, 3s. 6d. each; post 8vo, illustrated boards, 2s. each.
Gabriel Conroy.
A Waif of the Plains. With 60 Illustrations by STANLEY L. WOOD.
A Ward of the Golden Gate. With 59 Illustrations by STANLEY L. WOOD.

Crown 8vo, cloth, 3s. 6d. each.
Susy. With 2 Illusts. by J. A. CHRISTIE.
The Bell-Ringer of Angel's, &c. With 39 Illusts. by DUDLEY HARDY, &c.
Clarence: A Story of the American War. With 8 Illustrations by A. JULE GOODMAN.
Barker's Luck, &c. With 39 Illustrations by A. FORESTIER, PAUL HARDY, &c.
Devil's Ford, &c.
The Crusade of the 'Excelsior.' With Frontis. by J. BERNARD PARTRIDGE.
Tales of Trail and Town. With Frontispiece by G. P. JACOMB-HOOD.
Condensed Novels. New Series.
Three Partners; or, The Big Strike on Heavy Tree Hill. With 8 Illustrations by J. GULICH. Also the CHEAP EDITION, medium 8vo, 6d.

HARTE (BRET)—*continued.*
Crown 8vo, cloth, 3s. 6d. each; picture cloth, flat back, 2s. each.
A Sappho of Green Springs.
Colonel Starbottle's Client.
A Protégée of Jack Hamlin's.
With numerous Illustrations.
Sally Dows, &c. With 47 Illustrations by W. D. ALMOND and others.

Post 8vo, illustrated boards, 2s. each.
The Luck of Roaring Camp, and Sensation Novels Condensed.
(Also in picture cloth at same price.)
An Heiress of Red Dog.
The Luck of Roaring Camp.
Californian Stories.

Post 8vo, illus. bds., 2s. each; cloth, 2s. 6d. each.
Flip. | **A Phyllis of the Sierras.**

Maruja. Crown 8vo, cloth, 3s. 6d.; post 8vo, picture boards, 2s.; cloth limp, 2s. 6d.

HAWEIS (Mrs. H. R.), Books by.
The Art of Dress. With 32 Illustrations. Post 8vo, 1s.; cloth, 1s. 6d.
Chaucer for Schools. With Frontispiece. Demy 8vo, cloth, 2s. 6d.
Chaucer for Children. With 8 Coloured Plates and 30 Woodcuts. Crown 4to, cloth, 3s. 6d.

HAWEIS (Rev. H. R.).—**American Humorists:** WASHINGTON IRVING, OLIVER WENDELL HOLMES, JAMES RUSSELL LOWELL, ARTEMUS WARD, MARK TWAIN, and BRET HARTE. Crown 8vo, cloth, 6s.

HAWTHORNE (JULIAN), Novels by. Crown 8vo, cloth, 3s. 6d. each; post 8vo, illustrated boards, 2s. each.
Garth. | **Ellice Quentin.**
Fortune's Fool. | **Dust.** Four Illusts.
Beatrix Randolph. With Four Illusts.
D. Poindexter's Disappearance.
The Spectre of the Camera.

Crown 8vo, cloth, 3s. 6d. each.
Sebastian Strome.
Love—or a Name.
Miss Cadogna. Post 8vo, Illustrated boards, 2s.

HEALY (CHRIS), Books by.
Crown 8vo, cloth, 6s. each.
Confessions of a Journalist.
Heirs of Reuben.
Mara.

The Endless Heritage. Crown 8vo, cloth, 3s. 6d.

HELPS (Sir ARTHUR). — Ivan de Biron. Crown 8vo, cloth 3s. 6d.; post 8vo, illustrated boards, 2s.

HENTY (G. A.), Novels by.
Rujub, the Juggler. Post 8vo, cloth, 3s. 6d.; illustrated boards, 2s.

Crown 8vo, cloth, 3s. 6d. each.
The Queen's Cup.
Dorothy's Double.
Colonel Thorndyke's Secret.

HENDERSON (ISAAC).—Agatha Page. Crown 8vo, cloth, 3s. 6d.

HERBERTSON (JESSIE L.).— Junia. Crown 8vo, cloth, 6s.

HERMAN (HENRY).—A Leading Lady. Post 8vo cloth, 2s. 6d.

HILL (HEADON).—Zambra the Detective. Crown 8vo, cloth, 3s. 6d.; picture cloth, flat back, 2s.

HILL (JOHN), Works by.
Treason-Felony. Post 8vo, Illustrated boards, 2s.
The Common Ancestor. Crown 8vo, cloth, 3s. 6d.

HINKSON (H. A.), Novels by.
Crown 8vo, cloth, 6s. each.
Fan Fitzgerald. | **Silk and Steel.**

HOEY (Mrs. CASHEL). — The Lover's Creed. Crown 8vo, cloth, 3s. 6d.

HOFFMANN (PROFESSOR).— King Koko. A Magic Story. With 25 Illustrations. Crown 8vo, cloth, 1s. net.

HOLIDAY, Where to go for a. By E. P. SHOLL, Sir H. MAXWELL, JOHN WATSON, JANE BARLOW, MARY LOVETT CAMERON, JUSTIN H. McCARTHY, PAUL LANGE, J. W. GRAHAM, J. H. SALTER, PHŒBE ALLEN, S. J. BECKETT, L. RIVERS VINE, and C. F. GORDON CUMMING. Crown 8vo, cloth, 1s. 6d.

HOLMES (C. J., M.A.).—Notes on the Science of Picture-making. With Photogravure Frontispiece. Demy 8vo, cloth, 7s. 6d. net.

HOLMES (O. WENDELL).— The Autocrat of the Breakfast-Table. Illustrated by J. GORDON THOMSON. FINE PAPER EDITION, pott 8vo, cloth, gilt top, 2s. net.; leather, gilt edges, 3s. net.

HOOD'S (THOMAS) Choice Works in Prose and Verse. With Life of the Author, Portrait, and 200 Illustrations. Crown 8vo, cloth, 3s. 6d.

HOOK'S (THEODORE) Choice Humorous Works; including his Ludicrous Adventures, Bons Mots, Puns, Hoaxes. With Life and Frontispiece. Crown 8vo, cloth, 3s. 6d.

HOPKINS (TIGHE), Novels by.
For Freedom. Crown 8vo, cloth, 6s.

Crown 8vo, cloth, 3s. 6d. each.
'Twixt Love and Duty.
The Incomplete Adventurer.
The Nugents of Carriconna.
Nell Haffenden. With 8 Illustrations.

HORNE (R. HENGIST).—Orion. With Portrait. Crown 8vo, cloth, 7s.

HORNIMAN (ROY), Novels by.
Crown 8vo, cloth, 6s. each.
Bellamy the Magnificent.
Lord Cammarleigh's Secret.
Israel Rank. Crown 8vo, cloth, 3s. 6d.

HORNUNG (E. W.), Novels by.
The Shadow of the Rope. Crown 8vo, cloth, 3s. 6d.
Crown 8vo, cloth, 6s. each.
Stingaree. | A Thief in the Night.

HUGO (VICTOR).—The Outlaw of Iceland. Translated by Sir GILBERT CAMPBELL. Crown 8vo, cloth, 3s. 6d.

HUME (FERGUS), Novels by.
The Lady From Nowhere. Cr. 8vo, cloth, 3s. 6d.; picture cloth, flat back, 2s.
The Millionaire Mystery. Crown 8vo, cloth, 3s. 6d.
The Wheeling Light. Crown 8vo, cloth, gilt top, 6s.

HUNGERFORD (Mrs.), Novels by. Crown 8vo, cloth, 3s. 6d. each; post 8vo, illustrated boards, 2s. each; cloth limp, 2s. 6d. each.
The Professor's Experiment.
Nora Creina.
Lady Verner's Flight.
Lady Patty. | Peter's Wife.
The Red-House Mystery.
An Unsatisfactory Lover.
April's Lady.
A Maiden All Forlorn.
The Three Graces.
A Mental Struggle.
Marvel. | A Modern Circe.
In Durance Vile.
Crown 8vo, cloth, 3s. 6d. each.
An Anxious Moment.
A Point of Conscience.
The Coming of Chloe. | Lovice.
The Red-House Mystery. POPULAR EDITION, medium 8vo, 6d.

HUNT (Mrs. ALFRED), Novels by. Crown 8vo, cloth, 3s. 6d. each; post 8vo, illustrated boards, 2s. each.
The Leaden Casket.
Self-Condemned.
That Other Person.
Mrs. Juliet. Crown 8vo, cloth, 3s. 6d.

HUTCHINSON (W. M.)—Hints on Colt-Breaking. With 25 Illustrations. Crown 8vo, cloth, 3s. 6d.

HYAMSON (ALBERT).—A His- tory of the Jews in England. With 16 Portraits and Views and 2 Maps. Demy 8vo, cloth, 4s. 6d. net.

HYATT (A. H.), Topographical Anthologies by. Pott 8vo, cloth, gilt top, 2s. net each; leather, gilt edges, 3s. net each.
The Charm of London.
The Charm of Edinburgh.
The Charm of Venice.
The Charm of Paris.

INCHBOLD (A. C.), The Road of No Return. Crown 8vo, cloth, 6s.

INDOOR PAUPERS. By ONE OF THEM. Crown 8vo, 1s.; cloth, 1s. 6d.

INMAN (HERBERT) and HARTLEY ASPDEN.—The Tear of Kalee. Crown 8vo, cloth, gilt top, 6s.

INNKEEPER'S HANDBOOK (The) and Licensed Victualler's Manual. By J. TREVOR-DAVIES. Crown 8vo, cloth, 2s.

IRVING (WASHINGTON).—Old Christmas. Square 16mo, cloth, with Frontispiece, 1s. net.

JAMES (C. T. C.).—A Romance of the Queen's Hounds. Crown 8vo, cloth, 1s. 6d.

JAMES (G. W.). — Scraggles: The Story of a Sparrow. With 6 Illustrations. Post 8vo, cloth, 2s. 6d.

JAMESON (WILLIAM).—My Dead Self. Post 8vo, cloth, 2s. 6d.

JAPP (Dr. A. H.).—Dramatic Pictures. Crown 8vo, cloth, 5s.

JEFFERIES (RICHARD), by.
The Life of the Fields. Post 8vo, cloth, 2s. 6d.; LARGE TYPE, FINE PAPER EDITION, pott 8vo, cloth, gilt top, 2s. net; leather, gilt edges, 3s. net. *Also* a NEW EDITION, with 12 Illustrations in Colours by M. U. CLARKE, crown 8vo, cloth, 5s. net; parchment, 7s. 6d. net.
The Open Air. Post 8vo, cloth, 2s. 6d.; LARGE TYPE, FINE PAPER EDITION, pott 8vo, cloth, gilt top, 2s. net; leather, gilt edges, 3s. net. *Also* a NEW EDITION, with 12 Illustrations in Colours by RUTH DOLLMAN, crown 8vo, cloth, 5s. net; parchment, 7s. 6d. net.
Nature near London. Crown 8vo, buckram, 6s.; post 8vo, cl., 2s. 6d.; LARGE TYPE, FINE PAPER EDITION, pott 8vo, cl., gilt top, 2s. net; leather, gilt edges, 3s. net. *Also* a NEW EDITION, with 12 Illustrations in Colours by RUTH DOLLMAN, crown 8vo, cloth, 5s. net; parchment, 7s. 6d. net.
The Pocket Richard Jefferies: being Passages chosen from the Nature Writings of JEFFERIES by ALFRED H. HYATT. 16mo, cloth, gilt top, 2s. net.; leather, gilt top, 3s. net.
The Eulogy of Richard Jefferies. By Sir WALTER BESANT. Cr. 8vo, cl., 6s.

JEROME (JEROME K.).—Stage- land. With 64 Illustrations by J. BERNARD PARTRIDGE. Fcap. 4to, 1s.

JERROLD (TOM), Works by.
Post 8vo, 1s. each; cloth, 1s. 6d. each.
The Garden that Paid the Rent.
Household Horticulture.
Our Kitchen Garden: The Plants We Grow, and How We Cook Them. Post 8vo, cloth, 1s. net.

JOHNSTON (R.).—The Peril of
an Empire. Crown 8vo, cloth, 6s.

JONES (WILLIAM, F.S.A.).
—Finger-Ring Lore: Historical, Legendary, and Anecdotal. With numerous Illustrations. Crown 8vo, cloth, 3s. 6d.

JONSON'S (BEN) Works. With
Notes and Biographical Memoir by WILLIAM GIFFORD. Edited by Colonel CUNNINGHAM. Three Vols., crown 8vo, cloth, 3s. 6d. each.

JOSEPHUS, The Complete
Works of. Translated by WILLIAM WHISTON. Containing 'The Antiquities of the Jews,' and 'The Wars of the Jews.' With 52 Illustrations and Maps. Two Vols., demy 8vo, half-cloth, 12s. 6d.

KEATING (JOSEPH).—Maurice.
Crown 8vo, cloth, 6s.

KEMPLING (W. BAILEY).—The
Poets Royal of England and Scotland: Original Poems by Royal and Noble Persons. With Notes and 6 Photogravure Portraits. Small 8vo, parchment, 6s. net; vellum, 7s. 6d. net. Also an Edition in THE KING'S CLASSICS (No. 39).

KERSHAW (MARK).—Colonial
Facts and Fictions: Humorous Sketches. Post 8vo, illustrated boards, 2s.; cloth, 2s. 6d.

KING (LEONARD W., M.A.).—
A History of Babylonia and Assyria from the Earliest Times until the Persian Conquest. With Maps, Plans, and Illustrations after all the principal Monuments of the Period. In 3 volumes, royal 8vo, buckram. Each volume separately, 18s. net; or per set of 3 volumes, if subscribed for before the issue of Vol. I., £2 10s. net.

Vol. I.—**A History of Sumer and**
Akkad: An account of the Primitive Inhabitants of Babylonia from the Earliest Times to about B.C. 2000.

„ II.—**A History of Babylon** from
the First Dynasty, about B.C. 2000, until the Conquest by Cyrus, B.C. 539.

„ III.—**A History of Assyria** from
the Earliest Period until the Fall of Nineveh, B.C. 606. [*Preparing*

KING (R. ASHE), Novels by.
Post 8vo, illustrated boards, 2s.
'The Wearing of the Green.'
Passion's Slave. | **Bell Barry.**

A Drawn Game. Crown 8vo, cloth, 3s. 6d.; post 8vo, illustrated boards, 2s.

KINGS AND QUEENS OF ENG-
LAND. By E. G. RITCHIE and BASIL PROCTER. With 43 Illustrations. Small demy 8vo, 1s. net.

KING'S CLASSICS (The).
General Editor, Professor I. GOLLANCZ, Litt.D. Printed on laid paper, 16mo, each with Frontispiece, gilt top. Quarter bound grey boards or red cloth, 1s. 6d. net each; quarter vellum, cloth sides, 2s. 6d. net each; three-quarter vellum, 5s. net each.

Volumes now in course of publication:

35. **Wine, Women, and Song:**
Mediæval Latin Students' Songs. Translated into English, with an Introduction, by JOHN ADDINGTON SYMONDS.
36, 37. **George Pettie's Petite Palace of Pettie his Pleasure.** Edited by Prof. I. GOLLANCZ, 2 vols.
38. **Walpole's Castle of Otranto.** By Sir WALTER SCOTT. With Introduction and Preface by Miss SPURGEON.
39. **The Poets Royal of England and Scotland.** Original Poems by Kings and other Royal and Noble Persons, collected and edited by W. BAILEY KEMPLING.
40. **Sir Thomas More's Utopia.** Edited by ROBERT STEELE, F.S.A.
41.†**Chaucer's Legend of Good Women.** In Modern English, with Notes and Introduction by Professor W. W. SKEAT.
42. **Swift's Battle of the Books.** Edited, with Notes and Introduction, by A. GUTHKELCH.
43. **Sir William Temple upon the Gardens of Epicurus, with other 17th Century Garden Essays.** Edited, with Notes and Introduction, by A. FORBES SIEVEKING, F.S.A.
44. **The Four Last Things,** by Sir THOMAS MORE; together with **A Spiritual Consolation and other Treatises** by JOHN FISHER, Bishop of Rochester. Edited by DANIEL O'CONNOR.
45. **The Song of Roland.** Translated from the old French by Mrs. CROSLAND. With Introduction by Prof. BRANDIN.
46. **Dante's Vita Nuova.** The Italian text, with DANTE G. ROSSETTI's translation on opposite pages. With Introduction and Notes by Prof. H. OELSNER.
47.†**Chaucer's Prologue and Minor Poems.** In modern English, with Notes and Introduction by Prof. W. W. SKEAT.
48.†**Chaucer's Parliament of Birds and House of Fame.** In modern English, with Notes and Introduction by Prof. W. W. SKEAT.
49. **Mrs. Gaskell's Cranford.** With Introduction by R. BRIMLEY JOHNSON.
50.†**Pearl.** An English Poem of the Fourteenth Century. Edited, with a Modern Rendering and an Introduction, by Professor I. GOLLANCZ.
51, 52. **King's Letters.** Volumes III. and IV. Newly edited from the originals by ROBERT STEELE, F.S.A.
53. **The English Correspondence of Saint Boniface.** Translated and edited, with an Introductory Sketch of the Life of St. Boniface, by E. J. KYLIE, M.A.

KING'S CLASSICS (The)—*continued.*

56. The Cavalier to his Lady. Seventeenth Century Love Songs. Edited by F. SIDGWICK.

57. Asser's Life of King Alfred. Edited by L. C. JANE, M.A.

58. Translations from the Icelandic. By Rev. W. C. GREEN, M.A.

59. The Rule of St. Benet. Translated by Right Rev. ABBOT GASQUET.

60. Daniel's 'Delia' and Drayton's 'Idea.' Edited by ARUNDELL ESDAILE, M.A.

61. The Book of the Duke of True Lovers. A Romance of the Court, by CHRISTINE DE PISAN, translated, with Notes and Introduction, by ALICE KEMP-WELCH.

62. Of the Tumbler of Our Lady, and other Miracles. Translated, from the Middle French MSS., with Notes and Introduction, by ALICE KEMP-WELCH.

63. The Chatelaine of Vergi. A Romance of the Court, translated from the Middle French, by ALICE KEMP WELCH, with Introduction by L. BRANDIN, Ph.D., and with the original Text. Edition Raynaud.

84. Troubadour Poems. Edited by BARBARA SMYTHE.

85. An Anthology of French Verse. Selected by C. B. LEWIS.

Earlier Volumes in the Series are—
1. The Love of Books (The Philobiblon).
2. *Six Dramas of Calderon (FitzGerald's Translation). (Double vol.)
3. Chronicle of Jocelin of Brakelond.
4. The Life of Sir Thomas More.
5. Eikon Basilike.
6. Kings' Letters : Alfred to the coming of the Tudors.
7. Kings' Letters : From the Tudors to the Love Letters of Henry VIII.
8. †Chaucer's Knight's Tale (Prof. SKEAT).
9. †Chaucer's Man of Law's Tale (Prof SKEAT)
10. †Chaucer's Prioress's Tale (Prof. SKEAT).
11. The Romance of Fulke Fitzwarine.
12. The Story of Cupid and Psyche.
13. Evelyn's Life of Margaret Godolphin.
14. Early Lives of Dante.
15. The Falstaff Letters.
16. Polonius. By EDWARD FITZGERALD.
17. Mediaeval Lore.
18. The Vision of Piers the Plowman (Prof. SKEAT).
19. The Gull's Hornbook.
20. *The Nun's Rule, or Ancren Riwle. (Double vol.).
21. The Memoirs of Robert Cary, Earl of Monmouth.
22. Early Lives of Charlemagne.
23. Cicero's 'Friendship,' 'Old Age,' and 'Scipio's Dream.'
24. *Wordsworth's Prelude. (Double vol.)
25. The Defence of Guenevere.
26, 27. Browning's Men and Women.
28. Poe's Poems.
29. Shakespeare's Sonnets.
30. George Eliot's Silas Marner.
31. Goldsmith's Vicar of Wakefield.
32. Charles Reade's Peg Woffington.
33. The Household of Sir Thomas More.
34. Sappho : One Hundred Lyrics. By BLISS CARMAN.

* Numbers 2, 20, and 24 are Double Volumes and Double Price.
† The Chaucer Vols, and also No. 50, may be had in stiff paper covers at 1s. net each.

KING'S LIBRARY FOLIOS (The).

The Mirrour of Vertue in Worldly Greatnes, or The Life of Sir Thomas More, Knight. By his son-in-law, WILLIAM ROPER. 10s. 6d. net. (Seven copies of this volume alone remain, and are not to be sold apart from sets.)

Eikon Basilike, the Portraicture of His Sacred Majestie in his Solitudes and Sufferings. Edited by EDWARD ALMACK, F.S.A. £1 1s. net.

Shakespeare's Ovid, being Arthur Golding's Translation of the Metamorphoses. Edited by W. H. D. ROUSE, Litt.D. £1 11s. 6d. net.

The Percy Folio of Old English Ballads and Romances. Edited by the GENERAL EDITOR. In four volumes at £4 4s. the set. (Volumes I. and II. issued ; III. at Press; IV. in Preparation.)

** NOTE.—*Seven complete sets of the above folios remain for sale. Price, per set, £7 17s. 6d. net.*

KING'S LIBRARY QUARTOS (The).

The Alchemist. By BEN JONSON. Edited by H. C. HART. 5s. net ; Japanese vellum, £1 1s. net.

The Gull's Hornbook. By THOMAS DEKKER. Edited by R. B McKERROW. 5s. net ; Japanese vellum, 10s. 6d. net.

The Beggar's Opera. By JOHN GAY. Edited by HAMILTON MACLEOD. 5s. net ; Japanese vellum, 10s. 6d. net.

KIPLING PRIMER (A). Including Biographical and Critical Chapters, an Index to Mr. Kipling's principal Writings, and Bibliographies. By F. L. KNOWLES. With Two Portraits. Crown 8vo, cloth, 3s. 6d.

KNIGHT (WILLIAM and EDWARD).—The Patient's Vade Mecum: How to Get Most Benefit from Medical Advice. Crown 8vo, cloth, 1s. 6d.

LAMB'S (CHARLES) Complete Works in Prose and Verse, including 'Poetry for Children' and 'Prince Dorus.' Edited by R. H. SHEPHERD. With 2 Portraits and Facsimile of the 'Essay on Roast Pig.' Crown 8vo, cloth, 3s. 6d.

The Essays of Elia. (Both Series.) FINE PAPER EDITION, pott 8vo, cloth, gilt top, 2s. net ; leather, gilt edges, 3s. net.

LAMBERT (GEORGE). — The President of Boravia. Crown 8vo, cloth, 3s. 6d.

LANE (EDWARD WILLIAM).
—The Thousand and One Nights, commonly called in England The **Arabian Nights' Entertainments.** Translated from the Arabic and illustrated by many hundred Engravings from Designs by HARVEY. Edited by E. S. POOLE. With Preface by STANLEY LANE-POOLE. 3 Vols., 8vo, cl., 22s. 6d.

LAURISTOUN (PETER). The Painted Mountain. Cr. 8vo, cloth, 6s.

LEE (HOLME).—Legends from Fairy Land. With about 250 Illustrations by REGINALD L. and HORACE J. KNOWLES, and an Introduction by E. H. FREEMANTLE. Crown 8vo, cloth gilt, 5s. net.

LEES (DOROTHY N.).—Tuscan Feasts and Tuscan Friends. With 12 Illustrations. Large crown 8vo, cloth, 5s. net.

LEHMANN (R. C.). — Harry Fludyer at Cambridge, and Conversational Hints for Young Shooters. Crown 8vo, 1s.; cloth, 1s. 6d.

LEIGH (HENRY S.).—Carols of Cockayne. Crown 8vo, buckram, 5s.

LELAND (C. G.).—A Manual of Mending and Repairing. With Diagrams. Crown 8vo, cloth, 5s.

LEPELLETIER (EDMOND). — Madame Sans-Gêne. Translated by JOHN DE VILLIERS. Post 8vo, cloth, 3s. 6d.; illustrated boards, 2s.; POPULAR EDITION, medium 8vo, 6d.

LEYS (JOHN K.), Novels by. The Lindsays. Post 8vo, illust. bds.,2s. A Sore Temptation. Cr. 8vo, cl., 6s.

LILBURN (ADAM).—A Tragedy in Marble. Crown 8vo, cloth, 3s. 6d.

LINDSAY (HARRY), Novels by. Crown 8vo, cloth, 3s. 6d. each. Rhoda Roberts. | The Jacobite. Crown 8vo, cloth, 6s. each. Judah Pyecroft, Puritan. The Story of Leah.

LINTON (E. LYNN), Works by. Crown 8vo, cloth, 3s. 6d. each; post 8vo, illustrated boards, 2s. each.
Patricia Kemball. | Ione.
The Atonement of Leam Dundas.
The World Well Lost. 12 Illusts.
The One Too Many.
Under which Lord? With 12 Illusts.
'My Love.' | Sowing the Wind.
Paston Carew. | Dulcie Everton.
With a Silken Thread.
The Rebel of the Family.
An Octave of Friends. Crown 8vo, cloth, 3s. 6d.
Sowing the Wind. CHEAP EDITION, post 8vo, cloth, 1s. net.
Patricia Kemball. POPULAR EDITION, medium 8vo, 6d.

LORIMER (NORMA).—The Pagan Woman. Cr. 8vo, cloth, 3s. 6d.

LUCAS (ALICE). — Talmudic Legends, Hymns, and Paraphrases. Post 8vo, half-parchment, 2s. net.

LUCAS (E. V.), Books by.
Anne's Terrible Good Nature, and other Stories for Children. With 12 Illustrations by A. H. BUCKLAND, and Coloured End-Papers and Cover by F. D. BEDFORD. Crown 8vo, cloth, 6s.
A Book of Verses for Children. With Coloured Title-page. Crown 8vo, cloth, 6s.
Three Hundred Games and Pastimes. By E. V. LUCAS and ELIZABETH LUCAS. Pott 4to, cloth, 6s. net.
The Flamp, and other Stories. Royal 16mo, cloth, 1s. net.

LUCY (HENRY W.).—Gideon Fleyce. Crown 8vo, cloth, 3s. 6d.; post 8vo, illustrated boards, 2s.

MACAULAY (LORD).—The History of England. LARGE TYPE, FINE PAPER EDITION, in 5 vols. pott 8vo, cloth, gilt top, 2s. net per vol.; leather, gilt edges, 3s. net per vol.

MACCOLL (HUGH).—Mr. Stranger's Sealed Packet. Cr. 8vo, cloth, 3s. 6d.; post 8vo, illus. boards, 2s.

McCARTHY (JUSTIN), Books by.
The Reign of Queen Anne. Two Vols., demy 8vo, cloth, 12s. each.
A History of the Four Georges and of William the Fourth. Four Vols., demy 8vo, cloth, 12s each.
A History of Our Own Times from the Accession of Queen Victoria to the General Election of 1880. LIBRARY EDITION. Four Vols., demy 8vo, cloth, 12s. each.—Also the POPULAR EDITION, in Four Vols., crown 8vo, cloth, 6s. each. —And the JUBILEE EDITION, with an Appendix of Events to the end of 1886, in 2 Vols., demy 8vo, cloth, 7s. 6d. each.
A History of Our Own Times, Vol. V., from 1880 to the Diamond Jubilee. Demy 8vo, cloth, 12s.; crown 8vo, cloth 6s.
A History of Our Own Times, Vols. VI. and VII., from 1897 to Accession of Edward VII. 2 Vols., demy 8vo, cloth, 24s.; crown 8vo, cloth, 12s.
A Short History of Our Own Times, from the Accession of Queen Victoria to the Accession of King Edward VII. NEW EDITION, revised and enlarged. Crown 8vo, cloth, gilt top, 6s.; also the POPULAR EDITION, post 8vo, cloth, 2s. 6d.; and the CHEAP EDITION (to the year 1880), med. 8vo, 6d.

LARGE TYPE, FINE PAPER EDITIONS. Pott 8vo, cloth, gilt top, 2s. net per vol.; leather, gilt edges, 3s. net per vol.
The Reign of Queen Anne, in 1 Vol.
A History of the Four Georges and of William IV., in 2 vols.
A History of Our Own Times from Accession of Q. Victoria to 1897, in 3 Vols.

McCARTHY (JUSTIN)—*continued.*
Crown 8vo, cloth, 3s. 6d. each ; post 8vo, pict.
boards, 2s. each ; cloth limp, 2s. 6d. each.
The Waterdale Neighbours.
My Enemy's Daughter.
A Fair Saxon. | Linley Rochford.
Dear Lady Disdain. | The Dictator.
Miss Misanthrope. With 12 Illusts.
Donna Quixote. With 12 Illustrations.
The Comet of a Season.
Maid of Athens. With 12 Illustrations.
Camiola.
Red Diamonds. | The Riddle Ring.
Crown 8vo, cloth, 3s. 6d. each.
The Three Disgraces. | Mononia.
'The Right Honourable.' By JUSTIN
MCCARTHY and MRS. CAMPBELL PRAED.
Crown 8vo, cloth, 6s.
Julian Revelstone. Cr. 8vo, cloth, 6s.

McCARTHY (J. H.), Works by.
The French Revolution. (Consti-
tuent Assembly, 1789–91.) Four Vols.,
demy 8vo, cloth, 12s. each.
**An Outline of the History of
Ireland.** Crown 8vo, 1s. ; cloth, 1s. 6d.
**Ireland Since the Union—1798–
1886.** Crown 8vo, cloth, 6s.
Hafiz in London. 8vo, gold cloth, 3s. 6d.
Our Sensation Novel. Crown 8vo,
1s. ; cloth, 1s. 6d.
Doom: An Atlantic Episode. Crown 8vo, 1s.
Dolly: A Sketch. Crown 8vo, 1s.
Lily Lass. Crown 8vo, 1s. ; cloth, 1s. 6d.
A London Legend. Cr. 8vo, cloth, 3s. 6d.

**MACDONALD (Dr. GEORGE),
Books by.**
Works of Fancy and Imagination
Ten Vols., 16mo, cloth, gilt, in case, 21s. ;
or separately, Grolier cloth, 2s. 6d. each.
Also a NEW ISSUE in 16mo, cloth, gilt
top, 2s. net per Vol. ; leather, gilt top, 3s.
net per Vol.
Vol.   I. WITHIN AND WITHOUT—THE
       HIDDEN LIFE.
  „   II. THE DISCIPLE—THE GOSPEL
       WOMEN—BOOK OF SONNETS—
       ORGAN SONGS.
  „   III. VIOLIN SONGS—SONGS OF THE
       DAYS AND NIGHTS—A BOOK
       OF DREAMS—ROADSIDE POEMS
       —POEMS FOR CHILDREN.
  „   IV. PARABLES—BALLADS—SCOTCH
  „   V. & VI. PHANTASIES.   [SONGS.
  „   VII. THE PORTENT.
  „   VIII. THE LIGHT PRINCESS—THE
       GIANT'S HEART—SHADOWS.
  „   IX. CROSS PURPOSES—GOLDEN KEY
       CARASOYN—LITTLE DAYLIGHT.
  „   X. THE CRUEL PAINTER—THE WOW
       O'RIVVEN—THE CASTLE—THE
       BROKEN SWORDS—THE GRAY
       WOLF—UNCLE CORNELIUS.
**Poetical Works of George Mac-
Donald.** 2 Vols., cr. 8vo, buckram, 12s.
Heather and Snow. Crown 8vo, cloth,
3s. 6d. ; post 8vo, illustrated boards, 2s.
Lilith. Crown 8vo, cloth, 6s.
The Pocket George MacDonald:
Passages Chosen by A. H. HYATT. 16mo,
cloth gilt, 2s. net ; leather gilt, 3s. net.

**MACDONELL (AGNES).—
Quaker Cousins.** Post 8vo, boards, 2s.

**MACHRAY (ROBERT), Novels
by.** Crown 8vo, cloth, 6s. each.
A Blow over the Heart.
The Mystery of Lincoln's Inn.
The Private Detective.
Her Honour. Crown 8vo, cloth, 3s. 6d.

**MACKAY (Dr. CHAS.).—Inter-
ludes and Undertones.** Cr. 8vo, cloth, 6s.

**MACKAY (WILLIAM).—A
Mender of Nets.** Crown 8vo, cloth, 6s.

**MACKENZIE (W. A.).—The
Drexel Dream.** Crown 8vo, cloth, 6s.

MACLISE Portrait Gallery (The)
of Illustrious Literary Characters:
85 Portraits by DANIEL MACLISE ;
with Memoirs by WILLIAM BATES, B.A.
Crown 8vo, cloth, 3s. 6d.

MAGIC LANTERN, The, and its
Management. By T. C. HEPWORTH.
With 10 Illusts. Cr. 8vo, 1s. ; cloth, 1s. 6d.

MAGNA CHARTA: A Facsimile of
the Original, 3 ft. by 2 ft., with Arms and
Seals emblazoned in Gold and Colours, 5s.

MALLOCK (W. H.), Works by.
The New Republic. Post 8vo, cloth,
3s. 6d. ; illustrated boards, 2s. ; LARGE
TYPE, FINE PAPER EDITION, pott 8vo,
cloth, gilt top, 2s. net ; leather, gilt edges,
3s. net.

Poems. Small 4to, parchment, 8s.
Is Life Worth Living? Crown 8vo,
buckram, 6s.

**MALLORY (Sir THOMAS).—
Mort d'Arthur,** Selections from, edited
by B. M. RANKING. Post 8vo, cloth, 2s.

**MARGUERITTE (PAUL and
VICTOR), Novels by.**
Crown 8vo, cloth, 3s. 6d. each.
The Disaster. Translated by F. LEES.
Vanity. Translated by K. S. WEST. With
Portrait Frontispiece.

The Commune. Translated by F. LEES
and R. B. DOUGLAS. Cr. 8vo, cloth, 6s.

MARIE DE MEDICIS and the
Court of France in the XVIIth Century. Translated from the French of
LOUIS BATIFFOL by MARY KING. With
a Portrait. Demy 8vo, cloth, 7s. 6d. net.

MARLOWE'S Works, including
his Translations. Edited with Notes by
Col. CUNNINGHAM. Cr. 8vo, cloth, 3s. 6d.

**MARSH (RICHARD).—A
Spoiler of Men.** Cr. 8vo, cloth, 3s. 6d.

MASTER OF GAME (THE): The Oldest English Book on Hunting. By EDWARD, Second Duke of York. Edited by W. A. and F. BAILLIE-GROHMAN. With Introduction by THEODORE ROOSEVELT. Photogravure Frontispiece, and 23 Full-page Illustrations after Illuminations. Large cr. 8vo, cloth, 7s. 6d. net; parchment, 10s. 6d. net.

MASSINGER'S Plays. From the Text of WILLIAM GIFFORD. Edited by Col. CUNNINGHAM. Cr. 8vo, cloth, 3s. 6d.

MASTERMAN (J.).—Half-a-dozen Daughters. Post 8vo, bds., 2s.

MATTHEWS (BRANDER).—A Secret of the Sea. Post 8vo, illustrated boards, 2s. ; cloth, 2s. 6d.

MAX O'RELL, Books by. Crown 8vo, cloth, 3s. 6d. each.
Her Royal Highness Woman.
Between Ourselves.
Rambles in Womanland.

MEADE (L. T.), Novels by. A Soldier of Fortune. Crown 8vo, cloth, 3s. 6d. ; post 8vo, illust. boards, 2s.
Crown 8vo, cloth, 3s. 6d. each.
The Voice of the Charmer.
In an Iron Grip. | The Siren.
Dr. Rumsey's Patient.
On the Brink of a Chasm.
The Way of a Woman.
A Son of Ishmael.
An Adventuress. | Rosebury.
The Blue Diamond.
A Stumble by the Way.
This Troublesome World.

MEDICIS (Lives of the): from their Letters. By JANET ROSS. With Photogravure Frontispiece and other Illustrations. Demy 8vo, cloth, 7s. 6d. net. [Preparing.

MEDIEVAL LIBRARY (The New). Small crown 8vo, pure rag paper, boards, 5s. net per vol. ; pigskin with clasps, 7s. 6d. net per vol.
1. **The Book of the Duke of True Lovers.** Translated from the Middle French of CHRISTINE DE PISAN, with Notes by ALICE KEMP-WELCH. Woodcut Title and 6 Photogravures.
2. **Of the Tumbler of our Lady, and other Miracles.** Translated from the Middle French of GAUTIER DE COINCI, &c., with Notes and Introduction by ALICE KEMP-WELCH. Woodcut Title and 7 Photogravures.
3. **The Chatelaine of Vergi.** Translated from the Middle French by ALICE KEMP-WELCH, with the original Text, and an Introduction by Dr. L. BRANDIN. Woodcut Title and 5 Photogravures.
4. **The Babees' Book.** Edited from Dr. FURNIVALL's Texts, with Notes, by EDITH RICKERT. Woodcut Title and 6 Photogravures.

MEDIEVAL LIBRARY (The)—continued.
5. **The Book of the Divine Consolation of Saint Angela da Foligno.** Translated from the Italian by MARY G. STEEGMANN, with Introduction by ALGAR THOROLD. Woodcut Title and reproductions of Woodcuts.
6. **The Legend of the Holy Fina, Virgin of Santo Geminiano.** Translated from the 14th Century MS. by M. MANSFIELD. Woodcut Title and 6 Photogravures.
7. **Early English Romances of Love.** Edited in Modern English by EDITH RICKERT. 5 Photogravures.
8. **Early English Romances of Friendship.** Edited in Modern English, with Notes, by EDITH RICKERT. 6 Photogravures.
9. **The Cell of Self-Knowledge.** Seven Early Mystical Treatises printed in 1851. Edited, with Introduction and Notes, by EDMUND GARDNER, M.A. Coll. type Frontispiece in two colours.
10. **Ancient English Christmas Carols, 1400-1700.** Collected and arranged by EDITH RICKERT. With 8 Photogravures. Boards, 7s. 6d. net ; pigskin with clasps 10s. 6d. net.

MELBA: A Biography. By AGNES M. MURPHY. With Chapters by MADAME MELBA on THE ART OF SINGING and on THE SELECTION OF MUSIC AS A PROFESSION, Portraits, and Illustrations. Demy 8vo, cloth, 16s. net.

MERRICK (HOPE). — When a Girl's Engaged. Cr. 8vo, cloth, 3s. 6d.

MERRICK (LEONARD), Novels by.
The Man who was Good. Crown 8vo, cl., 3s. 6d. ; post 8vo, illust. bds., 2s.
Crown 8vo, cloth, 3s. 6d. each.
Cynthia. | This Stage of Fools.

METHVEN (PAUL). — Influences. Crown 8vo, cloth, 6s.

MEYNELL (ALICE).—The Flower of the Mind: a Choice among the Best Poems. In 16mo, cloth, gilt, 2s. n t ; leather, 3s. net.

MINTO (WM.).—Was She Good or Bad? Crown 8vo, cloth, 1s. 6d.

MITCHELL (EDM.), Novels by.
Crown 8vo, cloth 3s. 6d. each.
The Lone Star Rush. With 8 Illusts.
Only a Nigger.
The Belforts of Culben.
Crown 8vo, picture cloth, flat backs, 2s. each.
Plotters of Paris.
The Temple of Death.
Towards the Eternal Snows.

MITFORD (BERTRAM), Novels by. Crown 8vo, cloth, 3s. 6d. each.
Renshaw Fanning's Quest.
Triumph of Hilary Blachland.
Haviland's Chum.

MITFORD (BERTRAM)—*continued.*
Crown 8vo, cloth, 3s. 6d. each ; picture cloth, flat back, 2s. each.
The Luck of Gerard Ridgeley.
The King's Assegai. With 6 Illusts.
The Gun-Runner. Cr. 8vo, cl., 3s. 6d.; Cheap Edition, medium 8vo., 6d.
Harley Greenoak's Charge. Crown 8vo, cloth, 6s.

MOLESWORTH (Mrs.). —
Hathercourt Rectory. Crown 8vo, cloth, 3s. 6d. ; post 8vo, illust. boards, 2s.

MONCRIEFF (W. D. SCOTT-).—
The Abdication: A Drama. With 7 Etchings. Imperial 4to, buckram, 21s.

MORROW (W. C.).—Bohemian Paris of To-Day. With 106 Illusts. by EDOUARD CUCUEL. Small demy 8vo cl. 6s.

MUDDOCK (J. E.), Stories by.
Crown 8vo, cloth, 3s. 6d. each.
Basile the Jester.
Young Lochinvar.
The Golden Idol.

Post 8vo, illustrated boards, 2s. each.
The Dead Man's Secret.
From the Bosom of the Deep.
Stories Weird and Wonderful. Post 8vo, illust. boards, 2s. ; cloth, 2s. 6d.
Maid Marian and Robin Hood. With 12 Illus. by STANLEY L. WOOD. Cr. 8vo, cloth, 3s. 6d. ; picture cl. flat back 2s.

MURRAY (D. CHRISTIE),
Novels by. Crown 8vo, cloth, 3s. 6d. each ; post 8vo, illustrated boards, 2s. each.
A Life's Atonement.
Joseph's Coat. With 12 Illustrations.
Coals of Fire. With 3 Illustrations.
Val Strange. | **A Wasted Crime.**
A Capful o' Nails. **Hearts.**
The Way of the World.
Mount Despair. | **A Model Father.**
Old Blazer's Hero.
By the Gate of the Sea.
A Bit o' Human Nature.
First Person Singular.
Bob Martin's Little Girl.
Time's Revenges.
Cynic Fortune. | **In Direst Peril.**

Crown 8vo, cloth, 3s. 6d. each.
This Little World.
A Race for Millions.
The Church of Humanity.
Tales in Prose and Verse.
Despair's Last Journey.
V.C.: A Chronicle of Castle Barfield.

Verona's Father. Crown 8vo, cloth, 6s.
His Own Ghost. Crown 8vo, cloth, 3s. 6d. ; picture cloth, flat back, 2s.
Joseph's Coat. POPULAR EDITION, medium 8vo, 6d.

MURRAY (D. CHRISTIE) and HENRY HERMAN, Novels by.
Crown 8vo, cloth, 3s. 6d. each ; post 8vo, illustrated boards. 2s. each.
One Traveller Returns.
The Bishops' Bible.
Paul Jones's Alias. With Illustrations by A. FORESTIER and G. NICOLET.

MURRAY (HENRY), Novels by.
Post 8vo, cloth, 2s. 6d. each.
A Game of Bluff.
A Song of Sixpence.

NEWBOLT (HENRY). — Taken from the Enemy. Fcp. 8vo, pic. cov., 1s.

NISBET (HUME), Books by.
'**Bail Up!**' Crown 8vo, cloth, 3s. 6d. ; post 8vo, illustrated boards, 2s. ; POPULAR EDITION medium 8vo, 6d.
Dr. Bernard St. Vincent. Post 8vo, illustrated boards, 2s.

NORDAU (MAX).—Morganatic : A Romance. Translated by ELIZABETH LEE. Crown 8vo, cloth, gilt top. 6s.

NORRIS (W. E.), Novels by.
Crown 8vo, cloth, 3s. 6d. each ; post 8vo, illustrated boards, 2s. each.
Saint Ann's. | **Billy Bellew.**
Miss Wentworth's Idea. Crown 8vo, cloth, 3s. 6d.

OUIDA, Novels by. Crown 8vo, cloth, 3s. 6d. each ; post 8vo, illustrated boards, 2s. each.

Tricotrin.	**A Dog of Flanders.**
Ruffino.	**Cecil Castlemaine's**
Othmar.	**Gage.**
Frescoes.	**Princess Napraxine.**
Wanda.	**Held in Bondage.**
Ariadne.	**Under Two Flags.**
Pascarel.	**Folle-Farine.**
Chandos.	**Two Wooden Shoes.**
Moths.	**A Village Commune.**
Puck.	**In a Winter City.**
Idalia.	**Santa Barbara.**
Bimbi.	**In Maremma.**
Signa.	**Strathmore.**
Friendship.	**Pipistrello.**
Guilderoy.	**Syrlin.**

Crown 8vo, cloth, 3s. 6d. each.
A Rainy June. | **The Massarenes.**
The Waters of Edera.

Crown 8vo, picture cloth, flat back, 2s. each.
Syrlin. | **The Waters of Edera.**

POPULAR EDITIONS, medium 8vo, 6d. each.
Under Two Flags. | **Moths.**
Held in Bondage. | **Puck.**
Strathmore. | **Tricotrin.**
The Massarenes. | **Chandos.**
Friendship. | **Ariadne.**
Two Little Wooden Shoes.
Idalia. | **Othmar.** | **Pascarel.**
A Village Commune.
Two Little Wooden Shoes. LARGE TYPE EDITION. Fcap. 8vo, cloth, 1s. net ; leather, 1s. 6d. net.
Wisdom, Wit, and Pathos, selected from the Works of OUIDA by F. SYDNEY MORRIS. Post 8vo. cloth. 5s.

OHNET (GEORGES), Novels by.
Doctor Rameau. Post 8vo, illustrated boards. 2s.
A Weird Gift. Crown 8vo, cloth, 3s. 6d. ; post 8vo, illustrated boards, 2s.
A Last Love. Post 8vo, illust. bds., 2s.

OHNET (GEORGES)—*continued.*
Crown 8vo, cloth, 3s. 6d. each.
The Path of Glory.
Love's Depths.
The Money-maker.
The Woman of Mystery.
The Conqueress.

OLIPHANT (Mrs.), Novels by.
Post 8vo, illustrated boards, 2s. each.
The Primrose Path.
The Greatest Heiress in England

Whiteladies. Crown 8vo, cloth, with 12 Illustrations, 3s. 6d.; post 8vo, bds., 2s.
The Sorceress. Crown 8vo, cloth, 3s. 6d.

OSBOURNE (LLOYD), Stories by. Crown 8vo, cloth, 3s. 6d. each.
The Motormaniacs.
Three Speeds Forward. With Illustrations.

O'SHAUGHNESSY (ARTHUR).
Music & Moonlight. Fcp. 8vo. cl., 7s. 6d.

PAIN (BARRY).—Eliza's Husband. Fcap, 8vo, 1s.; cloth, 1s. 6d.

PANDURANG HARI; or, Memoirs of a Hindoo. With Preface by Sir BARTLE FRERE. Post 8vo, illustrated boards, 2s.

PARADISE (The) or Garden of the Holy Fathers: Histories of the Anchorites, Recluses, Cœnobites, Monks, and Ascetic Fathers of the Deserts of Egypt, between about A.D. 250 and 400. Compiled by ATHANASIUS, PALLADIUS, ST. JEROME, and others. Translated from the Syriac, with an Introduction, by E. A. WALLIS BUDGE, Litt.D. With 2 Frontispieces. 2 vols. large crown 8vo, buckram, 15s. net.

PARIS SALON, The Illustrated Catalogue of the. With about 300 Illustrations. Published annually. By 8vo, 3s.

PAYN (JAMES), Novels by.
Crown 8vo, cloth, 3s. 6d. each; post 8vo, illustrated boards, 2s. each.
Lost Sir Massingberd.
The Clyffards of Clyffe.
A County Family.
Less Black than We're Painted.
By Proxy. | For Cash Only.
High Spirits. | Sunny Stories.
A Confidential Agent.
A Grape from a Thorn. 12 Illusts.
The Family Scapegrace.
Holiday Tasks. | At Her Mercy.
The Talk of the Town. 12 Illusts.
The Mystery of Mirbridge.
The Word and the Will.
The Burnt Million.
A Trying Patient.
Gwendoline's Harvest.

Post 8vo, illustrated boards, 2s. each.
Humorous Stories. | From Exile.
The Foster Brothers.
Married Beneath Him.
Bentinck's Tutor.
Walter's Word. | Fallen Fortunes.
A Perfect Treasure.
Like Father, Like Son.
A Woman's Vengeance.
Carlyon's Year. | Cecil's Tryst.
Murphy's Master.
Some Private Views.
Found Dead. | Mirk Abbey.
A Marine Residence.
The Canon's Ward.
Not Wooed, But Won.
Two Hundred Pounds Reward.
The Best of Husbands.
Halves. | What He Cost Her.
Kit: A Memory. | Under One Roof.
Glow-Worm Tales.
A Prince of the Blood.

A Modern Dick Whittington. Crown 8vo, cloth, with Portrait of Author, 3s. 6d.; picture cloth, flat back, 2s.

The Burnt Million. CHEAP EDITION, post 8vo, cloth, 1s. net.

Notes from the 'News.' Crown 8vo, cloth, 1s. 6d.

POPULAR EDITIONS, medium 8vo, 6d. each.
Lost Sir Massingberd.
Walter's Word. | By Proxy.

PAYNE (WILL). — Jerry the Dreamer. Crown 8vo, cloth, 3s. 6d.

PAUL (MARGARET A.).—Gentle and Simple. Crown 8vo, cloth, 3s. 6d.; post 8vo, illustrated boards, 2s.

PEARS (CHARLES).—From the Thames to the Seine. With 40 Illustrations in Colours and Sepia. Large fcap. 4to, cloth, 12s. 6d. net. [Preparing.

PENNELL - ELMHIRST (Cap- tain E.).—The Best of the Fun. With 8 Coloured Illustrations and 48 others. Medium 8vo, cloth, 6s. net.

PENNY (F. E.), Novels by.
Crown 8vo, cloth, 3s. 6d. each.
The Sanyasi. | The Tea-Planter.
Caste and Creed. | The Inevitable Law.

Crown 8vo, cloth, 6s. each.
Dilys. | Dark Corners.
The Unlucky Mark.

PERRIN (ALICE), Novels by.
Idolatry. Crown 8vo, cloth, 6s.

Crown 8vo, cloth, 3s. 6d. each.
A Free Solitude. | East of Suez.
The Waters of Destruction.
Red Records.
The Stronger Claim.

POPULAR EDITIONS, medium 8vo, 6d. each.
The Stronger Claim.
The Waters of Destruction.

PETER PAN KEEPSAKE (The).
By D. S. O'CONNOR. With Introduction by W. T. STEAD, and Illustrations. Demy 4to, picture cover, 1s. net.

PHELPS (E. S.).—Jack the Fisherman. Illustrated by C. W. REED. Crown 8vo, cloth, 1s. 6d.

PHIL MAY'S Sketch-Book : 54 Cartoons. Crown folio, cloth, 2s. 6d.

PHIPSON (Dr. T. L.).—Famous Violinists and Fine Violins. Crown 8vo, cloth, 5s.

PICTURE-MAKING, Notes on the Science of. By PROFESSOR C. J. HOLMES, M.A. With Photogravure Frontispiece. Demy 8vo, cloth, 7s. 6d. net.

PILKINGTON (L. L.).—Mallender's Mistake. Crown 8vo, cloth, 6s.

PLANCHÉ (J. R.).—Songs and Poems. Edited by Mrs. MACKARNESS. Crown 8vo, cloth, 6s.

PLAYS OF OUR FORE-FATHERS, and some of the Traditions upon which they were founded. By C. M. GAYLEY, LL.D. With numerous illustrations Royal 8vo, cloth, 12s. 6d. net.

PLUTARCH'S Lives of Illustrious Men. With Life of PLUTARCH by J. and W. LANGHORNE, and Portraits. Two Vols., 8vo, half-cloth, 10s. 6d.

POE'S (EDGAR ALLAN) Choice Works : Poems, Stories, Essays. With an Introduction by CHARLES BAUDELAIRE. Crown 8vo, cloth, 3s. 6d.

POLLOCK (W. H.).—The Charm, and Other Drawing-Room Plays. By Sir WALTER BESANT and WALTER H. POLLOCK. With 50 Illustrations. Crown 8vo, cloth, 3s. 6d.

POTTS (HENRY). — His Final Flutter. Crown 8vo, cloth, 6s.

POWDER - PUFF (The) : a Ladies' Breviary. By FRANZ BLEI. Fcap. 8vo, cloth, 3s. 6d.

PRAED (Mrs. CAMPBELL), Novels by. Post 8vo, illus. boards, 2s. ea.
The Romance of a Station.
The Soul of Countess Adrian.
Crown 8vo, cloth, 3s. 6d. each ; post 8vo, illustrated boards, 2s. each.
Outlaw and Lawmaker.
Christina Chard.
Mrs. Tregaskiss. With 8 Illustrations. Crown 8vo, cloth, 3s. 6d. each.
Nulma. | Madame Izan.
'As a Watch in the Night.'
The Lost Earl of Ellan.
Christina Chard. CHEAP EDITION, post 8vo, cloth, 1s. net.

PRICE (E. C.). — Valentina.
Crown 8vo, cloth, 3s. 6d.

PROCTOR (RICHARD A.),
Works by. Crown 8vo, cloth, 3s. 6d. each.
Easy Star Lessons. With Star Maps for every Night in the Year.
Flowers of the Sky. With 55 Illusts.
Familiar Science Studies.
Mysteries of Time and Space.
The Universe of Suns.

Saturn and Its System. With 13 Steel Plates. Demy 8vo, cloth, 6s.
Wages and Wants of Science Workers. Crown 8vo, 1s. 6d.

PRYCE (RICHARD). — Miss Maxwell's Affections. Crown 8vo, cloth, 3s. 6d. ; post 8vo, illust. boards, 2s.

RAB AND HIS FRIENDS.— By Dr. JOHN BROWN. Square 16mo, with Frontispiece, cloth, 1s. net.

RAPPOPORT (A. S., M.A.).— The Curse of the Romanovs : A Study of the Reigns of Tsars Paul I. and Alexander I. of Russia, 1796-1825. With 23 Illustrations. Demy 8vo, cloth, 16s. net.

READE'S (CHARLES) Novels.
Collected LIBRARY EDITION, in Seventeen Volumes, crown 8vo, cloth, 3s. 6d each.
Peg Woffington ; and Christie Johnstone.
Hard Cash.
The Cloister and the Hearth. With a Preface by Sir WALTER BESANT.
'It is Never Too Late to Mend.'
The Course of True Love Never Did Run Smooth ; and Singleheart and Doubleface.
The Autobiography of a Thief ; Jack of all Trades ; A Hero and a Martyr ; The Wandering Heir.
Love Me Little, Love Me Long.
The Double Marriage.
Griffith Gaunt.
Foul Play.
Put Yourself in His Place.
A Terrible Temptation.
A Simpleton.
A Woman-Hater.
The Jilt ; and Good Stories of Man and other Animals.
A Perilous Secret.
Readiana ; and Bible Characters.

Also In Twenty-one Volumes, post 8vo, illustrated boards, 2s. each.
Peg Woffington. | A Simpleton.
Christie Johnstone.
'It is Never Too Late to Mend.'
The Course of True Love Never Did Run Smooth.
Autobiography of a Thief ; Jack of all Trades ; James Lambert.
Love Me Little, Love Me Long.
The Double Marriage.
The Cloister and the Hearth.
A Terrible Temptation.
Hard Cash. | Readiana.
Foul Play. | Griffith Gaunt.

READE (CHARLES)—*continued.*

Post 8vo, Illustrated Boards, 2s. each.
Put Yourself in His Place.
The Wandering Heir.
A Woman Hater.
Singleheart and Doubleface.
Good Stories of Man, &c.
The Jilt; and other Stories.
A Perilous Secret.

LARGE TYPE, FINE PAPER EDITIONS.
Pott 8vo, cloth, gilt top, 2s. net each; leather,
gilt edges, 3s. net each.
The Cloister and the Hearth. With
32 Illustrations by M. B. HEWERDINE.
'It is Never Too Late to Mend.'

POPULAR EDITIONS, medium 8vo, 6d. each.
The Cloister and the Hearth.
'It is Never Too Late to Mend.'
Foul Play. | Hard Cash.
Peg Woffington; and **Christie**
Johnstone.
Griffith Gaunt.
Put Yourself in His Place.
A Terrible Temptation.
The Double Marriage.
Love Me Little, Love Me Long.
A Perilous Secret.
A Woman Hater.

The Wandering Heir. LARGE TYPE
EDITION, fcap.8vo, cloth, 1s. net; leather,
1s. 6d. net.
The Cloister and the Hearth.
With 16 Photogravure and 84 half-tone
Illustrations by MATT B. HEWERDINE.
Small 4to, cloth, 6s. net.—Also a NEW
EDITION, with 20 Illustrations in 4
Colours and 16 in Black and White by
BYAM SHAW, R.I. Demy 8vo, cloth,
12s. 6d.; parchment, 16s. net.

RICHARDSON (FRANK), Novels
by. Crown 8vo, cloth, 3s. 6d. each.
The Man who Lost his Past. With
50 Illustrations by TOM BROWNE, R.I.
The Bayswater Miracle.

Crown 8vo, cloth, 6s. each.
The King's Counsel.
Semi-Society.
There and Back.

RIDDELL (Mrs.), Novels by.
A Rich Man's Daughter. Crown
8vo, cloth, 3s. 6d.
Weird Stories. Crown 8vo, cloth,
3s. 6d.; post 8vo, picture boards, 2s.

Post 8vo, Illustrated boards, 2s. each.
The Uninhabited House.
Prince of Wales's Garden Party.
The Mystery in Palace Gardens.
Fairy Water. | Idle Tales.
Her Mother's Darling.

RIVES (AMELIE), Stories by.
Crown 8vo, cloth, 3s. 6d. each.
Barbara Dering.
Meriel: A Love Story.

ROBINSON (F. W.), Novels by.
Woman are Strange. Post 8vo,
illustrated boards, 2s.
The Hands of Justice. Crown 8vo,
cloth, 3s. 6d.; post 8vo, illust. bds., 2s.
The Woman in the Dark. Crown
8vo, cloth, 3s. 6d.; post 8vo. illust. bds., 2s.

ROLFE (FR.), Novels by.
Crown 8vo, cloth, 6s. each.
Hadrian the Seventh.
Don Tarquinio.

ROLL OF BATTLE ABBEY,
THE: A List of Principal Warriors who
came from Normandy with William the
Conqueror, 1066. In Gold and Colours. 5s.

ROSENGARTEN (A.).—A Hand-
book of Architectural Styles. Translated by W. COLLETT-SANDARS. With
630 Illustrations. Cr. 8vo, cloth, 7s. 6d.

ROSS (ALBERT).—A Sugar
Princess. Crown 8vo, cloth, 3s. 6d.

ROWSELL (MARY C.).—
Monsieur de Paris. Crown 8vo,
cloth, 3s. 6d.

RUNCIMAN (JAS.), Stories by.
Schools and Scholars. Post 8vo,
cloth, 2s. 6d.
Skippers and Shellbacks. Crown
8vo, cloth, 3s. 6d.

RUSKIN SERIES (The). Square
16mo, cloth, coloured tops and decora-
tive End-papers, Frontispieces, and
Titles. 1s. net each.
The King of the Golden River.
By JOHN RUSKIN. Illustrated by
RICHARD DOYLE.
Bab and his Friends. By Dr. JOHN
BROWN.
Old Christmas. By WASHINGTON
IRVING.
Fairy Tales from Tuscany. By I.
M. ANDERTON.
Ruskin as a Religious Teacher.
By F. W. FARRAR, D.D.

RUSSELL (W. CLARK), Novels
by. Crown 8vo, cloth, 3s. 6d. each;
post 8vo, illustrated boards, 2s. each;
cloth, 2s. 6d. each.
Round the Galley-Fire.
In the Middle Watch.
On the Fo'k'sle Head.
A Voyage to the Cape.
A Book for the Hammock.
The Mystery of the 'Ocean Star.'
The Romance of Jenny Harlowe.
The Tale of the Ten.
An Ocean Tragedy.
My Shipmate Louise.
Alone on a Wide Wide Sea.
The Good Ship 'Mohock.'
The Phantom Death.
Is He the Man? | Heart of Oak.
The Convict Ship.
The Last Entry.

RUSSELL (W. CLARK)—*continued.*
Crown 8vo, cloth, 3s. 6d. each.
A Tale of Two Tunnels.
The Death Ship.
The 'Pretty Polly.' With 12 Illustrations by G. E. ROBERTSON.
Overdue. | **Wrong Side Out.**

The Convict Ship. POPULAR EDITION, medium 8vo, 6d.

RUSSELL (HERBERT).—True Blue. Crown 8vo, cloth, 3s. 6d.

RUSSELL (DORA), Novels by.
A Country Sweetheart. Crown 8vo, picture cloth, flat back, 2s.
The Drift of Fate. Crown 8vo, cloth, 3s. 6d.; picture cloth, flat back, 2s.

RUSSELL (Rev. JOHN) and his Out-of-door Life. By E. W. L. DAVIES. With Illustrations coloured by hand. Royal 8vo, cloth, 16s. net.

RUSSIAN BASTILLE, THE (The Fortress of Schluesselburg). By T. P. YOUVATSHEV. Translated by A. S. RAPPOPORT, M.A. With numerous Illustrations. Demy 8vo, cloth, 7s. 6d. net.

SAINT AUBYN (ALAN), Novels by. Crown 8vo, cloth, 3s. 6d. each; post 8vo, illustrated boards, 2s. each.
A Fellow of Trinity. With a Note by OLIVER WENDELL HOLMES.
The Junior Dean.
Orchard Damerel.
The Master of St. Benedict's.
In the Face of the World.
To His Own Master.
The Tremlett Diamonds.

Crown 8vo, cloth, 3s. 6d. each.
The Wooing of May.
Fortune's Gate.
A Tragic Honeymoon.
Gallantry Bower.
A Proctor's Wooing.
Bonnie Maggie Lauder.
Mrs. Dunbar's Secret.
Mary Unwin. With 8 Illustrations.

SAINT JOHN (BAYLE). — A Levantine Family. Cr. 8vo, cl., 3s. 6d.

SALA (G. A.).—Gaslight and Daylight. Post 8vo, illustrated boards, 2s.

SCOTLAND YARD, Past & Present By Ex-Chief-Inspector CAVANAGH. Post 8vo, illustrated boards, 2s.; cloth, 2s. 6d.

SERGEANT (ADELINE), Novels by. Crown 8vo, cloth 3s. 6d. each.
Under False Pretences.
Dr. Endicott's Experiment.

The Missing Elizabeth. Crown 8vo, cloth, 6s.

ST. MARTIN'S LIBRARY (The).
In pocket size, cloth, gilt top, 2s. net per Vol.; leather, gilt edges, 3s. net per Vol.

By SIR WALTER BESANT.
London. | **Westminster.**
Jerusalem. (In collaboration with Prof. E. H. PALMER.)
All Sorts and Conditions of Men.
Sir Richard Whittington.
Gaspard de Coligny.
By BOCCACCIO.
The Decameron.
By ROBERT BUCHANAN.
The Shadow of the Sword.
By HALL CAINE.
The Deemster.
By WILKIE COLLINS.
The Woman in White.
By DANIEL DEFOE.
Robinson Crusoe. With 37 Illustrations by G. CRUIKSHANK.
By CHARLES DICKENS.
Speeches. With Portrait.
By AUSTIN DOBSON.
Eighteenth Century Vignettes. Three Series, each Illustrated.
By W. S. GILBERT.
Original Plays. Three Series.
By THOMAS HARDY.
Under the Greenwood Tree.
By BRET HARTE.
Condensed Novels.
By OLIVER WENDELL HOLMES.
The Autocrat of the Breakfast-Table. Illustrated by J. G. THOMSON.
Compiled by A. H. HYATT.
The Charm of London: An Anthology.
The Charm of Edinburgh.
The Charm of Venice.
The Charm of Paris.
By RICHARD JEFFERIES.
The Life of the Fields.
The Open Air.
Nature near London.
By CHARLES LAMB.
The Essays of Elia.
By LORD MACAULAY.
History of England, in 5 Volumes.
By JUSTIN McCARTHY.
The Reign of Queen Anne, in 1 Vol.
A History of the Four Georges and of William IV., in 2 Vols.
A History of Our Own Times from Accession of Q. Victoria to 1897, in 3 Vols.
By GEORGE MACDONALD.
Works of Fancy and Imagination, in 10 Vols. 16mo. (For List, see p. 19.)
By W. H. MALLOCK.
The New Republic.
By CHARLES READE.
The Cloister and the Hearth. With 32 Illustrations by M. B. HEWERDINE.
'It is Never Too Late to Mend.'

ST. MARTIN'S LIBRARY—*continued.*

By ROBERT LOUIS STEVENSON.
An Inland Voyage.
Travels with a Donkey.
Memories and Portraits.
Virginibus Puerisque.
Men and Books.
New Arabian Nights.
Across the Plains.
The Merry Men.
Prince Otto.
In the South Seas.
Essays of Travel.
Weir of Hermiston.
Collected Poems.

By H. A. TAINE.
History of English Literature, in
4 Vols. With 32 Portraits.

By MARK TWAIN.—Sketches.
By WALTON and COTTON.
The Complete Angler.

SEYMOUR (CYRIL), Novels by.

Crown 8vo, cloth, 6s. each.
The Magic of To-Morrow.
Comet Chaos.

SHAKESPEARE LIBRARY.

PART I.
THE OLD-SPELLING SHAKESPEARE.

In FORTY VOLUMES, demy 8vo, cloth,
2s. 6d. net per vol.; or Library Edition,
pure rag paper, half-parchment, 5s. net
per vol. In course of publication.

The Works of William Shakespeare
with the spelling of the Quarto or the
Folio as the basis of the Text, and all
changes marked in heavy type. Edited,
with brief Introductions and Notes, by F.
J. FURNIVALL, M.A., D.Litt., and F. W.
CLARKE, M.A. A list of the volumes
already published may be had.

PART II.
THE SHAKESPEARE CLASSICS.

Small crown 8vo, quarter-bound antique
grey boards, 2s. 6d. net per vol.; whole
gold-brown velvet persian, 4s. net
per vol.; also 500 special sets on larger
paper, half parchment, gilt tops (to be
subscribed for only in sets), 5s. net. per
vol. Each volume with Frontispiece.

1. Lodge's 'Rosalynde': the
   original of Shakespeare's 'As
   You Like It." Edited by W. W.
   GREG, M.A.
2. Greene's 'Pandosto,' or 'Doras-
   tus and Fawnia': the original
   of Shakespeare's 'Winter's
   Tale.' Edited by P. G. THOMAS.
3. Brooke's Poem of 'Romeus and
   Juliet': the original of Shakespeare's 'Romeo and Juliet.'
   Edited by P. A. DANIEL. Modernised
   and re-edited by J. J. MUNRO.
4. 'The Troublesome Reign of
   King John': the Play rewritten
   by Shakespeare as 'King John.'
   Edited by F. J. FURNIVALL, D.Litt.

SHAKESPEARE LIBRARY—*cont.*
THE SHAKESPEARE CLASSICS—*continued.*

5,6. 'The History of Hamlet':
   With other Documents illustrative of
   the sources of Shakspeare's Play, and an
   Introductory Study of the LEGEND OF
   HAMLET by Prof. I. GOLLANCZ.
7. 'The Play of King Leir and His
   Three Daughters': the old play
   on the subject of King Lear.
   Edited by SIDNEY LEE, D.Litt.
8. 'The Taming of a Shrew':
   Being the old play used by Shakespeare
   in 'The Taming of the Shrew.' Edited
   by Professor F. S. BOAS, M.A.
9. The Sources and Analogues of
   'A Midsummer Night's Dream.'
   Edited by FRANK SIDGWICK.
10. 'The Famous Victories of
    Henry V.'
11. 'The Menæchmi': the original
    of Shakespeare's 'Comedy of
    Errors.' Latin text, with the Eliza-
    bethan Translation. Edited by W. H. D.
    ROUSE, Litt.D.
12. 'Promos and Cassandra':
    the source of 'Measure for
    Measure.'
13. 'Apolonius and Silla': the
    source of 'Twelfth Night.' Edited by
    MORTON LUCE.
14. 'The First Part of the Conten-
    tion betwixt the two famous
    Houses of York and Lancas-
    ter,' and 'The True Tragedy of
    Richard, Duke of York': the
    originals of the second and third parts of
    'King Henry VI.'
15. The Sources of 'The Tempest.'
16. The Sources of 'Cymbeline.'
17. The Sources and Analogues
    of 'The Merchant of Venice.'
    Edited by Professor I. GOLLANCZ.
18. Romantic Tales: the sources of
    'The Two Gentlemen of Verona,' 'Merry
    Wives,' 'Much Ado about Nothing,'
    'All's Well that Ends Well.'
19,20 Shakespeare's Plutarch: the
    sources of 'Julius Cæsar,' 'Antony and
    Cleopatra,' 'Coriolanus,' and 'Timon,'
    Edited by C. F. TUCKER BROOKE, M.A.

PART III.
THE LAMB SHAKESPEARE FOR YOUNG PEOPLE.

With Illustrations and Music. Based on
MARY AND CHARLES LAMB'S TALES FROM
SHAKESPEARE, an attempt being made
by Professor I. GOLLANCZ to insert within
the setting of prose those scenes and
passages from the Plays with which the
young reader should early become acquainted. The Music arranged by T.
MASKELL HARDY. Imperial 16mo, cloth,
1s. 6d. net per vol.; leather, 2s. 6d. net per
vol.; Special School Edition, linen, 8d.
net per vol.

I. The Tempest.
II. As You Like It.
III. A Midsummer Night's Dream.
IV. The Merchant of Venice.
V. The Winter's Tale.
VI. Twelfth Night.

SHAKESPEARE LIBRARY—*cont.*

THE LAMB SHAKESPEARE—*continued.*

VII. **Cymbeline.**
VIII. **Romeo and Juliet.**
IX. **Macbeth.**
X. **Much Ado About Nothing.**

XI. **A Life of Shakespeare for the Young.** *[Preparing.*

XII. **An Evening with Shakespeare:** 10 Dramatic Tableaux for Young People, with Music by T. MASKELL HARDY, and Illustrations. Cloth; 2s. net; leather, 3s. 6d. net; linen, 1s. 6d. net.

PART IV.

SHAKESPEARE'S ENGLAND.

A series of volumes illustrative of the life, thought, and letters of England in the time of Shakespeare. The first volumes are—

Robert Laneham's Letter, describing part of the Entertainment given to Queen Elizabeth at Kenilworth Castle in 1575. With Introduction by Dr. FURNIVALL, and Illustrations. Demy 8vo, cloth, 5s. net.

The Rogues and Vagabonds of Shakespeare's Youth: reprints of Awdeley's 'Fraternitye of Vacabondes,' Harman's 'Caveat for Common Cursetors,' Parson Haben's or Hyberdyne's 'Sermon in Praise of Thieves and Thievery,' &c. With many woodcuts. Edited, with Introduction, by EDWARD VILES and Dr. FURNIVALL. Demy 8vo, cloth, 5s. net.

Shakespeare's Holinshed: a reprint of all the passages in Holinshed's 'Chronicle' of which use was made in Shakespeare's Historical Plays, with Notes. Edited by W. G. BOSWELL STONE. Royal 8vo, cloth, 10s. 6d. net.

The Book of Elizabethan Verse. Edited, with Notes, by WILLIAM STANLEY BRAITHWAITE. With Frontispiece and Vignette. Small crown 8vo, cloth, 6s. net; vellum gilt, 12s. 6d. net.

The Shakespeare Allusion Book. Reprints of all references to Shakespeare and his Works before the close of the 17th century, collected by Dr. INGLEBY, Miss L. TOULMIN SMITH, Dr. FURNIVALL, and J. J. MUNRO. Two vols., roy. 8vo. 21s. net.

Harrison's Description of England. Part IV. Uniform with Parts I.-III. as issued by the New Shakspere Society. Edited by Dr. FURNIVALL. With additions by Mrs. C. C. STOPES. (250 copies only.) 17s. 6d. net.

A Study of Shakespeare. By A. C. SWINBURNE. Crown 8vo, cloth, 8s.

The Age of Shakespeare. By A. C. SWINBURNE. Crown 8vo, buckram, 6s. net.

Shakespeare's Sweetheart: a Romance. By SARAH H. STERLING. With 6 Coloured Illustrations by C. E. PECK. Square 8vo, cloth, 6s.

SHARP (WILLIAM).—Children of To-morrow. Crown 8vo, cloth, 3s. 6d.

SHERARD (R. H.).—Rogues. Crown 8vo, cloth, 1s. 6d.

SHERIDAN'S (RICHARD BRINSLEY) Complete Works. Crown 8vo, cloth, 3s. 6d.

SHERWOOD (MARGARET).— DAPHNE: a Pastoral. With Coloured Frontispiece. Crown 8vo, cloth, 3s. 6d.

SHIEL (M. P.), Novels by.
The Purple Cloud. Cr. 8vo, cloth, 3s. 6d.
Unto the Third Generation. Cr. 8vo cloth, 6s.

SIGNBOARDS: Their History, including Famous Taverns and Remarkable Characters. By JACOB LARWOOD and J. C. HOTTEN. With 95 Illustrations. Crown 8vo, cloth, 3s. 6d.

SIMS (GEORGE R.), Books by.
Post 8vo, illustrated boards, 2s. each; cloth limp, 2s. 6d. each.
The Ring o' Bells.
Tinkletop's Crime. | Zeph.
Dramas of Life. With 60 Illustrations.
My Two Wives. | Tales of To-day.
Memoirs of a Landlady.
Scenes from the Show.
The Ten Commandments.

Crown 8vo, picture cover, 1s. each; cloth, 1s. 6d. each.
The Dagonet Reciter and Reader.
The Case of George Candlemas.
Dagonet Ditties. | Life We Live.
Young Mrs. Caudle.
Li Ting of London.

Crown 8vo, cloth, 3s. 6d. each; post 8vo, picture boards, 2s. each; cloth, 2s. 6d. each.
Mary Jane's Memoirs.
Mary Jane Married.
Dagonet Abroad.
Rogues and Vagabonds.

Crown 8vo, cloth, 3s. 6d. each.
For Life—and After.
Once upon a Christmas Time. With 8 Illustrations by CHAS. GREEN, R.I.
In London's Heart.
A Blind Marriage.
Without the Limelight.
The Small-part Lady.
Biographs of Babylon.
His Wife's Revenge.
The Mystery of Mary Anne.
Picture cloth, flat back, 2s. each.
Rogues and Vagabonds.
In London's Heart.

POPULAR EDITIONS, medium 8vo, 6d. each.
Mary Jane's Memoirs.
Mary Jane Married.
Rogues and Vagabonds.
How the Poor Live; and Horrible London. Crown 8vo, leatherette, 1s.
Dagonet Dramas. Crown 8vo, 1s.

Joyce Pleasantry. With a Frontispiece by HUGH THOMSON. Crown 8vo, cloth, 6s.

SHELLEY'S Complete WORKS in Verse and Prose. Edited by R. HERNE SHEPHERD. Five Vols., crown 8vo, cloth, 3s. 6d. each.

Poetical Works, in Three Vols.:
Vol. I. Margaret Nicholson; Shelley's Correspondence with Stockdale; Wandering Jew; Queen Mab; Alastor; Rosalind and Helen; Prometheus Unbound; Adonais.
Vol. II. Laon and Cythna; The Cenci; Julian and Maddalo; Swellfoot the Tyrant; The Witch of Atlas; Epipsychidion; Hellas.
Vol. III. Posthumous Poems; The Masque of Anarchy; and other Pieces.

Prose Works, In Two Vols.:
Vol. I. Zastrozzi; St. Irvyne; Dublin and Marlow Pamphlets; Refutation of Deism; Letters to Leigh Hunt; Minor Writings.
Vol. II. Essays; Letters from Abroad; Translations and Fragments; a Biography

SISTER DORA. By M. LONSDALE. Demy 8vo, 4d.; cloth, 6d.

SLANG DICTIONARY (The): Historical and Anecdotal. Cr. 8vo, cl., 6s. 6d.

SMEDLEY (CONSTANCE).— The June Princess. Crown 8vo, cloth, 6s.

SOCIETY IN LONDON. Crown 8vo, 1s.; cloth, 1s. 6d.

SOMERSET (Lord HENRY).— Songs of Adieu. 4to, Jap. vellum, 6s.

SOWERBY (M. and G.), Children's Books by.
Bumbletoes: their Adventures with Belinda and the Buttonsboy, pictured in 12 Coloured Scenes and 18 other Illustrations by MILLICENT SOWERBY. With Verses by GITHA SOWERBY. Small crown 8vo, decorated boards 1s. 6d. net.
Childhood: Twelve Days from our Youth. Pictured in Colours by MILLICENT SOWERBY and written in Verse by GITHA SOWERBY. Crown 4to, cloth, 3s. 6d. net
Yesterday's Children. With 12 Illustrations in Colour and many in Line by MILLICENT SOWERBY; and Verses by GITHA SOWERBY. Crown 4to, cloth, 3s. 6d. net.

SPEIGHT (T. W.), Novels by.
Post 8vo, illustrated boards, 2s. each.
The Mysteries of Heron Dyke.
By Devious Ways.
Hoodwinked; & Sandycroft Mystery. | The Golden Hoop.
Back to Life. | Quittance in Full.
The Loudwater Tragedy.
Burgo's Romance.
A Husband from the Sea.
Crown 8vo, cloth, 3s. 6d. each.
Her Ladyship. | The Grey Monk.
The Master of Trenance.
The Secret of Wyvern Towers.
Doom of Siva. | As It was Written
The Web of Fate.
Experiences of Mr. Verschoyle.
Stepping Blindfold: Cr. 8vo, cloth, 6s.
Wife or No Wife. Post 8vo, cloth, 1s. 6d.

SPEIGHT (E. E.).—The Galleon of Torbay. Crown 8vo, cloth, 6s.

SPENSER for Children. By M. H. TOWRY. With Coloured Illustrations by W. J. MORGAN. Crown 4to, cloth, 3s. 6d.

SPETTIGUE (H. H.). — The Heritage of Eve. Cr. 8vo, cloth, 6s.

SPIELMANN (MRS. M. H.).— Margery Redford and her Friends. With numerous Illustrations by GORDON BROWNE. Large crown 8vo, cloth, 5s. net.
The Rainbow Book: Sixteen Tales of Fun and Fancy. With 37 Illustrations by ARTHUR RACKHAM, HUGH THOMSON, BERNARD PARTRIDGE, and other well-known artists. Large crown 8vo, cloth gilt, 5s. net,

SPRIGGE (S. SQUIRE). — An Industrious Chevalier. Crown 8vo, 3s. 6d.

STAFFORD (JOHN), Novels by. Doris and I. Crown 8vo, cloth, 3s. 6d.
Carlton Priors. Crown 8vo, cloth, 6s.

STANLEY (WINIFRED). — A Flash of the Will. Cr. 8vo, cloth, 6s.

STARRY HEAVENS Poetical Birthday Book. Pott 8vo, cloth, 2s. 6d.

STEDMAN (E. C.).—Victorian Poets. Crown 8vo, cloth, 9s.

STEPHENS (RICCARDO).—The Cruciform Mark. Cr. 8vo, cl., 3s. 6d.

STEPHENS (R. NEILSON).— Philip Winwood. Cr. 8vo cl., 3s. 6d.

STERLING (S. H.), Stories by.
Square 8vo, cloth, 6s. each.
Shakespeare's Sweetheart. With 6 Coloured Illustrations by C. E. PECK.
A Lady of King Arthur's Court. With Illustrations in Colours by CLARA ELSENE PECK, and other Decorations,

STERNDALE (R. ARMITAGE). —The Afghan Knife. Post 8vo, cloth, 3s. 6d.; Illustrated boards, 2s.

STERNE (LAURENCE).— A Sentimental Journey. With 89 Illustrations by T. H. ROBINSON, and a Photogravure Portrait. Crown 8vo, cloth gilt, 3s. 6d.

STEVENSON (BURTON E.).— Affairs of State. Crown 8vo, cloth, 3s. 6d.

STOCKTON (FRANK R.).—The Young Master of Hyson Hall. With 36 Illustrations. Crown 8vo, cloth, 3s. 6d.; picture cloth, flat back, 2s.

STODDARD (C. W.), Books by.
Post 8vo, cloth, gilt top, 6s. net each.
South-Sea Idyls: Summer Cruising.
The Island of Tranquil Delights.

STEVENSON (R. LOUIS), Works by. Cr. 8vo, buckram, 6s. each.

Travels with a Donkey. With a Frontispiece by WALTER CRANE.

An Inland Voyage. With a Frontispiece by WALTER CRANE.

Familiar Studies of Men & Books.

The Silverado Squatters.

The Merry Men.

Underwoods: Poems.

Memories and Portraits.

Virginibus Puerisque.

Ballads. | **Prince Otto.**

Across the Plains.

Weir of Hermiston.

In the South Seas.

Essays of Travel.

Tales and Fantasies.

Essays in the Art of Writing.

A Lowden Sabbath Morn. Illustrated by A. S. BOYD.

Songs of Travel. Cr. 8vo, buckram, 5s.

New Arabian Nights. Crown 8vo, buckram, 6s.; post 8vo, illust. boards, 2s.; POPULAR EDITION, medium 8vo, 6d.

Large crown 8vo, cloth, 7s. 6d. net each; parchment, 10s. 6d. net each; LARGE PAPER EDITION, pure rag paper, the Plates mounted, vellum, 21s. net each.

An Inland Voyage. With 12 Illustrations in Colour, 12 in Black and White, and other Decorations, by NOEL ROOKE.

Travels with a Donkey in the Cevennes. With 12 Illustrations in Colour, 12 in Black and White, and other Decorations, by NOEL ROOKE.

A Child's Garden of Verses. With 12 Illustrations in Colour and numerous Black and White Drawings by MILLICENT SOWERBY. Large crown 8vo, cloth, 5s. net; LARGE PAPER EDITION, parchment, 10s. 6d. net.

Post 8vo, cloth backs, 1s. net each; leather, 2s. net each.

A Christmas Sermon.

Prayers Written at Vailima. There is also a MINIATURE EDITION of the PRAYERS in velvet calf yapp (2¼ by 3½ in.), 1s. 6d. net.

The Suicide Club; and The Rajah's Diamond. (From NEW ARABIAN NIGHTS.) With 8 Illustrations by W. J. HENNESSY. Crown 8vo, cloth, 3s. 6d.

The Stevenson Reader. Edited by LLOYD OSBOURNE. Post 8vo, cloth, 2s. 6d.; buckram, gilt top, 3s. 6d.

The Pocket R.L.S.: Favourite Passages. 16mo, cl., 2s. net; leather, 3s. net.

LARGE TYPE, FINE PAPER EDITIONS. Pott 8vo, cloth, gilt top, 2s. net each; leather, gilt edges, 3s. net each.

An Inland Voyage.

Travels with a Donkey.

Virginibus Puerisque.

Familiar Studies of Men & Books.

New Arabian Nights.

Memories and Portraits.

Across the Plains.

The Merry Men. | **Prince Otto.**

In the South Seas.

STEVENSON (R. LOUIS)—continued.

Essays of Travel.

Weir of Hermiston.

Collected Poems of R. L. S.

R. L. Stevenson: A Study. By H. B. BAILDON. With 2 Portraits. Crown 8vo, buckram, 6s.

Recollections of R. L. Stevenson in the Pacific. By ARTHUR JOHNSTONE. With Portrait and Facsimile Letter. Crown 8vo, buckram, 6s. net.

STRAUS (RALPH), Novels by. Crown 8vo, cloth, 6s. each.

The Man Apart.

The Little God's Drum.

STRUTT (JOSEPH). — The Sports and Pastimes of the People of England. With 140 Illustrations. Crown 8vo, cloth, 3s. 6d.

STUART (H. LONGAN.)— Weeping Cross. Crown 8vo, cloth, 6s.

SULTAN (THE) AND HIS SUBJECTS. By RICHARD DAVEY. With Portrait. Demy 8vo, cloth, 7s. 6d. net.

SUNDOWNER, Stories by.

Told by the Taffrail. Cr. 8vo, 3s. 6d.

The Tale of the Serpent. Crown 8vo, cloth, flat back, 2s.

SUTRO (ALFRED). — The Foolish Virgins. Fcp. 8vo, 1s.; cl., 1s. 6d.

SWIFT'S (Dean) Choice Works, in Prose and Verse. With Memoir, Portrait, and Facsimiles. Cr. 8vo, cl., 3s. 6d.

Jonathan Swift: A Study. By J. CHURTON COLLINS. Cr. 8vo, cl., 3s. 6d.

SWINBURNE'S (ALGERNON CHARLES) Works.

Mr. Swinburne's Collected Poems. In 6 Vols., crown 8vo, 36s. net the set.

Mr. Swinburne's Collected Tragedies. In 5 Vols., cr. 8vo, 30s. net the set.

Selections from Mr. Swinburne's Works. With Preface by T. WATTS-DUNTON, and 2 Photogravure Plates. Fcap. 8vo, 6s.

The Queen-Mother; and Rosamond. Crown 8vo, 7s. 6d. net.

Atalanta in Calydon. Crown 8vo, 6s.

Chastelard: A Tragedy. Crown 8vo, 7s.

Poems and Ballads. FIRST SERIES. Crown 8vo, 9s.

Poems and Ballads. SECOND SERIES. Crown 8vo, 9s.

Poems and Ballads. THIRD SERIES. Crown 8vo, 7s.

Songs before Sunrise. Crown 8vo, 10s. 6d.

Bothwell: A Tragedy. Crown 8vo, 12s. 6d.

Songs of Two Nations. Crown 8vo, 6s.

George Chapman. (In Vol. II. of G. CHAPMAN's Works.) Crown 8vo, 3s. 6d.

Essays and Studies. Crown 8vo, 12s.

Erechtheus: A Tragedy. Crown 8vo, 6s.

A Note on Charlotte Bronte. Crown 8vo, 6s.

A Study of Shakespeare. Crown 8vo, 8s.

SWINBURNE (A. C.)—*continued.*
Songs of the Springtides. Crown 8vo, 6s.
Studies in Song. Crown 8vo, 7s.
Mary Stuart: A Tragedy. Crown 8vo, 8s.
Tristram of Lyonesse. Crown 8vo, 9s.
A Century of Roundels. Cr. 8vo, 6s.
A Midsummer Holiday. Cr. 8vo, 7s.
Marino Faliero: A Tragedy. Crown 8vo, 6s.
A Study of Victor Hugo. Cr 8vo, 6s.
Miscellanies. Crown 8vo, 12s.
Locrine: A Tragedy. Crown 8vo, 6s.
A Study of Ben Jonson. Cr. 8vo, 7s.
The Sisters: A Tragedy. Crown 8vo, 6s.
Astrophel, &c. Crown 8vo, 7s.
Studies in Prose and Poetry. Crown 8vo, 9s.
The Tale of Balen. Crown 8vo, 7s.
Rosamund, Queen of the Lombards: A Tragedy. Crown 8vo, 6s.
A Channel Passage. Crown 8vo, 7s.
Love's Cross-Currents: A Year's Letters. Crown 8vo, 6s. net.
William Blake. Crown 8vo, 6s. net.
The Duke of Gandia. Crown 8vo, 5s.
The Age of Shakespeare. Crown 8vo, 6s. net.

SWINNERTON (FRANK A.).—
The Merry Heart. Cr. 8vo, cloth, 6s.

SYRETT (NETTA), Novels by.
Anne Page. Crown 8vo, cloth, 3s. 6d.
A Castle of Dreams. Crown 8vo, cloth, 6s.

TAINE'S History of English
Literature. Trans. by HENRY VAN LAUN. Four Vols., demy 8vo, cl., 30s.—POPULAR EDITION, Two Vols., crown 8vo, cl., 15s.; FINE PAPER EDITION, in Four Vols., with 32 Portraits, pott 8vo, cloth, gilt top, 2s. net per vol.; leather, gilt edges, 3s. net per vol.

TALES FOR THE HOMES.
By TWENTY-SIX WELL-KNOWN AUTHORS. Edited by Rev. J. MARCHANT. Published for the benefit of the BARNARDO MEMORIAL FUND. With 3 Portraits. Crown 8vo, cloth, 5s. net

TAYLOR (TOM). — Historical
Dramas. Crown 8vo, 1s. each.
  'JEANNE DARC.'
  'TWIXT AXE AND CROWN.'
  'THE FOOL'S REVENGE.'
  'ARKWRIGHT'S WIFE.'
  'ANNE BOLEYN.'
  'PLOT AND PASSION.'

THACKERAY : The Rose and
The Ring. With Coloured Frontispiece, 44 Illustrations (12 in Two Tints) and Decorative End-papers by GORDON BROWNE. Demy 8vo, cloth, 3s. 6d. net.
Thackeray (The Pocket). Arranged by A. H. HYATT. 16mo, cloth, gilt top, 2s. net; leather, gilt top, 3s. net.

THOMAS (ANNIE), Novels by.
The Siren's Web. Cr. 8vo, cl., 3s. 6d.
Comrades True. Crown 8vo, cloth, 6s.

THOMAS (BERTHA), Novels by.
In a Cathedral City. Cr. 8vo, cl., 3s. 6d.

Crown 8vo, cloth, 6s. each.
The House on the Scar.
The Son of the House.

THOREAU: His Life and Aims.
By A. H. PAGE. With a Portrait. Post 8vo, buckram, 3s. 6d.

THORNBURY (WALTER).—
Tales for the Marines. Post 8vo, illustrated boards, 2s.

TIMBS (JOHN), Works by.
Crown 8vo, cloth, 3s. 6d. each.
Clubs and Club Life in London. With 41 Illustrations.
English Eccentrics and Eccentricities. With 48 Illustrations.

TREETON (ERNEST A.).—The
Instigator. Crown 8vo, cloth, 6s.

TROLLOPE (ANTHONY), Novels
by. Crown 8vo, cloth, 3s. 6d. each; post 8vo, illustrated boards, 2s. each.
The Way We Live Now.
Frau Frohmann. | Marion Fay.
The Land-Leaguers.

Post 8vo, illustrated boards, 2s. each.
Kept in the Dark.
The American Senator.
The Golden Lion of Granpere.

Crown 8vo, cloth, 3s. 6d. each.
Mr. Scarborough's Family.
John Caldigate.

TROLLOPE (FRANCES E.),
Novels by. Crown 8vo, cloth, 3s. 6d. each; post 8vo, illustrated boards, 2s. each.
Like Ships upon the Sea.
Mabel's Progress. | Anne Furness.

TROLLOPE (T. A.).—Diamond
Cut Diamond. Post 8vo, illus. bds., 2s.

TURENNE (RAYMOND).—The
Last of the Mammoths. Crown 8vo, cloth, 3s. 6d.

TWAIN'S (MARK) Books.
UNIFORM LIBRARY EDITION. Crown 8vo, cloth, 3s. 6d. each.
Mark Twain's Library of Humour. With 197 Illustrations by E. W. KEMBLE.
Roughing It: and The Innocents at Home. With 200 Illustrations by F. A. FRASER.
The American Claimant. With 81 Illustrations by HAL HURST and others.
Pudd'nhead Wilson. With Portrait and Six Illustrations by LOUIS LOEB.
*The Adventures of Tom Sawyer. With 111 Illustrations.

TWAIN (MARK)—*continued.*
Tom Sawyer Abroad. With 26 Illustrations by DAN BEARD.
Tom Sawyer, Detective, With Port.
* **A Tramp Abroad.** With 314 Illusts.
* **The Innocents Abroad:** or, New Pilgrim's Progress. With 234 Illusts.
* **The Gilded Age.** By MARK TWAIN and C. D. WARNER. With 212 Illusts.
* **The Prince and the Pauper.** With 190 Illustrations.
* **Life on the Mississippi.** 300 Illusts.
* **The Adventures of Huckleberry Finn.** 174 Illusts. by E. W. KEMBLE.
* **A Yankee at the Court of King Arthur.** 220 Illusts. by DAN BEARD.
* **The Stolen White Elephant.**
* **The £1,000,000 Bank-Note.**
A Double-barrelled Detective Story. With 7 Illustrations.
Personal Recollections of Joan of Arc. With 12 Illusts. by F. V. DU MOND
More Tramps Abroad.
The Man that Corrupted Hadleyburg. With Frontispiece.
The Choice Works of Mark Twain. With Life, Portrait, and Illustrations.
⁎ The Books marked * may be had also in post 8vo, cloth, 2s. each.

POPULAR EDITIONS, medium 8vo, 6d. each.
Tom Sawyer. | **A Tramp Abroad.**
The Prince and the Pauper.
Huckleberry Finn.

Mark Twain's Sketches. Pott 8vo, cloth, gilt top, 2s. net; leather, gilt edges 3s. net; post 8vo, cloth, 2s.

TWELLS (JULIA H.).—Et tu, Sejane! Crown 8vo, cloth, 6s.

TYTLER (SARAH), Novels by. Crown 8vo, cloth, 3s. 6d. each; post 8vo, illustrated boards, 2s. each.
Buried Diamonds.
The Blackhall Ghosts.
What She Came Through.

Post 8vo, illustrated boards, 2s. each.
Saint Mungo's City. | **Lady Bell.**
The Huguenot Family.
Disappeared. | **Noblesse Oblige.**
Beauty and the Beast.

Crown 8vo, cloth, 3s. 6d. each.
The Macdonald Lass.
The Witch-Wife.
Rachel Langton. | **Sapphira.**
Mrs. Carmichael's Goddesses.
A Honeymoon's Eclipse.
A Young Dragon.

Crown 8vo, cloth, 6s. each.
Three Men of Mark.
In Clarissa's Day.
Sir David's Visitors.
The Poet and His Guardian Angel.

Citoyenne Jacqueline. Crown 8vo, picture cloth, flat back, 2s.
The Bride's Pass. Post 8vo, illustrated boards, 2s.

TYTLER (C. C. FRASER-).—Mistress Judith. Crown 8vo, cloth, 3s. 6d.; post 8vo, illustrated boards, 2s.

UPWARD (ALLEN), Novels by.
The Queen against Owen. Crown 8vo, cloth, 3s. 6d.; picture cloth, flat back, 2s.; post 8vo, picture boards, 2s.
The Phantom Torpedo-Boats. Crown 8vo, cloth, 6s.

VANDAM (ALBERT D.).—A Court Tragedy. With 6 Illustrations by J. B. DAVIS. Crown 8vo, cloth, 3s. 6d.

VASHTI and ESTHER. By 'Belle' of *The World.* Cr. 8vo, cl., 3s. 6d.

VENICE IN THE EIGHTEENTH Century. By PHILIPPE MONNIER. Translated from the French, with a Frontispiece. Demy 8vo, cl., 7s. 6d. net.

VICENZA (The Painters of).— By TANCRED BORENIUS. With 15 Full-page Plates. Demy 8vo, cloth, 7s. 6d. net.

VIZETELLY (ERNEST A.), Books by. Crown 8vo, cloth, 3s. 6d. each.
The Scorpion.
The Lover's Progress.

A Path of Thorns. Crown 8vo, cloth, 6s.
The Wild Marquis: Life and Adventures of Armand Guerry de Maubreuil. Crown 8vo, cloth, 6s.

WALLACE (LEW.).—Ben-Hur: A Tale of the Christ. Crown 8vo, cloth, 3s. 6d.

WALLER (S. E.).—Sebastiani's Secret. With 9 Illusts. Cr. 8vo, cl., 6s.

WALTON and COTTON'S Complete Angler. Pott 8vo, cloth, gilt, 2s. net; leather, gilt edges, 3s. net.

WALT WHITMAN, Poems by. Edited, with Introduction, by W. M. ROSSETTI. With Port. Cr. 8vo, buckram, 6s.

WARDEN (FLORENCE), by.
Joan, the Curate. Crown 8vo, cloth, 3s. 6d.; picture cloth, flat back, 2s.

Crown 8vo, cloth, 6s. each.
The Heart of a Girl. With 8 Illusts.
Tom Dawson.
The Youngest Miss Brown.

Crown 8vo, cloth, 3s. 6d. each.
A Fight to a Finish.
The Old House at the Corner.
Love and Lordship.
What Ought She to Do?
My Lady of Whims.

WARMAN (CY).—The Express Messenger. Crown 8vo, cloth, 3s. 6d.

WASSERMANN (LILLIAS).—The Daffodils. Crown 8vo, cloth, 1s. 6d.

WESTALL (WILL.), Novels by.
Trust-Money. Crown 8vo, cloth, 3s. 6d.;
post 8vo, illustrated boards, 2s.

Crown 8vo, cloth, 6s. each.
Dr. Wynne's Revenge.
The Sacred Crescents.
A Very Queer Business.

Crown 8vo, cloth, 3s. 6d. each.
A Woman Tempted Him.
For Honour and Life.
Her Two Millions.
Two Pinches of Snuff.
With the Red Eagle.
A Red Bridal. | Nigel Fortescue.
Ben Clough. | Birch Dene.
The Old Factory.
Sons of Belial. | Strange Crimes.
Her Ladyship's Secret.
The Phantom City.
Ralph Norbreck's Trust.
A Queer Race. | Red Ryvington.
Roy of Roy's Court.
As Luck would have it.
As a Man Sows.
The Old Bank.

With the Red Eagle: POPULAR
EDITION, medium 8vo, 6d.

WARRANT to Execute Charles I.
A Facsimile, with the 59 Signatures and
Seals. 2s.
Warrant to Execute Mary Queen
of Scots. Including Queen Elizabeth's
Signature and the Great Seal. 2s.

WEBBER (BYRON).—Sport and
Spangles. Crown 8vo, cloth, 2s.

WERNER (A.). — Chapenga's
White Man. Crown 8vo, cloth, 3s. 6d.

WESTBURY (ATHA). — The
Shadow of Hilton Fernbrook. Crown
8vo, cloth, 3s. 6d

WHEELWRIGHT (E. G.).—A
Slow Awakening. Crown 8vo cloth, 6s.

WHISHAW (FRED.), Novels
by. Crown 8vo, cloth, 3s. 6d. each.
A Forbidden Name.
Many Ways of Love. With 8 Illusts.

Crown 8vo, cloth, 6s. each.
Mazeppa.
Near the Tsar, near Death.
A Splendid Impostor.

WILDE (LADY).—The Ancient
Legends, Charms, and Superstitions
of Ireland. Crown 8vo, cloth, 3s. 6d.

WILLIAMS (W. MATTIEU).—
The Chemistry of Cookery. Crown
8vo, cloth, 6s.

WILLIAMSON (Mrs. F. H.).—A
Child Widow. Post 8vo, illust. bds., 2s.

WILLS (C. J.), Novels by.
An Easy-going Fellow. Crown 8vo,
cloth 3s. 6d.
His Dead Past. Crown 8vo, cloth, 6s.

WILSON (Dr. ANDREW), by.
Chapters on Evolution. With 259
Illustrations. Crown 8vo, cloth, 7s. 6d.
Leisure-Time Studies. With Illustra-
tions. Crown 8vo, cloth, 6s.
Common Accidents, and how to
Treat Them. Cr. 8vo, 1s.; cloth, 1s. 6d.

WINTER (JOHN STRANGE),
by.
Regimental Legends. Post 8vo,
Illustrated boards, 2s.; cloth, 2s. 6d.
Cavalry Life; and Regimental
Legends. Crown 8vo, cloth, 3s. 6d.;
picture cloth, flat back, 2s.

WOOD (H. F.), Detective Stories
by. Post 8vo, illustrated boards 2s. each.
Passenger from Scotland Yard.
The Englishman of the Rue Cain.

WOOLLEY (CELIA PARKER).—
Rachel Armstrong. Post 8vo, 2s. 6d.

WRAGGE (CLEMENT L.).—
The Romance of the South Seas.
With 84 Illustrations. Crown 8vo, cloth,
7s. 6d. net.

WRIGHT (THOMAS).—History
of Caricature and of the Grotesque
in Art, Literature, Sculpture and
Painting. Illustrated by F. W.
FAIRHOLT. Crown 8vo, cloth, 7s. 6d.

ZANGWILL (LOUIS).—A Nine-
teenth Century Miracle. Crown 8vo,
cloth, 3s. 6d.; picture cloth, flat back, 2s.

ZOLA (EMILE), Novels by.
UNIFORM EDITION. Translated or Edited,
with Introductions, by ERNEST A. VIZE-
TELLY. Crown 8vo, cloth, 3s. 6d. each.
His Masterpiece. | The Joy of Life.
Germinal.
The Honour of the Army.
Abbe Mouret's Transgression.
The Fortune of the Rougons.
The Conquest of Plassans.
The Dram-Shop.
The Fat and the Thin. | Money.
His Excellency. | The Dream.
The Downfall. | Doctor Pascal.
Lourdes. | Fruitfulness.
Rome. | Work.
Paris. | Truth.

POPULAR EDITIONS, medium 8vo, 6d. each.
The Fortune of the Rougons.
Lourdes | Rome. | The Downfall.
Paris. | Money. | The Dram-
The Joy of Life. | shop.

UNWIN BROTHERS, Ltd., Printers, 27, Pilgrim Street, Ludgate Hill, London, E.C.